Burning Lamp

Amanda Quick

piatkus

PIATKUS

First published in the US in 2010 by G.P. Putnam's Sons,
A member of Penguin Group (USA) Inc., New York
First published in Great Britain in 2010 by Piatkus
This paperback edition published in 2011 by Piatkus

3 5 7 9 10 8 6 4

A CIP catalogue record for this book
is available from the British Library.

ISBN 978-0-7499-5296-9

Printed and bound in Great Britain by
Clays Ltd, St Ives plc

Papers used by Piatkus are from well-managed forests
and other responsible sources.

MIX
Paper from
responsible sources
FSC
www.fsc.org   FSC® C104740

Piatkus
An imprint of
Little, Brown Book Group
Carmelite House
50 Victoria Embankment
London EC4Y 0DZ

An Hachette UK Company
www.hachette.co.uk

www.piatkus.co.uk

For my brother, Jim Castle,

a man of great talent, with love

THE DREAMLIGHT TRILOGY

Dear Reader:

The Arcane Society was founded on secrets. Few of those secrets are more dangerous than those kept by the descendants of the alchemist Nicholas Winters, fierce rival of Sylvester Jones.

The legend of the Burning Lamp goes back to the earliest days of the Society. Nicholas Winters and Sylvester Jones started out as friends and eventually became deadly adversaries. Each sought the same goal: a way to enhance psychic talents. Sylvester chose the path of chemistry and plunged into illicit experiments with strange herbs and plants. Ultimately he concocted the flawed formula that bedevils the Society to this day.

Nicholas took the engineering approach and forged the Burning Lamp, a device with unknown powers. Radiation from the lamp produced a twist in his DNA, creating a psychic genetic "curse" destined to be passed down through the males of his bloodline.

The Winters Curse strikes very rarely, but when it does, the Arcane Society has good reason for grave concern. It is said that the Winters man who inherits Nicholas's genetically altered talent is destined to become a Cerberus—Arcane slang for an insane psychic who possesses multiple lethal abilities. Jones & Jones and the Governing Council are convinced that such human monsters must be hunted down and terminated as swiftly as possible.

There is only one hope for the men of the Burning Lamp. Each must find the artifact and a woman who can work the dreamlight energy that the device produces in order to reverse the dangerous psychic changes brought on by the curse.

In the Dreamlight Trilogy (Book One: *Fired Up*, Book Two: *Burning Lamp*, and Book Three: *Midnight Crystal*) you will meet the three men—past, present and future—of the Burning Lamp. These are the dangerous, passionate descendants of Nicholas Winters. Each will discover some of the deadly secrets of the lamp. Each will encounter the woman with the power to change his destiny.

And ultimately, far in the future, on a world called Harmony, one of them will unravel the lamp's final mystery, the secret of the Midnight Crystal. The destinies of both the Jones and the Winters families hang in the balance.

I hope you will enjoy the trilogy.

Sincerely,
Jayne

I shall not long survive but I will have my revenge, if not in this generation, then in some future time and place. For I am certain now that the
three talents are locked into the blood and will descend down through
my line.

Each talent comes at a great price. It is ever thus with power.

The first talent fills the mind with a rising tide of restlessness that
cannot be assuaged by endless hours in the laboratory or soothed with
strong drink or the milk of the poppy.

The second talent is accompanied by dark dreams and terrible
visions.

The third talent is the most powerful and the most dangerous. If
the key is not turned properly in the lock, this last psychical ability will
prove lethal, bringing on first insanity and then death.

Grave risk attends the onset of the third and final power. Those of
my line who would survive must find the Burning Lamp and a woman
who can work dreamlight energy. Only she can turn the key in the lock
that opens the door to the last talent. Only such a female can halt or
reverse the transformation once it has begun.

But beware: Women of power can prove treacherous. I know this
now, to my great cost.

It is done. My last and greatest creation, the Midnight Crystal, is finished. I have set it into the lamp together with the other crystals. It is a most astonishing stone. I have sealed great forces within it but even I, who forged it, cannot begin to guess at all of its properties, nor do I know how its light can be unleashed. That discovery must be left to one of the heirs of my blood.

But of this much I am certain: The one who controls the light of the Midnight Crystal will be the agent of my revenge. For I have infused the stone with a psychical command stronger than any act of magic or sorcery. The radiation of the crystal will compel the man who wields its power to destroy the descendants of Sylvester Jones.

Vengeance will be mine.

PROLOGUE

London, late in the reign of Queen Victoria . . .

It took Adelaide Pyne almost forty-eight hours to realize that the Rosestead Academy was not an exclusive school for orphaned young ladies. It was a brothel. By then it was too late; she had been sold to the frightening man known only as Mr. Smith.

The Chamber of Pleasure was in deep shadow, lit only by a single candle. The flame sparked and flared on the cream-colored satin drapery that billowed down from the wrought-iron frame above the canopied bed. In the pale glow the crimson rose petals scattered across the snowy white quilt looked like small pools of blood.

Adelaide huddled in the darkened confines of the wardrobe, all her senses heightened by dread. Through the crack between the doors she could see only a narrow slice of the room.

Smith entered the chamber. He barely glanced at the heavily draped bed. Locking the door immediately, he set his hat and a black satchel on the table, looking for all the world as though he were a doctor who had been summoned to attend a patient.

In spite of her heart-pounding fear, something about the satchel distracted Adelaide, riveting her attention. Dreamlight leaked out of the black bag. She could scarcely believe her senses. Great powerful currents of ominous energy seeped through the leather. She had the unnerving impression that it was calling to her in a thousand different ways. But that was impossible.

There was no time to contemplate the mystery. Her circumstances had just become far more desperate. Her plan, such as it was, had hinged on the assumption that she would be dealing with one of Mrs. Rosser's usual clients, an inebriated gentleman in a state of lust who possessed no significant degree of psychical talent. It had become obvious during the past two days that sexual desire tended to focus the average gentleman's brain in a way that, temporarily at least, obliterated his common sense and reduced the level of his intelligence. She had intended to take advantage of that observation tonight to make her escape.

But Smith was most certainly not an average brothel client. She was horrified to see the seething energy in the dreamprints he had tracked into the room. His hot paranormal fingerprints were all over the satchel, as well.

Everyone left some residue of dreamlight behind on the objects with which they came in contact. The currents seeped easily through shoe leather and gloves. Her talent allowed her to perceive the traces of such energy.

In general, dreamprints were faint and murky. But there were exceptions. Individuals in a state of intense emotion or excitement generated very distinct, very perceptible prints. So did those with strong psychical abilities. Mr. Smith fit into both categories. He was aroused, and he was a powerful talent. That was a very dangerous combination.

Even more unnerving was the realization that there was something wrong with his dreamlight patterns. The oily, iridescent currents of his tracks and prints were ever so faintly warped.

Smith turned toward the wardrobe. The pale glow of the candle gleamed on the black silk mask that concealed the upper half of his face. Whatever he intended to do in this room was of such a terrible nature that he did not wish to take the chance of being recognized by anyone on the premises.

He moved like a man in his prime. He was tall and slender. His clothes looked expensive, and he carried himself with the bred-in-the-cradle arrogance of a man accustomed to the privileges of wealth and high social rank.

He stripped off his leather gloves and unfastened the metal buckles of the satchel with a feverish haste that in another man might have indicated sexual lust. She had not yet had any practical experience of such matters. Mrs. Rosser, the manager of the brothel, had informed her that Smith would be her first client. But during the past two days she had seen the tracks the gentlemen left on the stairs when they followed the girls to their rooms. She now knew what desire looked like when it burned in a man.

What she saw in Smith's eerily luminous prints was different. There was most certainly a dark hunger pulsing in him but it did not seem related to sexual excitement. The strange, ultralight radiation indicated that it was some other kind of passion that consumed him tonight. The energy was terrifying to behold.

She held her breath when he opened the satchel and reached inside. She did not know what to expect. Some of the girls whispered about the bizarre, unnatural games many clients savored. But it was not a whip or a chain or leather manacles that Smith took out of the satchel. Rather it was a strange, vase-shaped artifact. The object was made of metal that glinted gold in the flickering candlelight. It rose about eighteen inches from a heavy base, flaring outward toward the top. Large, colorless crystals were set in a circle around the rim.

The waves of dark power whispering from the artifact stirred the hair on the nape of her neck. The object was infused with a storm of dreamlight that seemed to be trapped in a state of suspension. *Like a machine,* she thought, astonished; *a device designed to generate dreamlight.*

Even as she told herself that such a paranormal engine could not possibly exist, the memory of a tale her father had told her, an old Arcane legend, drifted, phantomlike through her thoughts. She could not recall the details but there had been something about a lamp and a curse.

Smith set the artifact on the table next to the candle. Then he went swiftly toward the bed.

"Let us get on with the business," he muttered, tension and impatience thickening the words.

He yanked aside the satin hangings. For a few seconds he stared at the empty sheets, evidently baffled. An instant later rage stiffened his body. He crushed a handful of the drapery in one fist and spun around, searching the shadows.

"Stupid girl. Where are you? I don't know what Rosser told you, but I am not one of her regular clients. I do not make a habit of sleeping with whores, and I certainly did not come here tonight to play games."

His voice was low and reptilian cold now. The words slithered down Adelaide's spine. At the same time the temperature in the chamber seemed to drop several degrees. She started to shiver, not just with terror but with the new chill in the atmosphere.

He'll check under the bed first.

Even as the thought whispered through her, Smith seized the candle off the table and crouched to peer into the shadows beneath the bed frame.

She knew that he would open the wardrobe as soon as he realized that she was not hiding under the bed. It was the only other item of furniture in the room that was large enough to conceal a person.

"Bloody hell." Smith shot to his feet so swiftly that the candle in his hand flickered and nearly died. "Come out, you foolish girl. I'll be quick about it, I promise. Trust me when I tell you that I have no plans to linger over this aspect of the thing."

He stilled when he saw the wardrobe.

"Did you think I wouldn't find you? Brainless female."

She could not even breathe now. There was nowhere to run.

The wardrobe door opened abruptly. Candlelight spilled into the darkness. Smith's eyes glittered between the slits in the black mask.

"Silly little whore."

He seized her arm to haul her out of the wardrobe. Her talent was flaring wildly, higher than it ever had since she had come into it a year ago. The result was predictable. She reacted to the physical contact as though she had been struck by invisible lightning. The shock was such that she could not even scream.

Frantically she dampened her talent. She hated to be touched when her senses were elevated. The experience of brushing up against the shadows and remnants of another person's dreams was horribly, gut-wrenchingly intimate and disturbing in the extreme, a waking nightmare.

Before she could catch her breath she heard a key in a lock. The door of the chamber slammed open. Mrs. Rosser loomed in the entrance. Her bony frame was darkly silhouetted against the low glare of the gaslight that illuminated the hallway behind her. At that moment she embodied the nickname that the women of the brothel had bestowed upon her: The Vulture.

"I'm afraid there's been a change of plans, sir," Rosser said. Her voice was as hard and pitiless as the rest of her. "You must leave the premises immediately."

"What the devil are you talking about?" Smith demanded. He tightened his grip on Adelaide's arm. "I paid Quinton an exorbitant price for the girl."

"I just received a message informing me that this establishment is now under new ownership," Rosser said. "It is my understanding that my former employer recently expired. Heart attack. His business enterprises have been taken over by another. There is no cause for concern. Rest assured your money will be refunded."

"I don't want a refund," Smith said. "I want this girl."

"Plenty more where she came from. I've got two downstairs right now who are younger and prettier. Never been touched. This one's fifteen if she's a day. Doubt that you'd be the first to bed her."

"Do you think I give a damn about the girl's virginity?"

Rosser was clearly startled. "But that's what you're paying for."

"Stupid woman. This concerns a vastly more important attribute. I made a bargain with your employer. I intend to hold him to it."

"I just told you, he is no longer among the living. I've got a new employer."

"The business affairs of crime lords are of no interest to me. The girl is now my property. I'm taking her out of here tonight, assuming the experiment is completed to my satisfaction."

"What's this about an experiment?" Mrs. Rosser was outraged. "I never heard of such a thing. This is a brothel, not a laboratory. In any event, you can't have the girl and that's final."

"It appears that the test will have to be conducted elsewhere," Smith said to Adelaide. "Come along."

He jerked her out of the wardrobe. She tumbled to the floor.

"Get up." He used his grip on her arm to haul her to her feet. "We're leaving this place immediately. Never fear, if it transpires that you are of no use to me, you'll be quite free to return to this establishment."

"You're not taking her away." Rosser reached for the bellpull just inside the door. "I'm going to summon the guards."

"You'll do nothing of the kind," Smith said. "I've had quite enough of this nonsense."

He removed a fist-sized crystal from the pocket of his coat. The object glowed blood red. The temperature dropped another few degrees. Adelaide sensed invisible ice-cold energy blazing in the chamber.

Mrs. Rosser opened her mouth but no sound emerged. She raised her arms as though she really were a great bird trying to take wing. Her head fell back. A violent spasm shot through her. She collapsed in the doorway and lay very still.

Adelaide was too stunned to speak. The Vulture was dead.

"Just as well," Smith said. "She is no great loss to anyone."

He was right, Adelaide thought. Heaven knew that she had no fondness for the brothel keeper but watching someone die in such a fashion was a horrifying experience.

Belatedly, the full impact of what had just occurred jolted through her. *Smith had used his talent and the crystal to commit murder.* She had never known that such a thing was possible.

"What did you do to her?" Adelaide whispered.

"The same thing I will do to you if you do not obey me." The ruby crystal had gone dark. "Damn things never last long," he muttered. He dropped the stone back into his pocket. "Come along. There is no time to waste. We must get out of here at once."

He drew her toward the table where he had left the artifact. She could feel the euphoric excitement flooding through him. He had just murdered a woman and he had enjoyed doing it; no, he had *rejoiced* in the experience.

She sensed something else as well. Whatever Smith had done with the crystal had required a great deal of energy. The psychical senses, like every other aspect of the mind and body, required time to recover after

7

one drew heavily on them. Smith would no doubt soon regain the full force of his great power, but at that moment he was probably at least somewhat weakened.

"I'm not going anywhere with you," she said.

He did not bother to respond with words. The next thing she knew, icy cold pain washed through her in searing waves.

She gasped, doubled over and sank to her knees beneath the weight of the chilling agony. So much for thinking that he had exhausted his psychical resources.

"Now you know what I did to Rosser," Smith said. "But in her case I used far more power. Such intense cold shatters the senses and then stops the heart. Behave yourself or you will get more of the same."

The pain stopped as abruptly as it had begun, leaving her dazed and breathless. Surely this time he had used the last of his reserves to punish her. She had to act quickly. Fortunately he was still gripping her arm. She required physical contact to manipulate another individual's dreamlight energy.

She raised her talent again, gritting her teeth against the dreadful sensations, and focused every ounce of energy she possessed on the currents of Smith's dreamlight. In the past year she had occasionally manipulated the wavelengths of other people's nightmares but she had never before attempted what she was about to try now.

For an instant Smith did not seem to realize that he was under attack. He stared at her, mouth partially open in confusion. Fury quickly ignited in him.

"What are you doing?" he demanded. "You will pay for this, whore. I will make you freeze in your own private hell for daring to defy me. *Stop.*"

He raised his other arm to strike her but it was too late; he was already sliding into a deep sleep. He started to crumple. At the last second he tried to grab the edge of the table. His flailing arm knocked the candle off the stand and onto the floor.

The taper rolled across the wooden floorboards toward the bed. There was a soft whoosh when the flame caught the trailing edge of the satin drapery.

Adelaide rushed back to the wardrobe and took out the cloak and shoes that she had stashed inside earlier in preparation for her escape. By the time she was dressed the bed skirt was fully ablaze, the flames licking at the white quilt. Smoke was drifting out into the hall. Soon someone would sound the alarm.

She pulled the hood of the cloak up over her head and went toward the door. But something made her stop. She turned reluctantly and looked back at the artifact. She knew then that she had to take the strange object with her. It was a foolish notion. It would only slow her down. But she could not leave it behind.

She stuffed the relic into the black satchel, fastened the buckles, and started once more toward the door. She paused a second time over Smith's motionless figure and quickly searched his pockets. There was money in one of them. The dark ruby-colored crystal was in another. She took the money but when she touched the crystal she got an uneasy feeling. Heeding her intuition, she left it where it was.

Straightening, she went to the door, stepped over Rosser's dead body and moved out into the corridor.

Behind her the white satin bed was now engulfed in crackling, snapping flames. Down the hall someone started screaming. Men and women in various stages of dress and undress burst out of nearby doorways, seeking the closest exits. No one paid any attention to Adelaide when she joined the frantic crush on the staircase.

Minutes later she was outside on the street. Clutching the satchel, she fled into the night, running for her life.

I

Thirteen years later . . .

"Got her." Griffin Winters drew a circle around Avery Street and set the pen back into the brass inkstand. He flattened his palms on the desk and studied the large map of London spread out before him. Intense satisfaction swept through him. The hunt was all but over. The lady did not know it yet, but from now on she belonged to him. "I'm certain of her next target."

"What makes you think that you can predict where she'll strike next?" Delbert Voyle asked. He reached into his pocket and took out a pair of spectacles.

A large, powerfully built man in his early forties, Delbert had only recently concluded that he needed spectacles. They had an oddly transformative effect on his appearance. Without them he looked like what he was: a hardened man of the streets who made his living as an enforcer for a crime lord. But whenever he plunked the gold-rimmed spectacles onto his lumpy nose he suddenly metamorphosed into a slightly overweight scholar who belonged in a library or behind the counter of a bookshop.

"I saw the pattern this morning after I read the account of last night's raid on the Avery Street brothel," Griffin explained. "It all became clear."

Delbert leaned over the desk to get a closer look at the locations of the brothels. He knew every alley and unmarked lane in both the good and bad neighborhoods. He had no difficulty comprehending the map. In fact, he could have drawn it.

Delbert possessed a sense of direction as well as a photographic memory of every location he had ever visited that was, in Griffin's opinion, probably psychical in nature. Delbert scoffed at the notion, although he took Griffin's talent for granted, just as Jed and Leggett did. To his men, Griffin knew, he was simply the Boss and, as such, he was expected to be different.

Delbert, Jed and Leggett were among the first members of the crew of young street thieves whom Griffin had recruited into his fledgling gang two decades earlier. They had all left the streets a long time ago. Now the three enforcers supervised and guarded the household.

Delbert was in charge of the kitchens. Jed took care of the grounds and the dogs and served as coachman. Leggett shouldered the responsibilities that would normally have fallen to a butler. A laundry maid came in twice a week and other day staff was employed as required, but all of the outsiders worked under strict supervision. None spent the night. Griffin was not concerned that someone might try to pinch the silver. The house held secrets, however, and he was single-mindedly obsessive when it came to concealing them. He had not become one of the most powerful crime lords in London by being careless.

Although Jed, Delbert and Leggett kept the big house running smoothly, that was not their primary responsibility. In reality they were Griffin's lieutenants. Each was charged with overseeing a specific aspect of the empire that Griffin had built.

The ragtag band of thieves he had formed years ago had matured into a well-organized business enterprise with a variety of holdings. Its tentacles reached deep into London's grittier neighborhoods and also into its most respectable streets. In the past several years Griffin had discovered that he had a knack for investing. He owned shares in a number of banking, shipping, and railroad companies and with those shares had come even more power.

None of his neighbors on St. Clare Street was aware that the big house built on the ruins of the ancient Abbey belonged to one of the most notorious figures in the city's criminal underworld. To those in the nearby mansions the owner of the pile of stone at the end of the street was simply a wealthy, if decidedly eccentric, recluse.

"You're still convinced that it's a woman who is organizing the raids?" Delbert asked, forehead wrinkling a little as he studied the map.

"There is no doubt in my mind," Griffin said.

Delbert removed his spectacles and put them carefully back into his pocket. "Well, I'll say this much for her, she's moving up in the world. The Peacock Lane and the Avery Street whorehouses are a good deal more elegant than the first three she hit. Do you think she knows that the latest two are owned by Luttrell?"

"I'd stake the Abbey on it. I'm sure she's had her sights set on Luttrell's brothels all along. The first three raids on the small, independent houses were staged to gain experience. Like any good general, she learned from those raids and refined her tactics. From now on, she'll concentrate on Luttrell's operations. She is nothing if not ambitious."

"That's a social reformer for you. No common sense at all." Delbert clicked his teeth in a tut-tutting sound. "Probably doesn't realize what kind of viper she's dealing with."

"She knows. That's why she's hitting his operations. Social reformers seem to be convinced that they are somehow protected by the righteousness of their cause. It would never occur to our little brothel raider that Luttrell would not hesitate to slit her throat."

"She appears to be focusing all of her attention on the whorehouses," Delbert mused.

"That's been obvious from the very first newspaper accounts."

Delbert shrugged. "No need for us to be concerned, in that case. We don't operate any whorehouses. She might become a nuisance if she decides to go after gaming clubs or taverns, but as long as she sticks to raiding brothels, she's Luttrell's problem."

"Unfortunately," Griffin said, "if she keeps on with her hobby, she's going to get herself killed."

Delbert shot him a searching look. "You're worried about a social reformer? They're nothing but pests, same as squirrels and pigeons, except that you can't roast them or make a decent stew out of them."

"I think this particular reformer might come in very handy if I can get to her before she ends up floating in the river."

Delbert was starting to become alarmed. "Bloody hell. She's caught your fancy, hasn't she, Boss? Why her?"

"It's difficult to explain."

Griffin looked at the portrait on the wall. It was akin to gazing into a dark mirror. Nicholas Winters was dressed in the style of the late seventeenth century, but his black velvet coat and elaborately tied cravat did nothing to obscure the startling similarity between the two of them. From the dark hair and brilliant green eyes to the fiercely etched planes and angles of their faces, the resemblance was uncanny.

The portrait had been completed shortly after Nicholas had come into his second talent. The nightmares and hallucinations had already begun. Every time Griffin examined the painting he found himself searching for some indication of the madness that would soon follow.

The image in the painting suddenly wavered and shimmered. Nicholas stirred to life. He fixed Griffin with his alchemist's eyes.

"You are my true heir," Nicholas said. *"The three talents will be yours. It's in the blood. Find the lamp. Find the woman."*

Griffin suppressed the vision with an effort of will. The disturbing daytime hallucinations had begun a few weeks earlier at about the same time that his new talent had appeared. The nightmares were so bad now that he dreaded sleep. There was no longer any way to deny the truth. He had been struck with the Winters Curse.

Delbert, blissfully unaware of the hallucination, contemplated Griffin with the knowing look of a longtime friend and confidant.

"You're bored," Delbert announced. "That's the real problem here. You haven't had a woman since you parted company with that pretty blond widow you were seeing a few months back. You're a healthy man in your prime. You need regular exercise. There's no shortage of willing females who would be more than pleased to scratch that particular itch for you. No need to pursue one who will surely cause you no end of trouble."

"Trust me, I'm not interested in bedding a social reformer," Griffin said.

But even as he spoke the words, he realized with a frisson of awareness that he was lying. He was very good when it came to lying. The skill had helped him rise to the top of his profession. But he conducted his life by a few, inflexible rules, one of which was that he never lied to himself.

Although he had no intention of explaining the situation to Delbert, the reality was that he was obsessed with the woman who was conducting the brothel raids. He had been fascinated by her since the first rumors from the street had reached him. Initially he had found the fixation inexplicable. Delbert was right, social reformers were just another form of urban pest.

"No offense, Boss, but I know that look," Delbert said grimly. "It's the same one you get whenever you decide to go after something you want. But use your head, man. For all you know this female, assuming she is a female, might be a little old gray-haired grandmother or a crazed religious zealot. Hell, she might prove to be one of those women who has no interest in men."

"I'm aware of that," Griffin said. Yet some part of him was convinced otherwise. It was, no doubt, the part that would soon be standing on an invisible edge looking down into the hell of insanity.

Find the lamp. Find the woman.

Delbert, glumly resigned, exhaled a deep sigh. "You're going to track her down, aren't you?"

"I don't have any choice." Griffin contemplated the circles he had drawn on the map. "But I need to do it quickly."

"Before Luttrell gets to her, do you mean?"

"Yes. She's found a strategy that works and she's sticking to it. Predictability is always a weakness."

"Once we locate her, Jed and I'll grab her for you."

"No, that approach won't work. I need the lady's full and willing cooperation. This situation calls for a proper social introduction."

Delbert snorted. "A respectable social reformer agrees to be introduced to a crime lord? Now that's a sight I'd pay good money to see. How do you plan to arrange that?"

"I believe the lady and I have a mutual acquaintance who can be persuaded to set up a meeting on neutral territory," Griffin said.

2

THE WIDOW SWEPT INTO THE CHARITY HOUSE KITCHEN JUST as Irene and the others were digging into mountains of scrambled eggs and sausages. Forks frozen in midair, the girls stared at the new arrival, astonished. Elegant ladies, even those devoted to good works, never, ever allowed themselves to be tainted by the presence of fallen women. And The Widow was clearly a very elegant person.

She was fashionably dressed from head to toe in striking shades of black, silver and gray. The black lace veil of her fine velvet hat concealed her features. The skirts of her gown were draped into intricate folds and trimmed with a street-sweeper ruffle at the hem to protect the expensive fabric from the dirt and grime of the pavement. The pointed toes of a pair of dainty gray leather high-button boots peeked out from beneath the ruffle. Black gloves sheathed the lady's hands.

"Good morning," The Widow said. "I'm delighted to see that you all have hearty appetites. That is a very good sign."

Belatedly, Irene Brinks got her mouth closed. She jumped up from the end of the bench and managed a small curtsy. There was a great deal of scraping of wood on floorboards as her four companions pushed back the bench and stood.

"Please sit down and return to your breakfasts," The Widow said. "I just wanted to have a word with Mrs. Mallory."

The small, stout, cheerful-looking woman at the stove wiped her hands on her apron and gave The Widow a radiant smile.

"Good morning, ma'am," Mrs. Mallory said. "You're here early today."

"I wanted to see how you were getting on after the excitement last night," The Widow said briskly. "All is well?"

"Yes, indeed." Mrs. Mallory glowed with satisfaction. "The young women are eating good breakfasts, as you noticed. I suspect it's the first decent meal most of them have had in a while."

"Just like last time," The Widow said. But she said it very softly. "The girls are half starved."

"I'm afraid so," Mrs. Mallory said. "But we'll soon fix that."

Irene did not move. Neither did the other girls. They stood rigidly at attention, unable to determine the correct course of action. They had some experience with social reformers like Mrs. Mallory but nothing in their lives had prepared them for The Widow.

The Widow looked at them. "Do sit down and finish your breakfast, ladies."

There was a moment of confusion while Irene and the others looked around to see if there were some actual ladies present in the kitchen. Belatedly realizing that The Widow had addressed them, they quickly took their seats on the bench.

Mrs. Mallory crossed the room to join The Widow. The two women continued to talk in quiet tones. But the charity house kitchen was not large. Irene could hear what they were saying. She was sure the other girls were listening, too. Like her, though, they pretended to concentrate on the food. It was not much of an act, Irene thought. They were all very hungry.

Last night they had panicked initially when, upon fleeing the burning brothel, they had been whisked into carriages and taken away. The men who had seized them had spoken in reassuring tones, but Irene and her companions knew better than to believe in the kindness of strangers. They concluded that they had been kidnapped by a rival brothel owner and would soon be employed again doing the same type of work they had done at the Avery Street whorehouse. They all knew that once a female started making her living on her back, there was no other future available.

It was not as though whores did not have dreams, Irene thought. A girl could always hope that some gentleman would take a fancy to her and perhaps give her a few pretty baubles or even set her up as his mistress. Admittedly, the chances of that happening were poor, but the possibility kept one going. When a girl gave up her dreams she turned to opium and gin. Irene was determined not to follow that path.

Upon arrival at the charity house they had been greeted with hot muffins and tea. It was obvious straight off that Mrs. Mallory was a typical social reformer, not a brothel manager. Irene and the others had been quick to take advantage of the food, aware that the charity house respite would be short-lived. Social reformers were always well intentioned but they lacked common sense. They did not begin to comprehend the realities of the world in which Irene and her friends lived.

The best the social reformers could offer a girl was the workhouse and, ultimately, a life of grinding servitude as a maid-of-all-work. Even that miserable existence was unlikely to last long. One could expect to be dismissed without a character reference the instant the lady of the house discovered that the new member of the staff was a former whore. Irene preferred to cling to her dreams, impossible though they sometimes seemed.

"The Avery Street brothel is more stingy than some when it comes to feeding the poor things," Mrs. Mallory said to The Widow. "The manager believes that if the girls are kept thin they will appear younger. As you know, that particular establishment caters to clients who prefer the young ones."

"If the girls survive they are old at eighteen," The Widow said. "And then they are tossed out onto the streets. We must try not to lose any of this lot, Mrs. Mallory. The eldest cannot be a day above fifteen."

Her voice was cool, soft and very even. Irene sensed that The Widow was not just another lady who dabbled in social reform work because it was considered the fashionable thing to do.

The Widow walked across the kitchen and halted at the head of the table. Once again the girls bolted awkwardly to their feet.

"I know that you are all anxious and confused," The Widow said, "but I want to assure you that you are safe here. Mrs. Mallory will take excellent care of you. No man is permitted to enter this house. The doors are all locked and bolted. Tomorrow morning, once you have been outfitted with proper dresses, you will be taken to my Academy for Young Ladies, a boarding school for girls like you."

Irene could not believe her ears. She knew the others were equally dumbfounded.

It was little Lizzie, the newest whore, who voiced the question that was on everyone's mind.

"Excuse me, ma'am," Lizzie said. "But would you be talking about sending us to another brothel?"

"No. I am talking about sending you to a respectable boarding school," The Widow said firmly. "You will have clean beds and uniforms and you will attend classes. When you are ready, you will go out into the world with some money of your own, enough to feel safe and secure. You will also be prepared to support yourselves as typists, telegraph operators, dressmakers or milliners. Some of you may choose to use your money to set yourself up in a business of your own. The point is that those of you who choose to take advantage of what I am offering will all have choices in the future."

Irene lowered her eyes to her unfinished eggs. The other girls did the same. The Widow might be passionate, even fierce in her zeal to save them, but upper-class ladies were not always as intelligent as one might expect.

Lizzie soldiered on bravely. "Begging your pardon, madam, but we can't go to a real boarding school."

"Why not?" The Widow asked. "Do any of you have families to which you wish to return? Any decent relatives who will care for you?"

The girls swallowed hard and looked at each other.

Lizzie cleared her throat. "No, ma'am. It was my pa who sold me to the Avery Street house. He won't be wanting me back."

"My parents died of a lung fever last year," Sally explained. "I was sent to the workhouse. The manager of the Avery Street brothel took me out of there. She said I was going to go into service as a house maid. But, well, that wasn't what happened."

Irene did not offer her own history. It was all too similar.

"As I thought," The Widow said. "Well, rest assured you will have every opportunity to embark upon new careers now."

"But, ma'am," Lizzie said, "we're *whores*. Whores can't go to a proper girls' school."

"I assure you they can go to this school," The Widow said. "I own the Academy. I make the rules."

Sally cleared her throat. "What good will it do? Don't you see, ma'am? Even if we learn to type or make fine hats no one will hire us because we were once whores."

"Trust me," The Widow said, "you are about to disappear forever. By the time you graduate from the Academy, you will be respectable young women with irreproachable backgrounds. You will have new names and new identities. No one will ever know that you once worked in a brothel."

That explained everything, Irene thought. The Widow was mad.

"What if someone recognizes one of us in the future?" Sally asked. "A former customer, perhaps?"

"That is highly unlikely to happen," The Widow said. "London is, after all, a very big place. What's more, you will be a few years older by the time you leave the Academy. You will look different. Furthermore, your new, *respectable* backgrounds will be fully documented all the way back to your birth. You will leave the school with excellent character references that will guarantee that you will find decent employment."

Sally widened her eyes. "Can you really make us disappear and come back as different people?"

"That is precisely why my Academy exists," The Widow said.

The lady was offering a dream. It was, Irene realized, a very different vision of her future, not the one that had sustained her since embarking on her career as a whore. But unlike those vague fantasies, this dream seemed almost real. It was as if all she had to do was reach out and seize it.

3

"IT'S AN INTERESTING ARTIFACT BUT THERE IS SOMETHING DE-cidedly unpleasant about that stone vessel, don't you agree? I suspect that is why the museum staff chose to tuck it away back here in a gallery where very few visitors are likely to stumble across it."

The words were uttered in a deep, masculine voice that stirred Adelaide's senses and sent a whisper of heat through her veins. Energy shivered in the atmosphere. The man was a talent of some kind, a powerful one at that. She had not anticipated such a turn of events.

Nor had she expected such a strong reaction from herself. She was unnerved. There was no other word for it. She had never met the man known throughout London's criminal underworld only as the Director of the Consortium, but she would have recognized him anywhere. Some part of her had been waiting for him since her fifteenth year.

For a few seconds she continued to look at the ancient vessel as though studying it. The truth was that she was using the time to pull herself together. She must not let the Director see how badly he had unsettled her senses.

It took a supreme effort of will for her to steady herself, but she managed a deep breath and turned slowly around in what she hoped was a cool, controlled manner. She was a woman of the world, she reminded herself. She would not let a crime lord rattle her.

"I assume that you asked that this meeting take place in this particular gallery because you don't want any visitors to stumble across you, either, sir," she said.

"I took it for granted that the leader of the notorious brothel raiders would appreciate a degree of privacy as well."

Although she recognized him in a psychical sense, she knew almost nothing about the Director, just some fragments of the mystery and legend that surrounded him. The women of the streets who showed up at the charity house talked about him in whispers.

She tried to get a better look at him but she could not make out his features. He lounged, arms folded, one shoulder propped against a stone pillar. He appeared to be enveloped in shadows. There was an eerie, phantomlike quality about him. It was as if she were seeing his reflection in a pool of dark water.

She sensed that he was contemplating her as though she were an interesting artifact in the museum's collection. Although she could not see him clearly, she could tell that he was expensively dressed in the manner of a respectable, high-ranking gentleman, a gentleman who patronized a very exclusive tailor.

It bothered her that she could not make out his features. Certainly the light was dim in the gallery, but her eyes had adjusted to the low level of illumination. In any event, the crime lord stood only a few feet away. She ought to be able to see his face quite plainly.

She slipped into her other sight. Understanding struck immediately when she saw that the stone floor glowed hot with darkly iridescent dreamprints. The Director was employing his talent, somehow using it to conceal himself. She could not identify the nature of his ability but the raw power of it was very clear.

"I am not the only one who came veiled to this appointment," she said. "That is a clever trick you are using. Are you an illusion-talent, sir?"

"Very observant, madam." He did not appear to be alarmed or irritated. If anything he sounded approving, even satisfied in a cold, calculating fashion. "No, I am not an illusion-talent but your guess is very close. I work shadow-energy."

"I have never heard of such a talent."

"It is rare but it certainly has its uses. If I employ a sufficient amount of power I can make myself virtually invisible to the human eye."

"I can understand how a talent of that sort would be helpful to one in your profession." She did not bother to conceal her disapproval.

"I have found it extremely useful since the earliest days of my career," he agreed, evidently not offended in the least. "The fact that you perceived my little disguise is very encouraging. I have never encountered anyone else who could do so. I believe we may be able to conduct some business together."

"I doubt that, sir. I cannot imagine that we have anything in common aside from our mutual acquaintance."

"Mr. Pierce." He inclined his head. "Yes. But before we discuss our connection to him, I would like to verify the conclusions that I have reached concerning the nature of your own talent."

She stilled. "I do not see that my talent is any concern of yours, sir."

"I'm sorry, madam, but the exact nature and strength of your own abilities is of considerable interest to me."

"Why?" she asked, very wary now.

"Because if I am correct, there is a possibility that you can save both my sanity and my life." He paused. "Although if you cannot salvage the former, I will have little use for the latter."

She caught her breath and glanced again at the seething energy in his prints. Power and control burned in the currents of his dreamlight. She saw none of the murky hues that indicated mental instability.

"You appear quite healthy to me, sir," she said crisply. She paused before adding, "Although I can see that you suffer from unpleasant dreams."

She sensed immediately that she had caught him off guard.

"You can tell that much just by reading my dreamlight patterns?" he asked.

"Illness of any kind shows strongly in dreamlight. I do not perceive any signs of mental or physical disease in your prints. But powerful nightmares also leave a distinctive residue."

"Can you *see* my dreams?" He did not sound pleased.

She understood. Dreams were among the most private of all human experiences.

"No one can view the actual scenes of another person's dreams," she said. "What I perceive is the psychical energy of the emotions and sensations experienced while dreaming. My talent translates that energy into impressions and sensations."

He contemplated her for a long moment. "Do you find your talent disturbing?"

"You have no idea." She slipped back into her normal senses. The trail of hot footsteps disappeared. "What is it that you want of me, sir?"

"It is not just your paranormal abilities that interest me. I am also intrigued by your passion for saving others."

"I don't understand."

"I realize that you specialize in rescuing young women from brothels. I am also aware that I am neither young nor female."

"I did notice," she said, her tone sharpening. "Are you trying to tell me that you need saving, sir? Because I very much doubt that there is anything I can do to assist a man in your, uh, position."

She could have sworn that he smiled at that, although she could not be certain because of the cloak of shadows that he wore.

"I am too far gone, is that what you are saying?" he asked. "I will admit that there is no vestige of innocence left in my nature for you to salvage. But that is not why I asked for this meeting."

"Why, then?"

"I turned thirty-six two months ago," he said.

"How is that significant?"

"Because it appears to be approximately the age at which the family curse strikes, if it does, indeed, strike. My father and grandfather and several generations before me were spared. I had dared to hope that I, too, had escaped. However, it appears that I am not so fortunate."

"Sir, I really do not see how I can help you," she said. "I am a modern thinker. I do not believe in curses and black magic."

"There is nothing of magic involved, I promise you. Just a great deal of damnably complicated para-physics. But I am hopeful that you can deal with it, Adelaide Pyne."

For a second or two, she did not grasp the significance of what he had just said. Then horrified comprehension crashed through her.

"You know my name?" she whispered.

"I am the Director of the Consortium," he said simply. "I know everything that happens on the streets of London. And you, Mrs. Pyne, have been very active on those streets of late."

4

HE COULD SEE THAT HE HAD DELIVERED A GREAT SHOCK TO her nerves. Her control was admirable—she scarcely flinched—but he sensed that she was fighting panic. He had overplayed his hand. That was unlike him.

"My apologies, Mrs. Pyne," he said. "The last thing I want to do is frighten you."

"I cannot believe that Mr. Pierce told you my name," she said, recovering her outward air of composure. "I thought I could trust him."

"You can. I have always found Pierce to be a man of his word." He smiled faintly. "Or should I say a woman of her word?"

"You know Pierce's secrets as well?" Disbelief echoed in Adelaide's words.

"I am aware that Pierce is a woman who chooses to live as a man, yes. We met years ago. She was orphaned as a girl and forced out onto the streets. She learned early on in life that she was not only safer when she went about dressed as a boy but also more powerful. How did the two of you become acquainted?"

"We met soon after I began my work with the young women of the streets," Adelaide said. "Pierce and his companion, Mr. Harrow, took an interest in my charity house. When I mentioned my plans to raid some brothels in order to engage the attention of the press, Mr. Harrow offered to assist. He invited two members of the Janus Club to help also. Do you know of the club, sir?"

"Pierce established it years ago. The members are all women who prefer to live as men. I assume that the volunteers from the club are the ones who spirit the girls away after you have emptied the house by crying fire?"

"Yes. But how do you know so much about Mr. Pierce?"

"Over the years we have found it mutually advantageous to form an alliance."

"I suppose I can understand why the two of you would have been obliged to arrive at certain arrangements and understandings regarding the control of the various shady businesses that you each operate. Open war would hardly benefit either of you."

He discovered to his surprise that he did not care for the disdain in her voice. He thought that he had long ago ceased to be concerned with the opinions of others, but Adelaide Pyne's obvious disapproval irritated him for some reason.

"Don't you find your position somewhat hypocritical, Mrs. Pyne?"

"I beg your pardon?"

"You are a lady who forms associations with crime lords when it suits you. What does that make you?"

He heard the quick intake of her breath and knew that he had finally scored a point. What the devil was the matter with him? He needed her help. Trading barbs was hardly the most intelligent way to go about the task.

"Let us be clear, sir," she said. "I have formed an alliance with one particular crime lord, Mr. Pierce, not with you or anyone else in that business."

"I stand corrected," he said. "One alliance with one crime lord, it is."

"Speaking of Pierce, you claim that he did not tell you my identity. How, then, did you discover it?"

"Your raids have created quite a sensation, not just in the press but on the streets as well. There were rumors that some of the young prostitutes who have disappeared in the past few months vanished shortly after visiting a certain charity house on Elm Street. I made some inquiries and learned that the establishment, which until recently had been struggling financially, was currently flourishing under a new, anonymous patron known only as The Widow."

"Your investigation led you directly to me?" She was aghast. "Was it really so simple to discover my identity?"

"You have concealed your connection to the charity house well. But while individuals may hide their identities easily enough, I regret to inform you that it is relatively simple to track the flow of money. That is especially true when it transpires that all of the bills and expenses of a certain charity house are paid for by a specific bank."

"Good heavens. My bankers gave you my name? Is nothing sacred?"

"In my extensive experience, no, at least not when money is involved. There is an individual employed at your bank who happened to owe me a favor. When he learned that I was seeking the identity of the new patron of a certain charity house he was kind enough to repay his debt to me by giving me your name."

"I see." Frost dripped from every word. "Do you always do business in such a manner?"

"Whenever possible. I have all the money I require, Mrs. Pyne. These days I find that a debt owed to me is a far more valuable commodity."

"So you threaten and intimidate innocent people such as that bank clerk?"

"I thought I made it clear. There were no threats involved. The clerk owed me a favor."

"It strikes me that a favor owed to a crime lord is little short of a threat or extortion."

"Were you born this self-righteous, Mrs. Pyne, or did you acquire the trait during your years in America?"

She stiffened. "You know that I lived in America?"

"The bank clerk mentioned it. But I would have guessed it in any event. I can hear the overtones of an accent in your voice. I'll wager you spent a good deal of time in the West."

"I do not see what that has to do with this conversation."

"Neither do I, so let us move on to the more important topic."

"Which is?" she asked warily.

"How you are going to save me."

"And just how will I accomplish that? Always assuming I am of a mind to do so."

"With luck, your ability to work dreamlight will be my salvation."

"I admit that I am a dreamlight reader," she said. "But there is a vast difference between being able to perceive the residue of dream energy and being able to manipulate the currents of that sort of ultralight."

"I am convinced that you can do both," he said.

"What makes you believe that?"

"My theory was confirmed yesterday morning when I heard about the man who was found unconscious in the alley behind the Avery Street brothel."

"He's not dead," she gasped. "I would have known . . ." She broke off abruptly, evidently aware that she had already said far too much.

"He's alive, but I'm told that his nerves were shattered by the nightmares he experienced while he was in a most profound sleep.

They say that his companions were unable to awaken him for several hours."

Adelaide's gloved fingers tightened around the handle of her umbrella. "He tried to seize me when I went downstairs into the alley to get away. Claimed he'd spotted me earlier in the evening and suspected that there was something *off* about me, as he put it. I recognized him as the enforcer the girls feared the most at that brothel. I was told that he could be quite brutal. But I fail to see how you made the connection to me."

"The rumors I heard made me think that whoever rendered him unconscious used psychical talent. There was not a mark on him, I'm told. The fact that he is even now babbling about vivid nightmares convinced me that the person responsible for his condition was in all likelihood a dreamlight worker."

"I see."

"That particular enforcer has killed men, Mrs. Pyne," he said evenly. "You were damned lucky to survive the encounter."

She said nothing.

He was wasting time trying to make her see the recklessness of her ways. Stick to the point, he thought. If the lady wants to take foolish risks, that's her affair. But for some reason, consigning Adelaide Pyne to her fate was easier said than done.

"If you knew my identity, what made you contact Mr. Pierce?" she asked.

"I desired a proper introduction. He agreed to arrange this meeting."

"Because the two of you are allies?"

He knew she was not going to like the answer.

"Mr. Pierce also owes me a few favors," he said.

"Like the poor man who works at my bank."

"Pierce would never have given you up to me, if that is what concerns you. He agreed only to suggest the meeting to you but he made it clear that whether or not you accepted the invitation would be your decision. Perhaps the more intriguing question is why you consented to come here today."

"Don't be ridiculous," she said. "I had little choice in the matter. It was obvious that if you had gotten as far as making inquiries of Mr. Pierce it would not be long before you found me."

He did not respond. Her conclusion was right. He would have come looking for her if Pierce had not agreed to set up the meeting.

"What is the precise nature of your problem, sir?" Adelaide asked. "I am well aware that you are not engaged in the brothel business so you have nothing to fear from a social reformer like me."

"What makes you so certain that I do not operate any brothels?"

She waved one hand in a dismissive gesture. "The girls who come to the charity house bring a river of gossip from the streets. They collect far more information than most people, including their customers and the brothel keepers, realize. They are aware of who engages in the business of selling flesh and who does not. There are many rumors about you, sir, but none of them link you to that despicable activity."

"I will take comfort in knowing that I needn't worry about an assault from your raiders," he said politely.

"Do you mock me, sir?"

"No, Mrs. Pyne. I fear for your life. It is evident that you are now going after Luttrell's whorehouses. He is a ruthless man who lacks any vestige of a conscience. He does not know the meaning of remorse. He is driven by greed and a lust for power."

"One generally expects those sterling qualities in a crime lord," she said coolly. "Do you claim to be from a different mold?"

"I thought we had just agreed that I do not make money from brothels."

He had to work to keep the edge out of his voice. If they were in each other's company much longer he would soon be looking for some effective way to silence her, at least temporarily. It occurred to him that kissing her would achieve that objective.

"My apologies, sir," Adelaide said. "I am well aware that your character is vastly different from Luttrell's. He is truly a monster. I see the damage he causes every time I take a girl out of one of his establishments."

"You got away with raiding two of his houses but I doubt that you will escape so easily the next time. Take my advice, Mrs. Pyne. Find another hobby."

"Is that a threat, sir? Are you implying that you will inform Luttrell of my identity if I do not agree to help you?"

Anger crackled through him. There was no logical reason why she should trust him, let alone place any faith in his character. Nevertheless, he did not like knowing that she believed he would stoop to blackmail.

"I am attempting to make you see reason, Mrs. Pyne," he said. He clung to his patience with an effort of will. "It did not take me long to understand that you are now targeting Luttrell's brothels. You may be assured that he will soon come to the same conclusion, if he has not already done so. The pattern is clear."

"How can that be? Three of the five raids were conducted on independent brothels."

"You practiced your strategy on those first three raids. When you believed that you were ready, you went after your real target. Now that you've tasted some success, you are planning to continue raiding Luttrell's operations."

"Why would I concentrate on him?"

"Probably because they employ the youngest women and cater to the most jaded clients. When you hit his whorehouses you also embarrass some of the most socially prominent men in London. By making

34

an example of Luttrell and his customers, you hope to frighten other, smaller brothel owners."

She sighed. "My plan is that obvious?"

He shrugged. "It is to me. There is no reason to think that Luttrell won't figure it out as well. He is not a stupid man. Furthermore, I am quite certain that he possesses a considerable degree of talent of his own. You would be wise to assume that his intuition is at least as good as mine."

She was silent for a moment.

"How well do you know Luttrell?" she asked finally.

"We are not friends, if that is what you mean," he said. "We are competitors. At one time we went to war with each other. The Truce settled certain matters between us but it does not mean that we trust each other. And a truce can always be broken."

"I have heard of this Truce," she said. "According to the rumors, you and Luttrell battled for months over the territories that each of you wanted to control. The two of you finally met in Craygate Cemetery and struck a bargain. In effect, you divided much of London's underworld empire between your two organizations."

"Something like that, yes."

"Good grief. Have you no shame, sir?"

"I leave the finer feelings to people like you, Mrs. Pyne. In my experience delicate sensibilities get in the way of making money."

"Is making a profit all that you care about?"

"That and staying sane. Both goals require that I keep you alive, at least until I have convinced you to help me. If you insist on forging ahead with your current pastime of raiding Luttrell's brothels, I expect your body will soon turn up in the river."

To his surprise she hesitated.

"I will admit that I have a few concerns about the strategy that I have been employing on the raids," she said reluctantly.

"Only a few concerns? How often do you think that the Trojan-horse strategy could have been repeated using the same damn horse? Sooner or later, even a fool will catch on, and I can promise you that Luttrell is no fool."

"The thing is, the fake smoke is so effective. It always empties out a house within minutes and it creates great confusion," she said.

"But it is also a very obvious tactic. You won't get away with it again, not if you use it against a Luttrell operation. He'll have his enforcers waiting for you next time."

"You sound very sure of that."

"Very likely because that is what I would do in his place. If I operated a string of brothels, trust me, I'd have enforcers watching the clients like hawks by now."

She cleared her throat. "You are nothing if not forthright, sir. But I refuse to believe that you would have me murdered in cold blood if I staged a raid against one of your operations. That is not your style."

He smiled at that. "You know little of my style. But I will promise you that nothing that ever happens between us will be in cold blood, Adelaide Pyne."

She stilled, evidently struck speechless.

"Fortunately, this is a hypothetical conversation," he added. "As you pointed out, I'm not in the brothel business."

"What if I raided one of your gambling clubs or taverns?" she asked icily. "Would my body end up in the river?"

"No. My methods tend to be a good deal more subtle than Luttrell's."

"Such as?"

He could be patient, he reminded himself. Patience was a virtue in his profession. The ability to wait for the proper moment to strike, combined with his natural intuition, had won him more victories than he could count. Impulse and strong passions were the greatest sins that could beset a crime lord. He had considered himself to be free of both for years . . . until Adelaide Pyne.

"We digress, Mrs. Pyne," he said, making a valiant effort not to grind his teeth. "Let's return to the point of this meeting."

"This meeting, as you call it, is not going well."

"That is because you are being difficult."

"It's a gift," she shot back.

"I have no trouble believing that."

She tapped the tip of her umbrella against the pedestal that held the ugly artifact. "Very well, sir. You said you needed my help on an urgent matter. Why don't you explain exactly what it is you wish me to do for you? Then, perhaps we can discuss the possibility of a mutually agreeable bargain."

The word *bargain* sparked a lightning-bright warning. He was willing to pay her for her services, but the notion of negotiating with her gave him considerable pause. On the other hand, it was not as though he had much choice in the matter. Adelaide Pyne was his only hope.

"I have a rather long and somewhat complicated story to tell you," he said carefully.

"Perhaps you will be able to cut your tale short when I inform you that I have an artifact in my possession that I believe belongs to you. A family heirloom, I suspect."

It was his turn to be stunned. Impossible, he thought. She could not possibly have the lamp.

"What are you talking about?" he asked finally.

"I refer to a rather odd antiquity shaped something like a vase. I believe it is about two hundred years old. It is fashioned of some metal that resembles gold. The rim is set with a number of cloudy gray crystals."

Anticipation flooded through him. For the first time in longer than he could remember, he allowed himself a measure of hope.

"Damn it to hell," he said very softly. "You found the Burning Lamp."

"Is that what it is called? Now that you mention it, I suppose it does resemble certain ancient oil lamps. But it is not made of alabaster in the Egyptian manner."

"How did you know that it belonged to me?"

"I didn't know it. Not until I met you a few minutes ago. It sounds impossible, but the artifact is infused with a formidable quantity of dreamlight. The patterns of the energy trapped in the lamp are nearly identical to your own. There are dreamprints on the device as well that are clearly from a man of your bloodline."

He could not believe his good fortune. He had come here today hoping to persuade her to help him search for the lamp. The possibility that she already had it in her possession left him feeling first light-headed and then—predictably enough given his nature—suspicious.

"How long have you had it?" he asked evenly, as though merely curious.

"I was fifteen when I acquired it."

Something in the very cool way she spoke told him that he was not going to get a complete answer to that question, not yet.

"How did it come into your possession?" he asked.

"I don't think that matters now," she said.

One thing at a time, he told himself. He could wait. The first step was to make certain that she possessed the real Burning Lamp.

"You mentioned that the artifact was not particularly attractive," he said. "I'm surprised you kept it around all these years."

"It has been a great nuisance, I assure you."

"Why is that?" He realized that he was still searching for the flaw in what appeared to be an incredible turn of luck.

"It took up valuable space in my luggage during my travels in America, for one thing," she said. "But the more serious problem is that the energy it gives off is quite disturbing, even to those who do not possess much talent. It is certainly not the sort of ornament that one wants sitting on the mantel. To be honest, I shall be delighted to get rid of it. And so will Mrs. Trevelyan."

"Who is she?"

"My housekeeper. She does not have any psychical ability, at least no more so than the average person, but just being in the presence of the lamp makes her anxious and uneasy. She is the one who banished it to the attic."

A torrent of questions flooded his mind. But one stood out.

"If you found the thing so disturbing, why did you keep it?" he asked.

"I have no idea." She glanced at the vessel displayed on the pedestal. "But you know how it is with paranormal artifacts of any sort. They hold a certain fascination, especially for those of us with some talent. And, as I told you, there is no question but that the lamp is infused with dreamlight. I have an affinity for that sort of energy. I simply could not let it go."

He exhaled slowly, still trying to dampen his sense of overwhelming relief. It seemed that the lamp had been found and he was standing in front of the woman who might be able to work it for him. But there was still the very real possibility that Adelaide Pyne might not be strong enough to manipulate the dangerous energies that Nicholas had locked inside the lamp.

There were other, equally unpleasant but plausible outcomes even if it transpired that Adelaide was sufficiently powerful. She might inadvertently or even deliberately murder him with the lamp's radiation. Short of that, she could destroy his talent, intentionally or otherwise.

Last, but by no means least, the lady might simply refuse to work the lamp for him because she did not approve of crime lords. But she was the one who had offered to bargain, he reminded himself. Evidently he had something she wanted. That gave him an edge. Once he knew what another person desired he could control the situation.

"It would appear that we are going to do business together, Mrs. Pyne," he said. "Allow me to introduce myself properly."

He lowered his talent and sank back into his normal senses, letting her see him clearly for the first time.

"I am Griffin Winters," he said, "a direct descendant of Nicholas Winters."

"Should I be impressed, sir?"

He was briefly disconcerted. "Not necessarily impressed, but I expected you to recognize the name."

"Why is that? Winters is not an uncommon name."

"You are aware of the Arcane Society, are you not, Mrs. Pyne?"

"Yes. My parents were members. My father had a passion for paranormal research. I was registered in the genealogical records of the Society shortly after I was born. But I have had no contact with the Society since the age of fifteen."

"Why is that?"

"My parents were killed in a train accident that year. I was sent off to an orphanage for young ladies. What with one thing and another I lost my connection to the Society."

"My condolences, madam. I lost my parents when I was sixteen." He realized that he had spoken on impulse. The knowledge worried him. He never did anything on impulse. Above all he did not discuss his own past, not even with his closest companions.

Adelaide inclined her head in a graceful gesture of silent sympathy. For a moment he had the sense that a delicate bond had been forged between them.

"As I said," she continued, "My father was fascinated with all things paranormal. I recall a few of the subjects he talked about but I do not recall him mentioning a Nicholas Winters."

"Nicholas Winters was a psychical alchemist. He was first a friend and later a rival and finally a mortal enemy of Sylvester Jones."

"You refer to the Jones who founded Arcane?"

"Yes. Like Jones, Nicholas was obsessed with discovering a way to enhance his talents. He constructed a device that he called the Burning Lamp. Somehow he succeeded in trapping a vast amount of dreamlight inside it. His goal was to employ the device to acquire a variety of powers."

"You think to follow in your ancestor's footsteps?" The disapproval was once again crisp in her voice. "I admit that I am not well acquainted with such matters, but I recall very clearly that my father often mentioned that individuals endowed with multiple talents are not only quite rare but also invariably mentally unstable. He said that within the Society there was a word for such people. It was the name of a creature in some ancient legend."

"The word is 'Cerberus,' the name of the monstrous, three-headed dog that guarded the gates of hell."

"Yes, I remember now," she said, appalled. "Surely you are not so lost to reason that you would wish to transform yourself into a psychical monster? If that is your objective, rest assured you will get no assistance from me."

"You misunderstand, Mrs. Pyne. I have no desire to become an insane rogue talent. On the contrary, I would very much like to avoid that fate."

"*What?*"

"You really don't know your Arcane history, do you?"

"I just explained—"

"Never mind. You will have to take my word for this. According to my ancestor's journal, I am doomed to become a Cerberus unless I can find the lamp and a dreamlight reader who can reverse the process of the transformation to a multitalent."

"Good grief. You actually believe this?"

"Yes."

"But how can you possibly know such a thing?"

"Because the transformation has already begun."

Her sudden stillness told him that she was starting to wonder about his sanity.

"I am in need of saving, Mrs. Pyne," he said. "It appears that you are the only one who can help me."

"I really don't think—"

Sensing weakness, he pounced. Like the predator that I am, he thought. Not that he would let that get in the way of achieving his objective.

"I am prepared to trust you," he said quietly. "I have allowed you to see me clearly. Will you honor me by returning the favor?"

For a moment he thought she would refuse. She tapped the tip of her umbrella against the pedestal again, thinking.

"I'm quite certain you could find me again if you wished to do so," she said finally. "So I suppose it no longer matters if you see my face."

It was not precisely the gracious capitulation he had hoped to provoke but he did not argue. She was right; he could find her again.

Everything inside him tightened as he watched her crumple the black netting up onto the brim of her hat. It was as if his entire future was about to be revealed to him.

Her intelligent, expressive features riveted his attention. Her whiskey-colored hair was pulled back into a chignon that was at once severe and stylish. But it was her hazel eyes that fascinated him most. They were the eyes of a woman who had seen something of the darkness in the world. He had expected as much. She was a widow, after all. In addition, she had spent several years abroad in the wilds of America. She conducted daring raids on brothels and rescued girls who were otherwise destined for short, hard lives as whores. She was acquainted with the rather dangerous Mr. Pierce, a remarkable accomplishment in itself.

She might be an irritating social reformer but Adelaide Pyne's gaze told him that she was far more aware of the hard truths of the world than most ladies of her class and station in life. Such forbidden knowledge always appeared in the eyes.

What astonished him was that there was also a bright, determined spirit about her. She was, he concluded, one of those foolish, willfully blind individuals who, even when confronted with harsh realities, continued to believe that goodness and right would ultimately prevail.

He could have told her otherwise. The war between Dark and Light was eternal. Victories were fleeting at best and went to whichever force happened to command the most power at any given moment. In his experience the elements that thrived in the shadows could be beaten back but only temporarily. Yet there were always those like Adelaide Pyne who would fight these battles regardless of the odds.

Such naïveté was incomprehensible to one of his nature, but he knew very well that it had its uses. The quality could be easily manipulated.

He smiled again, satisfied.

"Mrs. Pyne, you are the woman of my dreams."

5

"I SINCERELY HOPE THAT I AM NOT THE WOMAN OF YOUR dreams," she said.

He narrowed his eyes just a little. It seemed to her that the energy in the atmosphere around him grew heavier, more ominous. The hair on the nape of her neck lifted.

"You are offended?" he asked softly.

"Certainly, given that your dreamprints indicate that you suffer from nightmares," she said. "What woman would want to feature in a man's darkest, most unpleasant visions?"

He blinked. She knew she had surprised him. And then he started to smile. It was a slow, faint twist of his mouth but she sensed that the flash of amusement was genuine.

"Do you know, Mrs. Pyne, I think that we are going to get on very well together, in spite of the difference in our occupations and personal views."

It was all too easy to believe that Griffin Winters was the direct descendant of a dangerous alchemist. Adelaide told herself that her intense fascination with him was natural under the circumstances. He was not only a man of strong talent, he was also powerful in other ways as well. After all, he ruled a large portion of London's criminal underworld. But none of those facts explained the sparkling exhilaration she experienced in his presence.

He was not a handsome man but he was certainly the most compelling male she had ever encountered. His eyes were darkly brilliant and gem-green in color. His near-black hair was cut short in the current fashion. Sharply etched cheekbones, a high, intelligent forehead, an aquiline nose and an unforgiving jaw came together in a way that suited the aura of power that he wore so naturally.

There was something else about him as well: a sense of isolation, an abiding aloneness. Griffin Winters was a man who harbored secrets and kept them close.

She could well imagine him at work in a secret laboratory, stoking the fires of an alchemical furnace in search of arcane knowledge. Passion burned deep inside him but she sensed that it was securely locked behind an iron door. Griffin Winters would never allow that side of his nature to govern his actions. An oddly wistful sensation fluttered through her.

Don't be an idiot, she thought. The man is a crime lord, for heaven's sake, not a lost dog in search of a warm hearth and a kindly hand.

"At least I now know why I felt obliged to hang on to the lamp all these years," she said. "It appears that I was waiting for the rightful owner to claim it."

"Don't tell me that you believe in destiny, Mrs. Pyne?"

"No. But I have a great deal of respect for my own intuition. It told me that I ought to keep the lamp safe." She turned to walk away down the gallery. "My carriage is waiting in the street. My house is in Lexford Square. Number Five. I will meet you there. You shall have your lamp, Mr. Winters."

"And the woman who can work it?" he asked softly behind her.

"That remains to be negotiated."

HE ARRIVED in an anonymous black carriage that carried no markings or other identifying features. *One would hardly expect a man in his profession to go about in a vehicle inscribed with his initials or a family crest*, Adelaide thought, amused.

She watched from the drawing room window as Griffin opened the door of the cab and got out. He paused a moment, giving the square with its small park and respectable town houses an assessing glance.

She knew what he was doing. During her years in the American West she had seen others—lawmen, professional gamblers, gunfighters and outlaws—conduct the same quick analysis of their surroundings.

Griffin Winters no doubt possessed any number of enemies and rivals, she thought. She wondered what it was like living with the constant threat of violence. But he had chosen the path, she reminded herself.

Griffin went up the steps of Number Five and knocked once.

Mrs. Trevelyan's footsteps sounded in the hall. The housekeeper, excited by the unusual prospect of greeting a visitor to the household, was hurrying.

The door opened. Adelaide heard Griffin enter the front hall. A strange excitement fluttered through her in response to his presence in her home. She got the uneasy feeling that for the rest of her life she would know whenever he was in the vicinity. And, more disconcertingly, when he was not nearby. It was as if during that brief meeting in the museum she had somehow become attuned to him.

"My name is Winters," he said. "I believe I am expected."

"Yes, sir," Mrs. Trevelyan said. Her voice bubbled with enthusiasm and curiosity. "This way please, sir. Mrs. Pyne is in the drawing room. I'll bring in the tea tray."

Adelaide stepped quickly out into the hall. "No need for tea, Mrs. Trevelyan. Mr. Winters won't be staying long. He is here to collect an item that belongs to him, that's all. It's in the attic. I'll show him the way."

"Yes, ma'am." Mrs. Trevelyan's face fell, but she rallied swiftly. "It's very dusty up in the attic. I'm sure you'll both be wanting tea after you come back down."

"I don't think so," Adelaide said firmly. "Mr. Winters is a busy man. He'll wish to be on his way as soon as possible and as I have plans to go to the theater tonight, I don't have a great deal of time to spare, either." She looked at Griffin. "If you'll follow me, Mr. Winters, I'll show you to the attic."

She gripped the key ring tightly, whisked up her skirts and moved quickly toward the staircase. Griffin followed.

"Your housekeeper appears very eager to serve tea to your guests," he remarked halfway up the stairs.

"I suspect that she gets quite bored with only me and the daily maid for company."

"Yours is a small household, I take it?"

She reached the first landing and started up the next flight. "I live alone except for Mrs. Trevelyan."

"You must find it difficult without your husband. My condolences on your loss."

"Thank you. It has been several years now."

"Yet you still wear mourning."

"Sentiment aside, I find the veil useful, as I'm sure you noticed today at the museum."

"Yes," he said. "I can certainly understand the need for secrecy, given your hobby."

She ignored that. "As for the lack of visitors in this house that is due to the fact that I have only recently returned from America. I do not know many people here and I have no family."

"If you no longer have any connections to England why did you return?"

"I don't know," she admitted. She had been asking herself the very same question for weeks. "All I can tell you is that it seemed like the right time to come back."

She rounded another landing and climbed faster.

She set such a brisk pace on the last flight of stairs that by the time she reached the attic she was panting a little. Griffin, however, did not appear to be the least bit winded. In fact, it was obvious that he was in excellent physical condition.

It occurred to her that she had seen any number of gentlemen in various stages of undress in recent weeks, thanks to her new pastime, but very few had been endowed with the sort of manly physiques that made a lady want to look twice. She knew, however, that if she were ever to come upon a nude Griffin Winters she would not be able to resist a peek. Make that a thoroughly detailed scrutiny, she thought.

It was little wonder that Griffin was not breathless like her. He was not, after all, wearing several pounds of clothing. She had long ago eschewed the stiff bone corset and some of the multiple layers of undergarments that were currently fashionable. There was, however, no avoiding the great weight of the many yards of heavy fabric necessary to create a stylish gown, to say nothing of the petticoats required to support it. Her men's clothing was infinitely more comfortable and far less exhausting to wear.

"You were right," Griffin said. His voice was very soft. "I haven't seen the lamp since I was sixteen but the energy is unmistakable. I can feel the currents even out here in the hall."

She, too, was aware of the tendrils of dark energy leaking out from under the door. The dreamlight was so powerful that she could perceive it without raising her talent. But she was familiar with the lamp's currents, she reminded herself. She had been living with them since her fifteenth year. For Griffin, however, the power of the lamp likely came as something of a shock to the senses.

"Did you think I lied to you?" she asked. There was no logical reason why she should have been offended by his lack of trust. When had she come to care for the opinion of a crime lord?

"No, Mrs. Pyne," he said, studying the locked door. "I did not doubt that you believed you were telling the truth. But I had to allow for the possibility that you were mistaken."

"I understand." She gentled her tone. "You did not want to have your hopes raised only to see them dashed."

He looked at her, brows slightly elevated, as though he found her sympathy charmingly naive.

"Something like that," he agreed politely.

She cleared her throat. "I did warn you, it is not the sort of thing one keeps next to the bed," she said.

"As I recall, you mentioned that it was not the sort of ornament one kept on the *mantel*," Griffin said neutrally.

She felt herself turn very warm and knew that her cheeks were probably quite pink. She could not believe that he was making her blush. But to give Winters his due, he gallantly pretended the word *bed* was not now hanging between them like a razor-sharp sword.

She inserted the key into the lock and opened the door, revealing the heavily shadowed interior of the attic. The low-ceilinged room was crowded with the usual flotsam and jetsam that tended to gravitate upward in any household: odd pieces of furniture, old paintings in heavy frames, a cracked mirror and two large steamer trunks. The bulk of the stored items had been left behind by the previous tenant; only the trunks belonged to Adelaide. Thirteen years spent on the road did not allow one to collect a great many personal possessions.

"The lamp is inside that trunk," she said. She took one step into the room and nodded toward the second of the pair of steamers.

Griffin went past her and stopped at the large trunk. She watched him, aware of the seething energy swirling in the atmosphere. Not all of it was coming from the lamp. Much of it emanated from Griffin and for some inexplicable reason, she found it utterly enthralling.

"The artifact most certainly belongs to you, sir," she said. "There cannot be any doubt. It is obviously an object of enormous power. But I find it difficult to believe that your ancestor actually thought it could endow him with additional talents."

"I have translated the old bastard's journal and studied it for years but even I don't know the full truth about the lamp." Griffin did not take his eyes off the trunk. "I'm not sure that Nicholas, himself, understood what he had created. He was quite unstable at the end. But he did not doubt the lamp's power."

She moved a little farther into the room. "You said that Nicholas and Sylvester Jones were first close friends and later rivals?"

"Mortal enemies would be a more accurate description. I suspect that they were both driven at least partially mad by their lust for additional paranormal talents as well as by their own alchemical experiments. They were convinced that if they solved the secret of enhancing psychical powers they would add decades onto their normal life spans."

"The ultimate alchemical quest."

"Yes. They believed that the paranormal state was so entwined with the normal physical state that an increase in talent would have a therapeutic effect on all the body's organs."

"But researchers have discovered that too much psychical stimulation drives one mad."

"That's certainly what Arcane's experts have concluded."

"There is some logic to the theory. Overstimulation of any of the senses results in pain and physical as well as psychical damage."

"We're talking about a couple of mad alchemists, remember. They did not approach the problem the same way modern scientists do. Sylvester tried to achieve the goal through chemistry."

"The founder's formula. I remember my father mentioning it. But surely that is just another Arcane legend."

"I cannot say." Griffin leaned down to unlock the trunk. "But I do know that my ancestor was more of an engineer. He was skilled in crystals and metals. He forged the lamp with the intention of using its radiation to make himself more powerful. But when the device was completed he discovered that he needed a dreamlight reader to manipulate the energy he had succeeded in trapping inside the thing."

"Someone like me."

"He found such a woman." Griffin opened the trunk and contemplated the drawers built into each side. "Her name was Eleanor Fleming. According to the journal, Nicholas seduced her into working the device for him on three different occasions."

"Why didn't he just offer to pay her for her efforts?"

"He did. But the price she demanded was marriage. Nicholas had no intention of marrying a poor woman from a much lower class."

"So he lied to her."

"He agreed to the bargain, or so the story goes. He most certainly slept with her and produced offspring. I am living proof that that aspect of the legend is true. But because they had a sexual relationship there are still those within Arcane who believe that such an intimate connection is necessary before the artifact can be activated."

Memories of the night in the brothel slammed through her. She swallowed hard and then cleared her throat.

"Do you believe that?" she asked evenly.

"No, of course not." He glanced back at her, amused. "Calm your-

51

self, Mrs. Pyne. I have no designs on your ever so respectable virtue. From my reading of the journal, it's clear that a physical link of some kind is probably necessary, but I'm certain that it need not be anything more personal than a touching of the hands."

"I see." She told herself she should be greatly relieved. And she was. Most certainly. Ruthlessly she crushed the little flicker of excitement that had ignited somewhere deep inside her. "But you say there are those who are convinced that a more, ah, intimate connection is required?"

"You know how it is with legends, Mrs. Pyne. One way or another, a sexual encounter of some sort is always involved in the tale."

A great mystery had just been solved, although Griffin could not know it. After all this time, she finally understood why Smith had been determined to rape her that night thirteen years ago. He had believed that sexual intimacy with a dreamlight reader was required before he could acquire the powers of the artifact.

"What is it," she asked cautiously, "that makes you so certain that you are in danger of becoming an unstable multitalent?"

"Facts, Mrs. Pyne. I assure you, I base my concerns on hard evidence."

"Such as?"

"I came into my second talent a few weeks ago."

"Good heavens. You can't be serious, Mr. Winters."

"It was accompanied, just as the journal warned, by nightmares and hallucinations."

She watched him open a drawer, unable to believe what she was hearing. "Are you telling me that you have actually developed a new psychical ability?"

"That is exactly what I am saying, madam." He glanced curiously at the stack of old newspaper clippings and colorful advertising flyers he had uncovered.

"Not that drawer," she said quickly. "The next one down. What is your second talent?"

He closed the drawer full of papers and opened the one below it. "Let's just say that it is unpleasant."

"Mr. Winters, under the circumstances, I think I am entitled to something more in the way of an explanation. Do you refer to your shadow-talent?"

"No. That is my first talent, the one that developed when I was in my teens." He reached into the drawer and removed the velvet-shrouded object inside. "I have recently gained the ability to plunge another person straight into a waking nightmare."

She frowned. "I don't understand."

"Neither do I, at least not entirely." He examined the velvet sack. "For obvious reasons, there has not been much opportunity to experiment. All I can tell you is that I can trap a man in a nightmare. What he does while he is lost in the dream is unpredictable. On the one occasion I actually employed the talent, the individual collapsed and died."

"I see." A chill slithered through her. *Never forget that he is a crime lord.* Men in his profession were not above murdering people to achieve their objectives.

There was a muffled *thunk* when Griffin set the black velvet sack on top of the steamer.

"I have reason to believe that my victim had a weak heart," he said.

She recovered from the initial astonishment. "Well, that might explain a great deal."

"Certainly." His voice was cold and dry. "Another man might have merely been maddened by the visions and perhaps decided to jump out a window."

He began to untie the knot in the black cord that secured the sack.

"You are quite sure you generated nightmare energy?" she asked, curious now.

"There is no doubt in my mind."

"Actually, that is very interesting," she said.

He slanted her an unreadable look over his shoulder. "I have just told you that I can kill a man with my new talent, Mrs. Pyne. You do not sound suitably impressed, let alone horrified. Somehow I expected a stronger reaction from a social reformer."

She ignored his sarcasm, too intrigued with her own reasoning.

"What you describe is not unlike what I can do with my own senses," she said.

His smile was pure steel. "You are in the habit of dispatching people with your talent?"

"No, of course not. The most I can do is render an individual unconscious, as I did with that enforcer in the alley behind the brothel. But the principles of the para-physics involved may be similar."

"You sound like a scientist making an observation in a laboratory. We are talking about a *killing* talent, Mrs. Pyne."

"Hear me out, sir. Our mutual affinity for the energy in the lamp indicates that we both draw our powers from the dreamlight end of the spectrum. But it sounds as if you are simply capable of reaching much deeper into the dark ultralight regions than I can."

"Simply?"

"I do not mean to minimize your ability," she said quickly.

"Mrs. Pyne, when you put Luttrell's enforcer into that very deep sleep, did you touch him?"

"Yes, of course. That is the only way I can generate the level of energy required to do such a thing. Physical contact is required."

"The other night I killed a man who was standing a good three, maybe four paces away from where I stood. I never laid a hand on him."

She drew a sharp, startled breath. "That is a very powerful talent, indeed. How did you discover it?"

"While I was engaged in what you would no doubt consider the sort of hobby one would expect a crime lord to pursue."

"What hobby?"

"I was conducting some business in the study of a certain gentleman at about two o'clock in the morning. Suffice it to say that the gentleman in question was not aware of my presence in his household."

She drew a sharp breath. "You broke into someone's home and searched his study?"

"Does that surprise you?" The cold amusement was back in his voice. "Given my profession, that is?"

"Well, no. I suppose it doesn't. It's just that, considering your obvious rank and position in the criminal underworld, one would have thought that you no longer dabbled in such petty crimes, at least not personally. You control a vast criminal consortium. Surely you employ people who can do that sort of work for you?"

"You know the old saying 'If you want a job done properly, do it yourself.'"

"Nevertheless, to take such an unnecessary risk seems quite . . . extraordinary."

"No offense, Mrs. Pyne, but when it comes to risks, you are in no position to lecture me."

She discovered she did not have a ready response to that.

"To conclude my story," he said, "I was interrupted in the midst of the search by the homeowner and another man. There was no time to retreat back out the window and nowhere to hide. I used my shadow-talent to conceal myself. I was then obliged to witness a very heated argument between the two men. The gentleman reached into the drawer of the desk, pulled out a gun and prepared to shoot his visitor. That was when I intervened."

"Why?" she asked.

He got the cord untied. "Because the man who was about to be shot was a client of mine."

"A client? *Your* client?"

"He wanted answers to some questions. I had agreed to find them. In any event, I used my nightmare talent against the gentleman with the gun without even thinking about it. It was a reflexive, intuitive reaction."

"The way it always is the first time," she said quietly, remembering her own first experience with her talent.

"The man screamed," Griffin said, his voice very low. "It was unlike anything I have ever heard. An unearthly sound, as they say in sensation novels. And then he was on the floor. Dead."

"What of your client?"

"Not surprisingly, he fled the scene, thoroughly shaken. He never saw me. Later he and everyone else, including the police, concluded that the man who had tried to murder him had suffered a stroke. I saw no reason to correct that impression."

"*Hmm.*"

"I hear the scientist in your tone again, Mrs. Pyne."

"I believe I mentioned that my father specialized in paranormal research," she reminded him. "Perhaps I picked up a few of his character traits. You are convinced that this nightmare-generating talent of yours is new?"

"I think I would have noticed early on if people in my vicinity were plunging into states of abject terror for no apparent reason."

She refused to be put off course by his sarcasm. An idea had taken shape in her mind and she could not let it go.

"The thing is," she said, "I cannot help but wonder if perhaps your new ability is somehow linked to your first talent. In which case it would not necessarily be a second power, if you see what I mean. Maybe it is nothing more than an aspect of your original talent, one that took longer to develop."

"I told you, there are other symptoms that the curse has struck," he said, grim impatience edging his words. "When I am awake, I experience occasional hallucinations. I can deal with those. When I sleep, however, I endure nightmares so extreme that I awaken in a cold sweat, my heart pounding."

"I see," she said gently.

It occurred to her that a crime lord might have good reason to suffer from nightmares. She decided not to mention that it might be his conscience that was inflicting the bad dreams. She doubted that he would appreciate that observation. As for the hallucinations, she had no such easy explanation.

Griffin pulled down the sides of the velvet sack, revealing the artifact. He stood very quietly for a time. Adelaide sensed the energy swirling around him.

"There is no doubt," he said quietly. "This is the real Burning Lamp."

Adelaide moved closer to the relic. Her palms prickled. She had examined the relic any number of times over the years but it never ceased to fascinate her and send a frisson across her senses.

The lamp was about eighteen inches tall and gleamed like gold in the weak light. As she had told Griffin, it looked more like a metal vase than an old oil lamp. The tapered bottom section was anchored in a heavy base inscribed with alchemical symbols. The sides flared out as they rose upward. Murky gray crystals were embedded in a circle just below the rim.

"What do you sense?" Griffin asked. He did not take his eyes off the lamp.

"Dreamlight," she said. "A great deal of it."

"Can you work it?"

"Possibly," she said. "But not alone. From time to time over the years I have tried to access the energy in that lamp. I can make it glow faintly but that is all. But I can tell you one thing, if it is ever truly ignited, there may be no going back."

He picked up the artifact and carried it to the small attic window to get a better look. "How do I go about lighting it?"

"You don't know?"

"I handled the artifact a few times when I was younger but I was never able to activate it. My father believed that was because I had not inherited the curse. The lamp was stolen when I was fifteen. This is the first time in two decades that I have seen it."

"What about Nicholas's journal? Didn't he provide instructions on how to work the lamp?"

"If you know anything about the old alchemists you know that they were all obsessed with their secrets. Nicholas did not leave much in the way of specific instructions. I think he assumed that the man who tried to access the energy in the lamp would be guided by his own intuition and that of the dreamlight reader."

"I see."

"Well, Mrs. Pyne?" he said. "Will you work the lamp for me and reverse the process that has begun? Will you save me?"

She opened her senses and looked at his dreamprints. They burned on the wooden floorboards. He believed the legend, she thought. Whether or not it was true, he was convinced that he had inherited the Winters Curse.

"I will try to work the lamp for you," she said.

"Thank you."

"But I want to read your ancestor's journal before I attempt to manipulate the energy of the thing."

"I understand. I will bring it to you this evening."

"I'm afraid that will not be convenient. I am committed to attend the theater with friends tonight. Surely there is no great rush here. Judging by your dreamprints you are not on the brink of any sort of psychical disaster. Bring the journal to me tomorrow morning. I will study it and then decide how to proceed."

He did not look pleased by the short delay but he did not argue.

"Very well, perhaps you are right," he said. "My fate is in your hands. I will pay you whatever you ask."

"Yes, well, as to the matter of my fee," she said, "I really do not need your money. I am, as it happens, a rather wealthy woman."

"I understand. Please know that I am in your debt. If there's ever anything a man in my position can do for you, you have only to ask."

"As it happens, I do have a favor to request in exchange for my assistance with the lamp," she said.

He looked at her. His eyes were suddenly very, very green and as hot as his dreamprints. Energy floated across her nerves. She could have sworn that the shadows had deepened in the room.

"Ah, yes, the bargain you mentioned," he said very softly. "What do you want in exchange for saving me, Mrs. Pyne?"

She steeled her nerve. "Your expertise and professional advice."

Once again she could tell that she had caught him off guard.

"On what subject?" he asked, very wary now.

She tipped up her chin. Her intuition was warning her that she should never have started down this particular road but she refused to change course.

"You pointed out that the strategy I have been employing in the brothel raids has become predictable," she said. "I require a fresh approach."

"No." The single word was flat and unequivocal.

She ignored the interruption. "Mr. Pierce spoke very highly of your abilities in matters of strategy. Indeed, he said that no one is as skilled as you, sir."

"No."

"You know far more about Luttrell and the way he thinks than I do."

"No."

She drew herself up. "Therefore, in exchange for working the lamp I ask that you help me devise a new technique for conducting effective brothel raids."

"What you are asking, Mrs. Pyne, is that I assist you in devising a strategy that will surely get you killed. The answer is no."

"Give the matter some thought, sir," she urged.

"I may be bound for hell, madam, but at least when I arrive at the gates I will not have that particular sin on my conscience."

He turned and walked toward the door, the lamp gripped in one hand. He did not look back.

"Mr. Winters," she said quickly. "Think for a moment. You said, yourself, that you need me."

"I found one dreamlight reader. I will find another."

"Hah. You are bluffing."

"What makes you so certain of that?"

"I spent over a decade in the American West. Gambling is a popular pastime in that part of the world. I recognize a bluff when I see one. Even if you could locate another dreamlight reader I doubt very much you'll find one who is as powerful as I am."

"I'll just have to take my chances."

He went out into the hall.

The odds were staggeringly against him. She knew that, even if he did not. If he was right about what was happening to his senses, he might very well go mad and perhaps even die.

"Oh, bloody hell," she muttered. "Very well, sir, you win. I will work your lamp for you."

He stopped and turned around. "And the price, Mrs. Pyne?"

She twitched up her skirts and started toward the door. "I thought I made it clear. I do not need your money."

His jaw was rigid. "Damn it, Mrs. Pyne—"

She went past him into the hall and headed toward the stairs. "I will not charge you a fee for my services, Mr. Winters. Instead you will have to consider yourself in my debt from now until I think of some other favor to ask of you." She gave him her iciest smile over her shoulder. "Of course, you will likely decline to grant that one, too. For my own good, of course."

He followed her. "I will do anything you ask of me so long as it will not put you in harm's way."

"If repaying the favor to me hinges on your approval of whatever it is I choose to ask of you, I suspect you will be in my debt for a very long time. Possibly until it snows in that rather warm destination you mentioned a moment ago."

"I will find a way to repay you, Mrs. Pyne," he vowed.

"Don't bother. I shall take far more satisfaction in knowing that a notorious crime lord is in my debt."

"Damnation, Mrs. Pyne. Has anyone ever told you that you are stubborn, difficult, reckless and altogether lacking in sound judgment?"

"Certainly, sir. Those are the very qualities that enabled me to make my fortune in America."

"I can believe that," he said with great depth of feeling.

She reached the front hall and opened the door for him with a flourish.

"Before you hurl any more insults," she said, "you would do well to bear in mind that those are also the same character traits that have convinced me to work your damned lamp. Certainly only a stubborn, reckless, difficult woman lacking in *sound judgment* would have allowed a prominent member of the criminal class over the threshold of her home."

He paused on the front step and looked back at her. The flash of sensual heat combined with the dangerous irritation in his eyes sent a thrill through her. She caught her breath.

"You make an excellent point, Mrs. Pyne," he said, sounding very thoughtful. "I will do my best to remember it in our future dealings."

"Good day, Mr. Winters."

She closed the door with considerably more force than was necessary.

6

"DARE I ASK IF THE MEETING IN THE MUSEUM WENT WELL?"
Mr. Pierce inquired in his whiskey-and-cigar voice.

"It could best be described as *interesting*," Adelaide said. "Mr. Winters was not quite what I expected, to say the least."

She employed her black lace fan in a futile attempt to stir the still, stuffy air. It was intermission and the ornate, heavily gilded theater lobby was crowded with elegantly dressed people. She and Mr. Pierce and Adam Harrow had procured glasses of champagne and retreated to an alcove.

She told herself that it was the crush of theatergoers combined with the overheated atmosphere that was making her so uncomfortable. She felt stifled and edgy. The heavy veil of her hat was exacerbating the sensation, she thought. What should have been a pleasant evening had become an ordeal. She could not wait for it to end. But she did her best to conceal her unease from her companions.

"No one ever gets quite what they expect when they deal with Griffin

Winters." Pierce swallowed some champagne and lowered the glass. "That is likely one of the reasons for his extraordinary success."

"Did he let you get a close look at his face?" Adam Harrow asked in his languid manner.

"Yes, as a matter of fact, he did," Adelaide said.

She drank some more champagne in an attempt to quell her inexplicable tension. When she lowered her glass she realized that her companions were gazing at her with astonished expressions. They looked oddly impressed.

"Well, well, well," Pierce muttered. "An interesting meeting, indeed. Very few people are allowed to see Mr. Winters's face."

"And live to tell about it," Adam concluded dryly.

Pierce and Harrow were far more than very good friends. Adelaide could see from their dreamprints that the bond between them was deep and strong. It extended into every aspect of their lives, physical as well as emotional. They were women who lived as men and did it so successfully that they were accepted as gentlemen without question.

Pierce was short, square and as solid as a stone monument. His black hair was shot with silver. Although he had long ago banished the accents of the streets from his voice, the knowledge that he had gained in London's darkest alleys was still there in his startlingly blue eyes.

Adam Harrow, however, had come from an upper-class background. He was the very image of a modern, debonair man-about-town. He projected an effortless air of elegant ennui that marked him as well bred and fashionably jaded. His trousers and wing-collared shirt were in the very latest style. His light brown hair was brushed straight back from his forehead and gleamed with a judicious application of pomade.

Pierce studied Adelaide with an appraising look. "I will not pry but may I ask whether you and Winters arrived at a mutually satisfactory understanding?"

Of course he would not pry, Adelaide thought. In Pierce's secretive world, privacy was to be respected at all costs.

"I would not call it a mutually satisfactory understanding," Adelaide said. She fanned herself more briskly. "But I did agree to assist Mr. Winters with a certain project. In exchange I received a rather vague promise to repay the favor at some unspecified future date."

"I do not know why you are grumbling about such a bargain," Adam said. His eyes glinted with amusement. "Having Griffin Winters in your debt strikes me as no small thing. There are those who would give a fortune to be in your position."

"The problem with the bargain is that Mr. Winters made it quite clear that he will repay me only if he approves of the favor that I ask." Adelaide tried another sip of champagne and lowered the glass. "He has already refused my first request."

Pierce's brows shot up. "That does not sound like Winters. He may be as hard as granite but he has built an equally solid reputation as a man of his word."

"Precisely," Adam agreed smoothly. "If the Director of the Consortium lets it be known that a certain individual will disappear if said individual does not move his opium business to another neighborhood, one can place a secure bet on the result."

Adelaide glared at him through the veil. "You're trying to frighten me."

"Don't worry." Adam smiled. "You're not selling opium."

Pierce looked thoughtful. "Winters must have had a very compelling reason to deny you the first favor. He can deliver anything, except the impossible. And on occasion, he has been known to come through with that, as well."

"Did you request the impossible?" Adam inquired.

"Not at all," Adelaide said. "I merely asked him to help me revise my strategy for the brothel raids. He pointed out that they have become predictable. I had already reached the same conclusion."

"Ah," Pierce murmured. "Well, that explains it."

"Explains what?" Adelaide demanded.

"Winters knows that every time you go into a brothel you court disaster. He would never agree to help you take such a risk."

"Because if something goes wrong with a strategy that he had helped plot he would feel responsible?" Adelaide asked.

"Yes," Pierce said. "But there is another consideration as well. If word got out that he was behind an assault on one of Luttrell's establishments, it would shatter the Truce."

Adelaide flicked the fan, irritated. "He did mention the Craygate Cemetery Truce. Somehow, it is difficult to take an agreement between crime lords seriously."

"I assure you, the Cemetery Truce is an agreement that we all take extremely seriously," Pierce said evenly. "The open warfare that was going on between Winters and Luttrell in the months following Forrest Quinton's death affected many of us whose businesses were only on the sidelines."

"Who was Forrest Quinton?"

"The undisputed emperor of London's underworld," Pierce said. "He ruled for nearly three decades. Collapsed and died of a heart attack several years ago. It is generally assumed that the man who took over his organization arranged his very convenient death."

"Luttrell?" Adelaide asked.

"Yes. Luttrell was very busy for about a year securing what he could of Quinton's empire. But he was young and he lacked experience in management. Not surprisingly he lost a lot of territory."

"I assume he lost some of that territory to you?"

"Yes, but he lost far more to a young up-and-coming crime lord who called himself the Director," Pierce said.

"I see," Adelaide said. "You know, this story is a lot more interesting than the play we are watching. Please go on."

"Things remained fairly calm for a time. But Luttrell was nothing if not ambitious. When he decided he was ready, he went after his most serious competition."

"The Consortium?" Adelaide asked.

"Yes. If Luttrell had managed to crush Winters, there is no doubt but that I would have been next. I could not have mustered the army that would have been required to defeat Luttrell's enforcers. After me, the smaller players would have gone down easily enough."

"In the end, Luttrell would have been the last one standing," Adam said.

Pierce cocked a brow. "You can see that I am very much in Winters's debt."

"I understand," Adelaide said. "But it does leave me holding the bad end of the bargain I made with him."

"Who knows? The day may come when you will need another favor from Griffin Winters, one that he is willing to grant you."

Adelaide finished the last of her champagne and set the glass on a nearby tray.

"I cannot, for the life of me, imagine what that would be," she said.

THE CURTAIN CAME DOWN for the last time shortly before midnight and not a moment too soon as far as Adelaide was concerned. She walked outside with Pierce and Adam, eager to go home.

The scene in front of the theater was awash in the usual noisy chaos that always ensued when a play ended and the crowd spilled out of the lobby in search of carriages. In the street, the drivers of the private vehicles struggled to find their employers in the throng. Cabs and hansoms vied for fares.

"We're going for a late supper," Pierce said. "Will you join us?"

"I would love to but I think I will go home instead," Adelaide said. "I need my sleep. I have a feeling that Mr. Winters will be calling on me at an unfashionably early hour tomorrow morning. He is very eager to get started on his project."

"Winters is right about one thing," Pierce said quietly. "You are playing with fire when you stage those raids. Your goal may be admirable but you will not do the girls you have managed to rescue any good if you get yourself killed by one of Luttrell's enforcers. Who will finance the charity house and your Academy if you get your throat slit?"

The last thing she needed was another lecture on the subject, Adelaide thought.

"I am aware of the risks," she said.

Adam exhaled his jaded sigh. "You cannot save them all. A handful at most. As long as there is poverty and despair there will be young girls searching for a way out."

"Don't you think I understand that?" Adelaide whispered.

"The raids make excellent fodder for the sensation press," Pierce said. "But you could save more girls by spreading the word of your charity house and the Academy on the streets."

Adelaide wanted to argue but she was well aware that logic was not on her side. Maybe Pierce and Adam were right. Perhaps she had pushed her luck far enough.

"I will give the matter some thought," she promised.

Pierce nodded, satisfied. "I see your driver has found you. He is just across the street, waving madly. We will bid you good night."

Adelaide glanced in the direction Pierce indicated and saw the carriage and driver she had hired for the evening.

"Good night," she said. She gathered her cloak around her and made her way swiftly through the throng.

She was out of the theater at last. She should have been feeling some sense of relief from the too-close, slightly frazzled sensation that had been plaguing her all evening, she thought. But her senses were more agitated than ever. If she were back in the American West she would have been looking over her shoulder for a mountain lion or a rattlesnake or a man with a gun. But this was London and she was surrounded by respectable, well-dressed people. In London respectable people did not carry guns. Except for her, of course.

Perhaps her uneasiness was linked to her promise to work the Burning Lamp for Griffin Winters. It was bound to be a dangerous experience for both of them. Her intuition warned her that failure could be devastating.

If I had any sense I would have called his bluff, she thought. Just let him try to find another dreamlight reader.

But she had spoken the truth when she had told him that he was very unlikely to find another talent who could manipulate and control dreamlight as well as she could. Sending him off to find someone else who could work the lamp would have been tantamount to consigning him to whatever fate awaited him.

He had known that, she thought. Yet he had walked out of the attic rather than meet her terms. One had to admire such a gallant nature, even when it manifested itself in a villain. She had encountered any number of so-called gentlemen who would not have acted so nobly in such circumstances.

Rubbish. She must not allow herself to be seduced by romantic fantasies, she thought. Griffin Winters had not walked out of the attic because he was governed by his gallant nature. The truth was that he had called *her* bluff.

It served her right, she thought. In future she must not allow him to manipulate her. She would work the lamp for him, as agreed, but she would not allow him to play on her sympathies again. Above all she must not let him see that she was attracted to him. He would use that knowledge quite ruthlessly.

She forged a path through a gaggle of elderly matrons waiting for their carriages and started across the street. Her anxiety was growing stronger. She rarely raised her talent when there were a lot of people around. For one thing, in a public place like this there were bound to be any number of disturbing prints layered on the pavement. In addition she ran the risk of brushing up against another person, which would result in a stiff jolt of unpleasant dreamlight energy. She was still recovering from the encounter with Luttrell's enforcer. The last thing she needed was another dose of someone else's dreams.

She was so tense now that when she caught a fleeting movement at the corner of her eye she nearly screamed. She whirled, her cloak swirling around her, to face the threat.

The young boy standing beside a carriage horse ducked his head apologetically.

"Sorry, ma'am," he said. "Didn't mean to frighten you. Just trying to keep the horse calm. Old Ben, here, gets nervous in crowds."

"Old Ben and I have a good deal in common," she replied.

The boy grinned. "Watch out for the pickpockets, ma'am. They're always about in busy places like this."

"Thank you for the warning." She smiled, even though he could not see her face through the veil. Turning, she started again toward her own vehicle.

Her intuition was screaming at her now. She stopped fighting it and opened her talent. The pavement was suddenly illuminated by the eerie ultralight and the strange shadows cast by the radiation from the residue of decades of dreamprints. More prints fluoresced in icy hues on the sides of carriages. She concentrated on those that appeared both fresh and disturbing.

It was a formidable task. When she was fully in her senses energy sizzled in the atmosphere around her. Dreamprints glowed with lust, anger, pain, fear, anxiety and, most worrisome of all, spiking rage. Those endowed with her unusual ability generally saw far more of the world and of human nature than they wanted to see.

She paid especially close attention to a trail of prints that displayed the twisted currents of fury. They were being tracked across the street by a man in a top hat and a long black coat. He gripped a walking cane in one gloved fist. She shuddered, aware that it would take very little provocation to make him lash out with the cane.

She watched the man jump into a hansom. The small vehicle set off immediately, carrying its angry passenger away into the night. She breathed a sigh of relief.

Not much farther now. The driver of the carriage that she had hired for the evening jumped down from the box to open the door for her. It was all she could do not to break into an undignified run.

She was so intent on reaching the safety of the vehicle that she did not notice the unnatural shadows gliding toward her until a man's arm wrapped around her waist. She was dragged down to the pavement with such speed and force that she did not even have a chance to cry out.

The next thing she knew she was flat on her back. A man's heavy body was crushing her. Her senses were still flung wide open. Instinctively she tried to brace herself for what would surely be an explosion of nightmarish energy. It did not come.

She recognized the currents of hot, controlled energy instantly.

"Mr. Winters."

A gun roared somewhere in the night. Griffin shuddered violently. So much for her theory that no one in the crowd of respectable theatergoers would be carrying a gun.

The darkness erupted in screams and shrieks. Horses whinnied in terror. Hooves stamped and pounded on the pavement. Carriage wheels clattered.

Adelaide was nearly overwhelmed by the icy currents of energy slamming through her. Not her own, she realized.

"Griffin," she gasped. "You've been shot."

"Social reformers," Griffin muttered. "Damned nuisances, the lot of them."

7

HIS LEFT SHOULDER WAS DEATHLY COLD. HE'D BEEN SHOT
once before, back in his younger, more reckless days. Back when, like
other men in their early twenties, he had believed himself invincible.
He had learned several lessons from the incident, one of which was
that he was, indeed, mortal. Another was that although the wound felt
oddly cold now, the hot blaze of agony would hit him soon enough. In
the meantime he had things to do.

He looked down at Adelaide. She lay beneath him in a tangle of
skirts, petticoats and velvet cloak. Her hat and veil had come off and
her hair had fallen free of the pins that had secured it. The light of a
nearby carriage lamp slanted across her stricken features. Her eyes were
dark and deep with anxiety. Energy flared in the atmosphere around
them, hers and his own, he realized.

In that strange moment of shimmering awareness it seemed to him
that their currents were intertwined. The sensation of *intimacy*—there

was no other word for it—was unlike anything he had ever experienced, not even in a lover's arms.

It's the shock of the wound, he thought. Or maybe I'm hallucinating again.

"Mr. Winters," she said, more sternly this time. "Pay attention, sir. Where were you hit?"

"Shoulder, I think." His left arm was numb. He rolled to his feet and reached down with his good arm to pull her up beside him. Amidst the confusion that reigned in the street it was unlikely anyone would notice her, let alone recognize her, but he did not want to take any chances. He jerked the hood of her cloak up over her head and pulled a little more shadow-energy to veil his own features.

"This way," he ordered. He seized her hand and hauled her toward his carriage.

Mercifully, she did not argue or ask questions. He got her through the maze of rearing horses, frightened women and shouting men. By the time he reached the carriage, Jed had the door open and the stairs lowered.

"What happened, Boss?" Jed demanded. "Heard a gunshot. Are you and the lady all right?"

Adelaide was halfway through the door. She paused to look back at Jed. "Mr. Winters has been shot. We will need a doctor immediately."

"Is it true?" Jed asked, thoroughly alarmed now. "Are ye hurt, Boss?"

"I was in the wrong place at the wrong time." Griffin bundled Adelaide into the cab and got in beside her. "The lady is right. I'll need a doctor. Get back to the Abbey."

"Aye, Boss."

"First help me get Mr. Winters out of his coat," Adelaide said to Jed. It was an order, not a request. "I must see how badly he is bleeding."

73

She hiked up the skirts of her gown and started to tear wide strips out of her muslin petticoats.

Jed hesitated, uncertain whose orders to follow.

Griffin dropped down onto the seat across from Adelaide, closed his eyes and sagged back against the cushions. The interior of the cab was starting to swim around him.

"The Abbey, Jed."

"I believe you are sinking into shock, sir," Adelaide said. "You must let me deal with the wound at once."

Looking at her through slitted eyes, he said, "I want you away from here. The bastard may be hanging around in hopes of taking another shot."

Adelaide glanced out the window. "The prints of the man who shot you lead away from here down the street. He has fled, sir. You are safe, for now."

He had to work hard to focus on that astounding information. "You can see his footprints?"

"I can see the dreamlight energy in them, yes. It is very hot. Not surprising in view of the fact that he just attempted to commit murder."

"Son of a bitch," he whispered. "Would you recognize them if you saw them again?"

"Oh, yes. Dreamprints are quite distinctive. But this is no time to discuss my talent. I must see how badly you are bleeding. Jed, I will need your assistance."

"Yes, ma'am."

Griffin discovered that he lacked the strength to argue. That was not a good sign.

Jed scrambled up into the small cab and went to work. When he and Adelaide got the overcoat open and started to ease it off over one shoulder, Griffin was nearly engulfed in the flood tide of pain that washed over him. He closed his eyes again and clenched his back teeth to throttle the groan.

"Any idea who fired the shot, Boss?" Jed asked, struggling to work as gently as possible.

"No." Griffin sucked in another sharp breath.

"Have to work up a list," Jed growled. "You've made a number of enemies over the years. But I reckon we can put Luttrell at the top. Looks like he's decided to break the Truce."

Griffin started to respond but Adelaide was leaning in very close. Her fingertips touched his forehead. In spite of the rising tide of agony, it occurred to him that her hand felt very good on his skin. Soothing energy eased his senses.

"The pain only makes the shock worse," Adelaide said, leaning closer. "It places additional stress on the body and the senses. Forgive me, sir. I know you will not approve of what I am about to do."

He opened his eyes partway. "What the devil are you talking about?"

"Just relax, sir."

Energy pulsed lightly.

He wanted to reach up, capture her hand and hold on to her forever. The pulse of energy was growing stronger, urging him into a place where there would not be any pain. But there was something he had to do before he let the shadows take him.

"Jed," he said. He could not seem to get his eyes open. "Mrs. Pyne is coming to the Abbey with us. Keep her there, understand?"

"Yes, Boss," Jed said. He got the blood-soaked linen shirt open.

"What on earth do you mean, Mr. Winters?" Adelaide demanded. She snatched her fingers away from Griffin's forehead and began to apply pressure to the wound. "You cannot hold me against my wishes."

He ignored her. "Jed, tell the others that she is to be guarded night and day."

"I fear you are hallucinating, Mr. Winters," Adelaide said. "You did mention that you've had some problems with that sort of thing lately."

"The shooter wasn't aiming at me," he said to Jed. "Bastard was trying to kill Mrs. Pyne. If I don't wake up send word to Inspector Spellar at Scotland Yard. He owes me a few favors. He'll know what to do. Until then, I want the lady guarded around the clock. Is that clear?"

"Yes, Boss," Jed said.

"Dear heaven," Adelaide whispered, shocked. "You took the bullet meant for me."

She removed one hand from his shoulder long enough to touch his forehead again. Her fingertips were as light as butterflies and stained red with his blood.

He slid into sleep.

8

THE DREAM WELLS UP OUT OF THE DARKNESS, FEVER HOT AND glacial cold. It begins as they always do, at the foot of the stairs . . .

He climbs slowly upward to the horror he knows is waiting for him. He would give anything, including his soul, to be able to turn and run out of the house. But he knows that will not change the reality of what he is about to discover.

The silence on the floor above frightens him more than anything he has ever encountered in his sixteen years. Old houses are never so quiet. It is as if the once warm, cheerful home has become a tomb.

He reaches the landing and walks down the hall toward the closed door of his parents' bedroom. The shadows are denser on this floor. His pulse is skidding with fear. It is late afternoon outside but on this floor all is enveloped by night.

When he reaches the bedroom door he thinks once again of turning and fleeing back out into the light of day. But he knows that he cannot allow the terror to control him. He senses that running away from whatever awaits him on the other side of the door will constitute an act of betrayal.

The door is unlocked. He struggles to steady his nerve and then he opens the door.

He wants to look anywhere except at the bed. But there is no alternative. The white linen sheets are soaked in blood. One pale arm is draped languidly over the edge of the mattress.

Too late. He is always too late.

He opens his mouth to cry out his rage and despair and helplessness to an uncaring world . . .

"Calm yourself, Mr. Winters. You are dreaming again. I will ease the currents just as I did last time. Go back to sleep."

He has heard this gentle voice before. He trusts it now. The dream images evaporate, leaving a sense of peace unlike any he has known since he was sixteen years old.

He drifts back down into a deep healing sleep.

9

"HE WILL BE FINE," LUCINDA JONES SAID. "THE BALM THAT
I gave you will ensure that no infection takes hold while the wound
closes. Be sure to apply it twice daily. I will also leave you the ingredients for a tisane that will encourage healing. Make certain that he
drinks at least two cups a day, morning and night."

"Thank you, Mrs. Jones," Adelaide said.

She smiled at Lucinda across the width of the bed. Griffin was asleep
again. She did not sense any of the nightmarish energy that had ebbed
and flowed throughout the long night. He lay against the pillows, eyes
closed, dark hair matted with dried sweat. He was nude to the waist.
The bandage that covered his shoulder was fresh, the inside layers saturated with the therapeutic balm that Lucinda had prepared.

Immediately after the doctor had left, Adelaide made the decision
to send word to the newly wed Mrs. Jones, requesting a consultation
at the earliest possible hour. She had not been at all certain that there
would be a response but she could not think of anywhere else to turn.

The doctor who had closed the wound had scoffed at her concerns about infection. He was a good man, Adelaide had concluded, and quite deft with a needle and thread, but he was of an older generation. He gave no credence to modern notions of medicine.

"It was very kind of you to come out at such an early hour and in this dreadful weather," Adelaide said. "I cannot tell you how very grateful I am. The doctor got the bullet out and I insisted that he clean the wound quite thoroughly but I have seen such injuries before. I know what can happen."

"You were wise to be cautious." Lucinda closed and buckled the satchel that she had brought with her. "In my experience, infection often proves more lethal than the original wound. But I'm sure he will recover nicely."

"It is a relief to hear you say that. My housekeeper tells me that you possess great expertise in such matters."

Lucinda contemplated Griffin. Behind the lenses of her spectacles, curiosity glinted in her eyes.

"I must say, I'm amazed at how quietly he is sleeping," she said. "It is as if he had been given some opium concoction, but I do not detect any indication of the milk of the poppy."

"I have some small talent for dealing with pain," Adelaide explained.

Lucinda nodded, unsurprised. "Yes, I can sense that you possess some psychical ability, Mrs. Pyne. Do not worry overmuch about Mr. Winters. It is obvious that he is endowed with a very strong constitution."

Adelaide looked down at Griffin's broad, bare chest. So did Lucinda. There was a short pause while they both contemplated Griffin's strong constitution.

"Yes, indeed," Adelaide said. "Very strong." She cleared her throat and hastily pulled the sheet up to cover Griffin's chest.

Lucinda smiled. "Nevertheless, he will no doubt be in considerable discomfort when he does awaken. Men can get quite surly under those conditions." She opened her satchel again and removed another packet. "I will leave you something for the pain, just in case. Mix a spoonful into his tea or a glass of warm milk."

"Thank you."

Lucinda buckled the satchel again and hoisted it in one hand. "Very well, then. I must be off."

"A cup of tea before you leave?"

"Unfortunately I must decline. My husband is waiting for me in the carriage. We have another appointment this morning. Inspector Spellar from Scotland Yard has asked us to consult for him."

"I understand. I will see you out."

They left the bedroom and started down the staircase to the front hall of the big house.

"Again, allow me to express my gratitude, Mrs. Jones," Adelaide said.

"Nonsense. Delighted to be of some assistance," Lucinda said. "But I must admit I am surprised that you felt comfortable sending for me. My reputation in the press leads most people to believe that I am given to the pastime of poisoning people. How did you learn of my herbal skills?"

"I have had some experience of the press, Mrs. Jones. I am well aware of what it can do to a reputation. As for how I learned of your talent for concocting therapeutic remedies, I owe the knowledge to my housekeeper."

"And who might she be?"

"Her name is Mrs. Trevelyan. She is acquainted with your housekeeper."

"Mrs. Shute?"

"I believe that is her name, yes. The two have known each other since they started out in service together many years ago. Their world is a small one. Gossip flows through it just as freely as it does through the other social circles. Mrs. Trevelyan assured me that her friend would never have gone to work for an employer who was in the habit of poisoning the odd gentleman or two."

Lucinda chuckled. "In other words my housekeeper provided me with an excellent character reference. I must remember to thank her for that."

"It is a pleasure to meet you, Mrs. Jones. And congratulations on your recent marriage."

"Thank you." Lucinda appeared mildly surprised. "You are, I gather, a member of the Arcane community?"

"My parents were Arcane but they died a long time ago. I spent the past several years in America and have had no contact with the Society. Growing up I was well aware of the Jones family, however. When the announcement of your wedding to Mr. Caleb Jones appeared in the papers I recognized the name and made the connection. That was when Mrs. Trevelyan informed me that her old friend was in your employ."

"If you do not have any close connections within the Society, you may not be aware that Mr. Jones and I have recently founded a psychical investigation agency. Let me give you a card."

Lucinda reached into a hidden pocket sewn into the folds of her elegant skirts and pulled out a crisp pasteboard.

Adelaide took it from her and glanced at the name of the firm printed in very fine black script.

"Jones and Jones," she read.

"Should you ever feel the need of our services, I trust you will send word to our office. Jones and Jones prides itself on discretion."

"That is very good to know, Mrs. Jones."

Adelaide slipped the card into the pocket of the starched white apron that covered her from throat to ankle. Beneath the apron was a fresh, plain day dress. She had sent Jed to fetch Mrs. Trevelyan shortly after arriving at the Abbey. Demonstrating her considerable professional competence, the housekeeper had quickly packed a trunk that contained fresh clothes and a variety of personal toiletries. She had also put in a set of silk sheets and one of Adelaide's silk nightgowns.

Mrs. Trevelyan had never asked any questions about the silk sheets. She no doubt assumed that Adelaide's rule of sleeping only in silk was simply an eccentricity. The reality was that it was a necessity as far as Adelaide was concerned. The disturbing energy of other people's dreams and nightmares soaked into bedding and mattresses over the years and made sleep virtually impossible for someone with her unusual talent. She had discovered long ago that silk acted as a barrier to the unpleasant residue of old dreamlight.

Having seen to her employer's immediate needs, Mrs. Trevelyan had promptly sailed into the kitchen and taken charge of the household. She reported to Adelaide that the large man named Delbert had put up some resistance at first. But he and the other enforcers had been won over when the fragrant aromas of a hearty breakfast and strong coffee had begun to emanate from the kitchen.

"Men generally respond very well to a good meal," Mrs. Trevelyan explained to Adelaide. "Indeed, it has been my experience that they are more faithful to a good cook than they are to a lover."

Delbert waited now at the foot of the stairs with Lucinda's cloak. His coat was fastened around his bulky frame in a less than successful attempt to conceal the large revolver he carried in his shoulder holster. If Lucinda noticed the bulge she was too polite to question it.

Delbert was clearly unaccustomed to the business of assisting a lady into her cloak. He fumbled a bit with the long, sweeping length of fine wool and turned quite red when it did not settle properly around Lucinda's shoulders. But Mrs. Jones did not seem to notice.

"Thank you," she said politely.

"Yes, ma'am." Delbert turned even redder.

Out in the street, rain was falling steadily. Adelaide watched from the doorway as Delbert used a large umbrella to escort Lucinda down the steps to the waiting carriage. The vehicle's windows were securely closed against the damp weather.

The carriage door opened when Lucinda got close. A man dressed in a high-collared coat and a low-crowned hat kicked down the steps and got out. The heavy rain, combined with the hat, the coat and the fact that Delbert's broad back and the bobbing umbrella were in the way, made it difficult to get a clear view of the gentleman. Adelaide was certain, however, that she was looking at the other half of Jones & Jones.

There was a subtle intimacy in the way Caleb Jones handed Lucinda up into the cab. It spoke volumes. Mr. Jones, Adelaide thought, was very much in love with his wife and she with him.

The carriage door closed and the vehicle rolled off into the rain. Adelaide opened her senses and looked at the prints that the Joneses had left on the pavement. Hot energy burned in the rain.

Delbert lumbered back up the steps, paused to shake out the umbrella and then moved into the hall. He closed the door and looked at Adelaide. Anxiety scrunched his broad features into a grim mask.

"Will the Boss really be all right, ma'am?" he asked.

"Yes," Adelaide said. She was aware of the other two enforcers, Jed and Leggett, listening from the shadows of the hall. "Jed and I got the bleeding stopped very quickly and the doctor who was summoned appeared competent."

"He bloody well better be competent. Owes the Boss a favor, and that's a fact."

"I see. Well, rest assured, I called in Mrs. Jones merely as a precaution against infection."

"Yes, ma'am." Delbert hesitated, glancing up the staircase. "It's just that the Boss is sleeping so soundly. Has us a bit worried, if you want to know."

"Why? Sleep is what he needs now."

"The thing is, he hasn't been sleeping well for some time. The way he is at the moment, it strikes us as a bit unnatural is all."

"He'll awaken soon," she assured him. "When he does he will need some nourishing broth. Please ask Mrs. Trevelyan to send up a tray in an hour."

Delbert squinted. "How do you know the Boss will be awake by then?"

"Trust me."

She seized handfuls of her skirts and flew up the stairs. The last thing she and Mrs. Trevelyan needed just now was for Griffin's enforcers to wonder whether she was trying to murder their boss.

10

CALEB WATCHED LUCINDA LOWER THE HOOD OF HER CLOAK.
Her energy was a tonic to all of his senses. He still could not believe
that he was married to this remarkable woman.

"Obviously you were not immediately thrown out of the house as I
predicted," he observed. "Winters must, indeed, be in a bad way if he
allowed a woman named Jones to attend him."

"Mr. Winters does not even know that I was summoned," Lucinda
said. "He did not awaken during the time I was in the house."

Caleb whistled softly. "Well, that certainly explains why you got past
the front door. I wonder what he'll say when he wakes up and discovers
that he was treated by you." He paused a beat. "Always assuming that
he will wake up, of course. How bad is it?"

"Not as bad as it could have been. Mr. Winters was shot in the
shoulder. But it is clear that he did not lose a great amount of blood,
nor did he slide too far into shock, thanks to the quick actions of Mrs.
Pyne. The major danger now is, as always in such cases, infection. That

is why I was summoned. Mr. Winters is fortunate in his nurse. Mrs. Pyne seems well versed in modern notions of sickroom hygiene and cleanliness."

"Any clue to the identity of the man who shot him?"

"No, and I did not want to push the matter," Lucinda said. "It is obvious that the household is on guard, however. There are three men inside. They are all carrying American-style revolvers under their coats. I also noticed two very large dogs."

"There is nothing odd about the presence of armed guards in that household. As the Director of the Consortium, Winters has made a lot of enemies. I wonder which one got to him last night?"

"Do you think Jones and Jones should make some discreet inquiries?"

"I doubt if we would get far. Winters comes from a different world, my dear."

"The criminal underworld, you mean."

"It has its own rules, just as our world does. Winters's connections on the streets of his world are infinitely more impressive than our own. He will not need our assistance to discover the name of the shooter, nor would he welcome it."

Lucinda watched him very steadily. "What will happen when Mr. Winters discovers the identity of the man who tried to kill him?"

"I expect the would-be murderer will quietly disappear. I can also guarantee you that there will be no evidence left behind that could be traced back to the head of the Consortium. Winters is nothing if not subtle. Scotland Yard will never touch him. Spellar, I think, actually owes him a favor or two."

Lucinda shivered. "Mr. Winters is a very dangerous man."

"Yes, and possibly on the brink of becoming more so."

"Do you know him well?"

"Our families are linked through some ancient history, as you know, but the Winters and the Jones clans have steadfastly avoided each other for generations. I have never met Griffin Winters. He is the last of his bloodline. If he does not marry and produce a son, the legend of the Burning Lamp will end with him."

"He is not a young man," Lucinda said. "Midthirties I would say. I'm surprised that he is not married. Most men are at his age."

"He had a wife at one time. She died in childbirth. There was some speculation on the street to the effect that she was involved in an affair with one of his most trusted men. It was all very sordid. Shortly after the mother and babe died, the lover disappeared. Quietly."

"In true Winters style?"

"Yes. There have been rumors of discreet liaisons with other women over the years but no indication of offspring."

Lucinda's fine brows shot up above the rims of her spectacles. "It appears that you have kept an eye on him."

"We thought it wise."

"We? You mean your family?"

"Within Arcane, some legends must be taken seriously."

"I did notice one other odd thing in that household," Lucinda said.

"What is that?"

"Mr. Winters was sleeping very peacefully and quite soundly. It was not the sort of restless sleep that one expects after a serious injury."

"Perhaps the doctor gave him some opium or chloroform to dull the pain."

"No. It transpires that Mrs. Pyne is a woman of talent, very strong talent, I believe."

"Is she now?" Caleb asked softly. His intuition had stirred when the note requesting Lucinda's services had arrived earlier that morning. The information about Adelaide Pyne's talent caused it to surge like a fast-rising tide.

"She informed me that she has some ability to induce a healing state of sleep," Lucinda said. "She employed her abilities to put Mr. Winters into a deep slumber."

Caleb looked at her. "That is very interesting. I saw a woman in an apron standing in the doorway when we left a few minutes ago. She was not a housekeeper."

"That was Adelaide Pyne. Evidently she knew about my herbal skills because her housekeeper is acquainted with Mrs. Shute."

"So that is how she found you."

"Yes."

"Were Mrs. Pyne and Winters together at the theater last night? Are they lovers do you think?"

"I don't know," Lucinda said. "Mrs. Pyne seems to have felt some obligation to nurse him after the shooting, which implies they are quite close. Whether they are lovers, I cannot say." She drummed her gloved fingers on the satchel. "But there is most certainly something between them, some powerful connection, I think."

Caleb lounged back into the corner of the seat and looked out the window, absently searching for the patterns in the falling rain.

"There are a number of talents that can induce a sleeplike trance such as you describe," he said. "But under the circumstances, one in particular springs to mind. I wonder if Mrs. Pyne can read and manipulate dreamlight?"

"What would that tell you?"

He exhaled slowly. "It would indicate that Griffin Winters has either inherited the family curse or fears that he is going to inherit it. He appears to have found himself a dreamlight reader. I wonder if he has also discovered the lamp."

"Surely you are not going to sit there and tell me that you actually believe that Griffin Winters is in the process of transforming into a multitalent?" Lucinda was aghast. "That is nothing more than an old Arcane myth, Caleb."

"It is difficult to deny all of the ancient Arcane legends given that I am the direct descendant of one."

"Sylvester Jones." Lucinda clasped her hands together in her lap. "True. Very well, then, what do you suggest?"

"We will do the only thing we can for now. We will watch and we will wait."

"What, exactly, are we watching and waiting for?"

"Before I take this matter to Gabe I must have the answer to one more question."

"What is that?" Lucinda asked.

"If Winters has found both a dreamlight reader and the lamp, there are only two possibilities. Either he is trying to save himself from the curse . . ."

"Or?" Lucinda prompted.

"He wants to try to fulfill the legend and become a true Cerberus."

"That makes no sense," Lucinda insisted. "Why on earth would he wish to take the risk of driving himself mad with too much psychical energy?"

"Power is always seductive, my love. Nicholas Winters was certainly convinced that he could handle all three talents. He never got the chance to prove it because Eleanor Fleming destroyed his senses the last time she worked the lamp for him. It is entirely possible that Griffin Winters believes that he can achieve what his ancestor failed to accomplish."

"And if he does succeed?"

Caleb studied the intricate, glittering patterns created by the falling rain. "If he becomes the psychical monster that the Society has always believed to be the only possible outcome for a true multitalent, then Gabe and the Council will have no choice. They will conclude that

Winters must be destroyed. Such a vicious madman cannot be allowed to prey upon the public."

"The task will be assigned to Jones and Jones?"

"Yes."

Lucinda pulled her cloak more snugly around herself.

"Dear heaven," she whispered.

II

HE KNEW THAT SHE WAS IN THE ROOM. HER SCENT AND HER energy stirred his senses like a warm summer breeze. Another part of him stirred as well. The erection was reassuring on a number of levels, he concluded. For one thing it told him that he was still alive. The ache in his shoulder served the same purpose but it was not nearly so pleasant. He heard a low, muffled groan and realized it had come from his own throat. Getting shot always hurt like blazes.

"Bloody hell," he mumbled.

Adelaide's fingertips brushed his brow. The pain in his shoulder lessened. He sensed a deep, dreamless sleep creeping up on him, not for the first time.

He opened his eyes and looked at Adelaide.

"Put me under again, Mrs. Pyne, and I vow that the next time I wake up I will turn you over my knee."

She gasped and took a quick step back. "Good grief, sir. You startled me. How do you feel?"

"As though I'll most likely live." He sat up cautiously, wincing against the discomfort in his shoulder. He thought about it and was slightly amazed that the pain was not a good deal worse than it was. "What time is it?"

"Noon. I was just going to feed you some more broth."

Blurry images of previous awakenings flitted through his head. This was not the first time she had fed him broth. There were other vague recollections as well. He had some fleeting images of Delbert steadying him beside the bed while he made use of a chamber pot. He recalled Leggett and Jed helping him stagger weakly down the hall and back to the bedroom a few times.

After every awakening he had resisted sleep, knowing that the nightmares awaited him. But always Adelaide had reappeared to touch his brow. Each time he had tumbled back into the peaceful darkness. And there were no dreams.

No dreams.

"Maybe I should have asked what day is it?" he said.

"You were shot two nights ago," Adelaide said.

"You kept me out for damn near three days?" Anger surged through him. "Who the hell gave you the right to do that?"

For a second or two he thought she looked hurt. He felt something that might have been a twinge of guilt. Before he could worry about it, however, Adelaide assumed her righteous air.

"It was for your own good, Mr. Winters," she declared.

"Don't you dare use that excuse."

"Why not? I seem to recall you employing the very same reasoning when you told me that you would not help me raid Luttrell's brothels."

"That," he said through his teeth, "is an entirely different matter."

"Mr. Winters, allow me to inform you that I am not without experience in caring for those who have been injured. I discovered long ago that certain deep levels of sleep can be very beneficial when it comes to the healing process. In any event, you were not asleep the entire time. I let you wake up on several occasions. You needed food and a bit of exercise to stimulate the blood."

It dawned on him that at least some of his irritation was fueled by the knowledge that he was embarrassed. Adelaide had seen him in such a pitiful condition. She had nursed him intimately. He was naked to the waist. Below that, someone—please God, one of his men—had dressed him in some fresh cotton drawers.

Good lord. She had seen him in his drawers.

It was one thing to be naked with a woman while in the throes of passion. It was quite another to be in that condition when one was weak as a kitten.

He narrowed his eyes. "You may leave now, Mrs. Pyne, I want to take a bath and then I want to get dressed."

"Of course." She went toward the door. "I'll send Delbert in to assist you."

"I can manage on my own."

She clicked her tongue. "Do you know, Mr. Winters, your manners improve greatly when you are asleep. Delbert will be along in a moment. Just in case."

She opened the door.

He flexed his shoulder, testing uneasily for the heat and tenderness that signaled infection. There was pain, enough to make him suck in a harsh breath, but not the sort that was alarming.

"Mrs. Pyne?" he called after her.

She paused in the doorway and looked back at him. "What is it now?"

"Did the doctor take care to clean out the wound?"

"Rest assured, all precautions against infection have been taken. You are healing well. After your bath I will change the bandage again. I have some balm that promotes healing and ensures that the wound will not become feverish."

"Where the devil did you learn so much about gunshot wounds, Mrs. Pyne?"

"Spend a few years traveling with Monty Moore's Wild West Show and you, too, will learn a great deal about the subject. You would be amazed by the number of accidents that occur when there are a lot of guns lying about."

She stepped out into the hall and closed the door very firmly behind her.

12

FORTY-FIVE MINUTES LATER, GRIFFIN EMERGED FROM THE bath just in time to see Adelaide coming down the hall with a tray of fresh bandages. She was wearing a fresh, crisp white apron over a plain housedress. Her hair was pinned up in a severe chignon.

Delbert was lounging against the wall. He did not notice Griffin behind him. His full attention was focused on Adelaide. He straightened quickly at the sight of her.

"I told the Boss that you wanted me to help him with his bath, Mrs. Pyne," Delbert said, sounding anxious. "But he swore he could manage by himself."

"It's all right, Delbert." She gave him a reassuring smile before switching her gaze to Griffin. "Obviously Mr. Winters survived."

"I won't claim that I feel like a new man," Griffin said. "But I will say that I feel remarkably improved."

He tightened the sash of the black, embroidered dressing gown, uncomfortably aware that he wore nothing under it but a pair of drawers.

"You do appear to be a good deal stronger," Adelaide said, scrutinizing him closely.

He did not want her to look at him that way, he thought. The way a nurse looked at a patient. He wanted her to see him as a man: a fit, healthy man.

He inclined his head, taking refuge in the old, formal manners he had been taught as a boy.

"I believe that I owe you an apology for my display of temper earlier, Mrs. Pyne," he said. He knew he still sounded like an annoyed bear.

"I quite understand. You were not yourself, sir."

"If you say so. Could have sworn that was me snapping at you a short while ago but perhaps I was mistaken."

To his amazement, she blushed. But her tone remained as starched as her apron.

"I will change your bandage now," she said. She continued down the hall toward the bedroom. "Delbert will assist me. He has become quite expert."

Delbert opened the door for her. "Mrs. Pyne is very skilled at this nursing business, sir. Very impressive, she is."

Griffin followed Adelaide into the room. He watched her put down the tray.

"I agree, Delbert," he said. "Very impressive, indeed. Maybe it's the white apron. My very own Florence Nightingale."

Adelaide turned coolly to face him and pointed to a chair. "If you will please sit we will clean the wound, apply more of the balm and then put on a fresh bandage."

"Yes, ma'am." He sat down obediently. "But do keep in mind the warning I gave you earlier, Mrs. Pyne. I will be more than a little irritated if I find myself waking up from another unexpected bout of sleep."

"But the pain," she said uneasily.

"I will deal with it in a less dramatic fashion," he assured her. "Let's get on with it."

"I do have a tisane that might help."

"Change the bandage, Mrs. Pyne."

"Very well."

The process went smoothly enough. Griffin set his jaw a few times but the discomfort was not nearly as bad as he had anticipated. Adelaide was quick, efficient and very gentle. She applied the balm, wrapped a fresh bandage around his shoulder and secured it in place with cloth ties.

"Do you need me for anything else, ma'am?" Delbert asked. "Because if we're done here, I'll be on my way downstairs to the kitchen. Mrs. Trevelyan just took a lemon pound cake out of the oven and she's making a fresh pot of coffee."

Griffin was suddenly very hungry. "Sounds tasty."

Delbert paused at the door. "Don't worry, Boss; Mrs. Trevelyan has another pot of broth ready for you. I'll bring some up."

"Forget the damned broth," Griffin said. "Ask Mrs. Trevelyan to send a tray of real food to the library. I'll be downstairs in a few minutes."

"Right, Boss."

"Make sure there's plenty of coffee and a large slice of that pound cake on the tray," Griffin added.

Adelaide frowned. "You should eat lightly for a while yet, Mr. Winters." She looked at Delbert. "Ask Mrs. Trevelyan for some scrambled eggs and toast for Mr. Winters, please."

"Yes, ma'am."

"If I do not see lemon pound cake and coffee on that tray along with the eggs and toast," Griffin warned, "you will soon be looking for a new employer, Delbert."

"Yes, Boss."

Delbert escaped into the hall and hastily closed the door.

Adelaide gave Griffin a reproving glare. "That is no way to speak to Delbert. His loyalty to you is unquestionable and his concern for your well-being is genuine. I would think that an employer in your rather unique position would value such qualities in a member of your staff."

Griffin raised his brows. "An employer in my unique position?"

She cleared her throat. "I just meant that, given your unusual profession, it is obvious that you require great loyalty from those who work in this household."

"Ah, yes." He pulled the sleeve of his dressing gown up over his bandaged shoulder and retied the sash. "My unusual profession."

"Well, you are a crime lord, sir. One would think that you would be even more grateful than most employers to have someone like Delbert on staff. Such valuable employees should be treated with respect and civility in any household but most certainly in this one."

"Enough, Mrs. Pyne." He got to his feet and started toward her. "Good lord, woman. I have been out of my sickbed for less than an hour and already I am obliged to listen to a lecture. Do social reformers ever cease telling others how to behave?"

She blinked and took one step back.

"Really, sir," she said, her tone more severe than ever.

Griffin continued to prowl toward her.

"I find that your lectures have a disturbing effect on my senses," he said. He was aware that his voice had become a little rough around the edges. "Whenever you chastise me or berate me or give orders to me, I find that I am overcome with a compelling urge to kiss you until you stop talking."

She raised her chin. "I'll have you know that is the most outrageous thing any man has ever said to me."

"Obviously you have not met a great many crime lords." He stopped directly in front of her and planted his right hand on the door of the wardrobe behind her. "We tend to be an outrageous lot."

"I do not doubt that for a moment," she replied. "But if you think that you can intimidate me you are quite wrong."

"Actually, I'd rather kiss you," he said.

Her scent clouded his brain. Then again, maybe he was just feeling the effects of the lack of solid food. He leaned in a little closer, testing.

"I see," she said. "Well, I'm afraid that your reaction is only natural under the circumstances."

He pulled back a little. "What the devil are you talking about?"

"Allow me to explain." Her tone had become very cool, almost academic. "You are feeling grateful to me because I've been at your bedside, tending to your wound for the past three days. I have noticed that men who are ill or injured are inclined to view the women who care for them as angels, at least for a brief period of time. Not to worry, Mr. Winters. The impression generally wears off quickly once the man recovers."

"Trust me, Mrs. Pyne, in the entire time I have known you it has never once crossed my mind to think of you as an angel. What I am experiencing is simply the urge to kiss you until you cease lecturing. And if you don't run for the door right now, that is exactly what I am going to do."

She stood very still, watching him with her dream-filled eyes. Currents of heat swirled in the atmosphere. One did not have to be a talent to feel the intense frisson of awareness that occurred when the energy fields of two people who were sensually attracted to each other were forced into close proximity, he thought. The effects were similar to those of a small lightning storm.

The knowledge that she was aroused was more than gratifying. It was extremely motivating. And strengthening. A true tonic, he thought, one that was infinitely more effective than a nourishing broth.

"I cannot help but observe that you are not fleeing toward the door," he said.

"No." Her voice was low and breathless. "I'm not."

"May I ask why?"

"I'm not sure," she admitted. "Perhaps I'm curious."

"About what it would be like to kiss a man in my unique profession?"

"It is not often that one has such an unusual opportunity."

The not-so-subtle challenge only heightened his desire. "You're thinking that if you are not satisfied with the results of the experience you can always put me back to sleep again, right?"

"That is certainly an option for me," she said. "Under the circumstances, I'm surprised you are willing to risk the experiment."

"I'm a crime lord. Risk goes with the territory."

He brushed his mouth against hers, intending for the kiss to be a slow, seductive foray. But the instant he touched her, the energy that enveloped them suddenly ignited.

The kiss went from tempting to hot and searing in a heartbeat. Triumph and satisfaction slammed through him.

He had known it would be like this.

He felt the shock of realization and understanding flash through her at the same instant that it hit him. There was no chance for a slow heat to build between them. Without any warning they were both at the edge of control, shivering with the intensity of the experience.

He felt her arms steal around his neck just inside the collar of the dressing gown, bare skin on bare skin. He pressed closer, using the weight of his body to pin her to the wardrobe so that he could feel the curves of her breasts and the soft, feminine shape of her hips beneath the heavy fabric of her gown.

The bed was so close . . .

"No." Adelaide wrenched her mouth away from his. "We must not. Your shoulder."

He was vaguely aware that his shoulder was aching, but somehow it did not seem important. He leaned in again and kissed her throat. Tendrils of her hair came free of the pins and floated invitingly around her shoulders.

"Forget my shoulder," he said against her incredibly soft skin. "That's what I plan to do."

"Absolutely not." Her voice was firmer now. She planted her palms on his bare chest and pushed against him. "We cannot risk reopening the wound. It is healing so nicely. We must not take any chances."

She probably had a point but he did not want to consider it. Nevertheless, he could tell that the spell had been broken, at least for her. He exhaled heavily and reluctantly moved back a pace.

"I am going to dress now, Mrs. Pyne. You are welcome to stay and watch if you wish. I gather that you have already seen most if not all of me, so there is no need to concern ourselves with the proprieties, is there?"

Adelaide did not dignify that with a response. She went quickly toward the door.

"I'll meet you downstairs in the library," she said. "We have a great deal to discuss now that you are clearly on the road to recovery."

He waited until she got the door open.

"One question before you leave, Adelaide."

She gripped the knob very tightly and looked back at him. "What is it, Mr. Winters?"

"You indicated that you were curious about what it would be like to kiss a crime lord. I wonder if your curiosity was satisfied."

"Quite."

She went out into the hall. She was not precisely *running*, he concluded, but she was definitely moving at a very brisk trot.

THE EGGS, TOAST, CAKE AND COFFEE were waiting for him in the library. So was Adelaide. She had taken the time to pin her hair back into a strict twist. The large, white apron was gone and so was the functional housedress she had worn earlier. She was once again dressed in fashionable late mourning, an expertly tailored day dress this time, with a blouselike bodice and pleated skirts in a cloudy shade of gray.

At first glance it was as though the explosion of sensual and psychical fireworks upstairs had never occurred, he thought. Adelaide appeared to be cool and controlled once more. Her eyes were unreadable. But currents of tension swirled in the air between them. He took some satisfaction in that knowledge and then ambled over to the table where the breakfast tray awaited him.

"As you noted upstairs, we have a great deal to talk about," he said.

"Eat your breakfast first, sir," she said. "You need the sustenance."

"Thank you. I could not agree more."

He sat down and fell to the eggs and toast with a vengeance. While he ate he found himself wondering about the deceased Mr. Pyne. Had Adelaide loved him with all of her heart? So many questions and he had no right to ask a single one.

She poured coffee for both of them. "Your library is quite impressive."

"For a crime lord, do you mean? Believe it or not I can both read and write."

She set the pot down with a sharp bang that was loud enough to cause the dogs, dozing in front of the hearth, to raise their heads. The beasts studied the situation with some curiosity for a moment and then went back to sleep.

"Not only do you read and write," Adelaide said, "you speak with the accents of a man who was educated to be a gentleman."

"Some habits are hard to break."

"You did not grow up on the streets, did you?"

"No." He had overreacted, he decided. He tended to do that a great deal around Adelaide. What the devil had happened to his ironclad self-control, he wondered. He used his fork to cut a slice of lemon pound cake.

"I arrived on the streets at the age of sixteen," he said finally.

"Following the death of your parents?"

"Yes. My father was an investor. He had a talent for financial matters. But not even those possessed of a powerful, intuitive ability to determine the potential for profits and losses can predict storms. One of the ships in which he had invested not only a great deal of his own money but also funds from a consortium went down at sea. Had he lived there is no doubt but that he could have recovered and paid off the other investors. But he and my mother both . . . died a few weeks after the disaster. The creditors took everything."

"Your story is not unlike my own," Adelaide said quietly.

She drank coffee in silence while he finished the cake.

"Sorry," he said, vaguely embarrassed by his manners. "Haven't been this hungry since my days on the streets."

"A healthy appetite is always a good sign when one is recovering from a serious injury," she said. "I am glad that you are well enough to eat a full meal. I only hope you do not make yourself ill with that cake. Too much rich food on an empty stomach can have very unpleasant consequences."

He brushed crumbs from his hands. "You certainly know how to make sparkling mealtime conversation, madam."

"I am merely trying to give you the benefit of my advice, but I can see that you are not interested so I suggest that we move on to a more pressing subject."

He picked up his coffee cup, leaned back in the chair and stretched out his legs.

"You want to know why I happened to be at the theater the other night, don't you?" he said.

"Among other things. Do not mistake me. I owe you my life. But I cannot help but wonder how it is that you were conveniently at hand when someone pointed a gun at me."

"I think you know the answer." He swallowed more coffee, savoring the little rush of heat and energy. "I was keeping an eye on you."

Her eyes narrowed ever so faintly. "In other words you were following me."

"Of course. At the moment I have a great interest in your health and well-being." He kept his tone even. "If anything of an unfortunate nature were to occur to your person I would be in dire straits. As we have discussed, it is not easy to find someone with your sort of talent. Replacing you might prove difficult."

"I see," she said stiffly. "It is always nice to know that one is appreciated."

"I assure you, Adelaide, you are presently of the utmost value to me. I intend to take excellent care of you."

"Until I work the lamp for you."

"Do not concern yourself about your future. I will see to your safety after you work the lamp, as well. It is the least I can do to repay you."

Her mouth tightened at the corners. "Do you have any notion of who tried to murder me the other night?"

"Not yet. But now that I am feeling more fit I will get the word out on the streets that I am seeking answers to that very question. It will not take long to obtain a name."

She sighed. "I suppose it must have been one of the brothel owners whose establishments I raided."

"Very likely. It seems that you and I have something in common, Adelaide. We have both managed to acquire a few enemies. But you are safe in this household."

She smiled. "Because none of your enemies knows that the notorious Director lives amid the ruins of the St. Clare Street Abbey?"

"I suspect a few of them, Luttrell, for instance, is well aware of my address, just as I am aware of his. But I very much doubt that any of my competitors, including Luttrell, would dare to take you from this house. While you are here you are under my protection."

She grimaced. "In other words, whoever tried to get rid of me will not consider the objective worth risking the wrath of Griffin Winters."

"To be blunt, no."

"Not even Luttrell?"

Griffin shook his head, very sure. "He is nothing if not pragmatic. He won't break the Truce just to get rid of an annoying social reformer. He knows it would mean all out war again. What's more, I'm sure it has occurred to him that the next time I would not offer a second truce. The war would not end until one of us killed the other."

She stilled. "You would go to war for me?"

"In my world all I have is my reputation. I have spent twenty years crafting it. I cannot allow a rival to destroy it."

"No, of course not," she muttered. She reached for her coffee cup. It was his reputation that concerned him. There was nothing personal involved. She had no business feeling so deflated, she thought. Exactly what sort of answer had she expected?

"As I said, you are safe here, Adelaide." Griffin drank more coffee and lowered the cup. "I can protect you, assuming I don't turn into a Cerberus first. Once I am free of that problem I can concentrate on other business."

"At the risk of repeating myself," she said, "I doubt very much that you are in danger of becoming a monster."

"Unfortunately, there is no practical way to convince Arcane, specifically the Jones family, of the wisdom of your conviction."

Startled, she paused, her cup halfway to her lips. "What on earth does Arcane have to do with this situation?"

"If the Jones family discovers that I have inherited the Winters Curse it will do whatever it takes to destroy me."

She felt as though all the air had just been sucked out of the room. It took two tries before she could speak.

"I . . . I don't understand," she finally got out. "What do you mean?"

"Nicholas Winters was convinced that he was strong enough to handle the three talents."

"Yes. You explained that."

"He believed some of his offspring would also inherit that ability. But the Society does not abide by that theory. If the Joneses even suspect that I am showing symptoms of becoming a Cerberus, they'll hunt me down like the mad dog they will assume that I am. For obvious reasons I would prefer to avoid that outcome."

She took a deep breath. "Mr. Winters—"

"After what just transpired between us upstairs, I think you can call me Griffin."

Slowly she reached into a hidden pocket in her gown and withdrew a white card. "Mr. Winters, I have something to tell you. I fear you will not be pleased."

"What could be more displeasing than the prospect of turning into a monster?"

"While you were sleeping, you had a visitor. A consultant of sorts. To be clear, I'm afraid I'm the one who summoned her."

She handed him the card.

13

"LUCINDA JONES WAS HERE IN THE ABBEY?" GRIFFIN STORMED to the far end of the library, swung around and stalked back toward Adelaide. Hot energy simmered in the air around him. "Under my roof? You used the medicine that she gave you to treat my wound? How in bloody hell could such a thing happen?"

She watched him warily from the chair. There was a part of her that wanted to flee the room but she had already run from him once today. She would not do so again.

"Mr. Winters, calm yourself, sir," she said, employing her most soothing tones. "You have sustained a serious injury. You must not let your nerves become rattled like this. The stress will hinder the healing process."

Griffin shook his head. "If I didn't fully believe in the family curse, I most certainly do now. Congratulations, Adelaide. You have very likely succeeded in accomplishing what none of my many enemies have managed to achieve in twenty years. You have greatly increased the chances that I will be a dead man within the month."

"Surely you are dramatizing the situation. Winters is a common enough surname."

He shot her a scathing glance. "Like Jones?"

"Be reasonable, sir. To all outward appearances, you are a respectable gentleman living in a quiet, respectable neighborhood. You have evidently taken great pains to conceal your identity. Why, I have been told that very few people have ever seen your face clearly and, ah—" She stopped.

He glared at her. "And, ah what, Adelaide?"

"And lived to tell about it," she concluded hurriedly. "I realize that is a gross exaggeration but, then, you are something of a legend on the streets."

"Your point?" he said grimly.

She drew a steadying breath. "My point is that there is no reason why Mrs. Jones would have suspected that you are anything other than what you appear to be, a somewhat reclusive gentleman named Winters."

"We are talking about the Arcane Society Joneses," he said.

"I'm quite sure that they move in social circles very different from yours," Adelaide said.

He turned away from her and stood looking out the window into the garden. "I will allow that the Joneses move in far more elevated circles."

It dawned on her that she had offended him.

"I was only trying to explain why it is unlikely that Mrs. Jones would know who you are," she said quickly.

He ignored that. "What in blazes made you summon her here to the Abbey?"

"Well, as it happens, Mrs. Trevelyan recommended that I consult her. I was concerned about possible infection, you see."

"Your *housekeeper* advised you to send for her?"

"Mrs. Trevelyan is an old acquaintance of Mrs. Jones's housekeeper. Evidently they met when they went into service years ago."

"Good lord. I survived life on the streets and more enemies than I can recall and it comes to this. I have been undone by a couple of housekeepers and a social reformer."

Adelaide started to lose her temper. "You have not been undone by anyone, sir. But there is something I would very much like to know."

"What?"

"If the entire Jones family is forbidden to enter the Abbey, why on earth didn't one of your men speak up and mention the fact when I sent for Mrs. Jones?"

He gripped the edge of the window frame. "None of my men know about my family's connection to Arcane. I have kept the secret ever since . . . Never mind. What's done is done. Please do not tell me that Caleb Jones was also here in my house as well."

She coughed discreetly. "I believe he waited outside in the carriage."

"If it weren't for the fact that I may well be doomed, this might almost be an amusing comedy of errors."

"Damnation, Griffin, I have apologized."

"That certainly solves all my problems."

"I had no way of knowing that you were at odds with the Joneses. Really, sir, it has been two hundred years since the altercation between Sylvester Jones and your ancestor. That is a rather long time to carry on a feud."

"It's not a feud," he shot back. "It's considerably more complicated."

"What do you mean?"

"Nicholas Winters intended that one of his descendants would use the lamp not just to acquire enhanced talents but also to destroy the entire Jones bloodline. He even inserted a special crystal into the damn thing that is supposed to be infused with a psychical command that will ensure that outcome. The Midnight Crystal."

She frowned. "Do you really believe that is possible?"

"How the hell should I know? What matters is that the Joneses believe it. The question now is, does Caleb Jones suspect that I have found the lamp and a talent who can work it? Given the peculiar nature of his own talent, I must assume that he is already suspicious."

"But it was just a coincidence that I summoned Mrs. Jones to this household," Adelaide insisted.

"I'm told that Jones does not believe in coincidences, not when it comes to the old Arcane legends. For that matter, now that I have found you and the lamp, neither do I."

"But according to what you told me, the process of transformation can be reversed with the lamp."

"Yes."

"Surely Mr. Jones will assume that you will want to save yourself. He must realize that no sane man would take the risk of trying to become a Cerberus."

He looked back at her. "The promise of power is very seductive. Just ask any crime lord. Or any Jones, for that matter. That family has controlled Arcane for two hundred years."

"That is not amusing, sir. We both know that your objective is to save yourself and your sanity, not risk losing both. Mr. Jones is surely a logical man. He will assume that is your plan."

"Not bloody likely. Jones will believe that a man of my nature and profession will stop at nothing to acquire the full powers of the lamp."

"What makes you so certain of that?" she asked.

"In his place, it is what I would assume."

"Wouldn't you at least give your opponent the opportunity to reverse the process?"

Griffin did not answer immediately. A chill went through her.

"I'm not certain," he said finally. "I suppose it would depend on what I knew of the character of the man who possessed the lamp. Caleb Jones and I are not personally acquainted. He knows nothing about me except what he may have picked up from rumors on the streets."

"You never met when you were boys?"

"My family always took great care not to come in contact with the Jones clan. But now I must assume that Caleb Jones is aware of who I am and how I have made my living all these years." Griffin's mouth twisted coldly. "The particulars of my profession are not in my favor."

"No offense, sir, but you are allowing yourself to be overcome with suspicions. Are you hallucinating again?"

"Trust me, Adelaide. I would give a great deal to wake up and discover that this has all been a bad dream."

She told herself she had no grounds for feeling so crushed, but the memory of the kiss upstairs in the bedroom still burned. Evidently for Griffin the heated embrace was now just another scene in his ongoing nightmare.

One of the large dogs lumbered to his feet and padded across the room. He rested his massive head on her lap and waited patiently. She stroked him behind one ear. Dogs, she reflected, like other animals, had their own kind of paranormal senses. They were more acutely aware of psychical disturbances in the atmosphere than most humans.

She patted the beast for a moment. A thought struck her.

"There is one thing you might want to take into account, Griffin," she said.

"What?"

"Mrs. Jones has a psychical talent for botany. Indeed, the sensation press has portrayed her as a notorious poisoner. You say she would have known your identity before she stepped foot in this house."

"Given the current trend in my luck, almost certainly."

112

"If that was the case, and if Jones and Jones had wanted you dead, she had the perfect opportunity to poison you with the balm that she gave me to put on your wound or the tisane. Yet you are recovering remarkably well."

Griffin went very still for a few seconds. Then he nodded once.

"Do you know," he said, sounding suddenly intrigued, "that is a very interesting observation."

Encouraged, she hurried on. "Consider the matter closely, sir. The Joneses are either not nearly as well informed concerning your identity as you fear, or else they are not convinced that you are destined to become a Cerberus."

"There is one other possibility," Griffin said. "It should have occurred to me sooner."

She did not like the cold, calculating edge in his voice.

"What is that?" she asked.

"I know the history of Arcane almost as well as the Joneses know it. My father made certain that I was acquainted with the old legends, just in case the Curse struck me or one of my offspring."

"Well?"

Griffin resumed his prowl of the library. "Two hundred years ago Sylvester Jones was as obsessed with his psychical enhancement formula as Nicholas was with his Burning Lamp."

"So?"

"My father told me that, according to the old tales, Sylvester was partially successful in his attempts to expand his talent. But the formula was said to be fatally flawed. Ultimately every version of it becomes a slow-acting poison."

"Where are you going with this, Griffin?"

He halted again, this time in front of the hearth. "Perhaps the Joneses are deliberately holding back, waiting to see if Nicholas was, indeed, the more successful alchemist."

"Good heavens," she said, floored by his conclusion. "You can't be serious."

"My father told me that the members of the Jones family dare not use the founder's formula because it is so dangerous. But they might be very curious to learn if the lamp can safely be employed to enhance talents."

"Do you actually believe that they have decided to let you run an experiment on yourself?"

"Why not? After all, if the lamp turns me into a human monster they still have the option of destroying me. But if it actually works, if I become a stable multitalent, they can still destroy me, seize the lamp and try to use it on themselves. I doubt if they will have any trouble finding a dreamlight reader. They've got access to all of the Arcane membership records."

"Oh, for pity's sake. You really should have gone on the stage, sir. Your suspicious nature is nothing if not high drama. Very well, then, for the sake of argument, let us assume you are right. Where does your reasoning leave us?"

"For the moment, I'm afraid it leaves you something of a prisoner in this house."

"I was afraid you were going to say that."

14

THE TERRIBLE DREAM BEGAN AS IT ALWAYS DID . . .

*He stands at the foot of the staircase looking up into the dark shadows
above. The house is as still and silent as a tomb.*

*He knows that he will be too late but he has no choice. He starts
up the stairs, dread and despair icing his blood. The ghostly scene that
awaits him will shatter his world.*

He will be too late to save them . . .

"Wake up, Griffin. You are dreaming again."

Adelaide's voice pulled him out of the nightmare. He opened his
eyes and found her bending over him. In the pale light he could see
that she was dressed in a chintz dressing gown and a lacy little nightcap.
Tendrils of hair danced around her shoulders just as they had earlier
that afternoon when he had kissed her. She held a candle in an iron
stand in her left hand.

"Well, if it isn't Florence Nightingale." He pushed himself up against the pillows. He knew he sounded surly. He could not help it. He was perspiring, as though with fever, and his heart was still pounding. He hated having her see him this way again. An alarming thought struck. "Did I yell or cry out?"

"No," she assured him.

"Then how did you know that I was dreaming?"

"There is a connecting door between our bedrooms," she reminded him. "I sensed some of your dreamlight energy."

"Damnation. There is no privacy in this household anymore."

She touched his shoulder. "You are shivering but your skin is hot. Was the nightmare one of the sort that you associate with the onset of the second talent?"

"It is actually an old dream. I was plagued with it often when I was younger. But it faded with time. I thought that I was free of it. But since the onset of my new power it has returned with a vengeance."

"I can assure you that such psychical stress is not good for the healing process. Stop grumbling and allow me to give you some peaceful sleep."

"No."

"Please," she coaxed. "You want to recover as swiftly as possible. I can help you."

"I said no."

"Griffin, you are being ridiculously hardheaded about this and you know it."

"You think that my refusal to let you put me under again is the result of sheer stubbornness, but that's not the case," he said wearily. "I swear it."

"Then why won't you let me help you?"

"Because when I sleep that deeply, all of my senses sleep as well."

"I understand." Her voice softened. "You feel that you are not in control. You're afraid that if something happens you will not awaken in time to deal with it."

"I am not accustomed to sleeping so soundly, Adelaide. It is as if I am unconscious."

"Well, you are in a sense," she admitted. "But I have a solution to your concerns."

He eyed her warily. "What is that?"

"You only require a couple of hours of the deep, healing sleep each night to promote your recovery. If you allow me to put you under I promise that I will come back in precisely two hours to awaken you. Will that satisfy you?"

He thought about it. "This deep sleep, it really does promote healing?"

"Yes."

"I need my strength," he said.

"You'll recover it in half the time if you let me put you into the healing state for a couple of hours a day." She paused. "But I do understand that allowing such a therapy requires trust."

He made his decision. He lay back down on the pillows.

"Put me under," he said.

She touched her fingertips to his forehead. He felt her energy whisper across his senses.

He slept.

15

THE DOOR OF THE LABORATORY OPENED JUST AS BASIL HULSEY clipped a small frond off the *Ameliopteris amazonensis*. Luttrell and one of his enforcers, a heavily muscled man who moved like a beast of prey, walked into the room.

"Good morning, Dr. Hulsey," Luttrell said. "How goes the dream research?"

Hulsey gathered his shaken composure. The enforcer made him nervous but it was Luttrell who truly frightened him.

From a distance, one would never guess that the man was a powerful crime lord who, if the rumors were anywhere near accurate, controlled a string of brothels, opium dens and other disreputable enterprises. He certainly did not look like anyone's mental image of a master criminal.

Luttrell was in his late thirties, a handsome, well-built figure of a man who was always elegantly dressed. It was not until he opened his mouth that one caught the faint traces of the streets in his voice.

There was a chilling aura of power in the atmosphere around him. It was there in his ice-cold gaze, as well, Hulsey thought. Luttrell's eyes would have looked entirely appropriate in a viper, assuming snakes had blue eyes.

"The work is going very well, sir," Hulsey said. "Thanks to your great generosity and your keen appreciation for the complex nature of scientific investigation. I believe that we will be ready to run the first experiment on a human subject within a few days."

He put the frond down very carefully on the laboratory table. Thus far the experiments on the lacy fern that he had stolen had proved frustratingly inconclusive. He had developed one or two intriguing chemical concoctions from it, but his intuition told him that there was something vastly more important to be learned from the plant.

"I'm pleased to hear that," Luttrell said, clearly bored by the subject. "Meanwhile, I have come to see if the new devices are ready. You did say that they would be finished soon."

"Yes, of course, sir," Hulsey murmured.

He suppressed a sigh. A new month, a new employer. Lately he and Bertram seemed to be changing financial patrons more often than they changed their socks. It was becoming quite tiresome but there was little alternative. When one dedicated oneself to science one required money, a great deal of it. Money came from men such as Luttrell.

All in all, Hulsey thought, a crime lord was an improvement over his last patrons. At least Luttrell was honest about his profession and social status. The men of the Seventh Circle, on the other hand, had considered themselves gentlemen but had proved to be no better than the lowest sort of street criminals.

He looked toward the open doorway at the far end of the laboratory.

"Bertram," he called, "bring out the machines, if you would. Mr. Luttrell has come to collect them."

Bertram appeared. He gripped a large canvas bag in each hand. "I was able to prepare a half-dozen. I hope that will be sufficient."

Bertram, Hulsey thought, was a mirror image of himself at twenty-three: a scholarly-looking young man with spectacles and a receding hairline. But it was Bertram's talent that invoked a flush of paternal pride. His son's psychical abilities were not precisely the same as his own. No two talents were ever identical. But Bertram was as strong, if not stronger, than himself.

Together they would make vast strides in the field of dream research, assuming they could continue to obtain financing. And after he was gone, Hulsey thought, Bertram would not only carry on the Great Work but produce offspring who would inherit the Hulsey psychical gifts for scientific inquiry. Their bloodline would have an untold influence on future generations. It was an intoxicating notion.

"I'm sure six of the machines will be enough for what I have in mind," Luttrell said. "If they achieve the desired effects, I shall no doubt be in the market for several more, however."

"Certainly, sir," Bertram said politely. He hoisted the canvas bags onto the workbench.

Luttrell's face lit up with a disturbing air of excitement.

So far as Hulsey and Bertram were concerned, the vapor contained in the small machines was merely an accidental by-product of an experiment on the fern. But when Luttrell had viewed the results on a cage full of rats he had immediately seen the potential for creating weapons.

He watched hungrily as Bertram removed one of the metal canisters from the bag.

"Show me how it works," he said.

Bertram pointed. "You simply press here. The valve will open and the gas will be released immediately. The vapor is quite potent and spreads rapidly into the atmosphere. Whoever employs these devices should be advised to cover his nose and mouth with a thick cloth and stay well clear of the fumes until they have evaporated."

"Excellent." Luttrell picked up the canister and turned it in his hands. "I believe this will be a very handy tool, indeed."

Luttrell was pleased. Hulsey decided to take advantage of the moment. As he always did when he was feeling anxious, he took off his glasses and started to polish them with his dingy handkerchief.

"About the new microscope, Mr. Luttrell," he said cautiously.

"Yes, yes, go ahead and purchase it," Luttrell said. He smiled his reptilian smile. "I wouldn't want to stand in the way of scientific progress."

"We also require some new chemicals and herbs," Hulsey added.

"Make up a list and give it to Thacker, as usual. He is here to run errands for you."

Luttrell signaled the enforcer to pick up the canvas bags and then led the way out of the laboratory.

Hulsey watched the pair leave. When the door closed behind them Bertram heaved a deep sigh of resignation.

"I cannot believe that we are working for one of the city's most powerful master criminals," he said.

"Once again we are obliged to create dangerous toys for a patron who has no true appreciation for the Great Work." Hulsey positioned his glasses back on his nose. "But that seems to be the price of scientific discovery in the modern age."

"One can only hope that, in the future, there will be more respect paid to those of us committed to serious paranormal research," Bertram said.

16

FIVE DAYS LATER, DELBERT STOOD AT THE KITCHEN WINDOW,
drinking the rich hot chocolate that Mrs. Trevelyan had prepared. He
contemplated the scene in the garden. The Boss was sitting with Mrs.
Pyne on a green wrought-iron garden bench. They were examining the
old leather-bound journal that the Boss always kept close. The dogs
sprawled at their feet. It was a peaceful scene. But nothing about the
Boss was peaceful these days. *Never had been, come to that,* Delbert
thought.

"What do you think they are talking about?" he asked.

Mrs. Trevelyan did not look up from the mound of bread dough
that she was kneading.

"And just how would I know the answer to that question?" she
asked.

Delbert studied the couple in the garden. He had known Griffin
Winters for two decades, had watched the younger man grow up hard
and fast on the streets. There had always been a woman somewhere

in the background. The Boss liked women. But the word *background* was the key. That was where all the females in his life had remained until now.

But Mrs. Pyne was different. The Boss had never been like this with any other female, not even his wife. There was something in the atmosphere around the two people sitting on the bench, some sort of invisible energy. When he was in the same room as the pair, Delbert thought, he swore he could almost see little flashes of lightning.

He turned around to watch Mrs. Trevelyan work the dough. It was a pleasant sight. Her full bosom heaved against the apron as she leaned into her task.

"How did you come by your post in Mrs. Pyne's household?" he queried.

"The agency sent me around," she said. "I don't mind telling you, I was a bit desperate by the time she interviewed me. My old employer died a while back without bothering to leave me a reference, let alone a pension. Very hard to get a position in a respectable household without a good character, you know."

"I wouldn't know. Never tried to obtain a position in a respectable household."

She gave him a single head-to-toe glance. "Yes, well, judging by your very fine boots and your gold framed spectacles and that ring you wear I expect you've made a good deal more in your post here than I'll ever see in a lifetime."

Susan Trevelyan was a fine, handsome woman, he thought, not for the first time. Her broad, rounded thighs and full breasts put him in mind of a statue of some ancient goddess. She was strong and energetic, too. She hoisted the heavy iron cooking pots as though they were made of paper. It occurred to him that she might be equally vigorous in bed.

"Go on with your tale," he said.

"The agency hoped that, since Mrs. Pyne was recently arrived from America, the Wild West, no less, she might not be too particular in the matter of a character reference," Mrs. Trevelyan said.

"I've heard they're a bit odd out there in the West."

"I believe so. In any event, Mrs. Pyne interviewed me and hired me straight off. She never asked for a character reference, thank goodness."

"Does she ever talk about her time in America?"

"Sometimes." Mrs. Trevelyan settled the dough into a pan.

"Always been curious about the place, myself," Delbert said. "They make excellent guns."

Mrs. Trevelyan opened the oven door and inserted the pan of bread dough. "I think Mrs. Pyne gets a bit lonesome for the West at times. She had friends there and a great many adventures as well."

"Did she say why she came back to England?"

"No. I don't think she knows, herself, why she returned. To tell you the truth, until recently I thought she had made a mistake. I kept expecting her to book passage back to America."

"Why do you say that?"

"There was a strange restlessness in her spirits. Oh, she was always busy enough, what with her charity work and all, but it was as if some part of her was waiting for something to happen."

"Such as?"

"I had no notion and I don't think she did, either. Not until recently, that is." Mrs. Trevelyan wiped her hands on a towel and angled her head toward the scene in the garden. "A social reformer and a crime lord. Who would have believed it?"

Delbert smiled. "Who would have believed that a respectable woman like yourself would end up cooking for the Director of the Consortium and his lieutenants?"

She gave a gentle snort of laughter.

"Makes for an interesting change," she allowed.

There was a light sheen of sweat on her noble brow. Somehow it made her even more attractive.

"You're an unusual woman, Mrs. Trevelyan," he said.

"You are not quite what I expected in a member of the criminal class, yourself, sir. How long have you been with Mr. Winters?"

"Since the first days he arrived on the streets. He was just a boy. Barely sixteen years old and he'd been raised in a respectable home. He knew nothing about what he was facing but he learned fast. It was like he'd been born to create the Consortium."

"Consortium." Mrs. Trevelyan took a stew pot down from the wall. "Sounds more like a respectable investment firm than an underworld gang."

"That is exactly what the Boss said."

17

ADELAIDE MARKED HER PLACE AND CLOSED THE LEATHER-bound volume. "No offense, sir, but your ancestor was a peculiar individual."

"By all accounts, I take after him," Griffin said. "You've seen the portrait in the library. When I look at it, it is as if I am viewing my own reflection."

It was very pleasant sitting out here in the garden with Adelaide, he thought. A brief, tantalizing glimpse of what his life might have been like if his past had taken a different turn, if he were not who and what he was, if he had been free to marry and start a family.

"You do bear a striking resemblance to Nicholas Winters, but you are not at all the same man," Adelaide said.

The ringing certainty in her voice made him raise his brows.

"Why do you say that?" he asked. "The resemblance, both physical and psychical, is obvious."

"I've spent over a decade with that lamp," she reminded him. "Believe me when I tell you that I know every nuance of the heavy dreamprints on it. You are certainly a descendant of Nicholas Winters but you are your own man."

He sensed that there would be no arguing with her on the subject, so he let it drop.

"What else do the dreamprints on the lamp tell you?" he asked instead.

"Among other things, there was a very strong bond between Winters and the dreamlight reader, Eleanor Fleming." Adelaide hesitated a second before adding, "It was a bond of passion."

"I told you, they were lovers. She bore him a son. He betrayed her. She wanted revenge. It is an old and oft-told tale to be sure. The only thing that marks it as different from other such stories is that instead of trying to murder Nicholas, Eleanor used the energy of the lamp to destroy all of his talent."

"It was a harsh vengeance and she paid for it with her life," Adelaide said. "The energy unleashed by the lamp killed Eleanor, even as it shattered Nicholas's senses."

"Yes."

"She was a fool to trust him." Adelaide shook her head. "Nicholas Winters would have betrayed any woman. His real mistress was his obsession with power. Acquiring it was all he cared about until, at the end, he took up a new obsession."

"Revenge against the entire line of Sylvester Jones."

"Yes." She tapped the journal. "It is all here. Nicholas is nothing if not clear about his intention to destroy everything that Jones hoped to create even if it took generations upon generations to do so."

"Never let it be said that my ancestor did not make grandiose plans."

"He knew when he went to confront Sylvester for the last time that he would not survive the encounter," Adelaide continued. "Judging by what he wrote, I think he wanted Jones to kill him. It was a form of suicide."

"His senses were deteriorating rapidly because of what Eleanor Fleming had done with the lamp. He was sinking into insanity. Death was all that was left for him."

"Or so he believed."

Griffin looked at her. "When will you work the lamp for me?"

She glanced uneasily at the journal. "There is a great deal here that is not explained."

"You noticed that, did you? I told you, the old bastard was an alchemist. He was obsessed with secrecy. I did my best to decipher the code that he used in that journal, but it is possible I missed some vital element. I will never know for certain until you work the lamp."

"Do you have any idea what he meant when he wrote about the key in the lock?"

"I assume it's a warning. If things go wrong, there will be hell to pay."

She opened the journal and read aloud: *The third talent is the most powerful and the most dangerous. If the key is not turned properly in the lock, this last psychical ability will prove lethal, bringing on first insanity and then death."* She looked up. "He seems to be convinced that those of his line who inherit his powers will be able to handle the third talent but only if it is unlocked properly."

Griffin contemplated the pond. "Never forget that he was likely already quite mad when he wrote that."

"Or so legend has it." Adelaide closed the book again.

"As far as I'm concerned, the critical line in the journal is the one concerning a woman who can work dreamlight energy," he said. *"Only such a female can halt or reverse the transformation once it has begun."*

"He didn't like that, did he?"

"Knowing that the powers of the lamp cannot be accessed without the help of a woman who can manipulate dreamlight? No. He did not like that bit at all."

"It was his own fault. He's the one who created the device."

Griffin almost smiled. "True."

"No doubt he assumed that he could control the woman whose assistance he required."

"Nicholas may have been a psychical genius but he did not know much about women." Griffin looked at her. "Well, Adelaide? Do you think you can manipulate the power of the Burning Lamp?"

"Oh, yes."

Anticipation flashed through him.

"You can reverse the transformation?" he asked.

"I'm not at all certain about that aspect of the thing."

He exhaled heavily. "I hesitate to say this because you already think me inclined toward melodrama, but the truth is, you are my only hope."

Her intelligent, captivating face was shadowed and solemn. "If ever there was a situation that called for melodrama, this may be it. You do realize that if I work the lamp, it is quite possible that I will kill you in the process?"

"Yes."

"Do you truly wish to take that risk, sir?"

"I find it preferable to the alternative."

"You are so certain that you are destined to become mad if the transformation continues?"

He glanced at the journal. "All I have to go on is what Nicholas wrote in his notes and the legend as my father told it to me. You see my predicament, Adelaide."

"Yes," she said. "I understand."

"Well, then?"

"Tonight," she said. "Dreamlight energy is more powerful during the nighttime hours."

18

SHORTLY BEFORE MIDNIGHT ADELAIDE TUCKED THE JOURNAL into the crook of her arm and went to the door of her bedroom. She let herself out into the hall. The ancient stone walls seemed unnaturally still around her. Mrs. Trevelyan had retired to her bedroom after dinner and was presumably fast asleep. Delbert, Leggett and Jed were also abed.

After so many nights spent in the Abbey, Adelaide was now familiar with the evening rituals of the household. They all involved protection. Like sorcerers setting magical wards against supernatural forces, the three enforcers walked through the very modern locks and elaborately designed alarms. The dogs, the first line of defense, according to Jed, were turned loose in the garden.

She went down the shadowed staircase. When she reached the front hall she turned and made her way to the library.

Griffin was waiting for her. He stood in front of a low-burning fire, one hand on the mantel. Energy shifted in the atmosphere around him. It seemed to her that she could literally feel tendrils of his power reaching out to encircle her and draw her to him. The sensation stirred her senses. She had to suppress a sudden, nearly overwhelming desire to run to him.

Her fingers tightened on the journal. She must remain fully in control tonight, for both their sakes.

Griffin was dressed in dark trousers and a white linen shirt. The collar of the shirt was unfastened and the sleeves were rolled up on his forearms. He had not cloaked himself in his talent, yet there was a sense of darkness and shadow around him, as though he were about to go into a battle, which was, she thought, uncomfortably close to the truth.

But there were other powerful currents in the room, freighted with sexual awareness. Impossible though it seemed, Adelaide got the strange feeling that the wavelengths of desire were somehow resonating with the ominous energy leaking out of the Burning Lamp. The realization brought her to a halt just inside the doorway.

Griffin looked at her. "Come in, Adelaide."

That was all he said, but the husky sensuality in his voice sent a rush of excitement through her. He had never made any attempt to hide the fact that he was physically attracted to her, but even if he had tried to do so, she would have known. Just as he was surely aware of her desire for him, she thought. Such strong, primal forces generated a great amount of energy across the entire spectrum. Even people without much talent could usually sense the hot currents of passion. When such energy resonated between two individuals endowed with strong psychical sensitivities, it was impossible to conceal.

But that did not mean that one abandoned oneself willy-nilly to such elemental, potentially dangerous emotions, she reminded herself. She straightened her shoulders, closed the door and walked resolutely into the center of the room.

The heavy curtains were drawn closed against the night. Only a single gas lamp was turned up, leaving most of the library drenched in flickering shadows cast by the fire.

The artifact stood on a small round table in the center of the space. The gold-toned metal gleamed dully in the light. The crystals in the rim were cloudy.

"I have left instructions with the men that we are not to be disturbed under any circumstances," Griffin said.

For some reason that unnerved her as nothing else had. "They know we are meeting here tonight?"

"Yes."

"You told them what we planned to do with the lamp?"

"No, of course not," Griffin said. "I did not want to alarm them with talk of psychical experiments."

"Then what on earth will they think we are about?"

In spite of the tension in the room, he was amused. "What do you imagine they will conclude?"

She flushed. "Yes, of course. How . . . awkward."

"It is only natural that they believe us to be lovers, Adelaide." Impatience edged his tone. "They know full well that I have never before brought a woman into this house."

"Why not?" she asked before she could stop herself.

"Because this house holds far too many secrets."

She nodded, understanding at once. "You allow no one inside who cannot be trusted."

"The rule tends to limit houseguests quite dramatically."

"No doubt." She paused. "But you brought me here. And I summoned Mrs. Trevelyan."

The corner of his mouth kicked up in grim amusement. "And the next thing I know I've got a Jones under my roof: Mrs. Lucinda Bromley Jones, noted poisoner and one of the founders of Arcane's new psychical detective agency. You see what happens when the rules are broken?"

"I thought we had agreed that Jones and Jones was not an immediate threat."

"That does not mean I intend to make a habit of inviting the proprietors of the firm to tea."

"Mrs. Jones didn't stay for tea."

His brows rose. "Don't tell me you invited her?"

"It seemed the polite thing to do."

He shook his head in a resigned manner but he refrained from further comment on the subject.

"Fortunately, Mr. and Mrs. Jones are not here now," he said. "There is only you and me and the lamp. Let us get on with this business."

The words aroused old memories. Thirteen years ago Mr. Smith had said the same thing. *Let us get on with this business.* It was her intuition speaking tonight, she thought, warning her of danger. But, then, she already knew that what she and Griffin were about to attempt was very dangerous, indeed.

Griffin walked past her to the closed door. She heard the harsh rasp of iron-on-iron when he turned the key in the lock. There seemed to be an air of finality about the sound, a signal that there would be no turning back, the thought of which made her shiver and raised the hair on the nape of her neck. Dread? Fear? Foreboding? Whatever it was, there was no denying that it was tinged with excitement.

After all these years, she was about to discover the mysteries of the artifact that she had guarded for so long. A feverish surge of anticipation pulsed through her. She had been waiting for this moment, she thought. *And this man.*

She pushed that last thought aside. Tonight she must not be distracted. She had to concentrate solely on the work at hand. Griffin's life and her own, not to mention their senses and their sanity, hung in the balance. Everything would depend on her ability to control her talent.

She set the journal on a nearby table.

"Please turn down the gas lamp," she said. "I find it easier to focus on dreamlight when my senses are not too distracted by other forms of illumination."

Griffin did as she asked, plunging the room into even deeper shadows. "What of the fire?"

"That will not be a problem," she said.

Griffin crossed the short distance to the small table where the artifact stood.

"What now?" he asked.

"I have concluded after reading the journal that you were right when you deduced that there must be some physical contact between us in order to light the lamp and control the currents within it," she said. She reached across the table. "Take my hand, sir."

His fingers closed tightly around hers. Cautiously she put her free hand on the rim of the artifact, just above the crystals.

"Now touch the lamp with your other hand," she said.

He did as she instructed.

"I told you, I can make the lamp glow a little," she said, "but I am certain that only you can actually cause it to ignite."

"How do I do that?"

"I think it will be an intuitive thing," she said. "Start by opening your senses fully and feel your way into the pattern of the lamp's wavelengths."

"What will you do?"

"My task, as I understand it from the journal, is to make sure that the center holds. If the currents are not kept under firm control, they will become wild and chaotic. If that happens I doubt that we will survive."

"It occurs to me that neither one of us knows what we are about here."

"I had the same thought," Adelaide said.

She also knew that neither of them was going to suggest that they halt the experiment.

Griffin looked down at the artifact, his alchemist's face etched in the stark shadows cast by the fire. He said nothing but she felt energy pulse higher in the atmosphere. As yet his talent was unfocused so the extraordinary amount of dreamlight he generated crashed and roiled in harmless invisible waves in the space around them. The enthralling aura of his power threatened to further agitate her already aroused senses into a storm of sensual urgency. She struggled to control her response. She knew that Griffin was waging the same internal battle.

"It's the lamp," she informed him smoothly, as if she actually knew what she was talking about. "The energy it emits, even in the unlit state, appears to have a rather odd effect on our physical senses. Just ignore it."

He looked at her over the rim of the artifact. For a few heartbeats she could not move, so unnerved was she by the heat in his eyes.

"I don't know about you, but I find that ignoring these sensations is not an option," he said. "So perhaps we had best move forward with all due speed."

Entranced and compelled by the heat in his eyes, she could not breathe for a couple of heartbeats. She finally swallowed hard and took a grip on her nerves.

"Right," she said. "Try to connect with the patterns the lamp produces."

She knew immediately when he started to focus his energy in a deliberate fashion. Intuitively she did the same with her own talent, searching for a pattern in the paranormal storm that was trapped in the lamp. The power level in the room rose higher.

The artifact began to glow, faintly at first, but it soon brightened with the eerie hues of ultralight that came from the darkest end of the spectrum.

"Yes," Griffin said. There was soft triumph in his voice. "Yes, I can sense it now."

A shock of electricity seared Adelaide's senses. She took a sharp, startled breath. Griffin's hand clenched hers. She knew that the invisible lightning had jolted through him, as well. But the flash of dreamlight heat lasted less than a heartbeat. And then they were in the storm together.

She felt as if she were soaring on the currents of energy flooding the room. The sensation was intoxicating. On the other side of the table Griffin's eyes burned. His hand was a manacle around hers, chaining her to him.

A paranormal fire roared inside the lamp, flaring and flashing in colors that came from the heart of the dreamscape world. Like the flames of an alchemist's furnace they began to transform the artifact. The dull gold metal grew first opaque, then translucent and finally transparent. Adelaide stared at it, transfixed.

"It looks as if it is made of purest crystal," she whispered.

"The stones," Griffin said. "Look at them."

The crystals set in the rim of the artifact lost their murky quality. All but one began to glow with an intense inner fire. Each radiated a different color from across the dreamlight spectrum: diamond white, amber yellow, peridot and emerald greens, ruby red and exotic violets.

A senses-dazzling rainbow of ultralight lanced out across the room, spearing the walls, flashing off the mirror and illuminating the portrait of Nicholas Winters. Something shifted at the edges of Adelaide's vision. She realized that tendrils of her hair were floating in the air in response to the charged atmosphere.

She studied the currents produced by the artifact, noting the places here and there where the wavelengths did not resonate properly with Griffin's own patterns. The radiation in the lamp was beyond anything she had ever experienced but it was, still in all, dreamlight energy. She suddenly knew intuitively that what was required was a little fine-tuning.

She set to work coaxing the improperly oscillating sections of the currents into patterns that resonated smoothly with those that Griffin generated. It was subtle, delicate work. Like tuning a piano, she thought, delighted with her own analogy. One just knew when one got it right.

Now certain of what she was about, she made the little adjustments quickly, never letting go of Griffin's hand throughout the process. For his part he seemed unaware of what was happening. He stood very still, gazing at the lamp as though mesmerized.

An exultant sensation sizzled through her when she tuned the last of the slightly out-of-phase currents. Everything about the patterns, powerful though they were, felt right now. The music of the spheres, indeed, she thought. She started to tell Griffin that the task was completed and that he could shut down the lamp's power.

The words never left her mouth. Energy exploded across the wavelengths that oscillated between Griffin and the relic. Griffin uttered a choked, agonized groan. His eyes closed and his body shuddered violently in response to the hurricane reverberating between him and the lamp. His hand clutched hers, as though she was his lifeline in the storm.

The lamp was killing him, she thought, horrified. She had done this to him.

"Griffin," she said. "Listen to me. You must make it stop. Only you can light the lamp and only you can shut it down. I can hold the pattern constant for you but you must dampen the waves. Do you understand? Do it now."

He opened his eyes and looked at her through the tempest of shadows and raging dreamlight. Everything about him burned with power. There was something darkly sensual and utterly masculine in the energy that swept around her, imprisoning her.

"I understand," he said. The words were low, fierce and exultant. "You are the lady of the lamp and you belong to me."

"I think the lamp's energy is affecting your other senses," she said anxiously. "Try to stay focused here, Griffin."

His smile was slow and deeply compelling. For an instant she thought all was lost. Then, to her overwhelming relief, she sensed that he was lowering his own level of power. Slowly, deliberately, he suppressed the crashing waves of dreamlight.

The ultralight rainbow winked out as the stones lost their inner fire. The lamp stopped glowing. Within seconds it was no longer transparent. It grew quickly opaque and, at last, solid and metallic once more.

But Griffin's eyes were still lit with a fever. Adelaide watched him circle the table and come toward her, excitement flooding her senses.

When he pulled her into his arms she could no more have resisted him than she could have turned back the tides.

19

HE WAS BURNING HOTTER THAN THE LAMP AND ALL OF THE
energy he possessed was focused on Adelaide. The need to imprint
himself on her, to chain her to him in the most elemental way had been
building inside him since that first moment of psychical recognition in
the gallery of the museum. Now it demanded release and satisfaction.
He had to have her or he would go mad.

"Adelaide," he said. *"Adelaide."*

"Yes," she whispered.

He pulled her closer, crushing her against his chest with his good
arm, and brought his mouth down on hers. Her arms went around his
neck as though she was every bit as desperate to bind them together as
he was.

He sensed that the fire of the kiss was flashing and sparking through
both of them. Adelaide's half-choked cry of passion was a siren's song.
When her mouth opened under his, he was lost.

He got the front of her gown unfastened and pushed the stiff bodice off her shoulders and down over her hips. Her skirts crumpled around her ankles. He untied the petticoat and let it fall to a frothy heap at her feet, leaving her clothed only in a thin chemise and a pair of dainty, low-heeled, black satin mules.

"I cannot wait," he said against her throat.

"Your shoulder."

"Has never felt better."

Hands shaking with the force of his need, he yanked one of the folded blankets off the sofa, snapped it open and tossed it down onto the carpet in front of the fire. He pulled off his low boots, unfastened his trousers and opened his shirt.

"I have never needed anyone like this," he said. He kicked free of his clothing. "It is as if a fever has come over me and only you can quench it."

With a soft sigh she lay down on the blanket. He lowered himself beside her, pulled up the hem of her chemise and knelt between her legs. The scent of her arousal intoxicated his already inflamed senses. Her knees rose, inviting him closer. He leaned over her, bracing himself on his good arm.

She was so wet and hot and full that he could hardly breathe. He pushed himself deep into her body. She arched upward to meet him. He forced himself to retreat partway and then he surged back into her. Invisible flames burned higher in the room, threatening to consume him. He looked down at Adelaide's face. Her eyes were squeezed shut against the tidal waves of energy sweeping between them, around them and through them.

"Adelaide, look at me," he grated.

She raised her lashes partway. Her eyes glowed hot with a power that matched his own.

"Griffin," she whispered.

The sound of his name on her lips unleashed the last of his control.

He surged into her one more time. The climax slammed through his body and all of his senses, taking him beyond anything he had ever known. Adelaide convulsed beneath him.

"Griffin," she said again, breathless this time.

Together they flew into the center of the raging storm.

20

SHE SAT UP SLOWLY AND LOOKED DOWN AT GRIFFIN. HE SPRAWLED
on his stomach on the blanket, his face turned away from the fire.
He was sound asleep and he was dreaming, but she did not sense any
nightmare energy.

Carefully she disentangled herself from his arms. Something of critical importance had occurred when she had completed the process of
tuning the Burning Lamp. She had assumed that once the slight dis-
tortions in the oscillating rhythms had been corrected, Griffin's dreamlight currents would return to whatever pattern was normal for him.
But she was almost certain that that was not what had happened.

The key must be properly turned in the lock.

Good lord, what have I done?

She rose a little unsteadily, gathered up her clothing and dressed by
the light of the dying fire. When she had refastened the bodice of the
gown she took a deep breath and cautiously opened her senses.

Griffin's dreamprints were everywhere in the room but it was the trail of footsteps leading from the table where the lamp sat to the blanket in front of the hearth that made her catch her breath. The luminous energy flaring in the prints was more ominous and more powerful than that which glowed in any of the other psychical tracks.

She knew then that she had not saved Griffin from the fate he feared. When he awoke he would discover that he was now a full-blown Cerberus.

She tried to ponder the implications but for some reason she could not concentrate. A rising tide of unease was rattling her senses. This was a fine time to get an attack of nerves, she thought. She needed to understand what had occurred when she had worked the lamp so that she could explain it to Griffin. Then again, how did one explain a situation like this? Sorry, but you are now officially a psychical monster according to Arcane's definition.

Griffin stirred on the blanket. She flinched a little, startled, and turned quickly to look at him.

He folded his arms behind his head and contemplated her with the lazy satisfaction of a well-fed lion.

"You are so beautiful," he said.

She flushed. She knew full well that she was no beauty, but the fact that he found her attractive was ridiculously pleasing. He made her feel beautiful just by the way he looked at her. Of course, once she explained that she had failed him, his views would no doubt undergo a sea change. She collected herself.

"Griffin, there is something I must explain to you," she said. "It is rather complicated."

He got to his feet and started to pull on his clothes.

"I do not know how to thank you," he said.

"No need, really," she said quickly. "The thing is—"

She broke off because he was walking toward her, fastening his trousers. He stopped directly in front of her, cradled her chin in one hand

and tipped up her face for a staggeringly possessive kiss. When it was over, she had to remind herself to breathe.

"I know that what just happened between us was not the most romantic of encounters," he said. "But I swear it will be different next time."

She swallowed hard. "Next time? Well, as to that, sir—"

"Griffin." His smile was slow and sensual.

"Griffin. Perhaps we should allow for the fact that what just occurred between us may have been the result of the radiation from the lamp. It seemed to have a very arousing effect on our senses."

"Not a chance in hell of blaming it on the lamp," he said cheerfully. "I wanted you from the first moment I saw you. By the way, speaking of that damned artifact, you never told me how it came into your possession."

She blinked, caught off stride. "I explained that I found it when I was fifteen."

"Yes, you did say that." He used his fingers to shove his hair back off his high forehead. "But where did you find it? It doesn't seem to be the sort of object that one stumbles over in an antiquities shop." He paused, glancing at the lamp. "Or is it?"

"Does it matter?" she asked.

"I don't know. But I would like an answer."

She drew herself up and straightened her shoulders. It had been inevitable that sooner or later he would ask.

"I found it in a brothel," she said, daring him to leap to the obvious conclusion.

Startled disbelief lit his eyes. "What the devil were you doing in a whorehouse?"

She raised her chin. "I believe I mentioned that my parents died when I was fifteen. I received a rather large inheritance that was managed by my father's solicitor. He and the money both vanished within two months."

"And you wound up in a brothel?" he asked, his voice gentling.

She narrowed her eyes. "I assure you, I did not apply for a position in a house of prostitution."

"I did not mean to imply that you went willingly."

"I believe that the solicitor sold me to the brothel manager."

"Son of a bitch," Griffin said very, very softly.

"I thought I was being sent to a new boarding school," she added.

Energy flashed in the atmosphere.

"I'll kill every man who ever touched you in that place," Griffin said without inflection.

Astonishment left her speechless. He meant it, she thought. She had always known that there was something very dangerous lurking beneath the surface in him, but this was the first time she had glimpsed the shark's fin slicing through the dark waters.

An unfamiliar emotion swept over her. She had been on her own for so long, taking care of herself, relying on no one. It was difficult to believe that this man was willing to murder any number of gentlemen whom he did not even know in order to avenge her.

"Thank you, sir. Griffin." She brushed the moisture from her eyes with the edge of her hand and managed a shaky smile. "That is the most romantic thing anyone has ever said to me. Fortunately, no such violent action will be needed. I never actually went to work in the brothel, you see."

He watched her steadily. "Go on with your story."

"On the second night after my arrival I was informed that a man named Mr. Smith had purchased me for the evening. I knew that I would have only one chance to escape. I hid in the wardrobe. When Smith arrived he was carrying a satchel. I sensed the energy pouring out of the bag but I had no notion of what was inside."

"He had the lamp with him?" Griffin sounded incredulous.

"Yes."

"Damn it to hell," Griffin said softly. "That means that Smith bought you because he wanted a dreamlight reader. Somehow he knew you had the talent. He planned to work the lamp."

"Yes, I think so. But he was not absolutely certain that I could manipulate the energy of the thing. He seemed to think that he had to bed me first. Something about a test."

"Bastard. He believed that part of the legend."

She glanced at the crumpled blanket on the floor behind him and raised her brows. "There does appear to be something to the theory that a sexual bond is necessary, after all. It is certainly not beyond the realm of possibility. Passion generates a vast amount of psychical energy. Perhaps it is the key."

But he was no longer listening. He clamped a hand across her mouth.

"Quiet," he whispered.

It was a command, delivered in a voice as cold as the grave. She nodded once, signaling that she understood.

He took his palm away from her lips. He was not looking at her. His full attention was on the door. The battle-ready tension in him shivered in the atmosphere.

She wanted to ask him what had alarmed him. The dogs had not barked and none of the bells attached to the windows and doors had sounded. But the hair on the back of her neck was stirring and her senses were abuzz.

Griffin was already moving through the shadows, crossing the room toward his desk. His bare feet made no noise on the carpet.

A few seconds later she heard a faint squeak and knew that he had opened a drawer. She did not see the revolver in his hand until he came back to where she stood in front of the hearth. He put his mouth close to her ear.

"Lock the door behind me and do not come out until I return," he said.

He did not wait for her to acknowledge the order. He was already on his way to the door. She felt energy pulse in the atmosphere and suddenly she could no longer see Griffin clearly. He had pulled his cloak of shadows around himself, almost but not quite, vanishing.

She heard rather than saw him turn the key in the lock of the door. The sound seemed as loud as a gunshot but she knew that in reality it was no more than a soft metallic rasp.

The shadowy figure that was Griffin flattened himself against the side of the wall and eased the door open.

"Jed?" Griffin sounded relieved and a little irritated. "Bloody hell, man, you gave me a jolt. What in blazes is this about? I told you that we were not to be interrupted. Is something wrong?"

Adelaide looked into the hall and saw Jed. There was just enough light from the single wall sconce to make out his slight, wiry form and scarred features. Hot prints seared the floor at his feet.

Jed reached into his coat.

"It's not Jed," she shouted.

21

"*DOWN,*" GRIFFIN SHOUTED AT ADELAIDE.

Expecting gunshots, he fired twice through the doorway to give himself some cover while he got the door closed.

There was no answering fire from the man who looked like Jed. Instead, he yelped in alarm and dove to the floor. The object he had removed from his coat pocket glowed blood red in his fist.

"He's got a gun," the fake Jed screamed at an unseen companion.

Another man, moving with the telltale speed and lethal grace of a hunter-talent, appeared in the hall. He, too, gripped a fist-sized object that flared with a hellish crimson glare. In his other hand he held what appeared to be a cannon ball.

He rolled the ball across the floor through the rapidly narrowing doorway before the door finally slammed shut and Griffin turned the key in the lock.

The muffled voices of the two intruders reverberated through the heavy wooden door panels.

"He's trapped in there now," the hunter said. "This won't take long. The fog will get him soon enough. He'll be unconscious in a few minutes."

"The woman is in there with him," the first intruder responded.

"That will make it easy then. What the hell went wrong? You looked just like that bastard upstairs."

The first man was an illusion-talent, Griffin thought. That explained a few things.

"It was the woman," the illusion-talent muttered. "Somehow she knew."

The ball on the carpet was making a hissing sound. Griffin glanced at it as he went toward Adelaide. A faint plume of what looked like white smoke drifted upward from the dark metal canister. His heightened senses tingled in warning. He caught a whiff of the foglike vapor. It had a peculiar spicy-sweet scent. The room began to spin slowly around him.

Ignoring the gnawing ache in his left shoulder, he grabbed the artifact off the table and crossed to where Adelaide waited. She glanced questioningly at him. He gestured toward the section of the stone wall where the portrait of Nicholas Winters hung.

Adelaide sniffed faintly and then abruptly whipped a handkerchief out of a pocket in her gown.

"Cover your face," she whispered. "Don't breathe any of that vapor."

He handed the Burning Lamp to her and shoved the revolver into the waistband of his trousers. Plastering the front edge of his shirt across the lower half of his face, he used his free hand to push the portrait aside.

The room was ebbing and flowing around him but he managed to locate the chink in the stone by touch. He pressed the concealed lever. There was a soft sigh of hidden gears. A section of stone swung inward.

Cool currents of air wafted into the library from the concealed passage, pushing back the noxious vapor.

"Oh, dear," Adelaide muttered. For the first time, she sounded anxious. "A tunnel. I should have guessed. I don't do well in enclosed spaces, Griffin."

"I'm afraid you have no choice tonight."

"No," she said. "I can see that."

"Don't worry, we are not going far."

Mercifully she did not argue. She ducked into the dark entrance. He followed her, pulling the stone wall closed behind them.

The concealed door sighed shut, engulfing them in profound night. He took a cautious breath. The air in the stone corridor was stale but there was no trace of the gas.

"Don't move," he said.

"Believe me, I won't," Adelaide said. "I can't see my hand in front of my face. But I must tell you, I'm not sure how long I can wait here in the darkness like this without suffering an attack of nerves, Griffin."

He struck a light. The flame flared on the walls of the tunnel.

"Better?" he asked.

She looked around, her dread vivid in her eyes. "Not really," she said. "But I think I can manage for a while if I stay in my other senses. I understand now what you meant when you said that this house holds many secrets."

"The monks constructed the hidden passages in the walls. The concealed corridors are the chief reason I bought the place a few years ago. It is impossible to make any fortress one hundred percent impregnable. The tunnels were intended to be the last line of defense and an emergency escape route if ever one was needed. Come, we must hurry."

She followed him along the passageway. "Are we escaping?"

"Not yet. My objective is to take that pair by surprise."

"How?"

"These passageways run through every old wall of the house. There are several openings. One of them is in the kitchen. That's the one I'll use."

"Those men came here to kill you."

"Probably."

"Luttrell?"

"It would not come as a great surprise to discover that he has concluded that the Cemetery Truce is no longer useful to him. I've been certain that time would arrive sooner or later. Always knew that one day I would have to kill him. But there is another possibility."

"Arcane?" she asked, sounding wary.

"Both of the intruders are strong talents. They came armed with some kind of poisoned vapor and they are employing some odd red crystals. That doesn't sound like Luttrell. His methods are more traditional. Sounds more like a bunch of would-be psychical alchemists."

"What did you say about red crystals?"

"Each of those intruders has one. Have to assume they are some kind of weapon like the gas."

"Listen to me, Griffin. I believe that the red crystals may be tools that somehow focus a person's natural energy and make it stronger, at least temporarily."

"What do you mean?"

"Mr. Smith, the man with the Burning Lamp, had one. Believe me when I tell you that they are dangerous."

"After what happened in the library, I'll take your word for it."

The light flickered on the stone that marked the section that opened into the kitchen.

Adelaide moved to stand beside him. In the flaring light her eyes were haunted.

"Griffin, there is something else you must know before you deal with those two men," she whispered.

"What?" He reached out to press the triangle engraved on the marker stone.

"I think you still possess your second talent. In fact, I'm sure of it."

He went cold. "You worked the lamp. I felt the effects."

"I worked it but not in a way that reverses the process. I . . . . I think I just did a bit of tuning, if you see what I mean. Then I believe that we may have turned the key in the lock when we—" She broke off.

"Son of a bitch," he mumbled.

This was not the time to deal with the fact that he was still doomed. He would think about it later, assuming he stayed sane long enough to contemplate his future. The first priority was keeping Adelaide safe.

"I know that is not what you wanted to hear," she said earnestly. "But I am convinced that what I did is for the best."

"Any notion of how long I've got before I go mad?" he asked, amazed at how astonishingly calm he felt, almost as if the matter was merely academic.

"You are not going mad."

"We will discuss this later, assuming I'm still capable of carrying on a rational conversation. I will allow that tonight my second talent may come in handy."

"Griffin, wait—"

"Stay here. After I leave, press that stone with the mark on it. The wall will close again. That pair will never discover the interior passages in this house. You'll be safe in here until they are gone. When you emerge, see to Mrs. Trevelyan and my men."

"Yes, of course."

"And then send word to Jones and Jones."

"*What?*"

"Make it clear to Caleb Jones that you want to surrender the lamp. I do not trust Arcane when it comes to my own safety but the Joneses adhere to their own code of honor. They have no reason to harm you so long as they get their hands on the relic."

"All right." She touched his good shoulder. "But, please, promise me that you will be very careful."

He did not respond. There was no point making a promise that he could not keep. Instead, he leaned forward and brushed his mouth lightly across hers.

"I will never forget you, Adelaide Pyne," he said. "Even if I am fated to spend the rest of my days in an asylum."

"Damnation, Griffin, you are not going mad," she snapped. "I do not want to hear another word on the subject."

Her outrage was invigorating. He smiled a little and reached into a pocket. "Here. Take these."

"What are they?"

"A couple of spare lights just in case you end up spending a long time in this wall tonight."

"Oh." She seemed oddly disappointed but she rebounded immediately. "Thank you. Very thoughtful."

He got the feeling that she had been expecting something else in the way of a parting gesture. A touching keepsake, perhaps. It was a romantic notion. But if he did not return she would find the lights far more useful than a ring or an embroidered handkerchief.

He pushed hard on the marked stone. Deep inside the wall, gears and levers murmured in hushed tones. A crack of semidarkness appeared and widened steadily, revealing a long trestle table and the moonlit window.

He left Adelaide standing just inside the passage and went out into the kitchen. The odd thing was that he felt better psychically than he had in a very long time, more centered and in control of his talents. That was no doubt how all madmen felt as they sank deeper into the darkness.

He gathered a cloak of shadows around himself and proceeded bare-footed across the kitchen and out into the hall. Exhilaration slammed through him when he opened his talent to the fullest extent. He could not escape the sensation that he was *meant* to use this energy. Nature intended for him to employ it the same way that it intended for him to use his other senses.

The hunter-talent, with his preternatural hearing, sensed him first.

"Well, now, what have we got here?" the man asked softly from the shadows near the door of the library. "There were supposed to be only three guards in the house."

The hunter came out of the dimly lit front hall, moving with the speed and agility of a wolf taking down prey. The light from the lowered wall sconce revealed his savage grin and glinted on the knife in his hand. A crimson glare emanated from between the fingers of his other hand. Energy pulsed violently in the atmosphere.

Griffin held his fire. It was impossible to be certain of a shot when the target was moving so swiftly. He heightened his own talent, pulling more shadows around himself.

But the hunter did not hesitate. He rushed forward with unerring accuracy, showing no signs of confusion or bewilderment. The red crystal glowed hotter.

The bastard can see me with his heightened para-senses, Griffin thought. *I might as well be standing in the center of a spotlight on a stage.*

The intruder was almost upon him. There would be no chance of an accurate shot. He prayed that Adelaide was right, that he still possessed his second talent.

He reached into the darkest end of the dreamlight spectrum. There were things that even a hunter feared, things that lived only in the realm of nightmares.

The hunter was close now, so close that Griffin had no difficulty at all getting a fix on the other man's aura. He cast his talent like a whip.

The hunter floundered to a halt. Violent spasms stiffened his body. His arms flailed as though he were struggling with invisible demons. He screamed like a soul falling into the mouth of hell, screamed until the stone walls rang with his echoing cries. It seemed as though he screamed for all eternity before he fell silent and crumpled to the floor.

In the sudden, chilling silence, the sound of movement in the doorway just behind Griffin was as loud as thunder.

"F-F-Fergus?" The illusion-talent emerged from the breakfast room. He no longer bore any resemblance to Jed. Gaslight reflected off his gun and gleamed on the silver candlestick he clutched. He stared at the fallen man for a split second as though unable to comprehend. "Bloody hell, Fergus. What's the matter with you?"

He did not wait for a response from his stricken comrade. Spinning around, he disappeared back into the breakfast room.

Griffin followed. He needed only a second to acquire a focus but he had used a lot of energy to take down the hunter; he could not afford to waste any more power. He reached the entrance of the room just in time to see the pantry door swing closed behind his quarry.

The only exit from the pantry was the kitchen.

The gunshot exploded just as Griffin went through the swinging door into the kitchen. Fear unlike anything he had ever known even in his nightmares ripped through him.

"Adelaide," he shouted. "For God's sake, *Adelaide*."

"I'm right here, Griffin." She moved out of the darkened passageway, a small two-shot pocket pistol in her hand. The gun was pointed at the illusion-talent, who seemed frozen by the sight of the weapon. "I thought a warning shot might do the trick and it appears to have been effective."

Griffin looked at her. "I told you to remain hidden in the wall passage."

"And I seem to recall telling you that I do not do well in confined spaces." She studied her frozen victim. "I do believe this villain was trying to pinch the silver."

22

"THANK HEAVENS YOU'RE ALL SAFE." ADELAIDE SET THE KET-
tle on the stove. "Evidently whatever was in that vapor was only intended to induce unconsciousness. It was not designed to kill."

"Well, it appears they wanted you alive," Mrs. Trevelyan said. "So it
stands to reason they wouldn't use a deadly gas."

Adelaide winced. "An excellent point, Mrs. Trevelyan."

They were gathered in the kitchen, all except for Griffin. He was still
talking to the intruders who were secured in the library. Leggett had
reported that the hunter, Fergus, was still in a state of shock. Judging
by what she had seen of his dreamlight currents, Adelaide was not at all
certain that he would ever fully recover.

The illusion-talent, however, was babbling freely. Unfortunately, he
did not seem to know a great deal. The only thing he was certain of
was that he and his companion had been hired to steal the lamp and
kidnap Adelaide.

The two crystals the intruders had carried sat in the center of the trestle table. Now that they were no longer illuminated they appeared to be nothing more than red glass paperweights.

Mrs. Trevelyan, Leggett, Jed and Delbert occupied the benches on either side of the table. They were still groggy from the effects of the sleeping gas but their prints did not indicate any lasting damage. The dogs had awakened as well but they were listless and unsteady on their feet. That had not stopped them from gulping down several chunks of leftover roast that Adelaide had given them.

"I should be making the tea," Mrs. Trevelyan fretted. But the protest was halfhearted.

"Nonsense," Adelaide said. "I am perfectly capable of dealing with the tea."

Mrs. Trevelyan smiled weakly. "Yes, ma'am. I do believe that you are capable of dealing with just about anything that comes along. I had no idea that you carried a pistol about your person."

"An old habit I picked up during my time in the West," Adelaide explained. "Pocket pistols and derringers are commonly referred to as gamblers' guns but they fit nicely into a lady's skirts."

Delbert braced his elbows on the table and cradled his head in his big hands. "I can't believe they got past all of us, to say nothing of the traps and warning bells."

"My fault," Griffin said from the doorway. "As I told Mrs. Pyne, the Abbey is designed to withstand a variety of assaults but never one like the attack those two launched tonight. Clearly, I will have to have a chat with my architect."

Delbert and the others smiled wanly at the small joke.

"They took down the dogs, first, of course," Griffin continued. "Then the hunter went up onto the roof and lowered the gas canisters down through the chimneys into the bedrooms. Once you were all asleep, they broke the lock on the roof stairs and entered the house."

Jed frowned. "But there's an alarm on that door. Why didn't you hear it?"

Griffin looked at Adelaide. She blushed, remembering the paranormal storm they had unleashed in the library.

"We were otherwise occupied," Griffin said neutrally.

Delbert, Leggett, Jed and Mrs. Trevelyan exchanged glances.

Delbert cleared his throat. "No security system is perfect."

"No," Griffin agreed.

Adelaide looked at his grim face and then glanced at the floor near his feet. He had put on his boots but the exhaustion was still starkly evident in his prints. She knew that he must have used a vast amount of power to stop Fergus. She could also see the currents of the edgy energy that, in her experience, was common in the wake of violence. There was pain, as well. She knew his injured shoulder was aching badly.

All in all he needed some healing sleep. She was sure, however, that he would not rest until he was satisfied that the situation was under control and that she and the others were safe. Like the captain of a ship, Griffin Winters would always take care of those in his charge before he saw to his own needs.

"Surprised that pair was willing to break into the Director's personal residence," Leggett said. "Given your reputation, that took some nerve. Reckon they thought they could get away with it because they had those fancy weapons."

"They did not know the identity of this particular homeowner," Griffin said dryly. "Just that the house was well guarded."

Delbert snorted. "That explains it."

"The person who hired them probably assumed that they would not take the job if they knew the real identity of the target," Griffin added.

"No sensible man would," Leggett said.

Jed squinted at Griffin. "Did you learn anything useful from those two, Boss?"

"Such as who sent them, for starters?" Delbert growled.

Griffin shook his head. "No, and there's no point questioning them further. They don't have the answers I need. The one called Fergus cannot even remember why he came here tonight. The illusion-talent's name is Nate. He is desperate to offer information in exchange for his life but he doesn't know much. All he can tell me is that he and his companion were not only promised a great deal of money for grabbing Mrs. Pyne and the artifact but were told they would be given new crystals."

Mrs. Trevelyan's mouth tightened. "I don't understand it. How could they agree to take on such work without even knowing the name of their employer?"

"Fergus and Nate have been a team for years. They offer their skills for hire, no questions asked. They prefer not to know too much about those who employ them. As Nate says, it is usually safer that way."

"But what of the crystals?" Adelaide asked.

Griffin walked to the table, picked up one of the stones and held it to the light. "The man who hired them provided the crystals and the canisters of sleeping vapor. Nate and Fergus were told that if they focused their talent through the crystals, their natural abilities would be enhanced. According to Nate, that is exactly what happened. He said he always had a gift for altering his appearance in subtle ways that confused the eye but it was never so strong as it was tonight. Evidently the same was true for Fergus. He had been fast all his life but not like he was with the crystal."

The water was boiling. Adelaide plucked the kettle off the stove and began to fill the teapot.

"I sense no power in the crystals," she said. "I picked up one a short time ago and tried to determine if there was any energy in it. But it seemed like nothing more than a chunk of plain glass in my hand."

"Because it was exhausted," Griffin said. He put the crystal back down on the table. "Nate said that he and Fergus were warned that the stones would not work for long. They were told to use them sparingly."

Jed contemplated the red crystals. "Like a gun when you run out of bullets. Useless."

"Evidently," Griffin said.

Leggett frowned. "How does a person obtain fresh ammunition?"

A frisson of understanding whispered through Adelaide.

"I would imagine that they must be retuned," she said slowly, thinking it through. "Like a delicate musical instrument."

They all looked at her.

"Makes sense," Griffin said. "And doubtless only the individual who created them knows how to tune them. That would offer a measure of insurance, as well."

Mrs. Trevelyan was baffled. "What on earth do you mean, Mr. Winters?"

Griffin looked at her. "Consider the position of the man who put these crystals into the hands of a pair of street toughs like Nate and Fergus. He gave them very powerful weapons. He would not want those weapons turned against him."

Mrs. Trevelyan's eyes widened. "I see what you mean, sir. As long as they must go back to him for ammunition, so to speak, he need not fear that they will kill him to obtain the crystals."

"I'd like to know where they got those canisters of vapor," Delbert muttered. "My head still hurts."

"Mine, as well," Mrs. Trevelyan said. "And I had such unpleasant dreams. I suspect they will make sleep difficult for some time."

"Nightmares, they were," Jed said. "Unlike anything I've ever had. Everything seemed so real."

"I don't look forward to going to sleep again, that's a fact," Leggett added.

"I will take care of the nightmares," Adelaide said quietly.

The men looked at her.

She smiled. "I have a talent for that sort of thing."

"Where would they get such a noxious vapor?" Jed asked.

"I am very curious about that, myself," Griffin said.

"There are certainly chemicals such as chloroform and gases such as nitrous oxide that can render a person unconscious," Adelaide said. "But I have never heard of anything that could be effectively dispensed in the manner that vapor was tonight."

She picked up the pot and poured tea into the half-dozen heavy mugs on the counter.

Jed watched her with open admiration. "Never met a woman who could shoot a gun, Mrs. Pyne."

"I spent several years in the American West touring with Monty Moore's Wild West Show," she said. She put the teapot down. "One of the most popular acts was an exhibition of marksmanship by Monty Moore, himself. I was his assistant. He was kind enough to teach me how to use a variety of guns and rifles."

Delbert brightened. "I've heard of Monty Moore. There was an account of his sharpshooter skills in the press last year. His assistant tosses a playing card into the air and he shoots three holes in it before it hits the ground."

"From the back of a galloping horse, no less," Adelaide added.

Griffin raised his brows. "And if we believe that, you have some shares in a nice little California gold mine that you would be happy to sell to us for a very good price, correct?"

She smiled. "I will admit that Monty always took the precaution of putting holes in the cards before I threw them out for him. But he really was amazingly skilled with a gun. The audience loved him. In fact, I believe that he had a psychical talent for the business, although I don't think he realized it."

"A paranormal talent for handling a gun?" Leggett asked, intrigued. "Now that would come in handy."

"Trust me, I would never have agreed to hold the apples for him to shoot out of my hands if I hadn't been quite sure that he had a true gift for his art."

Griffin closed his eyes briefly as though in prayer and then looked at her. "You held the targets for an exhibition sharpshooter? I'm not sure my nerves can sustain the shock of that image."

"I'm sure you'll survive." She gave him the last mug of tea. "What will you do with those two men you captured tonight? Turn them over to the police?"

Jed, Leggett and Delbert stared at her as though she had spoken in tongues. But it was Mrs. Trevelyan who pointed out the glaring flaw in the suggestion.

"He can hardly go to the police now, can he?" Mrs. Trevelyan said. "Mr. Winters is a crime lord, after all. A man in his position doesn't summon Scotland Yard whenever someone breaks into his house."

"Sorry," Adelaide murmured. "I forgot myself."

Griffin ignored the byplay.

"As it happens, I've been giving the matter of Fergus and Nate some thought," he said. "The simplest thing to do is to set them free."

Mrs. Trevelyan bristled. "After what they did in this household?"

Griffin cradled his tea in both hands. "Something tells me they are going to do their best to disappear."

Delbert made a face. "If they know what's good for them, that's exactly what they'll do."

"It will be interesting to see who tries to find them after they leave here tonight," Griffin said.

Leggett pushed himself to his feet. "I'll take care of having them followed, Boss. Give me thirty minutes to get some men in place before you turn them loose."

Griffin looked at Adelaide. "And now, Mrs. Pyne, I have a few questions for you. But we will conduct our conversation in private."

23

THEY WENT BACK INTO THE LIBRARY AND CLOSED THE DOOR.
A cold draft wafted through the window that had been opened earlier
to clear out the last of the vapor.

Adelaide stopped in the center of the carpet. Heated memories
washed through her. She would never again be able to enter the room
without thinking about what had happened in it. For that matter, she
would very likely think about the passionate encounter every day for
the rest of her life.

Griffin closed the window. Then he crossed to the fireplace and re-
garded the embers of the fire with a brooding expression.

Adelaide did not sit down. She knew that it would be easier to argue
with Griffin if she remained on her feet.

"Do you have any notion of what you did tonight when you worked
the lamp?" he asked. His tone was chillingly cold and controlled.

"My intuition told me that some of the currents of your dreamlight
were not in harmony with those of the lamp," she said. She struggled

to keep her own voice calm and professional. "I simply did a little fine-tuning."

His jaw tightened. "Fine-tuning," he repeated. "Is that what you call it?"

"I do not think that the terrible nightmares and hallucinations will trouble you now," she ventured. "I believe they were caused by the slight disharmony in your patterns."

"Do you have any notion of what other surprises I might expect from the paranormal side of my nature, Adelaide?" he asked a little too politely.

She sighed. "I cannot say. But I must insist that all I did tonight was make some minor adjustments in your own natural wavelengths. The lack of harmony in the dreamlight portions of your aura was not surprising when you think about it."

He slanted a quick, hard look at her. "What the devil do you mean?"

She took a breath. "Griffin, please listen to me. I believe that when you came into what you call your second talent a few weeks ago some of your currents were temporarily disturbed. It seems only reasonable. Your paranormal senses suddenly had to deal with a lot more energy coming from the dreamlight end of the spectrum."

"Disturbed. Well, that is certainly one way to describe the effects of the Curse."

She warmed to her thesis. "I think that, given time, your currents would have gradually adjusted to the new level of power. All I did to-night was hurry things along, as it were."

His mouth twisted. "So that I can go merrily on my way to becoming a mad Cerberus?"

"I refuse to dignify that with an answer." She gave him her most reproving glare. "I have already made it clear that, in my opinion, you are not going mad."

He turned away from the dying fire and stalked to the window. He stood quietly for a moment looking out at the night.

"Then what in blazes is happening to me?" he asked after a time.

She looked at the glowing footprints on the floor and gently cleared her throat.

"Well, as to that I have a theory," she said.

"And just what is this theory of yours?"

"You are not becoming a Cerberus. Instead, you have simply developed the full potential of your own natural talent."

"Talent develops in the teens and early twenties." He shoved a hand through his hair. "I'm thirty-six."

"I suppose we must consider you a late bloomer, sir."

He turned at that and walked toward her, eyes very dangerous. "This is not a good time to make a joke out of what is happening to me, Adelaide Pyne."

She straightened her shoulders. "My apologies, sir. But I am convinced that what I am telling you is the truth. For whatever reason, possibly because your ancestor was not exposed to the lamp's radiation until he was the age that you are now, your own talent did not fully develop until you reached your thirty-sixth year. Regardless, I don't believe that you are a genuine multitalent. You are simply a much stronger version of what you have always been."

He stopped directly in front of her and searched her face. "I was a shadow-talent. Now I generate nightmares."

"Both abilities obviously come from the dreamlight end of the spectrum," she insisted.

"Is that right? You're an expert?"

She refused to let him intimidate her. "I'm a dreamlight reader. I have a great affinity for that kind of energy. Your talent is also based in dreamlight. Think about it. For years you have been able to cloak yourself in shadows. Now you can project those shadows at others.

When you do so your victims' senses are literally overwhelmed by the experience. They panic and their minds fill in the void with terrible visions and nightmares."

"Call it what you will, I doubt that Arcane will look upon my new ability as merely an extension of my first. And what of the third talent? When will I discover that one?"

"I don't think it's a third talent but rather a third *level* of talent," she said. "And you may not discover it unless or until you get into a situation in which you need it. Then your intuition will come to the fore and you will know what to do."

"No offense, Adelaide, but that is not particularly comforting."

"Well, if it helps, I would say, based on my reading of Nicholas's journal, that you would require the lamp in order to achieve something more dramatic in the way of power. You would also need my assistance. So the discovery of the third level of talent is unlikely to happen by accident. It would have to be planned, by both of us."

"But what the hell is the third level of talent?"

"I don't know," she admitted. "You are the one who translated the code your ancestor used to write the journal. Are you certain that there were no clues to the nature of the third level?"

"All I know is that the old bastard refers to it as the third and greatest talent. And then there is that unpleasant business regarding the Midnight Crystal and the psychical command to destroy anyone who happens to be descended from Sylvester Jones." He gripped the mantel very tightly. "Damn it, will I ever be free of this curse?"

"One of the stones remained dark tonight," she said. "And as you do not appear to be consumed by a great urge to attack the members of the Jones family, I think it is safe to say we did not activate the Midnight Crystal."

"I suppose I should be grateful for small favors. I have spent the greater part of my life avoiding the Joneses. You may believe me when I tell you that nothing has changed in that regard, especially now that they have decided that it is Arcane's responsibility to create an investigation agency that is the psychical version of Scotland Yard."

She pursed her lips, thinking about the red crystals Fergus and Nate had employed.

"There is another possibility," she said.

"What is that?"

"Perhaps the Midnight Crystal did not illuminate because Nicholas failed in his attempt to infuse it with power."

Griffin frowned, thinking about that. He nodded once, slowly.

"You may be right. It was the last crystal he added to the lamp. He was going mad and his talents were failing rapidly. In his rage and growing insanity he might well have convinced himself that he had created a powerful tool with which to secure his vengeance."

"But in reality it was just a piece of glass."

Griffin drummed his fingers on the mantel. "Regardless, if Caleb Jones suspects that I have used the lamp to stabilize the three talents—"

"The *three* levels of your *one* talent."

"Rather than to reverse the Cerberus process, he will likely err on the side of caution."

"Do you really think he will attempt to have you killed?"

Griffin shrugged. "It's the logical thing to do and Jones is nothing if not logical. If I were—"

"Yes, yes, I know." She silenced him with an impatient wave of her hand. "If you were in his place you would take that sort of drastic step. I told you to stop saying things like that."

"Sorry."

She sighed. "Has there always been this enmity and lack of trust between your family and the Joneses?"

"You could say it's in the blood." He looked at her. "Earlier, when we were in the wall passage, you said Smith had one of those red crystals when he tried to kidnap you."

"Yes. He used it to kill the brothel manager."

"That was several years ago. If those devices had been on the streets all this time I would have heard about them. I would have tried to buy some."

She frowned. "It would appear that the crystals are useful only to those who possess a fair amount of talent."

"I know this will come as a great shock, Adelaide, but there are actually some members of the criminal class who are talents."

She angled her chin. "There is no need for sarcasm, sir. I am well aware of that fact now." She hesitated. "You told me at our first meeting that very little happens on the streets of London without your knowledge."

"I may have exaggerated slightly for the sake of my reputation. Nevertheless, I cannot believe that devices as powerful as those crystals could have been floating around in the underworld all this time without coming to my attention."

"So the question becomes, after thirteen years, why have two more crystals suddenly appeared in the hands of a pair of street thieves?"

"Unfortunately, that is only one of many questions that must be answered, and quickly."

24

THE KNOCK ON THE CONNECTING DOOR CAME JUST AS SHE finished putting on her nightgown and robe.

She crossed the small space and opened the door. Griffin stood there. He was in his black dressing gown.

"I thought you were going to get some sleep," she said.

"I attempted to do just that." His mouth twisted. "Suffice it to say the effort was not a success."

"I could not sleep, either," she admitted. "I was thinking about going downstairs and helping myself to a glass of your excellent brandy. What have you been doing?"

"Thinking." He scrubbed his face in a weary gesture. "Although the brandy may be a more useful idea."

"You've been thinking about the intruders and those gas canisters and crystals?"

"No," he said. "As it happens, I was reflecting on the night I was shot."

Surprised, she opened the door wider. "I'm listening."

He moved into the room as though he had every right to be there. Like a husband, she thought, or a longtime lover. Then, again, it was his house.

"Initially it seemed logical to assume that Luttrell or one of the other brothel owners sent an assassin to the theater to kill you," he said. "But in view of what occurred here a few hours ago, I am inclined to believe that that assumption was wrong."

"What do you mean?"

"What if the gunman at the theater went there to kidnap you, not kill you?"

"If that was the case, why did he try to shoot me?"

"Maybe you weren't the target," Griffin said. "Maybe he was just trying to stop me from getting to you first."

A strange shock of understanding went through her. She moved away from the door and sank slowly down onto the dressing table chair.

"I think I see what you mean," she whispered.

Griffin began to pace the small space. "The episode at the theater was never about the brothel raids. It was about the damned lamp."

"But who could have known I had the lamp in my possession or that I could work it?" She spread her hands. "Who else besides you would even care about that blasted artifact?"

"The one other person we know for certain has previously displayed a keen interest in both you and the lamp."

"The man who purchased me when I was fifteen years old," she whispered. "Mr. Smith."

"Yes."

"But I do not know his real identity. He wore a mask that night, so I never even saw his face."

"You would recognize his dreamprints if you saw them again, though, correct?"

She shuddered. "Yes. But how can we go about finding him?"

"I think I know where to start the hunt." He started to turn away. He paused. "By the way, you'll want to pack a bag."

"Why on earth would I do that?"

"Because you and I are going to disappear for a while."

25

"THEY'RE NOT GOING ON A HONEYMOON, MRS. TREVELYAN," Delbert growled. "They're going into hiding."

"I'm aware of that," Susan Trevelyan said. She finished wrapping the large wedge of cheese in brown paper. "But there's no need for them to go hungry."

"They won't starve." Delbert eyed the fresh loaf of bread, the jar of pickles and the apples she had already packed in the bag. "Not with that amount of food."

"No telling how long they'll be gone."

"It's just for the evenings," Delbert said. "The Boss can't really disappear. He has to take care of Consortium business. Got a reputation to protect. He just wants to make certain that no one knows where Mrs. Pyne is at night."

"I understand." She positioned the package of cheese in the bag. "But you must admit, it is all rather romantic."

Delbert frowned. "How in blazes do you figure that?"

"Slipping off together. Spending the night in a secret location, just the two of them. It's like one of those lovers' trysts you read about in a sensation novel, don't you think?"

"Never read a sensation novel."

"You don't know what you've been missing."

"No, I reckon I don't." Delbert watched her closely. "What about yourself, Mrs. Trevelyan? Do you fancy slipping off for trysts and the like?"

"Heavens, no." She closed up the canvass bag. "I'm thirty-nine years old and I've been in service since the age of ten. I assure you, I gave up romantic notions years ago."

"What happened to Mr. Trevelyan?"

"There never was a Mr. Trevelyan. I took the title when I applied for my first post as a housekeeper. I thought it made me appear older and more experienced. Of course, now I am considerably older and considerably more experienced. I could probably drop the 'Missus,' but I've gotten used to it."

Delbert nodded. "I understand. Time has a strange way of passing, doesn't it? One day you're young with all your fine plans for the future. The next you're in the future and it doesn't look at all the way you thought it would."

"What about you, Mr. Voyle? Was there ever a Mrs. Voyle?"

"Yes. A long time ago. Lost her to an infection of the lungs."

"I'm sorry."

"Like I said, it was a long time ago."

"Would you like some more tea?"

"Yes, please."

She poured two cups and sat down at the table across from him. Delbert might be a member of the criminal class but there was a solid strength about him that she found inordinately appealing. He also possessed a very manly physique, she thought. A woman would no doubt get lost in those powerful arms.

"Do you ever think about making new plans for a different future?" she asked.

"Too late for that," Delbert said.

"Yes, I suppose so."

"I think about it sometimes, though," Delbert said. "You?"

"Sometimes." She picked up her tea. "But as you said, it's a bit too late. Dreams are for young people."

"Not too late for us to make plans for tonight, though."

"I beg your pardon?"

"Strikes me that with the Boss and Mrs. Pyne away for the evening, we'll have the Abbey to ourselves."

"Except for Leggett and Jed," she reminded him.

"Except for them," he agreed. "But I think they can be persuaded to stay out of our way."

"What did you have in mind, Mr. Voyle?"

"Some cards in the library, perhaps. And a bit of the Boss's excellent brandy."

"Mr. Winters won't care if you help yourself to his expensive spirits?"

"Got a feeling he'll have other things on his mind tonight."

She smiled slowly. "I think you're right. A game of cards and a spot of brandy sound like a very pleasant way to spend the evening."

"Not as exciting as a romantic tryst in a secret location."

"It will do nicely," she said.

26

"I GOT YOUR MESSAGE." MR. SMITH CLENCHED THE ARMS OF
the chair. "You said there would be no problem obtaining the woman
and the artifact. You told me that the two men you planned to hire
were specialists in this sort of thing."

Luttrell leaned back in his chair and contemplated Smith across
the broad expanse of the elegantly inlaid desk. Like everything else
in the office, the desk was of the finest quality and workmanship.
He took a great deal of satisfaction in surrounding himself with
only the sort of expensive furnishings and artwork that would have
graced the household of a true gentleman. The antiquities on display were all originals, with the exception of the small statue of the
Egyptian queen sitting on his desk. But he would soon deal with
that issue.

He had come a long way from the gutter in which he had been born.
He savored the knowledge.

"There was a small setback last night," he said.

"You call it a setback?" Smith was outraged. "We had a bargain, Luttrell."

His name was not really Smith, but until now Luttrell had allowed the polite fiction to stand.

Smith was tall, with angular features, and he carried himself with the sort of irritating upper-class arrogance that could only be bred in the cradle. At one time his hair had probably been quite dark, but it was now almost entirely silver and starting to thin.

He was a powerful talent of some kind but the energy that spiked and pulsed in the atmosphere around him was disturbed and erratic. Luttrell had survived the treacherous waters of London's underworld long enough to recognize the telltale indications of mental instability when he sensed them.

"Our arrangement still stands," Luttrell said coldly. "I told you that moving against the Director of the Consortium would be a tricky business. Nevertheless, you have my word that the project will go forward."

"Winters will be on his guard now."

"I think it is safe to say that he has been on his guard since the night your very inexperienced young villain botched the attempt to grab Pyne at the theater. That debacle is why you came back to me, remember? You did not know that it was Winters who took her that night. I'm the one who discovered that he was holding her prisoner in his household. Hell, you weren't even aware that Griffin Winters *was* the Director."

"I still find it astonishing to believe that Winters is this notorious crime lord you describe."

"But now that you know he has taken a great interest in the Pyne woman, everything has changed, hasn't it?"

"Yes, *yes*." Smith clenched his hands into fists. "If the Director truly is Griffin Winters, as you say—"

"He is. We inhabit the same world, Winters and I. We know each other as only two enemies can. Believe me when I tell you that the Director of the Consortium is Griffin Winters."

"Then, indeed, everything has altered," Smith whispered hoarsely. "If he was willing to risk his life to protect Adelaide Pyne it can only mean that he has the lamp and needs her to work it."

"And you want both, Pyne and the lamp."

"Don't you see? It is clear now that it is my destiny to succeed where Nicholas Winters and his descendants failed."

"I've got one question," Luttrell said. "Why did you want Pyne even before you suspected that the lamp had been found?"

Smith bristled. "I had recently concluded that I had another use for a strong dreamlight talent."

Luttrell's intuition hummed softly. "Something to do with the red crystals?"

"If you must know, I have gone as far as I can in perfecting them." Smith moved one hand in an irritated fashion. "But there is a possibility I can make greater advances with the focusing power of the devices if I have the assistance of a strong dreamlight reader. When you told me that Adelaide Pyne had reappeared in London, I thought I could make use of her. But now that I know that both she and the lamp are within reach—"

"I will get the artifact and the lady for you, never fear."

"What did those two thieves tell you?" Smith demanded. "What went wrong?"

"I have not had an opportunity to speak with the two men who were sent to the Abbey," he admitted. "They have disappeared."

"Disappeared?"

"That tends to happen to those who annoy the Director. It is the reason why I have gone to such great lengths to ensure that there is nothing about this venture that can be traced back to me." He paused for emphasis. "Or to you, either, of course."

Smith surged out of the chair and started to prowl the room. "I can assure you that the crystals were not at fault. Each was properly tuned."

"I have no idea what went wrong," Luttrell admitted. "Perhaps the vapor canisters did not function properly. All I know is that the two men are missing and will likely never be found."

He did not add that he had a man searching for the pair just in case they had escaped the Abbey. If they were found they would disappear again immediately. This time into the river. But it was unlikely they would ever turn up. Winters had a reputation, after all.

"There is no cause for alarm," he continued. "I assure you that I will have both the woman and the artifact by the end of the week."

Smith halted in front of the desk. "Are you certain?"

Luttrell smiled. "You have my word on it."

"I had given up hope of ever recovering the lamp, let alone of finding the dreamlight reader again. You have no notion of how long I have waited."

"You're wrong," Luttrell said softly. "I know exactly how long you have waited."

Smith scowled. "What the devil are you talking about?"

"You acquired the lamp twenty years ago. It took you another six years to locate Adelaide Pyne. You lost them both in a brothel fire."

Smith's mouth worked a few times before he recovered from the shock of the statement.

"You know about the brothel fire?" he hissed. "I very nearly died that night."

"I also know that the only reason you escaped the blaze was because one of the guards fleeing the scene found you unconscious and carried you to safety. He thought you might reward him, you see. Imagine his disappointment when you recovered consciousness and ran off without giving him so much as a penny. Left him with a very bad impression of the upper classes, I'm afraid."

"I can't believe you know all this."

"I make it a practice to know all the secrets of those with whom I do business. By the way, before you leave, I'll have the new crystal you promised to deliver today."

Smith's sallow features reddened with anger. "I'll thank you not to talk to me as if I were a carpenter or a tailor, Luttrell. I'm a man of science."

"I seem to be surrounded by scientists these days. The crystal, if you please. The first one you gave me is exhausted. Nothing but dead glass now."

"I warned you that they do not last long, especially if one attempts to focus a great deal of energy through them," Smith grumbled.

But he reached into the pocket of his overcoat, took out a red stone and handed it across the desk.

Luttrell took the stone. "I'll be in touch."

Smith hesitated, annoyed. It was obvious that he did not like being sent on his way as though he were a tradesman. On the other hand, he was no doubt relieved to escape the company of a man whom he considered his social inferior.

He picked up his hat and let himself out.

Luttrell examined the crystal, excitement pulsing through him. The stone had the bright clarity that indicated that it had never been used. It was the ultimate personal weapon for a man of great talent, he thought, a man like himself.

All things being equal he preferred to do business with those who were sane. Men who hovered on the border of madness were inherently unpredictable. But he was willing to make an exception in Smith's case.

In addition to his ability to forge the red crystals, Smith possessed one crowning attribute that more than compensated for the state of his mental health. In fact, it made him invaluable: Smith was a member of the General Council of the Arcane Society.

27

"ANOTHER TUNNEL," ADELAIDE SAID, RESIGNED. "I SHOULD have guessed."

"Sorry," Griffin said. He ducked his head to avoid the low stone ceiling of the underground passage. "If there were any other safe way to take you from the Abbey to our destination I would have used it."

"I understand. Just keep moving."

Maintaining a swift pace through the underground passage helped, she had discovered. So did elevating her talent. What did not help was the pack she had slung over her shoulder. As she had explained to Griffin, she refused to go into hiding without a change of clothes and a set of silk sheets. Griffin was also carrying a pack. It was considerably heavier than her own but it did not seem to slow him down.

They had entered the ancient tunnel from a concealed trapdoor in the basement of the Abbey. It was another convenient architectural legacy of the medieval monks. It was also, Griffin told her, yet another reason why he had purchased the tumbledown pile of stone.

With her senses flung wide she could see layer upon layer of murky dreamlight on the floor. Some of the prints were centuries old. Most were quite faint. But many still burned with fear and outright panic. A number of people who had been forced to make their way through the passage long ago had fought the same unnerving dread that plagued her. They would have been desperate if they felt obliged to use this passage.

Griffin's tracks, however, were hot and luminous with the unique energy of his talent. She could see that he had come this way many times over the years. It was also clear that the prints he was leaving today were more powerful than those that he had left in the past.

"You are most certainly stronger now," she said. "I can see it in your prints."

"But still no sign of madness?"

"None whatsoever," she assured him. "The slight disturbance that I detected when we first met, which led me to conclude that you suffered from chronic nightmares, is gone."

He did not respond but she sensed that he was willing to believe her, at least for the moment.

Water dripped. The air was dank. From time to time she could hear the skittering of rat feet in the darkness behind her.

At least she was appropriately dressed for the venture. The jacket and trousers she wore had been tailored to suit her slender frame. Her hair was tightly pinned beneath a masculine style wig. She was quite certain that when she and Griffin eventually emerged from the tunnel anyone who saw her would take her for a man.

"How did you discover this tunnel and the passages in the Abbey?" she asked.

"I found them years ago when I was living on the streets," Griffin said.

She thought about how hard life must have been for him back in the days when he was struggling to survive in the brutal realm of the city's underworld.

"It is no doubt the perfect hideout for a street gang," she observed, trying not to sound judgmental. "I can understand that it must hold a great deal of sentimental value."

"Crime lords don't put much stock in sentiment." He sounded amused. "But I find the tunnel convenient from time to time."

"Who else knows about it?"

"Only Delbert, Jed and Leggett."

"You have spent your entire life living in the shadows, haven't you, Griffin?"

"I've never thought of it that way but, yes, one could say that. It suits my talent, don't you think?"

"Perhaps."

He was silent for a moment or two.

"I got into the habit at the age of sixteen," he said.

"The year your parents died."

"The year they were murdered."

Shocked, she came to a sudden stop.

"Murdered?" she gasped. "You never said anything about murder."

"The press and the police concluded that my father shot my mother and then took his own life because he was despondent over his financial affairs. But I have never believed it."

He rounded a bend in the tunnel and disappeared from view.

Losing sight of him even for a few seconds iced her nerves. She hurried forward. When she turned the corner she saw that he had halted in front of an iron gate.

"Mind you don't step on that stone," he said, pointing to the floor of the tunnel. "It's a nasty trap. Involves a knife. Leggett designed it. He is very good with knives."

"I see. Thank you for mentioning it."

She edged cautiously around the stone and stopped beside Griffin. On the other side of the gate she could just make out a flight of stone steps.

Griffin reached up, pushed a loose stone aside and removed a key from a concealed space. He fitted the key into the lock of the gate. The heavy iron grill swung open with surprising ease.

"New hinges," Griffin explained. "I keep them well oiled."

He led the way through the opening and up the steps. At the top he put out the light and pushed open a thick wooden door. The air that wafted into the tunnel was only somewhat fresher. She saw a thin edge of foggy daylight beneath another door and realized that they had emerged into a stone-walled chamber. The walls and floor glowed with decades of very dark prints.

"It's a crypt," she whispered.

"It hasn't been used in years," Griffin assured her.

She decided that there was no point telling him that while the sad energy associated with generations of burials and mourning faded over time, it never entirely evaporated. To those like her who were sensitive to dreamlight, this place of entombment would always whisper of death and loss.

Griffin went past her and opened the door of the stone vault. Damp air flowed into the chamber. Adelaide closed down her senses and studied the gray scene outside.

Like the crypt, the entire graveyard had evidently been abandoned for years. It was choked with weeds, vines and overgrown grasses. The branches of the trees drooped like phantoms over the old monuments to the dead. A short distance away the remnants of the small church and a stone wall loomed in the mist. In the fog-shrouded light the crumbling stones and statuary resembled the ruins of an ancient dead city.

"Is this the cemetery where you and Luttrell agreed to the Truce?" she asked.

"No. I would never bring an enemy to this place. It is my secret. Craygate Cemetery is in a different part of town."

But he had brought her here, she thought. Griffin trusted her. For some reason she found that knowledge deeply gratifying.

"Our destination is not far from here," Griffin said.

They moved through the maze of tumbledown gravestones and climbed over a broken portion of the wall. A short time later they emerged into an old, dilapidated neighborhood of narrow streets and lanes. Here and there a light burned in a window but for the most part the buildings were dark. They kept walking, weaving a path through a maze of alleys and lanes.

It was not long before the surroundings altered, becoming noticeably more affluent. Streetlamps appeared at the entrances of houses. Carriages and hansoms rattled and clattered in the mist.

Griffin guided her through a small, neat park, around a corner and down a service lane. He stopped at the back of one of the walled gardens, took out another key and opened the gate.

She walked ahead of him into a garden that, like the graveyard, had gone unattended for years. There were no lights in the windows of the house.

"What is this place?" she asked softly.

"The house where I was born and raised." Griffin closed the gate very quietly. "The place where my parents were murdered. Immediately after their deaths it was sold to pay off my father's creditors. I was able to buy it back several years ago. No one lives here now."

"Why did you bring me here?" she asked quietly.

"I want you to see the room where my parents died."

At last she understood the reason for the strange journey. Astonished by his logic, she glanced at him.

"You hope that I will be able to tell you if the man who killed your mother and father is the same man who had me abducted and sent to the brothel, don't you," she said. "You believe there is a connection."

"You told me that you would recognize Smith's energy patterns if you ever saw them again."

"Yes, but why on earth would you expect me to see his prints here in your parent's house?"

"Because before he found you, he got his hands on the lamp. It was stolen from my father's safe on the night of the murders."

She calculated quickly. "But the two events, the theft and my abduction, took place several years apart."

"I'm aware of that." He unlocked the kitchen door. "At the very least, you may be able to tell me whether or not my conviction that my parents were murdered is the truth or some dark conspiracy theory that I have harbored all these years."

She stepped into the heavily shadowed room.

"I keep the curtains drawn at all times," Griffin said. "As far as the neighbors are concerned this house belongs to a family in the far North that rarely comes to the city. I am merely the caretaker who occasionally comes around to make sure that all is well."

"I understand."

"This way."

They dropped the packs on the kitchen floor and went up the back stairs to the floor above. When they reached the landing she opened her senses again.

And caught her breath at the sight of the dreamlight prints that burned in the bedroom hallway.

"Oh, Griffin," she whispered.

Even after two decades the energy of murderous violence shimmered and fluoresced ominously in the shadows.

He searched her face, his eyes as darkly brilliant as those of an alchemist gazing into his fires.

"You perceive the killer's prints?" he asked softly.

"Yes." She took a deep breath. "There is no doubt but that murder was done here. But the tracks I see were not left by the man I know as Smith."

"Damn," he said, his voice very low. "I was so sure."

"I'm sorry," she said gently.

"It does not mean that there is no link," he insisted. "There may well have been more than one man involved in this affair."

She did not argue with him. There was no point; he was obsessed with his theory.

"Well, at least I can assure you that you are right about the crime," she said. "I am certain that your parents were murdered." She shivered as she studied the luminous tracks. "As the old adage says, 'Murder leaves a stain.'"

"Did he come up the front staircase?" Griffin asked. There was an oddly flat quality in his voice. It was as if he had assumed a new role, that of disinterested observer.

"Yes. And left the same way as well. He did not go down the back stairs."

"Can you tell if my parents opened the front door for him?"

She glanced at him. "What would that say to you?"

"If they let him into the house it would indicate that they knew the killer."

She nodded. "Let me see if I can detect that much information."

She went to the top of the stairs and looked down into the front hall. Dark energy shimmered in the shadows but not on the threshold of the front door.

"He came from a room at the back of the house. But I did not see his prints in the kitchen."

Griffin moved to stand beside her. He gripped the railing and looked down. "The bastard let himself into the house through a window. He must have known that it was the servant's day off."

She examined the path of seething energy on the staircase. What she saw made her catch her breath.

"Griffin, something happened at the foot of the staircase. Your father collapsed, I think."

"But he was shot."

She shook her head. "Before that he fainted. Whatever occurred put him into a sleep state of some kind. He was unconscious."

"But that makes no sense. A blow to the head?"

"That might explain it." She turned to look back down the hall. "Something similar happened to your mother there at the door of the bedroom. She fell unconscious."

Griffin walked along the hall and opened the bedroom door.

She went slowly to stand beside him and looked into the room. When she studied the space with her normal senses she saw nothing out of the ordinary. The bed frame stood empty of mattress and linens. There was a large wardrobe in one corner. A dressing table mirror, clouded with years of dust, stood near the draped window.

On the surface there was no sign of the violence that had taken place in the chamber. But when she switched to her other senses the distinctive dreamlight prints left by the killer stained everything in sight.

"This is where they died," she whispered.

There was another set of tracks, as well. The disturbing energy radiating from them was so intense, even after so many years, that she had to drop back into her regular senses before she could talk about it.

"You found them, didn't you?" she asked. "I can see your prints mixed with the others."

"I was off with friends that day. I returned in the late afternoon. The servants were still out. When I walked through the door I knew at once that something terrible had happened. There was a strange stillness about the house. I can still feel it."

"You came upstairs and opened the bedroom door."

"Yes."

She touched his arm. "I cannot begin to imagine how dreadful it must have been for you," she said.

"Tell me what you see," he said in that same too-even voice.

He did not want her sympathy, she thought. He wanted answers. She took her fingers from his sleeve, composed herself and slipped back into her senses. She contemplated the psychical fluorescence that illuminated the room in eerie shades of ultralight.

"There are no signs of a struggle," she said. "I think that somehow the killer rendered them both unconscious, dragged them into this room and shot them here."

"Then he set the stage to make it appear that my father killed my mother and took his own life."

"Yes. I think that is exactly what happened." She hesitated, studying the floorboards near the bed. "There is something about the traces of energy left by your parents before they died. I do not think they were struck on the head. I cannot be absolutely positive, but I believe that the killer may have used some kind of talent to render your parents unconscious. It is as if they were in a trance just before their deaths."

"The killer was a talent." Griffin's eyes narrowed. "Only a powerful sensitive of some kind would be interested in the lamp in the first place."

"You said that the lamp was stored inside a safe?"

"Yes, in my father's study downstairs. The artifact was the only thing missing."

"Did anyone else know that the lamp was kept in the safe?"

"No, just my parents and me," Griffin said. "My father treated the artifact like the family secret that it is."

"What of Nicholas Winters's journal?"

"It was not in the safe at the time," Griffin said. "I kept it in my room in those days."

"Why?"

"My father had told me about the family curse. I was sixteen. Naturally, I was fascinated by the possibility that I might develop additional talents. I was determined to decipher the journal. I worked on it every evening. It was one of the few things I took with me when I disappeared into the streets."

"Why would anyone commit murder for the lamp? According to the old legends only a man of the Winters bloodline can handle the energy it generates."

"Why did Smith want it badly enough to kidnap you?" Griffin asked. "He obviously believed he could access the power of the artifact."

"You are right, of course. The prospect of acquiring enhanced psychical talents is evidently enough to make some people overlook the details of the legend."

"The trouble with Arcane legends," Griffin said, "is that one never knows which bits are true and which are false."

28

"I DO BELIEVE THAT YOU HAVE CHEATED ME, MR. HARPER."
Luttrell contemplated the small statue of the Egyptian queen that
stood on his desk. "I'm somewhat astonished, to be perfectly frank.
Not many men would have the nerve to take such a risk."

When he had been ushered into the office a short while ago,
Norwood Harper had been impressed with the elegance of the surroundings. The Aubusson carpet, the fine desk, the gilt mirror on the
wall and the collection of antiquities were not at all what one expected
from a master criminal. Initially Norwood had been thrilled with the
notion that his Egyptian queen would be displayed in such exquisite
surroundings.

But pleasure had transmuted into terror when he discovered why
Luttrell had sent for him. He had never been so frightened in his life.
His heart was pounding. His palms were ice cold. His intuition—the
invariably infallible Harper intuition—had warned him against doing
more business with Luttrell. So had his wife, for that matter. But, alas,
the artist in him had been unable to resist the challenge. Luttrell de-

manded the best and Norwood prided himself on creating only the finest antiquities.

"I assure you, s-sir, the statue is an original," he stammered. "Egyptian. Eighteenth dynasty. I obtained it from a most reliable source."

"I'm sure you did." Luttrell cocked a brow. "Your own workshop, I believe."

"Just look at the hieroglyphs on the base, sir. Marvelous."

"A nice touch," Luttrell said.

"And you will note the elegant form of the piece," Norwood added.

"The queen is a very attractive figure but that does not change the fact that it is a modern piece. I ordered a genuine Egyptian antiquity. That is what Harper Antiquities agreed to provide."

Professional pride inspired a momentary flash of righteous indignation in Norwood. "See here, sir, given your occupation I doubt very much that you can claim to be an expert on antiquities. What makes you so certain that the statue is a fake?"

Luttrell smiled. "I may be a lowly, uneducated crime lord in your estimation, Mr. Harper. But you engage in the business of fraudulent antiquities. I'm not at all certain that you are in any position to cast aspersions on my profession."

Horrified, Norwood flapped his hands. "I meant no offense, sir. I merely wondered how you acquired your, uh, expertise in antiquities."

"Do you know anything about the physics of the paranormal?"

Norwood froze. The Harper family was a large one and virtually every member had a psychical talent for forgery. Indeed, some of Norwood's own creations were currently on display in the British Museum, having been accepted as authentic antiquities by the foremost experts of the land. The fact that Luttrell had brought up the subject of the paranormal was more than a little ominous.

"I don't understand," Norwood said weakly.

"As it happens, Mr. Harper, I have a strong psychical talent that draws energy from the dreamlight end of the spectrum."

Norwood felt faint. He had sold one of his finest fakes to a master criminal possessed of some form of dreamlight talent. He could almost see an unmarked grave opening beneath his feet.

"Mr. Luttrell, I can explain—"

"Most people would have no notion of what I am talking about, but I can tell that you comprehend me quite clearly," Luttrell said. "Excellent. That will make things so much simpler."

"Sir, if you will allow me—"

"As I'm sure you are aware, dreamlight talent takes a wide variety of forms. But even someone with a weak version of the ability is usually capable of discerning the approximate age of an artifact such as your pretty little queen. Creativity generates a tremendous amount of psychical energy. Such energy always leaves an impression on the object that is produced. Embedded in that impression is some sense of the time that has passed since the act of creation. It is obvious to me that your queen was crafted quite recently."

Norwood knew then that his life depended on talking his way out of the horrific situation. He was a Harper. He had a great talent for deception. He drew himself up and assumed an air of offended dignity.

"Sir, if the statue is a fake, I promise you that I had no knowledge of it. As I told you I acquired it from a trusted source."

"Enough." Luttrell sat forward and pulled the black velvet bell cord that hung down the paneled wall. "Under other circumstances I would find it amusing to listen to what would no doubt be a very inventive piece of fiction. But I am rather pressed for time at the moment."

"Sir, I can assure you—"

The door of the office opened. A large, heavily muscled man with the face of a bulldog entered the room. His shaved head gleamed in the light.

"Yes, Mr. Luttrell?" he said.

"Please escort Mr. Harper to the guest quarters."

"Yes, sir." The big man gripped Norwood's arm and hauled him toward the door.

"One more thing," Luttrell said.

The burly enforcer paused. "Yes, sir?"

"Inform Dr. Hulsey that there is now a human subject available for his experiments. I'm certain that Mr. Harper will be only too pleased to help advance the cause of paranormal research."

29

ADELAIDE ADJUSTED HER VEIL TO MAKE CERTAIN THAT IT concealed her features. She contemplated the front window of the small, nondescript bookshop. The film of grime was so thick on the panes of glass that it was impossible to see the interior of the establishment.

"This is your office?" she asked, intrigued.

"One of several that I maintain throughout the city," Griffin said. "I rarely use the same one twice in a row. In my line it never pays to become too predictable in one's habits."

"I must say I'm impressed that you have no difficulty conducting business as usual even though we are in hiding."

"The Director or those who work for him must always appear to be omnipresent on the streets," Griffin said. "It's a vital aspect of my reputation."

He opened the door. A bell tinkled somewhere in the shadows. Adelaide whisked up her skirts and walked into the shop. A gas lamp burned behind the counter but its glow did little to drive back the shadows.

The premises looked as if they had not been swept or dusted in a very long time. The shelves were laden with an untidy assortment of unimpressive volumes.

She opened her own senses. Layers of Griffin's darkly iridescent dreamprints covered the dusty floor.

There were other tracks, as well. They formed a miasma of murky energy. What startled her was the strong emotion that burned in many of the tracks, almost all of it dark. She saw tendrils of fear, seething currents of desperation, the sad waves of despair and the acid-colored fluorescence indicative of dread.

Few people came to the bookshop to purchase the latest sensation novel, Adelaide thought. It was clear from the tumultuous energy on the floor that, for those who braved the nameless lane and the ominous shadows, the little shop was a place of last resort. Those who came here did so only when there was nowhere else to turn. She wondered what they hoped to find.

A gruff-looking gnome of a man appeared from the back room. He squinted at Griffin through a pair of gold-rimmed spectacles. He looked vaguely irritated. Evidently the sight of his employer standing there in the shop was not the highlight of his day.

"Eh, it's you, sir." The gnome adjusted his spectacles. "The Harpers are waiting."

"Thank you, Charles." Griffin looked at Adelaide. "Allow me to introduce you to Charles Pemberton. He is a scholar who does not like to be interrupted in his studies. But we have an arrangement. He manages this bookshop for me and, in turn, I see to it that his papers get published in a respectable journal."

Adelaide looked at Charles. "What is your field of research, sir?"

Charles grunted. "The paranormal."

Adelaide smiled. "I should have guessed."

Charles sat down behind a rolltop desk. "As it happens, I have a paper coming out in the next quarterly issue of the *Journal of Paranormal and Psychical Research*."

Adelaide stared at him, astonished. "That journal is published by the Arcane Society. Some of my father's work appeared in it."

"It is one of the very few legitimate publications in the field," Charles said, his attitude warming now that he could see that she was impressed. "My paper is on the controversy surrounding D. D. Home."

Adelaide nodded. "He was certainly a legend in the field. It was said that he was a man of great talent. Supposedly he could levitate and walk through fire, among other amazing feats."

"Rubbish." Charles snorted. "He was a complete fraud. In my paper I prove that all that levitating through the air and flying in and out of windows was just so much sleight-of-hand. *Bah*. The man was a charlatan to his fingertips."

"A very successful charlatan," Griffin said, amused. "He moved in the highest social circles. One must give him credit for carving out such an impressive career."

Charles glowered ferociously over the rims of his spectacles. "It's his sort that gives serious, legitimate paranormal research a bad name. My paper in the *Journal* will dispel the myths that surround his name."

"Don't count on it," Griffin said. He took Adelaide's arm and steered her toward the closed door of the back room. "In my experience, when given a choice between a good legend and a few boring facts, people will inevitably choose the legend."

"Having spent a number of years in show business, I can testify to that piece of wisdom," Adelaide said.

Charles snorted in disgust.

Adelaide glanced at Griffin. "How is it that you are able to get Mr.

Pemberton published in the Society's journal? I thought you avoided all connections to Arcane."

"One of the current editors owes me a favor."

"Yes, of course. I would be interested to know the nature of that particular debt."

"Someday I'll tell you. Meanwhile, I would like you to attend this meeting with my new clients with your senses open."

She watched him through the veil. "Why?"

"Your talent may prove helpful."

"Very well."

She walked into the other room. Energy shivered in the air behind her. She did not have to look at Griffin to know that he had drawn his cloak of psychical shadows around himself.

Two men and a woman waited in the small space. They were seated on plain wooden chairs. Their anxiety was well concealed behind politely composed faces but Adelaide sensed the panic just beneath the surface.

When she slipped into her other vision she saw the hot tension that radiated in their prints. Another kind of energy illuminated their dreamlight tracks as well. The three individuals were clearly persons of talent.

At the sight of Adelaide and Griffin the men got to their feet.

"Sir," the older of the two men said. He was silver-haired, well dressed and distinguished looking. He spoke in cultured tones. "Thank you for seeing us on such short notice. Allow me to introduce myself. I am Calvin Harper." He nodded toward the woman. "My wife, Mrs. Harper, and my brother, Ingram Harper."

They all looked expectantly at Adelaide but Griffin did not introduce her.

"We have not met but I know something of your extensive family," Griffin said. "I believe we have brushed up against one an-

198

other on occasion over the years. I congratulate you on the excellent vases in the Taggert Gallery. Taggert tried to sell one to me but I declined."

Calvin Harper affected an air of grave distress. "My dear sir, please accept my apologies if there is any past misunderstanding between us."

"None whatsoever," Griffin said easily. "Those phony Etruscan vases are Taggert's problem, not mine. As he appears to be content with them, I doubt that you have any need to be concerned."

Mrs. Harper peered at Griffin closely. Adelaide knew that she was trying to bring his face into sharp focus. Griffin was not invisible by any means but he seemed to be drenched in shadows, as though he stood in a dark, unlit hallway rather than the center of the room.

"What makes you think that Taggert's vases are fakes?" Mrs. Harper asked icily.

"I am aware that Taggert has acquired a number of his best pieces from the Harper family workshops," Griffin said.

Ingram Harper bridled. "Now, see here, sir, if you are implying that our family is in any way connected to the disreputable trade in fraudulent antiquities—"

"Ingram, that's enough," Calvin said firmly. "We have business with the Director. We do not have time for this. Norwood's very life is at stake."

"Indeed," Mrs. Harper said softly. She clutched a limp, damp handkerchief in her gloved fingers. "We can only hope that he is still alive. We came here today to plead with you to help us, Director. We don't know where else to turn."

Calvin squared his shoulders. "Rumor has it that you will occasionally assist those who find themselves in dire straits. We are prepared to pay whatever fee you ask."

"I take my fees in the form of favors that I expect to be repaid when I send word that I am in need of information or a service," Griffin said.

Calvin swallowed. "Yes, sir. We understand that."

Griffin inclined his head in an encouraging manner. "Why don't you start by telling me who Norwood is?"

"Yes, of course." Mrs. Harper composed herself. "Norwood is my nephew. Norwood's wife would have accompanied us but she is in a state of complete shock and unable to leave her bed."

"I am Norwood's father," Ingram added. "My son is an extremely talented sculptor. He is also the proprietor of a small antiquities shop."

"Harper Antiquities, I believe," Griffin said. "Yes, I have heard some rumors about the shop. Evidently some of Norwood's work is sitting in a number of respected private collections here and in America."

Ingram sighed. "In his defense, I can only say that it was Norwood's confidence in his own great talent that persuaded him to take the risk of selling the queen to such a dangerous man."

Griffin studied the Harpers' anxious faces. "Are you saying that Norwood sold a fraudulent artifact to a collector who was displeased to discover that he'd been cheated?"

Calvin's jaw tightened. "Evidently the collector concluded that the statue was not a genuine antiquity. It's all just a terrible misunderstanding, of course."

"Of course," Griffin said.

"But now Norwood has disappeared. When he left his shop he told his clerk that he had been asked to consult with the collector who purchased the queen. Norwood never returned from that meeting."

Mrs. Harper dabbed at her eyes with her handkerchief. "The past several hours have been a nightmare. We were expecting to learn at any moment that Norwood's body had been pulled out of the river."

Calvin put his hand on her shoulder in a soothing gesture before turning back to Griffin. "This morning we heard rumors to the effect that Norwood is being held prisoner."

"Have you received a ransom demand?" Griffin asked.

"No, no, nothing like that." Mrs. Harper dried her eyes. "There has been no word of any kind. That is what is making this situation so dreadful. It's why we came here to see you, sir. We could not think of anyone else who might have the connections necessary to discover what has happened to Norwood."

"Your concern seems a bit extreme," Griffin said. "Most collectors who believe they have been deceived simply demand a refund."

There was a short pause. The Harpers exchanged glances.

Ingram cleared his throat. "We have reason to think that the collector in question may be Mr. Luttrell."

"I'll be damned," Griffin said very softly. "Norwood Harper sold a fake antiquity to Luttrell? Now, there's an astonishing display of nerve for you."

"Will you help us, sir?" Ingram pleaded. "Our entire family is distraught."

"I will make some inquiries," Griffin said. "But this is Luttrell we're talking about. Norwood Harper may already be at the bottom of the river."

"We are aware of that, sir, although my intuition tells me that he is still alive, albeit in dreadful peril," Calvin said grimly. He squared his shoulders. "But regardless of the result of your inquiries, please know that we are in your debt. If there is ever anything you need that the Harper family can provide, you have only to ask."

Mrs. Harper rose and stepped forward. "And if it transpires that you do not require anything of a Harper in this generation, rest assured that the obligation will pass down through the family. Harpers do not forget a debt. If one of your descendants ever needs our assistance, we will stand ready to aid him in whatever way we can."

"I'll try to come up with something to request in my own lifetime," Griffin said. His tone lacked all emotion.

Adelaide's intuition tingled. She sensed that Griffin did not intend to produce any descendants. It certainly explained why he was not married, she thought. But he was a vigorous man as she had discovered last night. She wondered what had occurred to make him conclude that he did not want or could not have a family.

Then, again, she thought, she had made a very similar decision, herself.

30

"WE KNOW ONE THING FOR CERTAIN ABOUT NORWOOD Harper." Griffin unrolled a map on the small table near the window. "He is a fool."

"Because he sold one of his fakes to a vicious, ruthless crime lord who will not hesitate to make an example of him?" Adelaide asked.

"You will agree that such a transaction does not speak well for his common sense."

"I expect the artist in him got the upper hand," Adelaide said.

She set two mugs of tea on the table and watched Griffin draw a circle on the map.

"Do you do this sort of thing often?" she asked.

"Go to ground in rooms that no one knows I own while I try to decide how best to flush out the person or persons unknown who sent two talents equipped with a large number of infernal devices to subdue my entire household?" Griffin did not look up from the map. "As rarely as possible, I promise you. It is not at all convenient."

She sat down across from him and glanced around the small space. Griffin had brought her here following the meeting with the Harpers. After seeing the bookshop he used as an office, she had not been surprised to discover that his bolt-hole consisted of two small rooms above a shuttered shop on yet another nameless lane. Evidently crime lords did not concern themselves with luxuries and amenities when they went into hiding.

"I was not referring to our new quarters," she said. "I meant your new clients."

"Ah, yes, the Harpers." He sat down and picked up a mug. "I'll be honest. I'm not at all hopeful that Norwood is still alive."

"But if he is you will try to rescue him."

He swallowed some of the tea and lowered the cup. "I'll see what I can do. I may be able to negotiate with Luttrell."

"Why? Surely there is no favor you will ever need from a family of forgers."

"Psychically gifted forgers," he reminded her. He shrugged. "The Harpers have a true talent for the work. I might someday find myself in need of their skills."

"Or one of your descendants might need to call in the favor," she suggested gently.

She held her breath, aware that she was pushing against some invisible gate, but she could not resist. The urge to discover all of Griffin's secrets had become something of an obsession of late.

"Not likely," Griffin said. He set the cup down with an air of finality.

She frowned. "Why do you say that?"

"Mine is a dangerous world, Adelaide. I will not bring a wife into it, let alone a child. I tried that once, when I was younger and still somewhat inclined to take a romantic view of life."

"You were married?" She was taken aback. Somehow she had not expected to hear that particular fact.

"When I was twenty-two I fell in love. She was nineteen but she had been on her own for several years. She knew the ways of the streets. She knew my world."

"How did you meet?"

"Rowena had some talent for reading auras and a good head for business. She made her living as a fortune-teller. That put her into a position to learn many secrets. In those days, I was always in the market for information just as I am now. So I did her a favor."

"What kind of favor?"

"Got rid of a client who had begun to frighten her."

He watched her very steadily. She knew he was waiting to see some indication of shock or, at the very least, strong disapproval of the implied violence. She kept her expression calm, revealing only her curiosity.

"How did he scare Rowena?" she asked.

"Did I mention that Rowena was very beautiful?"

"No, you skipped that part," she said.

"Blond, blue-eyed. Ethereal."

"A real angel?" she asked politely.

"Some men certainly thought so."

Including you? she wanted to ask. But she already knew the answer. He had married the lovely Rowena, after all.

"A number of her male clients assumed that they could buy her favors as well as their fortunes," Griffin continued. "One particular gentleman took an unwholesome fancy to her. When she rebuffed his advances he began to stalk her. His approaches became more and more aggressive."

She folded her hands together on the table. "I have seen situations of that sort."

He raised his brows. "Have you, then?"

"Yes. Such men are difficult if not impossible to stop."

"The gentleman in question started to leave notes to the effect that if he could not have her, no man would ever have her. Rowena could read auras, remember. She saw enough to know that her life was in danger."

"So you took care of her problem."

"It was a delicate operation. The gentleman in question was not some nameless clerk who would never be missed if he disappeared. He was a man of rank and status, well known in social circles."

"He suffered an accident, I take it?" she said, raising her brows a little.

"It was tragic, really. Jumped off a bridge in a fit of despair. Family went to great lengths to keep it out of the press."

The gentleman in question had no doubt had some assistance getting off the bridge, she thought.

"I see," she said evenly. "And afterward?"

"Rowena repaid the favor by passing along odd bits and pieces of information. I started making excuses to visit her. After a time I asked her to marry me and she accepted."

"What happened?"

"A year and a half later she died in childbirth. The babe died with her."

"Oh, Griffin." She unfolded her hands, reached across the table and touched his arm. "I'm so very sorry."

He looked down at her hand. "It was a long time ago."

"Such losses fade with time but they never go away entirely. We both know that. In any event, it was not your world that killed Rowena. She died of natural causes, not because she married a crime lord. Why did the tragedy convince you that you could never marry and have a family?"

He raised his eyes to meet hers. "Men in my profession do not make good husbands, Adelaide. I was obsessed with building my empire and with keeping Rowena, myself and those who worked for me alive. I was not able to spend much time with Rowena but I was determined to keep her safe. In the end, she felt trapped. She grew . . . restless."

"She took a lover?"

"My lieutenant and closest friend," Griffin said. "We had been a team since our days on the streets. I trusted Ben more than I had ever trusted anyone in my life after my parents were killed."

And suddenly she understood.

"You trusted him to protect Rowena," she said.

"He was her bodyguard whenever she left the house." Griffin's mouth crooked. "I wanted my best man to look after her when I could not."

"That is so sad. It is the story of Lancelot and Guinevere."

Icy amusement glittered in Griffin's eyes. "With one significant difference. I'm not King Arthur."

"There is that," she agreed very seriously.

He startled her with one of his rare smiles. "What's this? Aren't you going to assure me that in my own way I'm a modern-day warrior king?"

She smiled, too. "I very much doubt that you even own a sword."

"You can say that after last night? I'm crushed."

She felt herself turning red. "Don't you dare try to turn this conversation in that direction."

He stopped smiling and drank some more tea. "In hindsight, assigning Rowena a bodyguard was a disaster that I should have seen in the making. During that year and a half she spent far more time with him than she did with me. I suppose she came to view Ben as her protector. Which is exactly what he was. Hell, I gave him the job."

"Stop right there, Griffin. It is one thing to regret the past, quite another to assume total responsibility for it. Rowena falling in love with her bodyguard was not your fault."

He smiled his faint smile but there was nothing of humor below the surface. "You absolve me of all guilt?"

"Not entirely. From the sound of it you were not an ideal husband. Your concern with your, ah, professional advancement and with keeping your family safe certainly did not help—" She broke off as another piece of the puzzle fell into place. "Oh, good grief. I see what's going on here. You were *obsessed* with protecting your family and associates. Later you wondered if that obsession was a sign that you had inherited the Winters family curse."

"*The first talent fills the mind with a rising tide of restlessness that cannot be assuaged by endless hours in the laboratory or soothed with strong drink or the milk of the poppy,*" he quoted. "That was how it was for me in those days. I did not spend hours in a laboratory, though. I spent them building an empire. But it came to the same thing in the end. And Rowena and the babe both died."

"That was when you first started to wonder if you really were fated to become a Cerberus," she concluded. "And that, in turn, made you believe that in some bizarre way, the curse was the real cause of the death of your wife and child."

"Perhaps."

"I probably should not ask but I must. Was the babe yours?"

"No. Rowena told me at the end. She knew that she was dying and I think she wanted to clear her conscience. She believed that if I knew the babe was another man's I would not grieve the loss."

"But of course you did. You grieved the loss of both of them and the loss of your friendship with Ben, as well. They were all the family you had. What's more, it was the second family you had lost. No wonder you started to take the curse so seriously."

And no wonder he had convinced himself that he could not protect a family, she thought.

Griffin drank some more tea. "Does it strike you that this conversation has become somewhat depressing?"

"Yes, it has," she said softly. "Shall we change subject?"

"I think that would be a wise idea."

"One thing before we leave the topic," she said. "I must know. What happened to Ben?"

He smiled a slow, icy smile. "What do you think happened to him?"

She wrinkled her nose. "If you're implying that you killed him in revenge for his betrayal, you're wasting your time. I don't believe that, not for a minute."

"Everyone else does." The feral smile disappeared. Griffin looked mildly disgusted. "I must be losing my touch. Not a good sign."

"Griffin, I know you did not kill Ben because you were too busy blaming yourself for what happened," she said patiently. "What became of your friend?"

"Well, it was immediately apparent to both of us that our business association, not to mention our friendship, had been somewhat altered by the situation," he said. "At the funeral he asked me if I was going to slit his throat. I told him no. He then informed me that he intended to move to Australia. We both agreed that was a brilliant notion. He sailed a week later."

"I'm glad."

"A rather dull ending to the tale, though, don't you think?"

"You're a crime lord," she said. "You have enough action and adventure in your life. A little dullness once in a while cleanses the palate."

"But what about the King Arthur analogy?"

"As I recall, Arthur did not kill Lancelot. I believe he banished him from the royal court, instead. Who knows? Maybe Lancelot went to Australia."

31

THEY MADE THE EVENING MEAL OUT OF THE FOOD THAT MRS.
Trevelyan had packed for them: bread, cheese, some pickles and boiled
eggs. There was also the bottle of wine that Griffin had grabbed from
his cellar before they went down into the underground tunnel.

He could see that the wine amused Adelaide.

"It is as though you waved a magic wand," she said. She looked at
him over the rim of the glass, her eyes sparkling. "With a mere bottle
of wine you have transformed our little adventure into a picnic. What
on earth made you think to bring it along?"

"I've had some experience in this business," he said. "Going into
hiding is never comfortable but there's no need to make the process
entirely uncivilized."

"I'll remember that."

She positioned a pickle on top of a small wedge of the cheese, placed
the cheese and pickle on a slice of bread and took a bite.

He watched her eat for a moment, enthralled. Something deep inside him stirred in response to her enthusiasm for the food. Then again, just being in her presence aroused him; the mere thought of her had the same effect. And in spite of everything that had happened, some part of him could not stop thinking about what it had been like to have her soft, warm and glowing in his arms.

"I can't help but notice that you seem to have adapted quite well to the poor accommodations I've provided," he said. "A lot of ladies would have been calling for their vinaigrettes by now."

She smiled. "Like you, I've had some experience in this line and often the accommodations were far more Spartan." She looked around, clearly satisfied. "We actually have a roof over our heads and a lavatory."

"What did you expect?"

She raised one shoulder in a dainty shrug. "A cave or an abandoned basement, perhaps."

"Why did you find it necessary to go into hiding?"

"It usually wasn't so much a case of having to hide out," she said with a judicious expression. "More often than not it was a matter of being obliged to leave town quickly under cover of night. I must admit that, on at least one memorable occasion, it was entirely my fault."

He picked up the knife and cut another slice off the loaf. "I cannot wait to hear the tale."

"My first post was working as an assistant to a medium named Mrs. Peck."

"There is no such thing as being able to speak to the dead." He bit off a chunk of the bread. "And, therefore, no real mediums."

"Yes, I know that. But you would be amazed by how many people are willing to believe such a power exists. Contacting spirits is a very profitable business. I met Mrs. Peck on the ship during the passage to New York. I started out as her assistant but when she realized I actually did have some genuine paranormal talent, she changed the billing and the act. I became the Mystical Zora."

"A fine stage name."

"I thought so. I got it out of a sensation novel. I gave amazing demonstrations of psychical talent and, for a handsome fee, I saw customers privately. I analyzed dreamlight and gave clients advice. I was quite good at it. But sometimes I made the cardinal show business mistake of telling people things they did not want to hear."

He ate some cheese. "A mistake in any profession."

"I learned that the hard way. And then there was the time I informed one customer that her husband was a brute who had already beaten her on a number of occasions and would likely someday murder her in a fit of rage. I advised her to leave him immediately and disappear. The woman took my advice. When his wife vanished, the husband blamed me. Mrs. Peck and I found it necessary to leave town in a rather hurried fashion."

"Did the husband try to pursue you?"

"I'm afraid he was in no condition to do so. He attacked me after the last performance. I had no choice but to put him to sleep, a very deep sleep. Something must have happened to his mind when I put him under. I was terrified at the time so I probably used more energy than was strictly necessary. In any event, when he woke up everyone assumed he'd had a stroke. He never really recovered."

"And the wife?"

Adelaide smiled slightly. "I believe she returned to see that her poor, bedridden husband was properly cared for until his timely death. Took about ten days for him to cock up his toes. I suspect the lady may have assisted him along his way, perhaps with a dose of arsenic. After he was gone she assumed control of his fortune."

"A happy ending."

Adelaide crunched another pickle. "My favorite kind."

"How did you end up in the Wild West Show?"

"Mrs. Peck and I made a great deal of money over the next few years. She eventually elected to retire to Chicago. I headed west with the act and made even more money. Monty Moore attended one of my performances in San Francisco. Afterward he came around to my dressing room and offered me the opportunity to join his Wild West Show. I declined initially because I was doing very nicely on my own. But when he promised to make me a full partner I decided to accept. His show was extremely popular but he thought it would do even better if he added some demonstrations of psychical talent. He was right."

"There were, however, more hurried midnight departures?"

She smiled. "Oh, yes. That sort of thing is part and parcel of the life of any traveling show. To the local people in a town the members of the cast and crew are always outsiders and not to be trusted. We were usually the first to be blamed for anything that went wrong. Washing stolen off the clothesline? Must have been one of the lads from the traveling show. Your wife's bracelet is missing? Everyone knows there are always pickpockets in the crowd at the show."

"I see what you mean."

"Frequently we found it necessary to load the horses, Willy and Buster, our two buffalo, and all the props and tents on board the train in the middle of the night. But it was never dull and always profitable. Eventually Monty and I sold the Wild West Show. He retired and I returned to England."

"What did you do with all the money you made?"

"I took Monty's advice and invested it in railroad shares, a couple of shipping companies and some property in San Francisco. Among other things, I own a large house with a very fine view of the bay. I had planned to make it my home."

"Instead you returned to England."

She helped herself to more cheese. "With the lamp."

"Why?"

"It was time." She glanced at the artifact with a reflective expression. "There are no coincidences, remember? I suppose it was my intuition that told me I needed to return to England."

"But you still own the house?"

"Oh, yes. A caretaker and his wife are looking after it."

He drank a little wine and then he smiled at her. "You have lived a very unusual life, Adelaide Pyne."

"So have you, Griffin Winters."

"There is, however, one thing that puzzles me."

"Only one thing?"

"Why did you never marry?"

"Ah." That was all she said. She sipped her wine.

He waited a moment. When it became obvious she was not going to continue he tried pushing a little.

"I will understand if it is something you wish to keep private," he said. "I did not mean to pry."

"Of course you did, just as I intended to pry when I asked you about your wife and best friend." She swirled the wine in her glass. "If you must know, it is the nature of my talent that makes marriage impossible for me."

He set his glass down and folded his arms on the table. "Of all the explanations you could have given, that is the very last one I expected. What is it about your talent that makes marriage impossible?"

"We both draw our talent from the dreamlight end of the spectrum, but my affinity for dream energy is not like your own."

"I am aware of that."

"I am very sensitive to the dreamlight currents of others. When people are awake that energy is usually suppressed to a level that I can handle quite easily, unless I open up my own senses. But when people sleep, their dreamlight floods their auras and the atmosphere around them." She moved one hand in a vague, uneasy gesture. "I find such

214

energy extremely disturbing. I cannot sleep in the same bed with someone who is dreaming. And everyone dreams."

He felt as if he'd been kicked in the gut. "Are you telling me that you cannot sleep with a man?"

"Yes." Her smile was wistful. "We are a pair, are we not? You dare not marry for fear of exposing a wife to your dangerous world. I cannot wed because I have never found a man I could love who, in turn, was capable of loving a woman with my unfortunate little eccentricity."

"But that's all it is, an eccentricity."

A wistful expression came and went in her eyes. "Over time my problem destroys any sense of closeness and intimacy. Certainly men think it a great convenience at first. They see me as the perfect mistress because I am delighted to live in a separate house and not demand marriage. But it doesn't take long for them to conclude that on some level I am rejecting them. And I suppose they are right."

"No," he said, very sure. "They realize that you will never truly belong to them. At first you are a challenge and that intrigues them, but when they comprehend that they will never be able to possess you, they become angry."

She raised one shoulder in a delicate shrug. "Perhaps. I do know that the damage goes both ways. I soon come to resent a lover whose dreamlight is so intolerable It ruins my sleep and disturbs all my senses."

His hand tightened around the wineglass. "Is that a subtle way of informing me that you do not want to sleep with me?"

She drew a sharp breath. "I did not mean that. Not exactly."

"Because you have my word that I will not impose my attentions on you tonight," he said. "You are under my protection. I will not take advantage of you."

She cleared her throat. "That is very noble of you. However, as it happens—"

He cut her off before she could complete the sentence, determined to say what needed to be said. "You have already made it clear that as far as you are concerned our encounter last night was brought on by paranormal forces."

"Good grief. You did not force yourself on me, Griffin. I am a woman of the world. And as you pointed out, there is an attraction between us."

"Which you attribute to the energy of the lamp."

"Not entirely." She was starting to sound cross.

"I realize that you had no intention of succumbing to passion when you worked the lamp for me. You were caught up in the energy that was sweeping through the room."

"Swept away by my bedazzled senses?" she asked in acid tones.

"In a manner of speaking."

"And what of yourself, sir? Were you also just a victim?"

"Hell, no," he muttered. "I knew exactly what I was doing."

"In other words, I'm the only weak-willed individual in this room? Is that what you are implying?"

"I meant nothing of the kind."

"If neither of us were victims of the effects of the Burning Lamp, then what are we supposed to make of what occurred? Just one of those things?"

He eyed her closely. "You're getting angry."

"Very astute of you." She gulped the last of her wine. "I am also trying to make it clear that I take full responsibility for my actions last night, just as you do. Nevertheless, I do agree that both of us were aroused in an unnatural manner."

"Unnatural," he repeated neutrally. Now his temper was starting to fray.

"What I'm trying to say is that I am well aware that it was not romantic love that brought us together."

"What was it, then?"

"Passion, of course. But I do assure you that the desire was mutual. You did *not* take advantage of me."

He let out his breath in a long, slow exhalation. "At least give me credit for trying to act the gentleman. It doesn't come easily to a professional crime lord."

Her smile was very cryptic. "It does to you, Griffin. Whether you will admit it or not."

He scowled. "I control the Consortium. I can control my own lusts."

"I never doubted that for a moment." Her voice softened. "I know that you would not dream of presuming on our relationship tonight."

He drank some more wine and tried again to quash the memories. "Wouldn't think of it."

But he would damn sure dream of it.

32

SHE AWOKE TO A STORM OF ENERGY. THE FORCE OF THE CUR-
rents jolted her from a dream. One moment she was holding the targets for Monty Moore and discovering that the man pointing the gun
at her was not Monty but Mr. Smith. In the next instant she was sitting
straight up on the cot, her hands knotted in the silk sheet.

Heart pounding, she struggled to separate the remnants of her own
dream energy from the gale that was howling soundlessly in the small
space. Not her own currents, she realized. Griffin was in the grip of a
savage nightmare. She would recognize his energy anywhere.

It was not just the moonlight filtering through the window that illuminated the outer room. She could see and sense the eerie glow of
hot dreamlight.

She scrambled free of the sheet and rose from the narrow bed. The
floor was cold beneath her bare feet. She went to the doorway and
looked out into the small sitting room area, expecting to see Griffin
asleep in his bedroll.

But he was not asleep. Instead he sat cross-legged on the open bed-roll. The Burning Lamp stood on the floor in front of him. He had one hand on the rim. The artifact was not yet fully transparent. The crystals were still dark. But energy stirred and flashed within the device, producing the ominous glow.

Griffin's eyes were open. They burned in the haunting glare of the artifact. He gave no indication that he saw her.

"Griffin?" She kept her tone low, barely a whisper. Her intuition warned her that it would be dangerous to startle him out of the dream state, especially now that he had ignited the lamp's power.

She went forward cautiously and stopped just short of the bedroll.

"Griffin," she said again, louder this time. "Can you hear me?"

He did not move but the violence of his dream energy altered slightly.

The artifact flared dangerously higher. That was not a good sign, she thought. Perhaps it was responding to her presence.

Unable to think of any other course of action, she crouched beside Griffin and very gingerly touched his arm.

She thought she was braced for the direct contact but nothing could have prepared her for the hurricane of nightmare energy that tore across her senses. She could not actually see the scenes of Griffin's hellish dream but the intuitive nature of her talent interpreted the energy in shatteringly clear images. Blood, a pale arm draped over the side of the bed, the ghostly reflection of his own image in the dressing table mirror and the knowledge that something horrible had been done. Above all was the soul-wrenching knowledge that he was too late to save his parents.

The visual impressions did not surprise her, given what she knew of Griffin's recurring nightmare. What stunned her was the realization that she was not sensing the usual seething chaos that was the signature of dream energy.

Griffin was in control of the nightmare. He could end it at any time. But she did not like what was happening to the lamp. The metal was translucent now. Soon the crystals would flare.

She took her fingers off his arm and reached toward the rim of the artifact.

Griffin slammed instantly into full awareness. She could tell that his senses were still aroused, still flooding the atmosphere with power. But the hot currents of nightmare energy altered dramatically with his awakening.

"*Adelaide.*" The harsh whisper sounded as though it came from the depths of a vast cavern.

His hand locked around her wrist, chaining her.

"Are you all right?" she asked, a little breathless because her own senses were soaring and whirling just as they had last night when he had taken her into his arms.

"I promised you that I would not touch you tonight," he said.

At last she understood. A moment ago he had been controlling the dark chaos of nightmare energy. When she had shattered his trance, the violent currents of power that he had been wielding had not suddenly evaporated. They simply had been transformed into another kind of energy. But he was still in control, she realized. It was astonishing.

Her own senses exalted in the dizzying excitement.

"I release you from your promise," she whispered.

"Are you sure you want to do that?"

"Yes. Oh, *yes.*"

She drew the fingertips of her free hand along the edge of his rigid jaw. His skin was feverish. So were his eyes. She felt the shudder that went through him. Instinctively she started to lean closer.

The lamp immediately brightened. She sensed that the forces unfurling inside the artifact would soon be beyond anyone's control.

She clamped her fingers around the rim. The shock that crackled through her made her grit her teeth. She knew that Griffin felt it too because his hand tightened convulsively around her wrist. But a heartbeat later she found the pattern of the wildly resonating currents. She wove her own energy into it, aware that she could not possibly assume control. The lamp was Griffin's to command. But if she worked subtly and carefully, she could hold the center of power for him.

Griffin looked at the lamp, the alchemist in him very close to the surface.

"I do believe we are playing with fire," he whispered.

She caught his chin with her free hand. "Griffin, listen to me. You must shut it down."

His smile was soul-shatteringly sensual. He used the grip on her wrist to draw her to him.

"It's all right," he said. "I'm in control."

A little flicker of panic seared off some of the heavy heat of passion.

"There is no knowing what the lamp might do in this state," she said. "It is extremely dangerous. You must shut it down."

"I want to know what lies at the heart of the storm. I need to understand."

"Please," she said. "Turn off the lamp. For my sake."

He smiled again and brushed his mouth across hers.

"For you, Adelaide, anything," he said.

The lamp winked out with startling suddenness, plunging the room back into moonlit darkness. The ominous energy that had been swirling in the atmosphere dropped back to what Adelaide knew to be a normal level in the proximity of the artifact.

There was a thud and a heavy clatter of metal on wood. Adelaide barely had time to register the fact that Griffin had swept the relic aside before she found herself flat on her back on the bedroll.

He came down on top of her, his body heavy and tight and hard against her own. His mouth closed over hers.

Energy flared again in the shadows but this time she recognized it and gloried in it. These were the exciting, unique currents that always shimmered in the atmosphere between them.

He opened his trousers and went to work unfastening her night-gown. She gripped his uninjured shoulder, digging her fingers into the sleek muscle there. His shirt was unbuttoned. She stroked her palm down his bare chest and then reached lower. She found the taut, full length of him and squeezed gently.

"Talk about playing with fire," he said.

He worked his way to her throat and then to her breasts, following the retreating tide of silk. Her nipples were so sensitive she cried out softly when she felt his tongue on them. Everything inside her clenched. She was damp and aching for him.

Griffin's hand flattened on her belly, warm and strong. She gasped when she felt his teeth sink very gently into the tender skin of the inside of her thigh. And then he was kissing her in the most shockingly intimate manner possible. She was a woman of the world, she reminded herself. Nevertheless, she had never allowed any of her small number of lovers such an intimate caress.

"Griffin."

"Anything for you, Adelaide," he said again, his voice as hard and tight as his body.

The climax spilled through her. She was still flying on the dazzling energy when Griffin entered her, thrusting deep and hard. Her body, already exquisitely tuned to the breaking point, responded to the impossibly full, impossibly tight sensation with another burst of stunning aftershocks.

Griffin braced himself above her and began to move slowly, heavily, deliberately. Every motion was an act of supreme control.

She wrapped herself around him. "You don't have to prove anything to me."

"Maybe this is for me," he said. His voice was hoarse and raw with the force of the effort he was exerting.

"No," she whispered.

She struggled a little, pushing at him until he obligingly rolled onto his back. She came down on top of him, fitting herself to him with great care.

"This is for you," she said.

For a moment she thought he would not be able to relinquish control to her. But with a groan he set himself free from his self-imposed restraints. She sensed that it was an act of trust. Thrilled, she took command of the passionate energy that flashed between them.

Griffin surrendered to his climax with an exultant shout. He surged into her for a timeless moment, his entire body wracked with the shudders of a raging release.

It seemed to Adelaide that the room had suddenly filled with a luminous mist. For a few timeless seconds she was acutely aware of the feeling that her aura was somehow fusing, however fleetingly, with Griffin's. It was as if they were touching each other's souls.

In the next breath it was over.

She felt Griffin sink slowly back into himself. She waited until he lay, damp and still, utterly relaxed, beneath her. Then, very gently, she eased herself away from him. She, too, was slick with perspiration and other fluids. Her inner thighs trembled a little, every muscle exhausted.

On the verge of sleep, Griffin encircled her with his arm and pulled her down beside him. She snuggled close. She would wait until he was fully asleep, she thought. Then she would retreat to her small cot and silk sheets in the other room.

Between one breath and the next she fell asleep.

33

GRIFFIN CAME OUT OF THE OTHER ROOM, FASTENING HIS shirt, just as she set the plate of leftover bread and cheese and two apples on the table. She studied him covertly, trying to determine what it was about him that seemed different this morning. Using water she had heated on the hearth, he had washed and shaved, but that was not it, she thought. He looked not only refreshed but also invigorated. All the hardness was still there but he seemed somehow younger, more carefree, as if he had discovered that life still had something to offer that was good.

Or maybe it was her own mood that rendered the atmosphere so buoyant and cheerful this morning. She still could not get over the fact that she had slept with Griffin, and peacefully at that. She had not opened her eyes until the morning sun had streamed through the window. It was the first time in her life that she had been able to spend an entire night with a lover.

Griffin inhaled with obvious pleasure. "The coffee smells good."

"Like the bottle of wine last night, it transforms everything," she said. She poured two cups and sat down across from him. "A fine example of genuine alchemy."

He laughed and sat down at the table.

She was intensely aware of the intimacy of the moment. The experience was such a delicious novelty that she could almost forget they were in hiding. She wanted to stay here with Griffin forever and forget that the real world even existed.

Good lord, she thought, maybe this is what Mrs. Trevelyan meant yesterday when she told me to enjoy myself.

Griffin's strong white teeth flashed briefly when he took a healthy bite out of an apple. He chewed, swallowed and smiled. Pure, unadulterated masculine satisfaction heated the atmosphere around him.

"You slept with me last night," he said.

She felt herself turn pink. "For pity's sake, Griffin, that is hardly fit conversation for the breakfast table."

"No, I meant you *slept* with me. You closed your eyes, went to sleep and probably even dreamed, didn't you?"

She cleared her throat. "Yes. I did sleep with you."

He waited a beat, radiating cool expectancy.

"What does that mean?" he said when she failed to carry on the conversation.

"I suspect it has something to do with the lamp," she said smoothly. "Both of us are, I think, tuned to its currents. Perhaps when it is in the same room with us it mutes other dreamlight wavelengths."

"In other words, you have no idea why you could sleep with me last night."

"None," she agreed. "Not a clue. Speaking of dreamlight, what in the world were you doing last night?"

"I'm not sure." He looked across the room to where the artifact stood on a small table. "All I can tell you is that there is something about that lamp that I need to discover. I feel as if I'm just on the brink of comprehension. I thought that if I pulsed a little energy into the damn thing I might be able to figure out what it is that is eluding me."

"Promise me that you won't ever again try to activate it without me."

"You have my word. I learned my lesson. That part of the legend is definitely true."

"The part that says that the lamp must be worked with a dreamlight reader?"

"Right." He took another bite of the apple. "I wonder what would have happened if you had not interrupted the process."

"Don't even think about it."

"Why? What do you suppose might have occurred?"

She glanced at the lamp. "I am convinced," she said very deliberately, "that if the energy in that lamp had gotten out of control, it might have fried all your senses and very possibly mine as well."

He looked interested rather than appalled. "Even if you were in the other room?"

She nodded somberly. "Even so. It might have killed both of us, Griffin. Or worse."

"Driven us mad?"

"Yes."

"Huh. All right. No more experiments." He finished the apple and drank some coffee. "I did some thinking while I was shaving."

"And?"

"It occurred to me that one of the many missing pieces in this puzzle is the mystery of the sleeping vapor that was in those canisters."

"There is also the mystery of the red crystals," she reminded him.

"Yes, but I have no notion of how to start looking for the person who forged those crystals. I do have an idea of how to go about finding the chemist who prepared the sleeping gas, however. There cannot be a large number of scientists around who would know how to concoct such an exotic gas. Whoever he is, I think there is an excellent possibility that he also created the crystals."

"But how do we go about finding one particular chemist in a city this size?"

"I hate to say it, but I'm afraid we need the advice of a certain lady known to possess a talent for poison."

"Good heavens. You want me to contact Lucinda Jones again?"

"I don't think you need to go so far as to offer tea this time."

34

"LOOK AT THEM," LUCINDA JONES SAID. "THEY MIGHT AS WELL be two gentlemen meeting at dawn to settle a point of honor with pistols."

Adelaide watched Griffin and Caleb Jones through the carriage window. A thick fog blanketed the park. The two men were no more than dark shadows in the heavy mist. They stood some distance apart, facing each other in a stance that would not have looked out of place at a traditional dawn appointment.

"You're right," she said. "They could well be a pair of duelists."

"Thank heavens gentlemen no longer conduct duels in this modern age," Lucinda said. "It is difficult to believe that such events were once commonplace. I wonder what made men give them up?"

"I suspect it was the improvement in the accuracy and reliability of the pistols," Adelaide said. "In the old days there was a very good chance that the guns would not fire at all or that the bullets would miss their targets. Either way, honor was satisfied."

Lucinda laughed. "It would be gratifying to think that common sense actually played a role in making duels unfashionable. Can I assume your expertise on the subject of guns comes from your experience in the American West?"

"Yes." Adelaide did not take her eyes off the men. "Unfortunately, there was still a form of dueling going on there until recently, although it was not nearly so commonplace as the novels and the press reported."

"I have heard the tales of the gunfights in the West." Lucinda studied Adelaide's trousers and jacket. "Do many women in America dress in men's clothes?"

"No. American women are as interested in fashion as women here in England, I assure you. The only reason I am wearing masculine attire now is because Mr. Winters made it plain that I must be able to run at a moment's notice."

"Mr. Winters obviously thinks ahead."

"I suspect it is how he has managed to survive this long in his profession."

"It must be a very difficult way to live," Lucinda said quietly.

"Intolerable, actually. But it is all he knows." She watched the men. "What do you suppose they are talking about?"

"I can't say, but I will tell you one thing."

"What is that?"

"Mr. Winters must love you very much."

Stunned, Adelaide jerked her attention from the scene outside the window. It took her a couple of seconds to find her tongue.

"What on earth makes you say that?" she managed, thoroughly flustered. "I assure you, Mr. Winters and I scarcely know each other. It is circumstances that have thrown us together."

"Really?" Lucinda surveyed her with a considering expression. "According to my husband, this is the first time he and Mr. Winters have met. Evidently after his parents were murdered, Mr. Winters vanished into the streets of London. By the time he resurfaced many things had changed."

"Yes, well, given the course Mr. Winters's life has taken, one can understand why they have not met prior to this occasion."

Lucinda's smile was all-knowing. "It is you who changed the equation, Mrs. Pyne."

"Actually, it's Miss Pyne. I altered it before I returned to England so that I would have a good excuse to wear widow's weeds. But please call me Adelaide."

"Very well, Adelaide. And you must call me Lucinda. I was about to say that I cannot think of any force other than love that would bring one of the most powerful men in London's criminal underworld to a meeting with Jones and Jones."

"Mr. Winters feels an obligation to protect me," Adelaide explained quickly.

"And that is not an indication of his love for you?"

"By no means. You must understand it is Mr. Winters's nature to protect those for whom he feels a responsibility. Love has nothing to do with it."

"*Hmm.*"

Adelaide eyed her with sharp suspicion. "What does that imply?"

"Nothing," Lucinda said airily. "I was merely trying to conjure the image of a crime lord who is secretly a knight in shining armor."

"It is a bit difficult to explain," Adelaide admitted.

35

"CONGRATULATIONS ON YOUR MARRIAGE, JONES," GRIFFIN SAID.

"Thank you."

"And on your new career as an investigator."

"The work suits me."

Griffin studied Caleb through the thin veil of fog that swirled between them. "From what I have heard of your psychical nature, that does not surprise me. They say you enjoy solving puzzles and finding patterns that lead to answers."

"By all accounts you are well suited to your own profession."

"We are what we are."

"The descendants of a pair of mad alchemists," Caleb said.

"Is that your rather obvious way of asking me if I'm turning into a Cerberus?"

"I'll assume the answer to the question is no." Caleb sounded unconcerned. "Mrs. Pyne worked the lamp successfully for you, didn't she?"

"Yes."

"Of course, even if things had not gone well with the lamp, you would certainly not stand here less than ten paces away and admit it."

"Very true."

Caleb glanced briefly toward the carriage, as if assuring himself that it had not vanished in the fog.

"You have the Burning Lamp and you have Mrs. Pyne. Matters seem to have gone well. Why did you ask to meet with me? I find it hard to believe that the Director of the Consortium would require the services of Jones and Jones."

"As a matter of fact, I do need your agency's services. I'm told your wife has a talent for detecting poison."

"What of it?"

Griffin reached into the canvas bag he carried. "I would like her opinion on the nature of the vapor that was once contained inside this canister."

He handed the metal ball to Caleb.

"Well, now." Caleb turned the canister in his gloved hands. His expression had been austere and unreadable but now intense interest lit his eyes. "What is this device?"

"The gas that was inside induced a profound sleep accompanied by unpleasant dreams in very short order, minutes only. Two nights ago a pair of intruders employed half a dozen canisters like that one to subdue my guards and the dogs. Mrs. Pyne and I were fortunate to escape the effects."

Caleb looked up, clearly astonished. "Are you telling that your enemies got inside your house?"

"It was embarrassing, to say the least."

Caleb smiled briefly. "For a man in your position? No doubt. But what the devil were they after? Why would anyone risk going up against you?"

"They wanted Mrs. Pyne and the lamp."

Caleb looked down at the canister. "That is a very disturbing development."

"And there is another thing, Jones. Both intruders were mid-level talents but they were armed with some odd red crystals that, for a short time, enhanced their natural abilities to a considerable degree."

"Hold on, are you telling me that there were *talents* involved?"

"A hunter and an illusion-talent." Griffin paused. "Not all of those with psychical ability were born into your world, Jones. Some were born into mine. When one comes from the streets one is rarely invited to join the Arcane Society."

"I am aware of that," Caleb said quietly. "I meant no insult. It is obvious that talent, like intelligence, is a trait that is not linked to one's social status."

"I'm glad someone within Arcane has noticed that biological fact."

"My cousin, Gabe, the new Master of the Society, is working hard to open up the organization and introduce an element of democracy into it. He does not give a damn about social class. No Jones does. But it will take some time to change things. Arcane is nothing if not hidebound."

"Sorry. I may be a bit sensitive on the subject." Griffin took one of the dead crystals out of the bag. He handed it to Caleb. "Each intruder carried one of these. Evidently the devices burn out quickly when used for even short periods of time. But they are effective. I can testify to that."

Caleb took the crystal and studied it closely. His curiosity charged the atmosphere around him. He looked at the device as though willing it to deliver answers.

"Someone knows that you have the lamp and a dreamlight reader," he said. "Whoever he is, he wants both badly enough to risk annoying you by sending two well-armed intruders into your household."

"I was certainly irritated. I came here today because I'm hoping that your wife can provide some insight. If she can identify the sleeping gas, I may be able to find the chemist who concocted it. It cannot be commonplace."

"Finding a chemist in this city is easier said than done. I recently had some experience along those lines."

"Those canisters came from my world, not yours," Griffin said quietly. "I know how to find answers in the underworld. But first I want to be sure that I am asking the right questions."

Caleb smiled a little at that. "We have more in common than you know, Winters. Come, let us see what Lucinda can tell us."

He turned and walked toward the carriage. Griffin fell into step beside him.

"I appreciate this, Jones."

"I assure you, this affair is of great interest to both of us. Now that we have finally become acquainted, there is something I wish to ask you."

"What is that?"

"There has always been one thing that has puzzled me about the events surrounding the deaths of your parents," Caleb said.

"What is that?"

"Why did you disappear that night?"

"Isn't it obvious?"

"No."

"I assumed that Arcane was responsible for the murders and for the theft of the lamp. It seemed logical to conclude that the Society might send someone after me, as well. I decided that my only hope was to disappear into the streets."

Caleb whistled appreciatively. "I admire the way you think, Winters. I do believe that you are the only man I have ever met who is as inclined toward conspiracy theories as myself. What makes you so sure that your parents were murdered? By all accounts it was a tragic case of murder and suicide."

"My father would never have shot my mother and taken his own life, certainly not because of financial problems. He had a talent for making money. He knew better than anyone else that he could easily recover his losses and repay his investors. In addition, the lamp was missing from the safe. There was no question in my mind about what happened that night."

"I see." Caleb sounded intrigued.

"Mrs. Pyne recently confirmed my theory with her talent. She detected the presence of the killer at the scene of the crime."

"Even after all these years?"

"As she said, murder leaves a stain, at least in dreamlight."

"Jones and Jones is now in the business of solving crimes," Caleb said. "I do not see why we could not take on some old cases as well as new ones."

"We are not dealing with two separate cases. The murder of my parents is connected to what is happening now."

"I really do admire your thinking processes, Winters. I agree, there are no coincidences. It is a relief to talk to someone who does not believe that I am half mad."

Griffin glanced at him. "How do you know that you are sane, Jones?"

"Simple. Whenever I am in doubt, I ask my wife."

The door of the carriage opened. Lucinda and Adelaide looked out.

"Mr. Winters would like you to examine this canister, my dear." Caleb handed the metal ball into the vehicle. Lucinda took it from him.

Griffin sensed the shifting energy in the atmosphere and knew that Mrs. Jones had just heightened her senses.

There was an outraged gasp from the interior of the carriage.

"My *fern*," Lucinda cried. "Whatever poison was in this canister was made with my *Ameliopteris amazonensis*."

"That explains a few things," Caleb said. "Basil Hulsey has found himself a new patron."

36

THEY SAT TOGETHER IN THE JONES CARRIAGE. IT WAS A TIGHT fit, Adelaide reflected. Furthermore with four people of talent gathered together in such close quarters it was impossible to ignore the level of power in the atmosphere. Energy shimmered invisibly even though everyone was careful to keep his or her senses lowered.

"Jones and Jones is a psychical investigation agency," Caleb explained. "Any member of the Society is welcome to bring a case to us. But the main reason J-and-J exists is to counter the forces of a dangerous new conspiracy."

"What is the nature of the conspiracy?" Adelaide asked.

"The conspirators refer to themselves as members of the Emerald Table," Caleb said. "We believe that the organization is structured in several circles or cells. We have taken apart two of the circles but we have not yet been able to identify the leaders. These are modern-day alchemists we are dealing with. They are obsessed with secrecy."

Adelaide frowned. "This is the modern era, Mr. Jones. Surely by now everyone knows alchemy is merely so much nonsense."

They all looked at her.

"Never forget that the great Newton took the study of alchemy seriously," Lucinda said politely.

"He may have been a brilliant man but he lived in the seventeenth century," Adelaide said.

"So did Sylvester Jones and Nicholas Winters," Caleb growled. "And we are all still dealing with the results of their alchemical experiments."

Adelaide cleared her throat. "Point taken, Mr. Jones. It is just that it is so difficult to believe that in the modern age there are still those who believe that they can discover how to transmute lead into gold."

"It is not the secret of turning base metals into gold that these modern alchemists seek," Lucinda explained. "They strive to perfect the founder's formula."

Adelaide's mouth went dry. "But I thought that was supposed to be just another Arcane legend."

"Like the Burning Lamp," Griffin said neutrally.

Adelaide winced. "Yes, of course."

"As far as we have been able to determine, the conspirators are working on various versions of the formula," Caleb said. "All of the recipes thus far appear to have had serious side effects. But that does not mean that those who use the drug do not cause us a good deal of trouble."

"One of their researchers is Dr. Basil Hulsey," Lucinda explained. "We believe that he is assisted by his son, Bertram. In any event, sometime back Basil Hulsey stole a fern from my greenhouse."

"The *Ameliopteris amazonensis* you mentioned?" Adelaide asked.

"Yes," Lucinda said. She studied the metal canister. "It has some unusual psychical properties. It appears that Hulsey has used it to produce a sleeping gas."

"The question," Caleb said, "is who the devil is the bastard working for now?"

"Someone from my world, it appears," Griffin said. He contemplated the canister. "I questioned the two intruders who invaded my household. They have been in business as a team for a number of years. They were convinced that they were working for someone in the underworld, not in society."

"Hulsey would require a fully equipped laboratory to produce the gas and the crystals," Caleb said.

"In my world there are very few who could or would finance such a project," Griffin said. "And very likely only one man who might also have a personal interest in such paranormal weaponry."

Caleb smiled faintly. "You mean, only one man other than yourself?"

"Yes." Griffin looked at him. "It appears that Luttrell has broken the Truce. That implies that something has happened to make him believe that he is now in a position to take the risk of attacking me."

Lucinda was clearly baffled. "What Truce?"

Caleb did not take his attention from Griffin. "Mr. Winters refers to the Truce of Craygate Cemetery, I believe."

Griffin was amused. "Jones and Jones is more in touch with the politics of my world than I would have guessed."

"In your world you are a legend," Caleb said simply. "So is the Truce. Legends have a way of making themselves known even to outsiders." He frowned. "You are convinced that Luttrell is a talent?"

"I have had some dealings with the man," Griffin said. "There is no doubt about it. Why do you think that Scotland Yard has never been able to get close to him?"

"For the same reason it has never been able to identify the Director of the Consortium," Caleb said. He looked at Lucinda. "You see what happens when men of talent become criminals, my dear?"

"Yes, indeed," Lucinda said. "They are remarkably good at the business."

Griffin waited politely, as though he had no interest in the discussion.

Caleb turned back to him. "Well, Winters? Will you assist us in locating Basil Hulsey?"

"I have no great interest in Hulsey," Griffin said. "But it is clear that I will have to do something about Luttrell. At the moment, the two problems appear to be connected."

"How do you propose to stop Luttrell?" Caleb asked, obviously fascinated. "By all accounts his organization is second only to your own in terms of power."

Griffin looked out the window at the fog-shrouded park.

"Cut off the head and the snake will die," he said.

240

37

"FOR PITY'S SAKE, GRIFFIN, I CAN'T BELIEVE YOU VOLUNTEERED to destroy Luttrell and his entire organization for Jones and Jones," Adelaide said.

"I'm not doing this as a favor to Arcane," Griffin said. "Luttrell broke the Truce when he sent that pair to grab you."

It was just after one in the morning. They were in the anonymous carriage he used to move around London. Jed was on the box. The light of a full moon infused the heavy fog with an eerie internal glow that reminded Griffin of the Burning Lamp. He felt the hair stir on the back of his neck.

It had taken only a day to obtain the first serious response to the offer that he had put out on the street, but he knew the clock was ticking. It would not take long for Luttrell to pick up the rumors.

"Luttrell will surely be prepared for you," Adelaide said. "You are one man, not an army."

"Sometimes one can do what many cannot. I seem to recall a very industrious social reformer who took down entire brothels from the inside with her Trojan-horse strategy."

"That is not the same thing at all," Adelaide insisted.

"Yes, it is. Just on a slightly different scale. But you can stop nagging me about it, at least for now. I'm not going to kill Luttrell this evening. My goal tonight is simply to meet with a man who wants to sell me some information."

"I don't like this."

"Well, I'll admit, it isn't the way I would normally choose to pass the evening hours either," he conceded. "I would much prefer to spend them with a bottle of claret and you in front of a fire."

As if we enjoyed a real home together, he added silently. He immediately pushed the entire notion into the place where old dreams go to languish. If nature were kind such phantom yearnings would simply be extinguished in that misty limbo. But he had learned long ago that nature was never concerned with kindness, only with life and death, and not always in the right order.

"Promise me you will be careful," Adelaide whispered urgently.

She did not understand about promises, he thought. One never made them unless one was absolutely certain that one could fulfill them.

"I fully intend to return in short order," he said instead. "If I don't come back in a few minutes, Jed knows what to do."

"Don't say that," she snapped. "I want your word that you will return safely."

He leaned forward, brushed his mouth across hers and cracked open the carriage door.

The familiar rush of energy that always came with the prospect of danger swept through him, heightening all of his senses. He moved off into the moonlit maze of narrow, crooked streets. At the corner, before turning into an alley, he stopped and looked back.

The carriage was only a shadow in the fog. He could just make out

Jed's wiry frame lounging on the box. Adelaide was invisible in the darkened interior of the cab. But he knew she was watching him.

Watching him as if she truly cared for his safety. The safety of a crime lord.

Social reformers, he thought. They had no common sense at all.

38

THE CHILL OF DEADLY ENERGY WAS SO FAINT AS TO BE AL-
most undetectable. Adelaide's first thought was that the temperature
had dropped a few degrees. Automatically she pulled up the high collar
of her gentleman's overcoat.

The trapdoor in the roof of the carriage was propped open so that
she could speak to Jed.

"Are you getting cold up there, Jed?" she asked softly. "There's a
blanket on the seat. Would you like it?"

There was no answer. Until a few minutes ago, she and Jed had
been conversing, sparingly to be sure, but in a comfortable fashion.
They shared something in common, after all, a deep concern for Jed's
employer.

Another thrill of ominously cold energy ruffled her senses. Like an
odor one had smelled long ago, it aroused memories.

"Jed?"

He did not respond.

She rose, knelt on the seat and reached up through the open trap-door to tap Jed's arm. When she touched his sleeve, an electrifying shock seared her partially heightened senses. Jed was rigid on the box, as stiff as though he had been frozen in place.

She gasped, and yanked her fingers back, as one would from a hot stove.

But in the next heartbeat, her intuition was shrieking at her. She knew beyond a shadow of a doubt that Jed was near death, that he *would* die if she did not counter some of the awful currents icing his senses.

She removed one glove, set her teeth together, heightened all of her talent, and reached up through the opening again. She caught hold of Jed's stiff arm. The heavy fabric of his coat muffled some of the force of the killing energy but not much.

She tugged on his arm and managed to drag his hand behind his back so that she could reach it. She stripped off his thick glove and interlaced her fingers with his own. His rough palm was as cold as a grave.

The waves of energy shooting through Jed flooded her own senses, chilling her blood.

The pattern of the currents had grown more warped and distorted over the years but she would have known them anywhere. Mr. Smith was stronger now, she thought, much stronger than he had been that night in the brothel.

But she was more powerful, too. At fifteen her talent had still been developing. She had been in the early stages of learning how to control and manipulate dreamlight. Tonight she fought for Jed's life with the full strength of her mature, refined power.

The cold was beyond anything she had ever known. It swirled straight through her, freezing her from the inside. No fire could warm her. The waves of icy energy were unrelenting. The only way to escape was to release her grip on Jed's hand but that was the one thing she would not do. If she let go of Jed he would be swept away into the killing currents.

She pulsed hot dreamlight energy directly into the icy waves in a desperate effort to disrupt the pattern. Her view was limited by the narrow opening of the trapdoor but she knew that the killer was standing somewhere nearby. Psychical energy could not be projected beyond a radius of fifteen or twenty feet at most. Nor could it be employed at such a violent level for long. A few minutes, Adelaide thought. She only had to hold on to Jed for a few minutes.

Jed was living through a soul-shattering nightmare. She had no choice but to live through it with him.

39

THE BODY LAY IN A POOL OF YELLOW LANTERN LIGHT. SO
much for the information that he had come here to purchase, Griffin
thought. But at least the murder explained the rising tide of unease
he had been experiencing since leaving Adelaide in the carriage. At
first he had told himself that his senses were naturally on edge because
as long as she was in danger he did not like to let her out of his sight.
Now, he realized, his intuition had likely been warning him that something had gone wrong with tonight's project.

He stood in the densest shadows of the alley, drawing the darkness
around himself, and studied the sprawled figure. It was clear that someone else had gotten to the would-be informant first. But sometimes the
dead could still talk.

He waited another moment, his senses heightened. The restless unease was still twisting through him. If anything it was growing stronger.

He had come here tonight to collect the information he needed to
keep Adelaide safe. He must not lose focus.

There were no traces of energy in the atmosphere to indicate that the killer was still in the vicinity. It was impossible to perpetrate such an extreme act of violence and then immediately disguise the psychical reaction. Even when a murderer enjoyed his work, his energy field remained hot for a considerable length of time afterward. In Griffin's experience the truly soulless killers were the ones most excited by the act. He supposed that in some freakish way, it made them feel more alive.

Satisfied that he was not about to walk into a trap, he pulled a little more energy around himself and went forward. He moved cautiously into the lantern light and stood looking down at the body for a moment, searching for signs of a wound. There were none.

He crouched and went swiftly through the dead man's pockets. There was a folded sheet of paper. In the weak light it appeared to be a list of ingredients. There was another paper in a different pocket, a receipt this time. He could just barely make out the firm. *S. J. Dalling, Apothecary.*

The sense of impending disaster was growing stronger by the second. He could no longer attribute it to the dead man.

Adelaide.

He turned and broke into a run.

When he emerged from the alley he saw the carriage. It was little more than a shadow in the fog but nothing appeared amiss. The horse was restless, however. The beast was shifting in his harness and tossing his head. Jed was on the box but he made no move to calm the uneasy horse.

Griffin drew his revolver and plunged forward, heart pounding with the overwhelming rush of urgency. He was vaguely aware that the night seemed colder than it had a moment ago.

"Jed."

There was no response. That was wrong; Jed could surely hear him from this distance.

It was Adelaide who responded.

"Smith is nearby," she shouted from inside the carriage. "Somewhere out there on the street. He's trying to kill Jed."

He heard the desperation in her voice and suddenly he understood everything, Jed's unnatural stillness as well as the chill across his own senses. He searched for the source of the cold sensation and found it almost at once.

The icy energy shivered from the dark mouth of a nearby alley, not more than fifteen paces from where Jed had parked the carriage. A fist-size ball of crimson light blazed in the darkness. Griffin used the blood-red glow as a beacon to acquire a focus on his target. He sent out a torrent of nightmare energy.

A violent storm of psychical fire flashed in the shadows when the two fields of energy collided. But it was no contest. Griffin could tell that Smith had already begun to exhaust his own senses. The red crystal abruptly dimmed and winked out.

The sensation of cold evaporated. Griffin heard footsteps pounding away down the alley. He fought the urge to go after his quarry. He had to get to Adelaide.

He raced back to the carriage and yanked open the door. In the shadows he could see Adelaide crouched on the seat. Her arm was extended through the trapdoor, gripping Jed's hand.

"Are you all right?" he asked.

"Yes." Her voice was flat, as if she was utterly exhausted. "And so is Jed. At least I think he is. Oh, Griffin, he was so cold."

She released Jed's hand and started to crumple.

Griffin vaulted up into the cab and caught her just before she collapsed onto the floor of the carriage. She was fever-hot in his arms, burning with dreamlight energy.

40

SMITH WAS TREMBLING SO VIOLENTLY WITH REACTION AND exhaustion that he could barely haul himself up onto the hansom cab. He managed to give the driver his address. Then he leaned forward and rested his feverish brow on his folded arms. The driver would assume he was just one more drunken gentleman on his way home after an evening spent with a mistress.

How could everything have gone so wrong? The plan had been brilliantly simple. According to Luttrell, Winters had put the word out on the streets that he was willing to pay well for information concerning a scientist named Basil Hulsey. One of Luttrell's enforcers had accepted the offer. Luttrell had informed him that he planned to take care of the man who had betrayed him tonight. He had explained that Winters would be drawn out of hiding and that there was an excellent chance that he would have the Pyne woman with him.

Luttrell had left the task of seizing her to Smith. The bastard had no interest in Adelaide Pyne and he was not yet ready to take the risk of making an obvious move against the Director. Luttrell did not care about the Burning Lamp. He was concerned only with the crystals.

Smith moaned in frustration. Grabbing the Pyne woman should have been simple. But first he'd had to dispatch the carriage driver who was very likely serving as a guard.

Such a simple strategy. Such a bloody disaster.

He might have succeeded if he'd had the assistance of the three young hunter-talents he was training. But when they had discovered that he expected them to go up against the Director, they had balked. Something to do with the man's reputation. *People who annoy him have a way of disappearing,* one of the hunters had explained. Not even the threat of depriving the three hunters of the red crystals had convinced them to assist in the kidnapping tonight.

Reliable help was always hard to find.

It was maddening to know that Adelaide Pyne had beaten him again tonight. She was just a woman, a dreamlight reader. According to his research her sort of talent was good only for perceiving the traces of dreamprints. Most females endowed with such a talent eked out pathetic livings as fortune-tellers. Pyne should not have been able to defeat him.

He forced himself to analyze all that had gone wrong. The answer became clear almost at once. He'd lost Pyne this time, just as he had on the first occasion, because he'd been forced to waste too much energy getting rid of someone who stood in the way. He'd made some improvements to the crystal devices over the years but they still burned out far too quickly.

He raised his head. He could not make the same mistake again. The next time he got an opportunity to acquire Adelaide Pyne he would make certain that he was not obliged to exhaust his talent first.

The hansom clattered to a stop in the street outside his town house. He dug into his pocket for a few coins for the driver and then climbed down from the cab. His hand was shaking so badly that it took three tries before he was able to get the key into the lock of the front door.

Once inside the town house he knew he would not be able to manage the stairs. He stumbled into the library, poured himself a stiff shot of brandy and collapsed into one of the reading chairs.

His last thought before he fell into a troubled sleep was that the night had not been a complete loss. He had learned one very important thing about Adelaide Pyne, a small, but intriguing fact that he could use the next time.

Everyone was vulnerable in some fashion. Tonight he had discovered Adelaide Pyne's great weakness.

41

SHE OPENED HER EYES TO THE LIGHT OF A GRAY DAWN. IT took her a moment to realize that she was back in her bedroom at the Abbey. Griffin was sprawled in a chair beside the bed, his left hand wrapped securely around the fingers of her own left hand, as though he feared she would slip away from him.

She lay quietly for a moment, watching him through half-closed eyes. He had a pen in his right hand and was making notes in a leather-bound notebook balanced on his knee. She could tell that he had slept very little, if at all. The dark stubble of a morning beard added another layer to the aura of shadows that always seemed to surround him, even when he was not deliberately cloaking himself.

"Good morning," she said.

His fingers tightened instantly around hers. He looked up from the notebook, eyes heating with relief.

"Good morning," he said. He leaned close and kissed her gently, as though he thought she was quite fragile.

"How is Jed?" she asked.

"He's fine." Griffin closed the notebook. "Sleeping like a baby. What about you?"

She took stock of her senses and sat up against the pillows. "Back to normal. I just needed time to recover. How long was I asleep?"

"I brought you and Jed here shortly after three this morning." He glanced at the clock on the dresser. "It's nearly ten."

She frowned. "Why did you bring us here? I thought you wanted to remain in hiding."

"Last night was a trap. I had to assume that whoever set it might have the capability of following the carriage back to the room in the lane where you and I stayed earlier. Those lodgings were designed to serve as a secret hideout, not a fortress."

"I understand."

"I have altered my strategy. Instead of trying to remain invisible, I have surrounded us with a small army. There are ten men patrolling the grounds at this moment. More will be summoned if needed. I doubt that Luttrell will try the same tactic twice, but just in case he elects to use the gas canisters again, Mrs. Trevelyan has fashioned masks from kitchen towels. Each man is carrying one."

She shook her head in admiration. "You accomplished all that in the few hours that I was asleep? Amazing. What did you learn from the informant?"

"Very little. He was dead by the time I got to him."

"Dear heaven," she whispered. "I didn't realize that."

"There was no sign of a wound. I believe that he was killed by psychical means. His name was Thacker."

"How did you discover that?"

"I found a list of herbs and a receipt for several items from an apothecary shop on his body. It was obvious that he had purchased supplies for a chemist. I sent someone around to the shop early this morning to make inquiries. The proprietor was quite helpful."

She got a vision of Delbert or Leggett intimidating a terrified shopkeeper.

"I see," she said, careful to keep her tone nonjudgmental.

Amusement gleamed briefly in Griffin's eyes. "There was no need for threats. An offer of money worked very well. The apothecary was only too happy to tell Delbert everything he knew about one of his best customers. It is only a matter of time now before we find someone who knew Thacker on a personal basis, perhaps a drinking companion. That individual will provide us with more information."

"How very efficient of you."

"I have been running the Consortium for some time now, Adelaide. In spite of appearances recently, I do know what I'm doing."

"Yes, of course." She frowned, thinking about what he had just told her. "Well, it all seems to indicate that Caleb Jones is right. Hulsey has found himself a new patron."

"Luttrell."

"But it was Smith I encountered last night. I am positive of it."

Griffin glanced at his notes. "I am convinced now that Smith and Luttrell have formed a partnership. Such a connection explains a great deal."

"Who do you think killed the informant? Smith?"

"I doubt it. Killing a man with para-energy would be an enormous drain on the senses, even with the aid of one of those red crystals. Thacker was a fresh kill. I do not think that Smith would have been able to murder him and then, a short time later, try to kill Jed and kidnap you."

"The killer was Luttrell, then?"

"Most likely. But this is the first time I have known him to kill in this fashion. I'm certain that he has not had the ability to commit murder psychically until quite recently. Believe me when I tell you that if he had possessed such a talent all this time, I would have heard rumors of it long ago. I suspect that he is now using the crystals to enhance his natural talent, whatever it is."

"So Luttrell is in league with the Hulseys and Smith."

"One can understand why he is interested in all three of them," Griffin said. "Any man in Luttrell's position would be very keen on a business arrangement with associates who can create weapons like those sleeping-gas canisters and crystals."

She raised her brows. "You mean any crime lord would be keen on such associates."

His smile was cold. "Let me rephrase that. Any man or woman in a position of power, or any man or woman who wished to acquire power, would be very pleased to go into partnership with those who can provide such weapons."

She wrinkled her nose. "You're right, of course. It isn't just crime lords who would be interested in the Hulseys and Smith."

"Well, the list of those who might want to do business with the Hulseys would likely be a long one. But only someone of talent would be attracted to Smith."

She nodded. "Because only a person of talent would find the crystals useful."

"Yes."

"I would like you to view the dreamprints of the person who tried to murder Jed last night. That will confirm that we are dealing with the same man who tried to kidnap you thirteen years ago."

"Very well, although I am sure the prints will belong to the man I knew as Smith."

"I don't doubt it. But I want to be certain."

"I understand," she said.

"I would also like you to look at the prints around Thacker's body."

"Of course," she said. She paused. "Griffin, there is one thing I do not understand about last night."

"What is that?"

She wrapped her arms around her knees. "It is obvious that Smith intended to kidnap me. But what of the Burning Lamp? I'm no good to him without it. How did he intend to get his hands on the artifact?"

"Once Smith had you, he would most likely have tried to negotiate for the lamp."

Everything inside her warmed gently. "You'd give up the lamp if you thought my life depended on it?"

"Without a second thought."

"Oh, Griffin, I'm truly touched. I know how important the lamp is to you."

"And then I'd slit the bastard's throat."

She groaned and rested her forehead on her knees. "Two birds with one lamp. Who says a crime lord can't be a romantic at heart?"

ADELAIDE BATHED AND DRESSED in a fresh pair of trousers and a clean shirt that Mrs. Trevelyan had meticulously pressed. Before going down to breakfast she went to the room where Jed was sleeping. Leggett hovered on the opposite side of the bed. He noticed her in the doorway.

"Good morning, Mrs. Pyne," he said. "You're looking a good deal more fit now than you did last night and that's a fact. When the Boss came through the door with you in his arms I swear, you looked just like one of those heroines in a sensation play. You know, the sort that is always fainting dead away from some terrible shock to the nerves."

"How embarrassing." She walked to the bed. "How is Jed?"

"Still asleep."

"He'll be fine," she said. She touched Jed's brow, trying not to wince when the churning waves of dreamlight whispered across her senses. "His temperature feels normal and although he's dreaming, he's not having any severe nightmares. The damage Smith did to his senses is healing."

"You saved his life last night," Leggett said. "He's my best friend. We've been together since our days on the streets."

"I understand," she said.

"I just want you to know that if there's ever anything I can do for you, anything at all, you only have to ask," Leggett said earnestly. "I'm real good with a knife."

That made twice in one morning that a man had offered to slit a throat for her.

She blinked back the moisture that had suddenly blurred her vision. "Thank you, Leggett. That is very sweet of you. I'll remember that."

42

ADELAIDE RAISED HER SENSES AND STUDIED THE PRINTS IN
the alley. Decades of dreamlight tracks fluoresced on the rain-slick
pavement but the most recent prints gave off disturbing currents of
dark ultragreen and unwholesome ultraviolet.

"It was most certainly Smith," she said. "I see his prints in my
dreams. I know them well, even after all these years."

Griffin looked toward the far end of the narrow alley. "He ran off
in that direction last night. There was a vehicle waiting for him. I'm
certain that I heard a hansom one street over."

"He is . . . not entirely sane, Griffin. I can see the taint of madness.
It is much stronger now than it was all those years ago."

"A powerful talent who is armed with a crystal that enables him to
commit murder and who is going mad. That has to be J-and-J's worst
nightmare."

"Do you really think Smith is a member of the Society?"

"There is so much that is explained if one accepts that assumption. Let us see what you can tell us about the murdered informant."

They walked out of the alley and headed down the street. Delbert and three other enforcers fanned out around Adelaide.

Griffin led the way into the small courtyard. The body was gone.

"A shopkeeper or a street lad probably found Thacker this morning and summoned the authorities," Griffin said. "It doesn't matter. We are only concerned with dreamprints."

"Dear heaven," Adelaide whispered. She stared at the wet pavement, unable to believe what she was seeing. "I know these prints, Griffin. I recognize them."

He frowned. "Are you going to tell me that it was Smith, after all?"

"No, not Smith." She looked up. "But I have most certainly seen this killer's prints somewhere else."

"Where?"

"In the house where your parents died. Whoever killed Thacker murdered your mother and father."

"Luttrell," Griffin said. "Son of a bitch. Should have killed him years ago."

43

"THE TIMING FITS," GRIFFIN SAID. "LUTTRELL WAS WORKING for Quinton during those years, a young man on the way up in the organization. Luttrell was two or three years older than me, probably eighteen or nineteen. He already had a fierce reputation on the streets."

They were sitting on the green wrought iron bench in the Abbey garden, the dogs dozing at their feet. Adelaide was growing increasingly concerned about Griffin. It seemed to her that he was sinking so deeply into the shadows that she might never be able to pull him back out into the light.

And just what was she thinking, anyway? The man was a crime lord. One did not go around trying to rescue such people.

"Why would Luttrell murder your parents and steal the Burning Lamp?" she asked. "How could he have even known about the artifact, come to that? He grew up on the streets, not within the Arcane Society."

"I told you, he possesses some kind of powerful psychical ability. Any strong talent who got close to the lamp would no doubt sense something of its paranormal nature and be intrigued."

"I cannot believe that Luttrell just happened across the lamp in the course of breaking into your parents' house. That is simply too much of a coincidence. If Luttrell did steal it during a routine burglary, why didn't he take your mother's jewelry? You said the lamp was the only thing missing from the safe."

"There is no question but that he went there for the sole purpose of stealing the lamp. I told you, he was working for Quinton in those days. So Quinton must have given him the order to obtain the artifact."

"Was Quinton a talent of some kind?" she asked.

"No, I don't think so. He was endowed with the kind of primitive intuition that allowed him to stay alive on the streets. In addition, he possessed the raw intelligence and the streak of ruthlessness required to build a strong organization. But I never heard any rumors that would have made me think he was a talent."

"So the question then becomes, how could Quinton have known about the lamp and, if he was not a talent himself, why would he have sent Luttrell to steal it?"

"I can't be absolutely certain but I can concoct an interesting little play that would explain a great deal."

"Tell me the story," she said.

"Act One opens twenty years ago. Our mysterious Mr. Smith, who is likely a member of Arcane, is aware of the legend of the Burning Lamp. He knows something of crystals and therefore thinks that he can access the artifact's power. He also knows that the lamp is probably in the hands of the descendants of Nicholas Winters. But he has no experience with the sort of criminal skills required to steal the artifact and he doesn't dare take the risk of trying to rob a respectable gentleman's house. He requires professional assistance."

"Go on."

"He makes a few inquiries and discovers the name of the most powerful crime lord in London."

She looked at him. "Would that have been hard to do?"

"No. Quinton was notorious. Owned half the brothels in the city, not to mention three-quarters of the opium dens. The police could not touch him but they certainly knew who he was."

"All right, so Smith somehow gets word to Quinton that he wishes to hire a thief."

Griffin massaged his injured left shoulder in an absent manner.

"Quinton was a very wealthy man," he said. "He would not have been interested in Smith's money. What's more, he was a cautious man. He would not have liked the idea of sending one of his enforcers to break into the household of a prominent investor simply to obtain an antiquity."

"Something must have convinced Quinton that stealing the lamp for Smith was worth the risk."

"Quinton might well have been intrigued by the notion of controlling a member of the Arcane Society, especially if Smith moved at the higher levels of the organization." Griffin stopped massaging his shoulder. He leaned forward and rested his forearms on his thighs. "Obtaining the lamp for Smith would have given Quinton a powerful hold over him."

"So Quinton agreed to the bargain."

"He sent his top enforcer, Luttrell, to carry out the task."

The utter lack of emotion in Griffin's words frightened Adelaide more than any scowl or bunched fist.

"Assuming that is the way it happened," she said gently, "Luttrell would have given the lamp to his employer."

"Who, in turn, would have handed it over to Smith. But Smith was unable to work the artifact. He must have discovered that at least one aspect of the legend was true. He required the services of a strong dreamlight reader. Which brings us to Act Two: It took him six more years to find you."

"But by then my parents were dead and I had gone into an orphanage," Adelaide said.

Griffin turned his head to look at her. "I do not think it was any coincidence that your parents died shortly after they registered the nature of your talent with the officials of the Society."

For a few heartbeats she could not comprehend what he was saying. When understanding did dawn, she felt oddly light-headed with the shock of it all. Her stomach roiled. For a moment she wondered if she was actually about to faint.

"Are you saying that Smith identified me as a dreamlight talent using the Arcane records and then arranged the death of my parents?" she whispered.

"I think it likely, yes. He had to get your family out of the way. How else could he hope to get his hands on you?"

"Do you think he went back to Quinton to commission the murder of my mother and father?"

"Yes."

She shivered. "But I was sent to an orphanage after they were killed."

"Not for long. I'll wager Smith arranged for you to end up in that brothel. He made another bargain with Quinton."

Her hands ached. She looked down and saw that her fingers were so tightly clenched together her knuckles had gone white.

"But at the last minute, when Smith came to test me, as he put it, the brothel keeper told him that he could not have me," she said.

"Something happened that night that made Quinton change his mind about selling you to Smith," Griffin said. "Perhaps he discovered that you were worth more to someone else."

"I don't see how that could be. I'm no good to any of these people without the lamp. And Smith was the one with the artifact."

"There is another possibility," Griffin said slowly. "Do you remember the exact date that Smith showed up at the brothel?"

"As if I could ever forget." She shuddered. "It will have been thirteen years ago, come the third of next month. I was on a ship bound for America three days later."

Griffin nodded slightly, evidently satisfied.

"That, too, fits," he said.

"What do you mean?"

"Quinton died a week earlier that same year. That was when those in my world woke up to discover that his organization had been taken over by his most trusted enforcer."

"Luttrell."

"Yes. Luttrell was very busy trying to gain control of his new empire during those first days and weeks."

"In other words, he might not have discovered the arrangement that his old employer had made with Smith until the very last minute?" she asked.

"Yes."

"I think you're right. I remember that when the brothel manager came back to the room she informed Smith that the establishment was under new management."

"Luttrell would most certainly have wanted to renegotiate the terms of the bargain that Smith and Quinton had made."

Griffin fell silent. Adelaide waited a moment.

"Well?" she said finally. "What do we do now?"

"Nothing has changed in this equation," Griffin said. "I know how to hunt in my world. I will deal with Luttrell. But if I'm right in concluding that Smith is a member of Arcane, Jones and Jones is better positioned to identify him."

Boots crunched on the gravel path behind Adelaide. She turned her head and saw Delbert approaching.

"Sorry to interrupt, Boss." Delbert stopped in front of the bench. "Leggett just got back from talking to Thacker's old pals at what used to be his favorite tavern."

Griffin straightened. "Any news?"

"Thacker was one of Luttrell's men, all right. A few weeks ago he was given what all of his friends considered a very comfortable assignment. He was running errands for a couple of scientists Luttrell has tucked away in Hidden Moon Lane."

Griffin was already on his feet, heading toward the house. "Get the carriage ready."

"Jed is bringing it around now, Boss."

Adelaide rose quickly. "You're going to Hidden Moon Lane?"

Griffin glanced back over his shoulder. "It may already be too late."

She hurried after him. "I'm coming with you."

"Yes, of course," he said. "I have discovered the hard way last night that I cannot let you out of my sight."

44

HIDDEN MOON LANE MIGHT AS WELL HAVE BEEN NAMED HID-
den Sun Lane, Griffin thought, especially when the fog was as thick
as it was that afternoon. The buildings were crowded so close together
that the narrow strip of pavement was trapped in perpetual twilight.
There were no signs of life. The windows of the looming structures
were closed and shuttered.

He stood in the small park with Adelaide and Delbert and surveyed the tiny street from its far end while Jed and the carriage waited
nearby.

"It looks like just the sort of neighborhood where one could conceal
a couple of rogue chemists and a secret laboratory," Adelaide offered.

"It does," Griffin agreed.

"There will probably be guards," Delbert warned.

"I don't think so," Griffin said.

Adelaide looked at him. "What makes you say that?"

"Because I suspect that Luttrell has already abandoned the operation. He must have known that it wouldn't take me long to discover Thacker's identity and trace his comings and goings to this address. But with luck he will not have bothered to inform Hulsey and Son that he no longer requires their services. There is a possibility, at least, that they are still on the premises."

"You believe Luttrell would simply abandon them to their fate?" Adelaide asked. "But we have concluded that they are valuable to him."

"It's called cutting one's losses," Griffin said. "I suppose it's possible that Luttrell took the time to kill the Hulseys, but I'm inclined to doubt it."

"Why wouldn't he get rid of them?" Delbert asked. "Seems like the sensible thing to do."

"Because they constitute a very convenient distraction. Luttrell knows that Arcane is hunting them. Makes sense to let J-and-J focus its attention on the Hulseys rather than on him. I doubt if Luttrell is eager to tangle with Arcane."

"Assuming the Hulseys are still alive," Adelaide said, "what are we going to do with them?"

"Turn them over to J-and-J. The Hulseys are a problem for Arcane, not me. All I want from them is information."

"Are we all going in together?" Delbert asked. "Bit of a crowd, don't you think?"

Griffin looked at him. "You will stay here with Mrs. Pyne. I'll go in and take a quick look around. If I don't return within fifteen minutes you know what to do."

"One moment if you please," Adelaide said coolly. "No one told me there was a contingency plan. What is it?"

"If I don't come back Delbert and Jed will see to it that you are escorted immediately to Caleb Jones's house. Jones will protect you."

"You said you weren't going to let me out of your sight," Adelaide said uneasily. "I think I should go with you. My talent could prove useful."

"I can conceal myself, but not someone else," he explained. "You will stay here with Delbert."

He knew she was going to launch into another argument so he pulled the shadows around himself, effectively disappearing. He started down the lane.

"It is so annoying when he does that," Adelaide said behind him.

"You get accustomed to it," Delbert said.

HE PRIED OPEN THE WINDOW on the upper floor and moved soundlessly into the darkened room. The lessons of his youth had not been wasted, he thought with some satisfaction. He still had the skills that had made him a legendary second-story man in his teens. His motto in those days had been simple: *Never go in through the ground floor. If there's a trap or an alarm, that's where it will be set.*

There was an air of emptiness about the room in which he stood, as if no one had lived there in a very long time. He took a moment to secure one end of a length of rope to the heavy bed frame. Then he crossed to the door and looked out into a long, narrow hall.

He stood quietly for a moment, listening with all of his senses. At first he heard nothing. Perhaps he was too late, after all. Maybe the Hulseys had received some warning or their intuition had told them it was time to find a new employer. Or perhaps Luttrell had indeed decided to kill them.

Then he heard the faint, muffled thuds from deep within the bowels of the house. Someone was at home.

He went down the stairs into the front hall, turned and went past a small drawing room and breakfast room. The ground floor was empty, just like the one above. But there was a crack of light under what looked like a closet door just inside the kitchen.

He opened the door and discovered another flight of stairs that descended into a basement. The room below was dimly illuminated by gaslight. Pulling the shadows more tightly around himself, he went down the steps.

The underground room at the foot of the stairs was old. Judging by the stonework, he knew it was at least a couple of centuries older than the house. London had been building and remodeling itself since the days of the Romans. There were layers upon layers of ruins beneath the city streets. Entire rivers were hidden beneath the pavement. The city's architectural past was a great convenience to those in his profession.

There was an entrance to a corridor on one side of the underground chamber. He flattened himself against the wall just to the side of the opening and looked down a short stone passage into another room.

Shadows bounced wildly in the second chamber. Urgent voices echoed.

"Are you sure this is necessary, sir? I was just starting to see some progress in my experiments with the mice. I thought we might move on to our human subject in a day or two."

A young man, Griffin concluded. Bertram Hulsey.

"We have no choice." The voice belonged to an older man. "Something has gone wrong, I tell you. The guard did not return with the supplies I ordered and there has been no word from our patron. I have been in circumstances like this on prior occasions. We must get out of here as quickly as possible."

"But the chemistry apparatus and all of the instruments and glassware. We cannot afford to replace so much fine equipment."

"We will find a new patron. There is always someone looking for men endowed with our talents. Hurry, Bertram. Leave everything except the notebooks and the fern."

Griffin lowered his talent a little. He was no longer nearly invisible but he knew that Bertram and Basil would not be able to make out his features.

He reached inside his overcoat and took the revolver out of his shoulder holster. He had discovered long ago that a large gun always commanded attention in these sorts of situations. He walked quietly along the hallway and stepped into the second chamber.

"Don't rush off on my account," he said. "Basil and Bertram Hulsey, I presume?"

The two men froze in the act of gathering up notebooks. The older man bore an uncanny resemblance to a large, spindly insect wearing glasses. The younger man appeared to be in his early twenties. Bertram was not yet completely bald like his father, but there was no mistaking the family resemblance.

"Who are you?" Bertram demanded. He peered sharply at Griffin, squinting a little.

"So this is where the firm of Hulsey and Son does business." Griffin picked up a glass vial off the workbench and examined the contents.

"What are you doing?" Basil squeaked. "Have a care, sir. There are some volatile chemicals on that workbench."

"Are there, indeed?" Griffin set the vial down and moved to the straw basket suspended on an iron chain from the ceiling. The delicate, graceful fronds of an unusual-looking fern spilled over the edges of the container.

"Don't touch that fern," Basil snapped. "It's extremely rare and absolutely vital to our current research."

Griffin unhooked the basket from the chain. "Constructing paranormal weapons for crime lords is no doubt a very profitable line. Pity you chose the wrong client. You should have come to me first. I would have paid much better than Luttrell."

"Are you the Director of the organization Luttrell calls the Consortium?" Basil stammered.

"I'm afraid so." Griffin smiled. "It was my personal residence that was attacked with those vapor canisters you constructed for Luttrell. I tend to take that kind of thing personally. Petty of me, perhaps, but there you have it."

Bertram went even paler than he already was. "We had no way of knowing how Luttrell would use the sleeping fog, sir."

"What you must understand is that I've spent years building my reputation," Griffin said. "It is my stock in trade. I cannot allow a couple of scientists to destroy it."

"Now, see here," Basil said. "My son just explained to you that we merely designed the canisters and concocted the gas. We are not responsible for what Mr. Luttrell did with them."

"In future you might want to give that aspect of your business some consideration," Griffin said.

Basil's eyes glittered behind the lenses of his spectacles. "Are you offering employment, sir? Because if so, I am pleased to tell you that our services are available for hire."

"Sadly, I must decline the opportunity," Griffin said. "I understand Arcane is on your trail and I do not want to attract any more attention from that quarter."

"Arcane?" Basil's eyes widened. "They know that we have been working for Luttrell?"

"They do now," Griffin said. "You see my problem. Hiring you would bring Jones and Jones to my door. I prefer to avoid those sorts of complications."

Bertram's mouth worked. "See . . . see here, sir, we are scientists, not criminals. It is not our fault that our former employer proved to be one of your competitors. What do you want from us?"

"Information," Griffin said. "You have already explained that you are responsible for the sleeping vapor. Tell me about the red crystals."

Basil blinked owlishly. "I don't know what you're talking about. What crystals?"

"Help."

The cry came from the far end of another passageway.

"Help, please. I can hear someone out there. Save me, I beg you."

"Who the devil is that?" Griffin asked.

"No one important," Basil assured him. "Merely the experimental subject that Mr. Luttrell provided for us."

"Damnation," Griffin said. "I knew this was going to get complicated. What is the subject's name?"

Bertram frowned. "Harper, I think. Why?"

"Let us hope for both your sakes that Mr. Harper is still in good health. Otherwise—" Griffin ceased talking and made a vague motion with the revolver.

Bertram and Basil reacted as if he had suddenly released a deadly serpent into the room. Both men stared at the gun in horror.

"Where, exactly, is Mr. Harper?" Griffin asked.

"He's in a chamber just down that hall," Bertram said quickly. "He's fine, really. We hadn't got around to running any experiments on him yet. I was hoping that perhaps in a day or two when we were certain that no more mice had died—"

"Go and get him," Griffin said.

Bertram dropped his stack of notebooks and bolted toward the entrance of the hallway. Basil started to follow him.

"You will stay here, Dr. Hulsey," Griffin said. "Think of yourself as insurance for your son's good behavior."

Hulsey's thin shoulders slumped. He watched Bertram disappear into the hallway.

A short time later Griffin heard scrambling sounds at the end of the corridor.

"Where are you taking me?" Harper demanded. He sounded terrified. "What's going on? You have no right—"

Bertram reappeared. He had a man of about forty in tow. Norwood

Harper was evidently still wearing the same clothes he'd had on when he disappeared after the ill-fated visit to Luttrell. His excellently cut coat and trousers were badly wrinkled. His shirt was crumpled and he had lost his tie at some point. In addition, he was unshaven and his hair was matted. His hands were bound.

"This is Harper," Bertram said. "He's all yours."

Norwood Harper shuddered and stared, terrified, at Griffin. "Who are you?"

"The Director of the Consortium," Griffin said. "Your family asked me to find you. Frankly, I assumed that you were probably dead."

"The Director?" Norwood appeared stunned.

"Correct." Griffin gestured at Bertram. "Untie him."

Bertram hastily freed Norwood's hands.

"I cannot express the depths of my gratitude, sir," Norwood said to Griffin. "I believe these two were about to carry out some diabolical experiment on me. There was talk of a drug."

"We will discuss the details later," Griffin said. He angled his head toward the corridor that led to the kitchen stairs. "Wait for me in the kitchen."

Harper needed no further urging. He broke into an awkward trot and disappeared down the passage.

Griffin looked at the anxious Hulseys. "Let us return to the subject of the crystals."

"We know nothing about any crystals," Basil said, affronted. "We have been conducting chemical experiments, not working with crystals."

"Oddly enough, I actually believe you. Well, gentlemen, I think that brings this conversation to a close." He motioned again with the revolver. "Let's go."

"Where are you taking us?" Bertram asked.

"Not far. I'm going to leave you in the cell where you imprisoned Norwood Harper. Never fear, someone from Jones and Jones will be along soon. I'm sure the agency will have some questions for you."

"No," Basil shrieked. "You can't do this to us. We're at a critical point in our research—"

The muffled roar of the explosion on the floor above cut off the last of the sentence. From somewhere in the vicinity of the kitchen, Norwood Harper screamed.

"Damn it to hell," Griffin said, mostly to himself. "Should have seen that coming. Amateurs. They never follow orders."

He hoisted the fern basket in his free hand and headed for the kitchen stairs, running hard.

"My fern," Basil called out.

Griffin ignored him. He pounded up the stairs. The exterior wall of the kitchen was already in flames. The fire blocked the window and the door that opened onto the small garden. Norwood stood statue-still in the center of the room.

"I told you to wait for me in the kitchen," Griffin said. "Why the hell did you open the back door? It was bound to be trapped."

Norwood's mouth worked but he was clearly unable to form a coherent sentence.

"The front door will also be trapped," Griffin said. "We'll go out from the floor above. Move, man."

Harper needed no urging. He fled down the hall to the main staircase, seized the banister and took the stairs two at a time. Griffin was only a pace behind him.

By the time they arrived on the landing smoke was drifting down the ground floor hall.

"Bedroom at the far end," Griffin said.

Norwood rushed forward. "How will we get out from up here?"

"By doing exactly as I say." Griffin followed him into the bedroom. "Take these." He stripped off his leather gloves and tossed them at Norwood. "Put them on. You'll need them to go down the rope."

He went to the window and uncoiled the length of rope he had secured to the bed. He tossed one end down toward the ground.

"Go," he said to Norwood. "Hurry."

Harper did not ask questions. He pulled on the gloves, took a deep breath and scrambled out the window. Clinging to the rope, he half slid, half lowered himself to the ground. He landed hard on his rear but he got to his feet, unhurt.

When Harper released the rope, Griffin yanked it back up, attached the basket to the free end and lowered the fern into Harper's hands.

He was about to follow Harper and the fern when the blast of killing energy scorched his senses. Out of the corner of his eye he caught a glimpse of a dark figure in the bedroom doorway. A crimson light glowed in the shadows.

"You almost escaped me, Winters," Luttrell said. He raised the red crystal. "I must admit, I'm impressed that you got this far. Thought for sure my little surprise in the kitchen would be the end of the matter. Most men would have made a dash for the nearest exit. But you do not think like most men, do you?"

Should have left Harper and the damn fern in the basement, Griffin thought.

45

THE RUSH OF PANIC CRACKLED THROUGH ADELAIDE LIKE A
lightning-ignited wildfire in desert brush.

"Something has gone wrong," she said.

Delbert looked at her. "How do you know that?"

"I just know it," she said. She started forward at a run. "We must
hurry."

Delbert leaped to follow her. "Come back, Mrs. Pync. The Boss
gave strict orders to keep you safe."

She paid no attention to him. Flames were licking out a window at
the end of the street.

"No," she whispered. *"No."*

"Bloody hell," Delbert muttered.

She ran faster. So did Delbert.

By the time they reached the house a plume of dark smoke was
thickening the fog. The first floor was half awash in flames.

"Dear heaven," Adelaide breathed. "Where is he? Where is Griffin?"

"The Boss will come out the same way he went in," Delbert said. He sounded as if he was trying to reassure himself rather than her. "From one of the upper floors. The Boss never goes in through the ground floor. Got a rule about it. He's probably around back in the garden by now."

"No, he's still inside," Adelaide said. "In mortal danger. I can feel it. We must get to him."

"There's no way we can go into that house now. The Boss can take care of himself. He's had a lot of practice, believe me."

"I must get to him," Adelaide said. She started toward the front steps.

Delbert gripped her arm and yanked her back with considerable force.

"I'm sorry, Mrs. Pyne," he said, his voice roughening. "I can't let you do that. The Boss would slit my throat himself if I allowed you to enter that house. The whole first floor will be in flames in a few minutes."

"But he's still in there."

She was frantic now. Delbert's hand tightened on her arm.

"Help."

The voice came from the walk that separated the burning house from the neighboring building.

"Help."

Adelaide saw a man running toward them. A large, bulky object swung wildly from his hand.

"What the bloody hell?" Delbert asked softly. "That's not the Boss. It's someone else. What's that he's got?"

"I think it's a fern," Adelaide said.

46

THE SEARING BLAST OF ENERGY WAS UNRELENTING, A GREAT
weight crushing his senses. For a few seconds Griffin struggled to pull
more shadows around himself but he knew he was wasting his strength.
The same was true of what he knew he would always think of as his
second talent. He could not project a wave of nightmares, not against
the psychical torrent that was roaring over him.

No one could maintain such a level of power for long, he thought.
He had to stay conscious until Luttrell exhausted himself.

"How do you like my new toy?" Luttrell asked. "I don't pretend
to understand the para-physics involved, but you must admit that it
produces an impressive result. It enhances my natural talent to an astonishing degree."

Griffin could not force his muscles to do anything so he tried the
opposite approach. He stopped fighting the overpowering energy altogether and immediately crumpled to the floor in front of the window.

The sudden, unexpected movement must have caught Luttrell by surprise, because for a heartbeat or two he lost his focus through the crystal.

Griffin could breathe again. The mountain that had been sitting on his senses lightened briefly. He pulled a tiny bit of energy along with a deep breath. He managed to cloak himself in some shadow light, not enough to make himself invisible but perhaps enough to make it harder for Luttrell to see him clearly.

Luttrell responded with rage.

"Don't move," he shouted.

Luttrell found his focus again almost immediately but it seemed to Griffin that the crushing weight of energy was not as steady nor as stable as it had been a moment ago.

There it was again, a tiny flicker in the resonating pattern of the currents. Either the shadow light was throwing off Luttrell's focus or the crystal itself was losing power. The human mind was not a machine that gave off energy at a constant rate. Talent was no different from hearing, sight, touch or smell. Like the normal senses, the psychical senses were affected by everything from strong emotion to the rate of one's pulse.

"I'm going to miss the Hulseys," Luttrell said. "They have been useful, but I have concluded that they are more trouble than they are worth. I always knew that sooner or later Arcane would come looking for them. I don't need that particular problem just now. I'm going to have my hands full taking over your organization."

Griffin sensed another short spasm in the currents of energy Luttrell was throwing at him. He used the short interlude to gather a few more shadows.

"My parents," he managed in a hoarse whisper. "Why did you kill them?"

"I had no choice," Luttrell said. "Believe it or not, I didn't know they were at home that day. I thought the house was empty. But as it turned out your mother and father were enjoying a few private moments upstairs. Your father heard me when I cracked the safe and came down to investigate. He had a gun. What was I to do?"

"Bastard."

"No argument there." Luttrell walked closer and stood looking down at Griffin. "I never had the opportunity to meet my own father. I understand he died in a knife fight a few months before I was born. But, then, we all have our sad little stories, don't we? Lucky for the social reformers. Just think where they'd be without so many to save."

"Some of us aren't worth saving."

Luttrell smiled. "You're probably right. On the other hand, some of us don't want to be saved, do we? Can you imagine either one of us living a quiet, boring, respectable life? What a waste of talent."

"The Truce. Why did you break it?"

"Our agreement has had its uses for the past few years. But unlike you I'm not content with only a portion of an empire. I am now ready to take it all. You and Pierce are the only major obstacles in my path. After tonight only Pierce will remain. I do not anticipate any trouble in that quarter."

"You're forgetting about Arcane."

Luttrell smiled. "The Society is composed of our betters. None of them were forced to survive on the streets the way you and I did. What do they know of our world? They have been weakened by generations of comfortable living."

"Don't count on it."

"I know they have some strong talents in their ranks, and that is why I am in no rush to take them on just yet. But soon I will own some of the most powerful men in that organization. I will know their secrets, and with that knowledge I will control Arcane. Think what I can accomplish with that kind of power."

"You don't know what you're dealing with," Griffin said. "Trust me."

"Now that is where you are wrong. I know exactly what I'm dealing with. I have a spy within the very heart of Arcane."

"You're a fool."

"Which one of us is lying helpless on the floor?" Luttrell asked. "But before I end this, there is one thing I would like to know. Did the Pyne woman work the Burning Lamp for you? According to that old legend you should have a couple of additional talents by now. I don't see any indication of extra powers, though."

"You know how it is with legends. Ninety-five percent of the tale is usually false."

"Yes, I was certain that would turn out to be the case with the Burning Lamp myth. How unfortunate for you. What matters to me is that my Arcane connection believes that he can access the energy of the lamp. He is obsessed with the damn thing. And I have become quite fond of these crystals that he creates for me. Thus, we have arrived at an agreement."

Luttrell's focus flickered again. Griffin grabbed a few more shadows. The natural gloom inside the room was a great asset. He knew that he was rapidly becoming a vague object in the poorly illuminated space.

"On your feet," Luttrell ordered. "Stand up where I can see you, damn it."

Griffin went very still and very silent. Luttrell was getting nervous.

"You heard me," Luttrell shouted. "Get on your feet."

Anger and a trace of fear reverberated in the words. Luttrell swung the crystal in an arc, searching for the target he could no longer see.

Griffin abruptly found himself free. His senses roared back at full power. He sent out a heavy wave of his nightmare talent.

Luttrell screamed, a high, keening cry that soared above the howl of the fire. The red crystal blazed once, weakly, and then went dark.

Griffin staggered to his feet.

"No," Luttrell shouted. "Stay away from me." He whirled and started toward the door.

Griffin slammed into him. They crashed to the floor. Griffin was remotely aware of pain in his left shoulder but it did not seem important. Luttrell flailed wildly. Griffin pulsed more energy.

Luttrell screamed again. In the next instant his heart stopped. So did the scream.

Griffin did not stop the floodtide of nightmares until there was nothing left on which to focus. The shock of the death splashed like acid across his senses. It was not the first time he had experienced it. He knew he would pay a price later but he considered it a fair bargain.

The fire was louder now. Smoke was drifting into the bedroom. He scrambled free of Luttrell's body, grabbed the crystal and ran for the window. He paused a moment to strip off his coat. He would need it to protect his hands from the friction created when he went down the rope.

He got one leg over the sill. The rope went taut. He looked down and saw Adelaide. She had seized the trailing end and was starting up the stone wall of the house.

"I should have known you'd show up sooner or later," he said.

"Griffin. Thank God."

She released her grip on the rope and dropped the short distance into the garden. He went over the edge of the window and lowered himself quickly down beside her.

Delbert came around the corner of the house, revolver in hand. He was breathing hard.

"Sorry, Boss. She got away from me."

"She's good at that kind of thing." Griffin grabbed Adelaide's hand. *"Run."*

They raced around the corner of the house and out into the lane.

Norwood Harper was waiting for them, the fern clutched in his hands. Griffin snatched the basket out of his fingers.

"Move, Harper. The house is coming down."

The stone walls stood but the interior of the house crumbled in on itself in a whirlpool of flames. Griffin could hear the fire brigade in the distance.

He brought Adelaide and the others to a halt next to the carriage. Jed looked down from the box. "Bit of trouble, Boss?"

"Just the usual," Griffin said.

Together they watched the fire wagons rumble past. No one spoke for several minutes.

Finally Griffin looked at Adelaide. "Where did you learn to climb a rope? Wait, let me guess. Monty Moore's Wild West Show."

"We had a regular feature that involved a gang of outlaws who escape from jail," she said. She was breathless from running. "The villains escaped by climbing a rope."

"How did it end?"

"The sheriff and his posse always caught the outlaws. But not before they robbed a bank."

"The outlaws *always* got caught?"

"I'm afraid so," Adelaide said.

"Obviously they were working for a poor excuse for a crime lord."

"I always played the role of the leader of the outlaw gang," she said. "I was the crime lord."

47

JED USHERED LUCINDA AND CALEB JONES INTO THE LIBRARY. Griffin rose from behind his desk to greet them.

"Imagine, Mr. and Mrs. Jones consorting with a known crime lord," he said. "This cannot be good for my reputation."

"Probably won't benefit ours much, either," Caleb muttered darkly.

Adelaide smiled at Lucinda.

"Ignore them both," she said. "Please sit down."

"Thank you." Lucinda took one of the chairs. She surveyed Adelaide with a worried glance and then she looked at Griffin. "Are you both all right? The man who brought the message said there was some sort of fire. No offense, but the two of you look as though you got a bit too close to a poorly vented hearth."

Adelaide glanced down at her soot-stained shirt and trousers and grimaced. Griffin's clothes were in worse condition. His face was smudged with smoky residue.

"We do look a sight, don't we?" Adelaide said. "We have not yet had a chance to bathe."

Mrs. Trevelyan brought in a tea tray. Griffin gave a brief account of what had happened in Hidden Moon Lane. At the conclusion he produced the fern from behind his desk with a theatrical flourish that made Adelaide roll her eyes. He winked at her.

"My *Ameliopteris*," Lucinda exclaimed. She leaped to her feet to take the basket from Griffin. Anxiously she surveyed the plant and then gave a relieved sigh. "Hulsey cut off several fronds but the poor thing appears to be in good health. It will grow back." She looked at Griffin. "I cannot tell you how much this means to me. Thank you, Mr. Winters. I hope that someday I can repay the favor."

Caleb's jaw tightened. He cleared his throat.

"My dear," he said to Lucinda, "There is no need to get overly emotional about this."

"But I truly am grateful," Lucinda insisted. "I am, indeed, in Mr. Winters's debt."

Griffin was already smiling his slow, cold smile. "As you wish, Mrs. Jones. I collect favors. It is something of a hobby of mine."

Caleb shot Griffin a wary glance. "It's just a fern, Lucinda. It was your property to start with. Winters merely returned it to you. No favors involved."

"I disagree," Lucinda said. "My *Ameliopteris* is very special to me. I will be forever grateful to Mr. Winters."

"I'm glad you are pleased, Mrs. Jones," Griffin said.

Adelaide gave him a repressive glare and then turned back to Lucinda. "Ignore Mr. Winters. You do not owe him anything just because he rescued your fern. Isn't that right, Mr. Winters?"

Griffin inclined his head in a gallant gesture. "Always happy to be of service to one of the proprietors of Jones and Jones."

Caleb fixed Griffin with a steely expression. "You say the Hulseys got away?"

"I think it would be prudent to assume that is the case," Griffin said. "That underground laboratory of theirs was connected to some old medieval tunnels."

"Given their history with various employers, I think it likely that they had some emergency escape plans prepared," Caleb said. He sounded resigned. "It's certainly what we would have done."

"Yes," Griffin said. "It is."

Caleb exhaled thoughtfully. "We do think alike, you and I."

Griffin did not respond to that statement but he did not deny it, either, Adelaide noticed.

"Well, on a positive note," she said briskly, "if the Hulseys did get away it will mean more work for Jones and Jones."

Caleb looked grim. "I assure you, Mrs. Pyne, the firm does not lack for clients. Damned nuisance they are, too."

"Don't believe a word he says." Lucinda patted his arm affectionately. "He loves the challenge of an investigation. And so do I. Now, then, with Luttrell dead, what will become of the underworld empire that he controlled?"

Griffin lounged back in his desk chair. "As neither Mr. Pierce nor I are interested in the brothel or opium business, I expect that there will soon be some squabbling over the remains."

Adelaide poured some tea for Lucinda. "In the meantime, my charity house and the Academy will take in as many of the women who worked in Luttrell's establishments as can be convinced to leave the streets."

Lucinda looked impressed. "Congratulations, Adelaide. Just think, in one fell swoop, all of those notorious brothels have been destroyed. That is a very impressive accomplishment for any social reformer."

"I cannot take the credit," Adelaide said. "Mr. Winters is the amazing social reformer who succeeded in leveling Luttrell's empire. I can't wait to read the account in *The Flying Intelligencer.*"

Griffin fixed her with a dangerous look. His eyes heated a little. "I will be more than a little displeased if my name appears in the sensation press."

"Really, sir, there is no need to issue dire threats and warnings," Adelaide said. She set the teapot back down on the tray. "I assure you, I will not mention a word to Gilbert Otford or any of the other gentlemen of the press. But I cannot be held responsible for any rumors that might even now be circulating."

"Yes," Griffin vowed, "you can and will be held accountable."

Adelaide smiled. "More tea?"

Caleb frowned at the chunk of red glass sitting on the corner of the desk. "What can you tell us about the crystal?"

"Very little." Griffin got to his feet and went around to the front of the desk. He propped himself against the edge and picked up the crystal. "The devices appear to be able to enhance the focus of one's natural psychical currents, at least temporarily. But the crystals burn out quickly."

Caleb rose and took the crystal from him. He held the device up to the light for a closer look. "You say the Hulseys did not take credit for them?"

"No. Luttrell made it clear that he obtained them from Smith, who, according to Luttrell, is Arcane. Smith moves in your world, Jones, not mine."

"You're quite right, Mr. Winters," Lucinda said. "Smith is our responsibility. We will investigate immediately."

Caleb frowned. "Tell me exactly how Luttrell described Smith's position in Arcane."

"He claimed that Smith was at the very heart of the organization."

Caleb nodded, grim-faced. "Odds are excellent that he's on the Council, then. That is the heart of Arcane."

"Well, at least that narrows our list of suspects," Lucinda pointed out.

"I did warn Gabe that some of those half-mad old alchemists on the Council would prove to be troublesome," Caleb said.

"I can help you identify the right man when you do find him," Adelaide offered. "I know his dreamprints."

"That will be extremely useful," Lucinda said. "Is there anything else you or Mr. Winters can tell us about him?"

"One thing, perhaps," Griffin said slowly. "I think that your Mr. Smith may have an obsession with the genealogical records of the Society. I believe that is how he found Adelaide the first time thirteen years ago."

A great stillness came over Caleb. He exchanged a look with Lucinda. She nodded somberly.

"Samuel Lodge," Caleb said very quietly.

HALF AN HOUR LATER, the length of time it took them to reach Lodge's town house in a fast hansom, Griffin and Caleb stood together in Lodge's bedroom. The wardrobe was open but it was only partially empty. Lodge had evidently taken only as many clothes as he could stuff into a pack or a small suitcase. There was a leather-bound note-book on one shelf.

Caleb looked at the nervous housekeeper. "When did he leave?"

"Mr. L-lodge left about an hour ago," the woman stuttered nervously. "He said there was a family emergency at his estates in the North."

"Did he receive any visitors before he left?" Griffin asked. "Were any messages delivered?"

"Y-yes, sir. A boy brought a message to the kitchen door. Said it was urgent. That was when Mr. Lodge told me that he had to leave immediately."

"Damn," Caleb muttered. "The Hulseys must have sent word to him after they escaped."

"They are no doubt hoping for future employment," Griffin said. He walked to the wardrobe and picked up the notebook. He opened it and studied some of the entries. "It appears that Lodge has been very busy with Arcane's genealogical records of late."

Caleb frowned. "What do you mean?"

"According to these notes he recently searched for and found three young men, all hunter-talents. All three grew up in orphanages. They were experimental subjects of a sort. He was curious to see if the crystals would work for other kinds of talents, but he did not want anyone within Arcane to become aware of his experiments. After he started doing business with Luttrell he realized he might need the three as bodyguards."

"How in blazes did Lodge find the three hunters?"

"The same way he found Adelaide. Through the genealogical records. The three men he identified as probably having some strong talent were all fathered by members of the Society. But the babes were illegitimate. They disappeared into orphanages."

"So Lodge now has some well-armed hunters protecting him."

Griffin closed the notebook. "Makes one wonder how many children of Arcane have vanished into the streets over the years because they were orphaned or born illegitimate."

Caleb exhaled deeply. "Arcane needs to do a better job of looking after its own."

A SHORT TIME LATER Adelaide stepped into the front hall of the town house and raised her talent. Decades of warped dreamprints were thickly layered on the marble tiles. The psychical footsteps shimmered with an oily luminescence. Her stomach tightened. She was suddenly aware of Griffin's hand on her arm, steadying her.

"Lodge is most certainly Mr. Smith," she said. "There is no question about it."

Caleb looked satisfied. "I made a few inquiries. It appears that he has fled to the Continent. I doubt very much that he will risk coming back. He knows that Jones and Jones will be waiting."

"What I do not understand," Adelaide said, "is why Lodge's dreamlight patterns are so disturbed." She studied the floor. "The instability appears to have grown worse over the years."

Caleb looked at Lucinda. "Do you sense any signs of the formula?"

"No," Lucinda said. "None whatsoever. There is no hint of poison here, at least not the sort that I can detect."

"The crystals," Griffin suggested. "Perhaps something about using them affects the resonating patterns of one's dreamlight energy over time."

Caleb was impressed. "Do you know, Winters, I think your talents have been wasted as a crime lord. You would have made an excellent detective."

"Why is it," Griffin asked, "that lately everyone seems to think that I chose the wrong career?"

48

SHE UNDRESSED, GOT INTO HER SILK NIGHTGOWN, TURNED down the sheets and then stood looking at the bed, undecided. It had been an exhausting day. She knew she desperately needed sleep but she doubted that she would even be able to close her eyes. The unpleasant shivers that always accompanied the aftermath of danger and violence were still fluttering through her, putting her senses on edge.

A large glass of brandy might help, she thought. She was contemplating that thought when she heard the single knock on the connecting door. Hot energy swept through her, momentarily driving out the shivers.

She drew a breath, crossed the room and opened the door. Griffin stood there. He had started to undress but had not completed the process. He still wore his trousers. His shirt hung open. She knew that he needed sleep even more than she did. But when she opened her senses she saw that his dreamprints burned.

"Griffin," she whispered. She opened her arms.

Without a word, he moved into the room, swept her up and fell with her onto the silk sheets.

He made love to her with an intensity and a single-mindedness that took her breath away.

When her body clenched in release, Griffin went rigid.

"Hold me," he said. "Don't let go."

They were the first and only words he had spoken since he had entered the room. She wrapped herself around him and held him with all of her strength while he shuddered through his climax.

The psychical fireworks dazzled all of her senses. Griffin finally collapsed beside her; she followed him into sleep.

SHE AWOKE SOME TIME LATER to discover that she was alone in the bed. But she sensed Griffin's presence. She opened her eyes and saw him standing at the window looking out into the night.

"Griffin?" she said softly. "What is wrong?"

He did not take his attention off the darkness on the other side of the window. "Are you truly convinced that my dreamlight currents are stable?"

"Yes. You must trust me on this."

"But how is it possible that I am able to control two different talents without driving myself mad?"

"I told you, I believe your second talent is not new at all. Rather it is a different aspect of your original ability. Furthermore, although you are a direct descendant of Nicholas Winters, his is not the only powerful bloodline you inherited."

"You refer to Eleanor Fleming, the woman who worked the lamp for Nicholas."

"She was an extremely strong talent, too. Perhaps it is the combination of bloodlines that makes it possible for you to control such a powerful talent. Or perhaps your ability is a result of the effects the lamp's radiation had on your ancestor. I don't know. All I can tell you is that you are completely stable."

Griffin contemplated the night, not speaking.

Adelaide got up and went to stand beside him.

"I have some early memories of my father discussing his research with my mother," she said. "One of those recollections is his opinion of the Jones family tree."

"What did he have to say about it?"

"Papa speculated on more than one occasion that he would not be at all surprised to learn that Sylvester ran a few experiments on himself with some early versions of the formula before he set about producing offspring."

Griffin was silent for a long moment. Then he turned to look at her. In the pale glow of the moonlight his smile was very cold.

"Not that any Jones would ever admit that the founder's formula might have irrevocably altered the bloodline," he said.

"Of course not. Such an admission would be tantamount to saying that at least one early version of the formula had been perfected and that it worked."

"If the Joneses know or even suspect that their bloodline is living proof that the original formula was successful, they would have every reason to believe that the Burning Lamp was also effective." Griffin's hand tightened on the edge of the window. "No wonder they have always kept a wary eye on my family."

"It would explain their long-standing concern with Nicholas's descendants and the lamp, yes."

"The Joneses no doubt fear the creation of another organization of strong talents that would rival the Arcane Society and its own power."

She smiled. "Well, I'm not sure you can leap to that conclusion. Are all crime lords so suspicious of the motives of others?"

"Crime lords who are not steeped in suspicion generally do not survive long."

"Are you suspicious of me?"

"No." He turned to face her. "Never. I would trust you with my life, Adelaide."

It was not exactly a declaration of love, she thought, but for a crime lord it was no doubt the next best thing.

49

AT THREE O'CLOCK THE FOLLOWING AFTERNOON, THE DOOR of the bedroom opened with such force that it crashed against the wall. It bounced so hard it would have slammed shut again had it not been for Griffin's booted foot in the opening.

"Oh, dear," Mrs. Trevelyan murmured. She put the neatly folded silk nightgown into the trunk. "I had a feeling this was going to happen."

"What the devil is going on here?" Griffin strode into the room and came to a halt directly in front of Adelaide. The heat in his eyes could have set fire to the bed along with everything else in the vicinity. "I just found Jed and Leggett in front of the Abbey with the carriage. They told me that you are leaving."

Adelaide turned back to the wardrobe and took out a petticoat. "Mrs. Trevelyan and I are moving back to Lexford Square."

"You can't leave here yet," Griffin said. "It isn't safe. J-and-J hasn't found Samuel Lodge."

"You heard Mr. Jones." Adelaide stepped around Griffin and carried the petticoat to the trunk. "Lodge has fled to the Continent and is unlikely to return. If he does, Arcane will be waiting. What's more, Lodge knows that. I will be quite safe."

"What if Caleb Jones is wrong?"

She placed the petticoat on top of her nightgown. "I understand that Mr. Jones is rarely wrong. Regardless, we both know that I cannot spend the rest of my life here at the Abbey. I have to return to my own house sooner or later. I think sooner is best."

There was a sudden silence.

Mrs. Trevelyan cleared her throat. "I believe I'll go downstairs and put the kettle on."

She sailed out into the hall, closing the door quietly but firmly behind her.

Griffin looked hard at Adelaide. "What is this all about?"

"It's time for me to leave," she said gently. She swept back past him. The ruffles at the hem of her skirts drifted over the toe of one of his black leather boots. She went to the dressing table and picked up her silver-backed brush and comb. "I will admit that being the mistress of a crime lord has a certain, shall we say, exotic aspect. Nevertheless, a mistress is a mistress. She does not live in her lover's house."

"You're not my mistress, damn it."

"Really?" She put the brush and comb into the trunk. "What word would you use to describe my position in your life?"

"You're my—" He stopped. "You're mine."

"I love you, Griffin," she said.

He looked at her with his fevered eyes. "You must know that I love you."

She smiled. "I hoped that was the case. Neither of us has had a real home for a very long time. It is up to us to make one for each other."

"You want marriage," he said, his voice very flat and cold.

"I think that is what we both want. Am I wrong?"

"It is the one thing that I cannot give you. Ask anything else of me."
His hands tightened at his sides. "*Anything.*"

She touched the side of his hard face with her fingertips and
smiled.

"There is nothing else I want," she said.

"For God's sake, Adelaide." He clamped his hands around her shoulders. "Don't you understand? Marriage to me would put you at risk. As
my wife you would be in constant danger."

"Surely you don't think that I would betray you with one of your
men as your first wife did."

"No. Never. That is not the problem and you know it. But marriage
to me will make you a target for all of my enemies."

"Do you have that many enemies, then?"

"I have been in this business a very long time," he said. "Things
have occurred that cannot be changed. There are those who dream of
vengeance. Yes, I have enemies. What is more, I have forged a certain
reputation. There will always be some who will seek to prove themselves by trying to destroy me."

"You are like one of those notorious gunfighters in the Wild West
who must forever be prepared to defend himself against the hot-blooded
younger males who wish to challenge him."

"There are men who will stop at nothing in order to take what I
have built. If they believe that you are important to me they will not
hesitate to use you to try to achieve their objectives."

"Would you give up your underworld kingdom for me, Griffin?"

He gripped her wrists. "In a heartbeat."

She smiled. "Yes, of course you would, because you know that you
could always rebuild it."

"That is not the point, Adelaide."

"I agree. Well, then, my darling crime lord, if you are willing to walk away from your empire and all that goes with it, including your formidable reputation, then I believe I have the solution to our dilemma."

"There is no solution. That is what I am trying to explain to you. I created this nightmare for myself and now I have no choice but to live in it."

" 'Better to reign in hell?' " she quoted offhandedly. "But you are not a devil, Griffin, and London isn't exactly Paradise Lost."

"I'm no fallen angel, either. I am what I am and there is no going back."

"Ah, but I am not suggesting that we go back. We will go forward to a place where no one will even think of being so rude as to inquire about your past, because everyone there is far more obsessed with the future. It is a place where your reputation is unknown and will not matter. A place where we can forge a home and a family together."

"Is this some dreamlight fantasy you have created?" he asked. "I am sorry, my love, but I learned a long time ago that dreams always evaporate in the light of day."

"This one won't. You have my word as a social reformer. I suggest you start packing, yourself."

"Why?"

"Because we are going to purchase tickets on a steamship bound for America. There is much to be done before we sail, of course, but I'm sure you can have your business affairs settled in short order. You have a great talent for management and organization."

50

"YOU'RE MOVING TO AMERICA?" CALEB ASKED. HE LOOKED first dumbfounded and then, almost immediately, intrigued.

"Our ship sails the first of the week," Griffin said. "Mrs. Trevelyan, Jed, Leggett and Delbert are going with us. Oh, and the dogs, as well."

They stood together in the park where they had met a few days earlier. But they were alone this time. The ladies had not accompanied them on this occasion.

"To say I am stunned would be the understatement of the year," Caleb said. But he sounded thoughtful, not stunned. "America is a big place. Where will you live?"

"Adelaide seems to think that San Francisco would be a good location for us." Griffin smiled. "She tells me that the fog will make me feel right at home."

"What about your various enterprises here in London?"

"I am selling my most profitable businesses to Mr. Pierce. There is no lack of buyers for the others."

"You will no doubt make a great deal of money from the sale of the Consortium's holdings. You certainly won't be destitute when you arrive in America."

"I have always found that it is far more convenient to be rich than it is to be poor," Griffin said.

"What of Adelaide's social reform work?"

"Evidently London is not the only city on the face of the earth that is in need of some social reform. Adelaide seems to feel that there will be plenty of opportunity for her to carry on her work in San Francisco."

"What will become of her charity house and the Academy?"

"Brace yourself, Jones. As we speak, she is making plans to turn over the responsibility for both charities to Arcane. Evidently some of the women of the Jones family are eager to assume the projects."

Caleb's smile was rueful. "No doubt. Keeping an eye on Miss Pyne will very likely prove to be a full-time occupation for you."

"She will be Mrs. Winters soon. You and Mrs. Jones are invited to attend the wedding."

"I am not generally keen on weddings, but in this case I will make an exception," Caleb said. "It is not often that one gets an opportunity to see a notorious crime lord wed a social reformer. We must make sure that Gabe's wife, Venetia, brings her camera."

"Any word on the whereabouts of Samuel Lodge?" Griffin asked.

"Not yet. But I have put a hunter-talent on his trail. We will find him."

"And when you do locate him?" Griffin asked. "What then?"

Caleb contemplated the sun-lit park with the air of a man whose dreams were troubled. "Adelaide and Lucinda are of the opinion that he is mad."

"Yes."

"I suppose we could arrange to have him locked up in an asylum. That sort of thing can usually be handled discreetly."

"Lodge is not only mad, he is also a powerful talent. How long do you think it will take him to escape an asylum?" Griffin asked quietly.

Caleb met his eyes.

"I know what you are saying, Winters. There really is no option, is there? Lodge will have to be put down like the mad dog that he is."

"And you will do what needs to be done because you cannot ask another to do it for you."

Caleb said nothing.

"There will be others like Lodge in the years ahead," Griffin said.

Caleb exhaled deeply. "I am well aware of that."

"You cannot kill them all. I do not believe that you were born for the work of a professional assassin."

"What is my role, then?"

"You are a general waging a war," Griffin said. "Your task is to collect and analyze information, devise strategies and then select the most skilled agents to carry out those strategies."

"And when I find myself confronting those like Samuel Lodge? What am I to do, Winters?"

Griffin reached into his pocket, took out a small, white calling card and handed it to Caleb.

"What is this?" Caleb examined the single name on the card. "Sweetwater?"

"It is an old family business. The members of the Sweetwater clan are all powerful talents of one kind or another. Very expensive but very discreet. The firm specializes in disposing of dangerous rubbish like Samuel Lodge."

Caleb frowned. "Are you telling me that the Sweetwaters are assassins for hire?"

"One could say that. But in their own way, they are an honorable lot. They adhere to a strict code. Done some work for the Crown."

"And for the Consortium?"

Griffin chose not to answer that.

"One cannot simply hire a Sweetwater off the street," he said instead. "They work strictly by referral."

"You are offering to make such a referral for Jones and Jones?"

"I will be happy to supply you with a character reference," Griffin said. "Consider it a favor."

51

IRENE BRINKS SAT AT A DESK IN FRONT OF ONE OF THE TEN typing machines arranged in the schoolroom. Her spine was straight, her shoulders were properly aligned and her fingers were poised over the keys in a graceful manner. *"Just as if you are playing a piano,"* Miss Wickford, the instructor, had said.

It was precisely that image, Miss Wickford had gone on to explain— that of a woman playing a piano—that had caused the public and employers, in general, to conclude that a career as a typist was a respectable profession for a female.

The vision of herself as a respectable, professional woman had inspired Irene. After three days at the Academy she had begun to imagine herself working in an office, gracefully producing elegant letters and neat reports for an employer.

But now, after several more days of instruction, her dreams had expanded. She was currently contemplating the possibility of opening a business of her own, an agency that supplied typists to firms and offices all over London. She would recruit from the Academy, she decided.

She was halfway through the sample letter, an order for fabric, needles and thread for a fictional tailor, when the door burst open.

A man strode through the doorway. He was accompanied by three other, much younger men, two of whom carried pistols. The third gripped a knife. There was a woman with the group as well. Irene recognized her as the social reformer from the charity house: Mrs. Mallory.

"You will all stay right where you are at your desks," the man declared. "The first woman who moves will be shot. Do I make myself clear?"

Irene, Miss Wickford and the other nine students froze in their chairs.

"My name is Mr. Smith," the intruder announced. He shoved Mrs. Mallory with such force that the woman stumbled and fell on the floor. "Get up," he ordered. "Sit at one of the desks."

Mrs. Mallory scrambled slowly to her feet and sat down. She was pale with terror.

"What do you want?" Miss Wickford asked Smith. She sounded as calm and unflustered as if she were giving a typing lesson.

"Nothing from you," Smith said. "Whether you live or die depends entirely on Adelaide Pyne. She has two choices, you see. Either she comes here to give me what I want or she will flee, leaving you all to your fates."

"Who is Adelaide Pyne?" Irene asked.

"I believe you know her as The Widow."

Irene remembered the formidable lady who had descended on the charity house kitchen the morning after the brothel raid.

"The Widow will rescue us," Irene said.

"Let us hope you are right." Mr. Smith removed an object from his pocket. It looked like a large chunk of blood-red glass. "Because if you are wrong, you will be the first to die."

52

THE FRONT DOOR OF THE CHARITY HOUSE WAS UNLOCKED.
That was so unusual that Adelaide paused, one gloved hand on the
knob, and opened her senses.

Jed, waiting patiently on the driver's seat of the carriage, reached a
hand inside his coat in a reflexive move.

"Something wrong, ma'am?" he asked.

There were layers upon layers of dreamprints on the front steps but
nothing out of the ordinary.

"No," she said, speaking over her shoulder. "I'll be out in a few
minutes."

The constant presence of a bodyguard was decidedly awkward but she
tolerated the inconvenience, aware that, until they sailed for America, it
was the only way that Griffin could have some peace of mind. She had
to admit that, as bodyguards went, Jed was a pleasant enough companion. Nevertheless, she could not wait until they were all aboard the ship
and she would once again be free of the rigorous protection.

She opened the door and stepped into the front hall. There were no unusually disturbing prints on the floor, but a curious silence gripped the entire house.

Another frisson of awareness shivered through her. It was still early in the day, she reminded herself. The women and girls of the streets did not usually drift in for their hot meals until mid-afternoon. Nevertheless, there should have been sounds from the kitchen. Mrs. Mallory was forever either preparing new pots of soup or cleaning up.

"Mrs. Mallory?" she called. "Are you here?"

It dawned on her that the woman might be outside in the kitchen garden collecting vegetables and herbs for the next meal.

Her senses still wide open, she walked into the kitchen. Shock swept through her at the sight of the dark, twisted dreamprints that radiated from the floor. Samuel Lodge had been in this room and not long ago.

"Mrs. Mallory," she shouted. "Where are you? Please answer me."

The front door slammed open. She heard Jed pounding down the hall. A few seconds later, he exploded into the kitchen, revolver in hand.

"I heard you call out," he said. He swung the revolver in a wide arc that covered every inch of the room. "Are you all right, ma'am?"

"Yes, I'm fine. But Lodge was here. And Mrs. Mallory is gone."

"Bloody hell," Jed muttered. "The Boss isn't going to like this."

"I'm not exactly thrilled, myself. Caleb Jones assured us all that Lodge had fled to the Continent."

Then she saw the folded sheet of paper on the kitchen table. It was stained with Lodge's foul dreamprints.

53

"HE DISCOVERED THE LOCATION OF THE ACADEMY," ADELAIDE whispered. She sank slowly down onto one of the kitchen chairs. Still a little numb, she stared at Griffin who was studying the note. "He probably frightened Mrs. Mallory into telling him the address. He has taken her and some of the girls hostage at my school."

"I can read, my love." Griffin did not look up from the note.

"He's going to murder them one by one unless I give him the lamp and agree to work it for him. In the note he says I mustn't tell anyone. If he finds out that I sent for you—"

"Calm yourself, Adelaide." Griffin refolded the note. "No one saw me enter this place. My first talent does have its uses."

His cold, casual confidence was oddly reassuring.

"Yes, of course." She took a deep breath and got a firm grip on her nerves. "It's just that the girls at the Academy are there because they trusted me, you see. They feel safe in the school. And they would have remained safe if not for me. I am the one responsible for bringing this monster down upon them."

Griffin dropped the folded note into the pocket of his long, black coat. "You are not responsible for what Lodge has done. He alone must take the blame. And the consequences."

"We have to rescue the students and Mrs. Mallory."

"Certainly."

"Do you think we should ask J-and-J for help?" she ventured.

"No. The risk is too great. We must assume that Lodge still has friends and connections at the highest levels of Arcane. If we take the time to contact Jones and Jones, someone may discover what has happened and send word to him."

"You have a plan?"

"I always have a plan."

In spite of her badly frayed nerves, she managed a small, albeit shaky smile. "You just discovered this disaster a few minutes ago. How could you have crafted a plan so quickly?"

"Plans for situations such as this all work off one core principle. It comes down to calculating the opposition's weaknesses. It is obvious that Lodge's obsession with the lamp is his Achilles' heel. We will use that against him."

"This is how you have lived your life all these years? Forever calculating weaknesses and vulnerabilities in yourself and others?"

"It's in the blood," he said.

54

ADELAIDE WALKED THROUGH THE FRONT DOOR OF THE ACAD-
emy three hours later. Behind her she heard the hired carriage rumble
away down the street. Griffin had concluded that they could not risk
using his private carriage or one of his men as a driver.

She wore her customary widow's attire, a heavily veiled hat, a steel
gray gown and a long black cloak. The Burning Lamp was concealed
in a canvas bag that she carried in both hands.

A rough-looking young man met her in the front hall. He bran-
dished a gun.

"About time ye got here," he growled. "Mr. Smith is getting impatient. Already picked out the first girl he's going to kill, just in case ye
need some assurance that he means business."

She looked at the enforcer's dreamprints and was not surprised to see
the dark energy of his currents. The disturbance in the iridescent tracks
was still faint but it was visible. He was a talent of some kind and he
had been employing one of Lodge's crystal devices. The damage had
already begun. It would only grow worse over time.

What did surprise her was that the prints were familiar.

"You're the one who tried to kidnap me at the theater," she said.

His face crunched in anger. "I would have had you, too, if some bastard hadn't gotten in my way."

"That bastard was the Director of the Consortium."

"Nah. If that were true, I'd have disappeared by now."

"It's never too late," she said. "You may still get the opportunity to disappear. Where is Lodge?"

"Lodge? Who are you talking about?"

"Never mind. Take me to Smith."

"Upstairs in the schoolroom with the women." The enforcer snorted, amused. "Bloody hell. Smith said you'd bring the relic but to tell you the truth, I didn't believe him. You must be a proper fool. Why didn't you run?"

"I doubt that you would understand."

"Social reformers." He shook his head. "You're all mad."

She went briskly up the staircase ahead of the armed man, the folds of her long black cloak billowing around her.

A moment later she swept into the schoolroom and stopped just inside the doorway. Miss Wickford, Mrs. Mallory and the students sat, tense and still, in two rows of chairs arranged at the far end of the room. They stared at her, varying degrees of shock and relief on their faces.

Two more young enforcers stood guard over them. One carried a pistol, the other a knife. But the slightly unstable currents of their dreamprints told Adelaide that they were also armed with crystals.

"Has anyone been hurt?" she demanded.

The women silently shook their heads.

Samuel Lodge was at the window. He turned quickly. An unwholesome excitement flared in his eyes and in the atmosphere around him.

"I knew you would come," he said hoarsely. "After the way you fought to protect the driver of the carriage the other night, I knew that you would not allow even these whores to die if you thought that you could prevent it. Social reformers have no common sense."

He clutched one of the ruby crystals in one hand. Blood-red light pulsed faintly, seeping between his fingers. His tracks were all over the floor, woven into a restless, agitated pattern that spoke more loudly than words. Lodge was a man on the edge of some psychical abyss.

"You do know that Jones and Jones is even now hunting for you, Mr. Lodge," she said calmly. "Arcane will stop at nothing to track you down."

"Once I have acquired the powers of the lamp, Arcane will cease to be a problem." His gaze went to the canvas bag. "You brought it with you, I assume?"

"Of course." She placed the bag on one of the desks.

Lodge hurried forward. The crimson stone in his hand brightened a little. Cold energy shivered in the atmosphere. The women in the chairs trembled in response. One girl started to weep silently.

"Take it out of the bag," Lodge ordered.

"As you wish." Adelaide opened the sack and removed the lamp. She set it on the desk. "I admit that I am curious to know what makes you think that you can access the power of the artifact. According to the legend, only a man of the Winters bloodline can handle such a vast amount of psychical stimulation."

"Or a man who studied the early work of Nicholas Winters and was able to successfully duplicate some of his first crystal experiments." Lodge touched the lamp, his eyes feverish with excitement.

She sensed more icy energy. The crystal he held pulsed a little hotter. The room got colder.

"Well, that explains how you managed to forge the red focusing crystals," she said. "How did you obtain one of Nicholas's notebooks?"

"I discovered it decades ago in the course of my research in the old library at Arcane House. It took me five years to decipher the alchemical code, but once I cracked it I discovered that the secret of creating a crystal that can focus strong energy was astoundingly simple and quite straightforward."

"Just because you learned one of Nicholas's secrets does not mean that you will be able to control the energy of the lamp," she warned.

Lodge grimaced, disgusted. "You are a dreamlight reader. You know nothing of the para-physics involved."

"I may be a dreamlight reader, but even when I was barely fifteen years old I was able to put you into a very deep sleep."

He rounded on her, molten fury heating his eyes. "Only because I was forced to expend so much energy getting rid of the brothel keeper."

"And because you did not anticipate that a woman who could read dreamlight would be able to defend herself against a man of your nature."

"You will not work your tricks on me a second time. If I sense that you are attempting to use your talent against me I will have my men start killing the whores."

He meant it, she realized. The women seated in the chairs stiffened with dread.

"There is no need to hurt anyone," she said, keeping her tone calm and subdued. "I have done as you asked. I have brought the lamp to you. You have certainly been a great mystery until recently, Mr. Lodge. I think most of the questions in this affair have been answered, but there is one that remains."

"I am not here to answer your questions," he muttered.

"Nevertheless, it is a question even Jones and Jones has not been able to answer," she said.

He was clearly flattered.

"What is it?" he asked.

"I know how you found me the first time. You used the genealogical records of the Society. But I don't know how you found me a few weeks ago, after I returned to England."

"It was that bastard, Luttrell, who found you, not me. He concluded that someone was targeting his whorehouses. He tracked you down to that charity house in Elm Street and then had someone follow you back to your address in Lexford Square."

"I see," she murmured. "Well, Mr. Winters did warn me that if he could find me, Luttrell could also."

"Luttrell recognized your name. Calling yourself Mrs. Pyne did not fool him for long. He remembered that I had once been willing to pay a fortune for you. He contacted me immediately to see if I was still in the market for a dreamlight reader. As it happened I was in need of a woman possessed of your talent."

"Why? You did not have the lamp, nor did you know that I had it."

"A few problems have developed with my focusing crystals."

She suddenly understood. "Your crystals are based on dreamlight and you have noticed the ill effects they are having on your talent."

His face tightened. "The difficulties I am having appear to be similar to those Nicholas Winters encountered. I hoped that a strong dreamlight reader could help me adjust the focusing powers of the crystals. I paid Luttrell another fortune for your address and had one of my men follow you to the theater that night. He tried to grab you but Winters got in the way."

"You knew it was Winters your man had shot?"

"No, not at the time. But Luttrell soon discovered who took you that night. It was then that I understood the full extent of my good fortune."

"You knew there was only one reason why Griffin Winters would risk his life for me. You realized that he had got hold of the Burning Lamp and needed me to work it for him. You went back to Luttrell because you knew you could not deal with the Director of the Consortium on your own."

"He agreed to obtain both you and the lamp for me in exchange for a supply of my focusing crystals. I believe the bastard actually thought he could use me as a spy within Arcane. As if I would lower myself to providing information to a man of his sort. Regardless, in the end he failed to carry out his side of the bargain."

"He is dead because he underestimated Mr. Winters. You are making the same mistake."

"Once I have acquired the three powers Winters, like Arcane, will no longer be a problem. Let us get on with the business."

"You want me to work the artifact here? In this room?"

"I have waited long enough for this moment, Adelaide Pyne."

"Not to be indelicate," she said, "but what of the physical connection with the dreamlight reader that is said to be required before a man can command the powers of the lamp? Surely you do not intend for us to fornicate here on the floor of the schoolroom in front of an audience?"

Lodge's face went as red as the crystal he was holding. His outrage would have been humorous in other circumstances. It also struck her as an overreaction. Her intuition gave her a possible reason: He has become impotent in the past fifteen years, she thought. She wondered if it was another side effect of the crystals.

"I have concluded that a sexual encounter will not be necessary after all," he grated. "All that is needed is for both of us to touch the lamp and each other."

She had come to a similar conclusion after reading Nicholas's journal. Her heart sank. Griffin had assumed that Lodge would attempt to bed her before she worked the lamp. It would have meant that, for a time, at least, she and Lodge would have been alone. That prospect had made for a very simple plan. Now things had become considerably more complicated.

"If a sexual connection is not required, why on earth did you go to the trouble of having me sold into a brothel all those years ago?" she asked, trying to buy some time.

"I had not yet mastered all of Nicholas's secrets at that point," Lodge replied. "I admit that in those days I still put some credence in that aspect of the legend."

"What if the energy of the lamp proves too strong for you to control?" she asked.

"That is no longer a risk," he said. He was shockingly self-confident. "My crystals will enable me to channel whatever energy is infused into the lamp."

"If all your conclusions are true, why do you still need me? You have the lamp."

"*You stupid woman,*" Lodge hissed. "I need you because it is clear from my research that part of the legend is true. Only a woman who can work dreamlight can manipulate the currents of the lamp so that they resonate properly with my own energy patterns."

"I'm amazed that you would trust me to carry out such a delicate task. One false move on my part and all of your senses might well be permanently shattered."

Lodge took a deep breath and made a visible effort to regain his control. "I have given orders to my men. If anything goes wrong, Adelaide Pyne, anything at all, your students, their instructor and the charity house social reformer will all die. Is that clear? The lives of all of these women are in your hands."

She shuddered. "I cannot tell you how relieved I am to know that no contact of an intimate nature between us will be involved."

"Believe me when I say that you cannot be any more relieved than I am. There is one thing I must know before we begin."

"Yes?"

"What occurred when you worked the lamp for Griffin Winters?"

"Mr. Winters was not particularly taken with the notion of risking his senses and his sanity. He did not wish to become a Cerberus. He asked me to employ the lamp to reverse the process. I did as he requested."

Lodge nodded, satisfied. "Yes, I thought that must have been it."

"Really? What led you to that conclusion?"

"The fact that Jones and Jones made no effort to kill Winters. The entire Jones family would have taken drastic measures if they had had any reason to believe that Winters was becoming a multitalent. The rumors of such an action would have spread throughout Arcane within hours."

"Instead, the Joneses will now employ those drastic measures to get rid of you," she said.

"Don't you think I made plans for an eventuality such as this? J-and-J believes that I am in Italy. By the time the agency discovers the truth, I will have acquired the powers of the lamp. There will be nothing they can do to stop me. Come, let us get on with the business."

"Very well," she said.

Lodge studied the lamp, scowling in concentration. Somewhat gingerly he touched the rim.

"Put your hand on the artifact," he ordered.

She rested her fingertips lightly on the rim. "Based on my experience with Mr. Winters I can tell you that the first step is for you to light the lamp. Once the energy has been ignited, I can proceed to make it resonate properly with the currents of your own dreamlight patterns."

"According to my theory, the process of lighting the lamp should be similar to what occurs when I focus energy through my crystals."

"Except that it requires an extremely powerful talent," she said.

Lodge shot her a disdainful glance. "I have always been one of the most powerful men in Arcane. But the crystal devices have enhanced my talents beyond those of anyone else in the Society, including the members of the Jones family."

"You are aware, though, that using the crystals all these years has disturbed your natural energy patterns."

317

"A small price to pay considering how the crystals have strengthened my talent."

Lodge raised the ruby stone, aiming it at the lamp as though it were a weapon. Adelaide sensed the surge of his energy field and knew that he was focusing all of his talent on the artifact.

There was a moment of tense silence.

Nothing happened.

"I require more power," Lodge announced, disgruntled. "I do not want to waste too much of my own energy in firing up the device. I will need my strength later." He signaled to one of the enforcers. "You. Come here. Touch the lamp and use your crystal to focus all of your talent on it."

"Yes, sir." The man hurried forward, eager to be part of the grand experiment. He put one hand on the lamp and took a crystal out of his pocket.

"*Now*," Lodge ordered.

Dreamlight swirled violently in the artifact. The lamp glowed palely and then ignited with a flash of paranormal lightning. Currents of raw power sizzled across Adelaide's senses. The lamp quickly became translucent and then fully transparent. Energy exploded in the atmosphere.

It all happened so quickly that Lodge and the enforcer were caught off guard.

The enforcer screamed and reeled back at the first shock. He crumpled to the floor, unconscious. His red crystal flared high and then went abruptly dark.

But Lodge managed to cling to the lamp, his fingers clenched around the glowing rim. His lips were drawn back in a death's-head grin. The red crystal in his hand blazed wildly.

The dark shadows in the corner of the schoolroom took on shape and substance. Griffin appeared. He walked toward the desk where Lodge and Adelaide stood gripping the artifact.

"Did you really think that you could control the lamp, Samuel Lodge?" he asked.

Lodge stared at him, a savage, desperate expression heating his eyes. "I *am* controlling it. You aren't even touching it. The lamp is responding to my power, not yours."

"I don't need to touch the artifact in order to access its energy," Griffin said. "Not when I am this close to it and there is a dreamlight reader to steady the currents. I am a Winters. The lamp is mine to command."

"*No.*" Lodge's shriek of fury and defiance reverberated off the walls.

Lightning crackled in the atmosphere. More energy swirled through the room, lifting tendrils of Adelaide's hair. She was in the pattern now, riding the heavy currents of power. All but one of the stones set in the rim of the artifact blazed, creating a senses-dazzling rainbow.

She knew the instant that Griffin accessed the third level of power. She had no notion what kind of talent he was about to unleash but she knew that together they could control the artifact. That was the only thing that mattered.

Lodge clung to the lamp, his knuckles bloodless. His warped dreamprints were growing more disturbed by the second. The red crystal he had been clutching flared out and went dark. But in the next instant, he pulled another one from his coat pocket. A fresh tide of energy spilled into the atmosphere.

She realized that Lodge was struggling to project his killing talent at Griffin. She almost laughed at the absurdity of the attempt.

Lodge abandoned the effort.

"Kill him," he shouted to the two remaining enforcers. "Do it now. Then kill all of the whores and The Widow, as well."

The two enforcers leaped forward, their crystals glowing hot in their hands.

The spears of light cast by the Burning Lamp intensified briefly.

Griffin was reaching for more power. Adelaide fought to hold the center of the storm.

Fleeting specters of terrible nightmares pulsed in the darkness inside the lamp. A high, shrill scream echoed through the schoolroom.

Adelaide risked a glance at the hostages. The women sat, frozen, on their chairs. But the two enforcers who had been charging Griffin were sprawled on the floorboards, unconscious, their crystals opaque and lifeless.

Lodge panicked. He tried to free his fingers from the lamp but it was soon evident that he could not let go of the artifact.

"This is all your fault," he screamed at Adelaide. "The legend is true. Dreamlight talents are all whores and cheats who cannot be trusted."

He aimed the ruby crystal at her. A wave of ice-cold energy slammed across her senses but she kept her grip on the lamp's currents. She could not let go. Her intuition told her that if the energy in the artifact escaped her control everyone in the room, including Griffin and the hostages would die. She had to hold on.

The killing cold ceased abruptly. Adelaide heard another shrill, howling cry of despair as Lodge arched in mortal agony. In the next heartbeat he collapsed on the floor. His dreamlight energy winked out of existence.

A few seconds later the howling power inside the Burning Lamp abated. The fiery glow faded. The rainbow disappeared. The artifact became solid metal once more.

A hushed silence descended. For a timeless moment, no one moved.

Then one of the young women in the first row of chairs spoke up.

"I told you The Widow would find a way to save us," Irene Brinks said.

55

THAT EVENING ADELAIDE SAT WITH GRIFFIN IN THE LIBRARY at the Abbey. The bookshelves were empty. Mrs. Trevelyan and the men had finished packing and crating the volumes in preparation for the move to America.

The Burning Lamp stood, dark and ominous once more, on a small end table. Griffin had let it be known that he did not intend to trust it to the cargo hold of the steamship. He would carry it on board.

"How did you know what you could do with the artifact when the time came?" Adelaide asked.

"I've been able to sense the latent power in the lamp all along," Griffin said. "But I did not know how to employ it until today when I was confronted with the necessity of using it. There was no other way to deal with three psychically enhanced enforcers and Samuel Lodge at the same time, not when they were all armed with those ruby crystals. I would have exhausted my own talent trying to take down just one or two of them."

"Your Winters intuition guided you," Adelaide said. "I thought that would be the case."

Griffin got to his feet and went to the table where the lamp stood. He examined the artifact for a long moment.

"It is a weapon, Adelaide," he said eventually. "It not only greatly magnified my talent, but it also allowed me to focus it so that I was able to use it against a number of men at the same time. I could have killed all of them and several more besides had I been of a mind to do so. I was able to control the energy of the device with your assistance but had that not been the case—" He broke off abruptly.

"If the lamp had burned out of control no one in that room would have survived," she said.

"No," he agreed. "What is more, even after the experience today, I still do not know the full extent of what the lamp is capable of doing. I accessed only a portion of its power to do what I did."

She sipped some brandy. "That is a chilling thought. There is something else, as well. The Midnight Crystal did not illuminate today. I know we have concluded that it may not contain any energy but given what did occur, we might want to reconsider that theory."

Griffin touched the crystal that had failed to ignite. "I think it would be best to assume that everything about this device is very, very dangerous."

She wrinkled her nose. "In other words, the Joneses are right to be concerned."

"Unfortunately, yes."

She looked at him. "You said you could have killed all of those men today. But in the end the enforcers survived, although their senses appear to be shattered, at least temporarily. I wonder why Lodge is the only one who died? Perhaps it had something to do with the distortion in the pattern of his currents."

322

Griffin said nothing. He drank some brandy and looked at the lamp. She took a breath. "I see."

"I could not allow him to live, Adelaide. He was too dangerous."

"I understand." She frowned a little. "I'm not sure how much longer he would have survived in any event. Using the crystals over a long period of time was not only affecting his mind. I believe the damage was physical, as well."

Griffin turned to face her. The shadows around him seemed to deepen. "I used all but one of the crystals in the lamp today. What of my senses and my mind? Will I suffer the same fate as Lodge?"

She shook her head, very certain. "You need not worry. The energy of the lamp and that of the crystals is tuned to you and those who inherit your particular talent. It is that tuning, I believe, that makes all the difference."

"So much power," Griffin said. "And all of it intended only for destruction. What a waste of Nicholas's intellect and talent."

"You said yourself, power is incredibly seductive."

The ensuing silence hummed gently.

After a while Adelaide stirred. "I will write down everything we have discovered about the lamp in a journal. That way if one of our children or grandchildren or great-grandchildren inherits your talent he will have some notion of what to expect. I will leave instructions for the dreamlight reader as well."

Griffin put aside his empty glass. He walked to the chair where she sat, reached down and raised her gently to her feet.

"Our children?" he said. "Grandchildren? Great-grandchildren?"

"We are going to make a home together, you and I." She touched the hard planes and angles of his alchemist's face. "And that means children."

"Until I met you, Adelaide Pyne, I had convinced myself that such a future was not to be. Not for me."

"And now?"

"You have saved me from the extremely unpleasant and no doubt rather violent fate that awaited me." He smiled. "Crime lords rarely die in bed. I believe that anything is possible as long as I have you."

They held each other very tightly for a long time.

56

THE WEDDING TOOK PLACE IN THE MORNING, AS WAS THE custom. The ceremony was brief, brisk and efficient. Caleb Jones, Delbert, Jed and Leggett acted as Griffin's groomsmen.

Lucinda Jones and Mrs. Trevelyan served as Adelaide's bridal attendants.

Following the first ceremony there was a second. Several members of the wedding party changed places so that Delbert and Mrs. Trevelyan could be married.

Afterward everyone piled back into carriages and set off for Caleb and Lucinda's home, where a traditional wedding breakfast had been set out in lavish style. The table was heavily laden with dishes of cold salmon, lobster salad, eggs, roast chicken, savory pies, fruit tarts, blancmange and a magnificent wedding cake.

Some time later Griffin stood with Caleb on the front steps of the big house.

"One thing before you go," Caleb said.

Griffin watched Delbert, Jed and Leggett organize the luggage on the roofs of the two heavily laden carriages. Adelaide occupied one vehicle. A radiant Mrs. Trevelyan and the two dogs were visible inside the other. The women were busy exchanging farewells with those who stood around the front steps.

"You want to know how much of the legend of the lamp is true," Griffin said.

"Do you blame me for being curious?" Caleb asked.

"No. In your place I would also ask questions. But I'm afraid I cannot give you all the answers, Jones."

"Cannot or will not?"

"Cannot." Griffin did not take his eyes off Adelaide. "I do not have all of them. But I can tell you that some parts of the story are accurate. It takes a man of my bloodline to light the lamp and it requires a powerful dreamlight talent to maintain control of the energy."

"And if that energy escapes control?"

"I don't know exactly what would happen," Griffin admitted. "Just as I cannot tell you why one of the crystals remained dark when I used the artifact to rescue the women at the Academy."

"The Midnight Crystal?"

"I think so, yes."

"Perhaps it is powerless?"

"That is certainly one possibility."

Caleb was silent for a moment.

"At the third level of power the lamp becomes a weapon of some sort, doesn't it?" he asked finally.

"Yes."

"But you are certain that only a man of your bloodline can activate it?"

"Adelaide assures me that is the case."

"Huh," Caleb said. "Perhaps it would be best to store the artifact at

Arcane House. Security is much tighter there now than it was in the old days. Gabe has made that a priority."

"The lamp stays in the Winters family."

"I thought you would say that," Caleb said. "Well, it was worth a try. I suppose the Joneses will just have to trust the Winters family to take damn good care of the thing in the future."

"We intend to do just that."

"What will you do in America?" Caleb asked.

"I don't know yet. Whatever it is, it appears that it will likely be an occupation of a somewhat respectable nature."

"That's what you get for marrying a social reformer."

"A small price to pay. Fortunately, I have a talent for investments."

"Lucinda and I are planning a trip to America later this summer," Caleb said. "The crossing to New York is about five days. We would want to see something of that city, naturally. Then, of course, there would be the train trip to San Francisco. Another four or five days, I believe. How do you feel about houseguests?"

Griffin felt oddly stunned. "*Houseguests?*"

"Arcane has a small office on the East Coast but Gabe feels it's past time that we paid attention to the rest of the country, especially the West. He wants me to study the situation there and devise some long-term plans for setting up additional branches of the Society as well as regional offices for Jones and Jones."

Griffin looked at Adelaide. She smiled at him through the open window of the carriage. Entertaining houseguests was one of the things that normal, married people did, he thought.

"I'm sure we'll be able to find room for you and Mrs. Jones," he heard himself say.

"Excellent. In that case, plan on seeing us on your doorstep in a few weeks."

Griffin smiled. "I'll do that."

He went down the steps and got into the carriage. Jed flicked the reins. On the other box, Leggett did the same. The two vehicles set off down the street.

"What were you and Mr. Jones discussing a moment ago?" Adelaide asked. "You had a rather strange expression."

"Jones and his wife are planning to visit San Francisco in a few weeks. They'll be staying with us."

"Of course they will," Adelaide said. "They are practically family, after all."

"I wouldn't go that far."

She laughed.

He pulled her off the seat and into his arms. "What you and I will build together will be a real family."

"Yes," she said.

He was aware of the dark energy of the artifact leaking out of one of the trunks on the roof of the carriage. The paranormal forces infused into the artifact were forever linked to him. The connection to the lamp was in his blood and could not be denied. But the bright, strong love he shared with the woman of his dreams was far more powerful than the dangerous currents trapped in the Burning Lamp, more powerful than any curse.

"I love you, Adelaide," he said.

"I love you, Griffin, with all my heart."

He was holding his future in his arms, Griffin thought. He would hang on to what was his.

MIDNIGHT CRYSTAL

BOOK THREE IN THE DREAMLIGHT TRILOGY

Available now from Piatkus

The lady from Jones & Jones looked very good in black leather.

Adam Winters waited for Marlowe Jones in the shadows of the ancient ruins. He had heard the trademark growl of the big Raleigh-Stark motorcycle for almost a full minute before the bike rounded the last curve of the narrow, winding road. Sound carried in the mountains.

The nightmares and hallucinations that had struck a few weeks ago had destroyed his sleep. He was living on the edge of exhaustion these days, fighting off the worst of the effects with short bouts of edgy rest, a lot of caffeine, and a little psi. But in spite of the toll the change had taken on him, a surge of exhilaration coursed through him when the newly appointed director of the Frequency City offices of J&J brought the bike to a stop and derezzed the engine.

She was close enough now for him to feel the power in her aura.

Her energy sang a siren song to his senses. Too bad she was a Jones. He would just have to work around that awkward fact.

She kicked down the stand with a leg clad in leather chaps, planted one booted foot on the ground, and raised the faceplate of the gleaming black helmet.

"Adam Winters," she said.

It was not a question. He was the new boss of the Frequency City Ghost Hunters Guild. Anyone who had bothered to glance at a newspaper or watch the evening news in the past month could recognize him.

"You're late, Miss Jones," he said. He did not move out of the quartz doorway.

"I made a few detours." She unfastened the helmet and removed it. Her hair was the color of dark amber. It was caught in a ponytail at the nape of her neck and secured with a black leather band. "Wanted to be sure I wasn't followed."

He watched her, trying to conceal his fascination. Objectively speaking, she certainly qualified as attractive, but she lacked the bland symmetry of real beauty. Marlowe Jones did not need a cover model's looks to rivet the eye, however. She was striking. There was no other word to describe the strength, intelligence, and passion that illuminated her features. Her eyes were a deep, mysterious shade that bordered on blue, almost violet. *The color of midnight,* he thought. *Midnight and dreams.*

And just where in hell had that poetic image come from? He really needed to get more sleep.

She was watching him now with those enthralling, knowing eyes. Energy shivered in the atmosphere. He knew that she was checking him out with her talent. Everything inside him got a little hotter in response to the stimulation of her psi.

When she had called him that morning to request the clandestine meeting, she had explained, in passing, that she was a dreamlight reader. She had no way of knowing just how much that information had stunned him.

A small chortling sound distracted him. For the first time he noticed the passenger on the bike. A small, scruffy-looking creature studied him from the leather saddlebag with a pair of deceptively innocent baby blue eyes. A studded leather collar was draped around its neck, half buried in the fluffy, spiky cotton-candy fur.

"You brought a dust bunny?" Adam asked.

"This is Gibson," Marlowe said. She held out her arm to the dust bunny.

Gibson chortled again and bounced out of the saddlebag and up the length of her arm to perch on the shoulder of her leather jacket. He blinked his baby blues at Adam.

"Didn't know they made good pets," Adam said.

"They don't. Gibson and I are a team. Different relationship altogether."

"Looks like you've got a collar on him."

"The folks at the gear shop where I buy my leathers made it for him. Gibson likes studs. He takes it off when he wants to play with it."

People, even smart, savvy people like Marlowe Jones, could be downright weird about their pets, Adam reminded himself. Then again, being a Jones, she was bound to be a little different anyway. Not that he had any room to criticize. During the past few weeks he had become pretty damn weird himself. *Always nice to start off with something in common,* he thought.

"I'll take your word for it," he said. "So, you were worried about being followed?"

"I thought it best not to take any chances," she said, very serious.

He got the feeling that she did very serious a lot. For some reason that amused him. "Sounds like you're as paranoid as all the other Joneses who ever ran a branch of J-and-J."

331

"It's a job requirement. But I prefer to think of it as being careful."

Her voice was rich, assured, and infused with a slightly husky quality that heated his senses like a shot of good brandy. The edgy thrill of anticipation that he had experienced when he'd taken her call early that morning became crystalline certainty.

She's the one, he thought.

This was the first time he had met Marlowe Jones in person, but something deep inside him recognized and responded to her. He knew beyond a shadow of a doubt that this was the woman he had been searching for these past few weeks.

As fate would have it, in the end she had found him. That was probably not a good sign. She was potentially a lot more dangerous than the people who had been trying to kill him lately. But somehow that did not seem to matter much at the moment. Maybe a few weeks of sleep deprivation had started to impact his powers of logic and common sense.

"I wasn't criticizing the paranoia," he said. "I'm a Guild boss. I consider paranoia to be a sterling virtue."

"Right up there with frequent hand washing?"

"I was thinking more along the lines of obsessive suspicion and a chronic inability to trust."

"Which explains why you got here early," she said. She surveyed the heavily wooded forest that surrounded them. "You wanted to check out the terrain. Make sure you weren't walking into a trap."

"It seemed a reasonable precaution under the circumstances. I have to admit, I got nervous after I discovered that these ruins are situated over a vortex."

She looked skeptical. "Can't picture you nervous."

"Everyone knows standard resonating amber doesn't work underground in the vicinity of vortex energy. Even the strongest ghost hunter can't pull any ghost fire when he's standing on top of that kind of storm."

"I am well aware that Guild men don't like to go anywhere near a vortex," she said.

"It's like asking a cop to leave his gun at the door. After I arrived it struck me that if I were inclined to take out a ghost hunter, I'd sure like to lure him to a vortex site."

"If you were really that worried, you wouldn't have stuck around."

He smiled. "Guess I'm more trusting than I look."

She eyed his smile with a dubious expression. "Somehow I doubt that."

At that moment Gibson chattered enthusiastically and tumbled down from Marlowe's shoulder to the ground. He hopped up on the toe of Adam's boot and stood on his hind paws. There was more chortling.

"He wants you to pick him up," Marlowe said. "He likes you. That's a good sign."

"Yeah? Of what?"

She gave a small, graceful shrug. "Never mind. Just a figure of speech."

Like hell, he thought. The dust bunny's reaction to him was important to her. When he leaned down to scoop up Gibson, the hair on the nape of his neck stirred. The heightening of energy in the atmosphere was unmistakable.

"See anything interesting?" he asked, straightening.

Marlowe blinked, frowning a little, as though she did not like the fact that he had realized that she was using her talent.

"How did you know?" she asked.

He plopped the dust bunny on his shoulder. "When it comes to talent, it takes one to know one."

She walked toward him, her boots crunching on the rough ground. "When I spoke with you this morning, I explained that I'm a dreamlight reader."

"Yes, you did. Not often I get a call from the head of J-and-J. Can't remember the last time, in fact."

"Your family hasn't had much connection with Arcane since the Era of Discord," she said.

"According to the legends, things have always been somewhat rocky between our two clans."

"I'm hoping we can put the old history behind us today," she said.

"Hard to do when there's so damn much of it. How did you get the job as the head of Arcane's Frequency office of J-and-J? Your predecessors at the agency were mostly chaos-theory talents of one kind or another, weren't they?"

To his surprise, she flushed a little as if she'd taken the comment as a personal affront.

"Yes," she said. "Most of them were chaos-theory talents. But it turns out that the ability to read dreamlight is also a very useful talent for an investigator."

She was definitely on the defensive. Interesting.

"I'm sure it is," he said.

Wistful regret came and went in her expression. "Besides, it's not like the old days. Things have been very quiet for J-and-J since the Era of Discord. Mostly we handle routine private investigations for members of the Society. I've been on the job for nearly three months and I haven't had to deal with a single rogue psychic. It's not like there's not a lot of competition out there. Anyone with a little sensitivity thinks he can go into business as a psychic PI."

"The glory days of J-and-J are in the past, is that it?"

"That's certainly what everyone in Arcane says."

"You think that's why they put you in charge," he said. "Arcane doesn't need high-end chaos-theory talents running J-and-J these days, so they went with a dreamlight reader."

Her brows snapped together. "I didn't come here to discuss my career path."

"So why all the secrecy?"

"I'm afraid that you are not going to be happy to hear what I have to tell you."

"Believe it or not, I figured that out about a second and a half after you informed me that you wanted to hold this meeting in the middle of nowhere. Speaking of which, why don't you come inside the gate?"

For the first time she seemed to realize that he had not emerged from the shadows of the narrow opening in the green quartz wall. She looked puzzled, but she walked through the gate and stopped just inside the ancient compound.

The design of the ruins followed the pattern that had characterized most of the other outposts built by the long-vanished aliens. The only feature that distinguished it was the fact that it had been constructed over a vortex. Then again, Adam thought, unlike humans the aliens probably hadn't had any problems with vortices. Their paranormal senses had been far more powerful than those of the descendants of the colonists from Earth. On the other hand, the humans had survived, he reminded himself. The aliens were long gone.

A high, fortresslike wall marked the perimeter of the compound. The handful of graceful towers inside the barricades were windowless. Narrow openings provided access to the various buildings, but it was obvious that the former inhabitants had not been keen on sunlight and fresh air, at least not the kind that was available aboveground.

Like the vast majority of the other ruins left by the long-vanished people who had first colonized Harmony, everything in the compound from the protective outer wall to the smallest building had been constructed of solid psi-green quartz. Even the ground was covered with a thick layer of the stone.

The quartz was impervious to everything the human colonists had thrown at it. Heavy construction equipment could not put a dent in the stone. Fire had no effect. Neither did the most violent storms. A bullet from a mag-rez gun could not even chip it.

Nothing grew on or within the walls or around the outside perimeter. The structures had stood for aeons, but there was no moss, no creeping vines, no vegetation on any of the emerald surfaces. The same went for animal life. No insects or snakes had ever invaded the sites that had been discovered to date. Even the rats stayed clear.

The fact that Gibson did not appear to be having any problems with the atmosphere inside the compound was interesting, Adam thought. Like most of the human population, he seemed comfortable in the vicinity of green quartz.

Adam looked at Marlowe. "I think I've had enough suspense for one day. Let's have it. Why did you drag me out here?"

She visibly steeled herself, squaring her shoulders.

"The Burning Lamp was stolen from the Arcane Society vault sometime between midnight and seven A.M. this morning," she said.

"I'll be damned. Arcane managed to lose the lamp. Again."

She blinked. Her eyes narrowed. "I thought you'd be a little more pissed off. I realize that your family entrusted the lamp to the Society after the Era of Discord."

"Obviously a mistake."

She ignored that. "I went to the scene this morning immediately after I was notified of the breach in security. It took a while to even figure out what was missing."

"No offense, but the museum's cataloging system sounds like it's in need of an overhaul, as well as its security system."

"Yes, it does," she agreed, her tone very neutral. "However, from what I was able to see in the way of dreamprints at the scene I'm sorry to say that it was evidently an inside job."

"Yeah? I'm amazed that you didn't leap to the conclusion that I was the thief. According to the legend, only a direct descendant of Nicholas Winters can access the energy of the lamp. There's no reason for anyone else to steal it."

"I am aware of that," she said. "The possibility that you were the one who took the lamp did occur to me. Your dreamprints do not match those of the thief, however. As I said, all indications are that whoever took the artifact was a member of the museum staff."

"You're that good?"

"I'm that good." There was a note of professional pride in her voice. "I believe I mentioned that even though I'm not a chaos-theory talent, I do have certain skills that are of use in an investigation."

"Now that you've seen my dreamprints, you can eliminate me from your list of suspects. Is that it?"

She cleared her throat. "There are other possibilities."

"Sure. Maybe I bribed or coerced someone on the museum staff to steal the lamp for me."

"That did occur to me, yes. Which is why you are still at the top of my list of suspects, Mr. Winters."

"I'm honored, of course. But there's one small flaw in your theory of the crime."

She studied him with her midnight eyes. "I'm sure you'll explain that to me."

"The Burning Lamp in the Arcane Museum was a fake."

She looked stricken. He realized that he had managed to shock her. The knowledge bothered him. She shouldn't have been quite so stunned. After all, it wasn't the first time Arcane had found itself with a fake lamp.

"Are you serious?" she said.

"My family has never trusted Arcane to take care of the lamp. When the Era of Discord ended, my multi-great-grandfather John Cabot Winters made certain that the Society got a very nice replica for their collection."

"Your ancestors here on Harmony had a fake made?"

"It was one of many my family has been obliged to commission over the years. Whenever the damn thing goes missing, which happens periodically, Arcane starts breathing down our necks. Sooner or later, we give the Society a fake lamp, and that usually satisfies everyone for another century or so."

"You mean until the Winters Curse strikes again," she said.

"Don't tell me you believe in family curses."

"No, but do I believe in genetics. Several centuries ago, Nicholas Winters managed to fry his own DNA with the Burning Lamp, and once in a while the results show up in one of his male descendants."

"That's the legend, all right," he agreed.

"Are you telling me that you have the real lamp in your possession?"

"No," he said. "It's gone missing again."

Comprehension lit her eyes. "Good grief, now I understand. You're looking for it, aren't you? That explains the rumors among the antiquities dealers in the Old Quarter. I've been picking them up for a couple of weeks now. In fact, I was getting set to launch an investigation."

"What rumors?" he asked, trying to buy a little time.

"Some of the dealers have been making very discreet inquiries about an Old World artifact. Word on the street is that a high-ranking Guild man was willing to pay well for it. According to the gossip, the relic possesses paranormal attributes."

"Why were you going to investigate?"

She moved one hand slightly. "Any artifact from Earth that is connected to the paranormal is automatically of interest to Arcane. Combine that with a mysterious collector who is highly placed in the Guild, and you better believe that J-and-J is going to get curious."

He stilled, aware of the extremely treacherous footing beneath his feet.

"What makes you think I'm the one searching for the lamp?" he asked.

"When did the nightmares and hallucinations start?"

The question blindsided him. She knew about the nightmares and waking dreams.

"What are you talking about?" he said.

"I can see the signs of some ghastly dream energy in your prints," she said. "According to the legend, nightmares and hallucinations are the first signs of the change. I think you've been on the trail of the real lamp a lot longer than I have. Time is running out for you, isn't it?"

"Okay, Marlowe Jones," he said. "Now you've got my full attention."

She walked forward to stand directly behind him.

"If there is one thing about the Winters legend that appears to be true, it's that the Winters male who inherits the problem—"

"We in the Winters clan call it a family curse."

She ignored that. "The descendant of Nicholas Winters who inherits the genetic twist needs a strong dreamlight reader to help him find and work the lamp."

All of his senses were jacked now.

"You know," he said, "this whole scene seems just a little too good to be true. Why don't you tell me what's really going on here, Miss Jones?"

"I've explained. I asked you to meet me here today because I assumed you had arranged for the theft of the lamp. Now I find out that you evidently didn't steal it, which raises all sorts of other problems. But right now we need to concentrate on the first priority."

"Which is?"

"I can see that you need the lamp," she said. "If that's true, then you need me."

"You're from J-and-J, and you're here to help, is that it?"

"I don't have time to play games, and neither do you. You need me or someone like me." She broke off, frowning a little. "Wait a second, is that it? You've found yourself another dreamlight reader? Do you think she's strong enough to handle the lamp's energy? Because if she isn't, you're both going to be taking a huge risk when you try to fire up the artifact."

Before he could respond, a small spark of light flashed at the very edge of his vision. It came from deep within the dense stand of trees outside, just beyond the barren perimeter that surrounded the quartz walls. He was vaguely aware that Gibson was growling in his ear.

His reflexes took over. He got an arm around Marlowe's waist and propelled them both out of the doorway.

He tried to take the brunt of the hard landing on the stone floor, but he heard a pained *Oomph* from Marlowe and knew that she was going to be bruised. *Lucky she was wearing a lot of leather,* he thought.

The glint of a studded collar flying past his field of vision told him that Gibson had leaped nimbly off his shoulder and alighted nearby.

The bullet seared a path straight through the gate. As soon as it entered the heavy psi environment inside the compound, it became wildly erratic, quickly lost velocity, and dropped harmlessly onto the floor. The crack of the rifle seemed to echo forever in the high mountains around the ruins.

Adam looked down at Marlowe, intensely aware of her soft, sleek body under the leather. Some of her hair had come free. She gazed up at him through a veil of dark amber tendrils.

"You're right," he said. "I do need you, and I need the lamp. But there's this complication."

"Someone is trying to kill you?"

"You noticed. I wasn't too worried about the problem. Figured it came with the territory when I took over the Frequency Guild. But now I have to wonder if maybe I've been keeping an eye on the wrong people. Maybe Arcane has decided to take me out before I go rogue."